DREAMER OF DESTINY

Barbara Woster

© 2018 All Rights Reserved
US ISBN 13: 978-0-9884617-4-1
US/INTERNATIONAL ISBN **13: 978-1-7336602-9-7**
ISBN eBook 978-1-7328433-5-6

~ PART ONE ~

HAND OF DESTINY

Some pray to marry the man they love.
My prayer will somewhat vary:
I humbly pray to heaven above,
That I love the man I marry.

Rose P. Stokes
My Prayer

CHAPTER 1

Christina made a full turning sweep, hope of locating her wagon and her family waning. She knew now that it had been foolish to wander away, and all she wanted was to get back to the haven of the wagons. She stood upon her tiptoes and began another swirling revolution, as graceful as a ballerina's pirouette; however, the wagons remained elusive. All that lingered in view were wheat-like stalks of grass, swaying in the breeze as if happily mocking her in her distress.

Upon the start of a third revolution, a stand of trees appeared at the edge of the prairie. As with the grass, the branches swayed to the silent rhythm of the wind, but instead of appearing blissful in their dance, the twisted branches seemed an evil that beckoned her. A violent shiver quavered throughout her body. Sweat broke out upon her brow and began trickling down toward her eyes, wide with sudden disquiet.

With a determined will, she turned her body from the tree line, and sank to her knees, a feeling of misery bullying her confidence. She scolded herself for foolishly unheeding her brother's warning. He bade her not to wander from the safety provided by the encircled wagons. Why had she not listened to his wisdom? Though younger than she, he was more aware of dangers lurking on this trip—far more than she. Though younger, she respected his knowledge and appreciated his loving concern for her safety—so then why did she not listen? What was it that made her disregard his warnings; disregard her own safety?

It is entirely the giant rabbit's fault, with those horns upon its head! That is where the blame lay! *She huffed at her deflection, but was certain that she would not have gone wandering were it not for the strange-looking beast hopping past her, flaunting it unusualness.* After all, hadn't Alice also followed an unusual animal and ended hopelessly wandering in Wonderland? *Well, her rabbit may not have been wearing a waistcoat and timepiece, but it* was *sporting antlers, which certainly gave just cause for further inspection. Perhaps these rabbit-like creatures were the cause of all ill-fated happenings, or perhaps she had followed the strange animal to her own Wonderland.*

Maybe she was dreaming, as Alice had been, and she was but within her musty Conestoga, safely ensconced within her scratchy woolen blanket. Perhaps, when her story played out, she'd waken to find she'd never left the safety of the wagon's enclosure after all.

As if thinking of the four-legged, horned-eared hopper made it suddenly appear, it stood but a few feet in front of her, sniffing the air with its delicate pink nose, absurd in contrast to its giant back thumpers and its deer-like horns.

"Well, what say you then? Your presence led me away from the wagons, so perhaps you'd be kind enough to hop back the way we came? I thought as much!" *Christina watched the Jackalope as it continued sniffing the air.* "I must say that it *is* rather unsporting of you though. After all, I would not be sitting in the middle of a field, had it not been for you, so the least you could do is assist me in finding my way back to where I belong."

The Jackalope did look at her then, and Christina decided its sudden attentiveness was granting her permission to resume her monologue, "Well, if you don't intend to return me to my wagon, could you perchance explain where this little escapade is leading me? Especially as I cannot see how standing in a field could possibly be considered adventurous."

She huffed at the Jackalope's refusal to respond, and stood with a flourish, "Well then, I suppose I will simply have to take matters into my own hands. I can't risk not getting home before nightfall, and I certainly can't accomplish my goal sitting here feeling sorry for myself, so I guess it's just a matter of determining which course to set out on." *Her sudden shift startled the Jackalope and it bounded away faster than she could blink, leaving her to wonder whether it was merely a figment of imagination. Its speed, she finally concluded, could only be the result of imagination and thus convinced herself that she was in a sort of Wonderland dream state. One from which she was more than ready to waken.*

She glanced up at the sun, her brow furrowing in confusion. If she were sleeping, why was it daylight? Her self-assurance spiraled away again, replaced with indecision—running amok inside her mind. Was this real? Had she really followed a creature out into the middle of nowhere? Was that even like her to do something so foolish? Try as she might to recall, her memory failed her.

Well, it appeared that if she was going to return to her family, she would just have to set course, and pray her decision was true.

She lifted her skirt and started pushing along through the tall grass, but a movement in her periphery stopped her. "Not this time, Mr. Rabbit! You are not going to distract me yet again!" *Yet her feet acted in direct defiance to her words, stopping their forward momentum.* "Traitors!" *She accused, staring down at her feet.*

The distraction moved again and she turned toward the tree line once more. She determined not to follow the rabbit further, but that did not mean it did not hold a fascination for her, for she'd never seen anything like it in all her years back east. It was truly a marvel to behold.

She scanned the trees, but the movements had stopped. She squinted against the sun, lifting her hand to block out the bright rays, and peered between the trees. Something was there. She could feel it watching her.

There!

Beside one of the trees were two eyes staring back at her, the sun's rays creating a haunting red glow where eyes should sit. The sight had her backing away, which restarted the movement that had brought her to a halt to begin with—only now that movement was directly on course with where she stood. When the beast moved from beneath the shadow of the trees, Christina gasped and stumbled, falling on her derriere, frozen in terror.

The beast looked to be half man, half bear, and white as newly fallen snow, with eyes pitch as night, yet somehow familiar in their frostiness. It lumbered toward her, its gaze, unfeeling, daring her to run, goading her to succumb to her fate as fodder. It reared onto its hind legs and let out an ear-piercing bellow that shook the earth underneath her bottom. The shudder beneath the earth jarred her from her daze, and she scrambled to her feet.

Run! Her mind yelled at her, but her feet were slow to respond. She stared in hapless wonder as the creature closed the gap, one slow, inelegant step a time, determination in its stride.

With an abruptness, it stopped its pursuit, raised upon its hind legs, and began sniffing the air, much as the Jackalope had done. Something unseen had gotten its attention, much as her attention had been snared twice during this dreadful escapade.

Slowly, to draw no renewed attention to herself, she turned her head to seek out what had caused the distraction. As before, she raised her hand to shield them from the sunlight, and squinted, peering into the darkness between the trees. She did not have to search hard or long, for the beast moved stealthily from the trees and into her line of sight—and the white beast's. Her knees quivered and threatened to collapse beneath her again.

Standing at the edge of the tree line, in all of its ferocious magnificence, teeth bared and snarling, was a Goliath-sized gray wolf, the likes of which she'd never seen. Albeit, as the only gray wolf she had ever seen, she was certain that its size was relative to her fear.

Although not nearly as gargantuan as the white creature—now snarling a warning in reply to the wolf's cautioning growl—its menace to her was just as great, for no matter which proved the victor in combat, she would be helpless to defend against becoming a next meal.

Christina began silent supplications—not to God, but to Mother Earth—in the hopes she would open the ground beneath her and swallow her whole. To God she prayed that He would place a shield between her and the two hostile beasts.

When the wolf and the white creature removed their attentions from her and began circling each other in preparation for battle, she didn't know whether to laugh or cry. Instead, she did what any lady of breeding would do—

She fainted.

CHAPTER 2

January 1861

Baying Wolf's mind was restless. He should be sleeping peacefully after the long hunt, but instead he found himself awake in the early morning hours needlessly examining the paintings that covered the walls of his tepee.

His gaze swept the many accomplishments permanently painted there with the wild berries that grew in the surrounding forest, although he didn't need to gaze upon them to know what each represented. He knew them all very well. Depictions of bravery, courage, and triumphs of which any warrior would be proud. His first kill of the mighty buffalo, his vision quest that took him from boyhood to manhood, and of Wolf—his spirit animal—leading him into battle against his enemies. All of these things and more he'd stared at for the past five hours, trying to ease his restless spirit.

If he closed his eyes, he could fall asleep, for sleep did not elude him—he eluded sleep. It was not fear that kept him awake, but a desire to avoid the woman, with skin the color of wheat, that haunted his dreams.

Just this night, although he felt exhausted from the hunt, he had followed the dream path until his mind journeyed along with hers. His body transformed to that of the wolf, in preparation for whatever it was the Great Spirit wanted him to face. Yet the whys of it all evaded him, much as sleep did.

In the dream, he'd watched from a distance as a white beast reared up, threatening her. He sensed her fear, sensed the evil stalking her; and sensing that this was why the Great Spirit sent him to her dreams; he commanded his spirit animal to defend her.

He stepped forth and glanced at her, tried to ease her fear with his presence. It was a futile effort, for one glance at Wolf had generated even more fear in her than he'd sensed before. A fear of him. A fear he could not accept or explain. Surely, the Great Spirit would have reached out to the white woman with a word of comfort; let her know that Wolf was sent as protector and friend. Perhaps she was closed off from the spirit world and could not receive comfort.

He held to that thought as he turned his concentration on the beast, circling, threatening. Ready to do battle to defend a woman who did not appear to want defending. Ready to do battle nonetheless.

The beast, however, was not ready—or not willing—to engage him, so turned and lumbered away into the stand of trees.

Wolf sat down heavily, allowing his mind to relax and peace to envelop his spirit. He glanced to where the woman had stood. She was gone. No doubt fled. Wolf closed his eyes and transformed again into his true being, returned to the recesses of the woods, down the dream path, and back to wakefulness.

He had not seen what had transpired after he left; could not recall seeing her as he slipped among the trees—nor should he care. She did not belong to his people and should not be his concern.

Now, lying here in the dark he tried desperately to avoid the sleep that could send his spirit animal back along the dream path. Back to her. It took too much energy to enter the dreams of another and already most of his energy was gone because of the hunt.

Nevertheless, he was restless.

Why did the Great Spirit send warnings to him about someone more enemy than ally? Why did he not seek out one of her own to protect her? There had to be someone within her own race with the courage to stand and face the beast that was trying to harm her. She was not his concern.

Her people were of no concern to him. *She* was of no concern to him. Her people had broken treaties and promises, and were encroaching on every part of their land, destroying their buffalo, and killing their people. They did not care for the Indian maiden, so why should he care about one of their women. There were no answers to the endless questions bounding through his mind; however, there was something about this woman that spoke to him, and that alone angered him—for he found himself wanting to shield her. This woman with her hair the color of fire and eyes the color of palest emeralds. He spat out a string of quiet-spoken curses and threw back the buffalo skin covering his body. Perhaps it was time to seek the counsel of his uncle, Fire Dreamer, the Shaman of his people. Maybe Fire Dreamer could tell him what this woman meant and why she invaded his nights, leaving him sleepless and frustrated.

Before he could move, the woman sleeping next to him drew his attention. She squirmed closer, seeking warmth from the blanket he'd removed—and something more, he had no doubt. He watched her nestle closer and grinned as a keening whimper escaped. Were his mind not preoccupied and his heart heavy with concern, he would be happy to oblige her needs, or so he thought until her hand moved innately along his upper thigh. He flinched and leapt from the bedding. Never before had her touch created shivers of repulsion inside him. He groaned in anger and frustration as he jerked his clothing on. It was the woman in his dreams that was causing him distraction, creating anger where there should be peace, frustration where he should find pleasure. He needed answers and soon. He stepped into the early morning air and closed his eyes against the onslaught of cold.

He moved across camp feeling rejuvenated from the chilliness. Hopeful. Now he only hoped that his uncle would provide the soothing balm that he needed so that he could return to the comfort of Prairie Heart's arms.

CHAPTER 3

Christina crawled wearily out of bed and shuffled to her washbasin on unsteady legs. Weakly, wearily, she poured lukewarm water from the porcelain pitcher into a bowl of the same blue-floral design, her arm quivering beneath the insignificant weight. With a sigh, she lifted the sponge, dipped it into the room-temperature water, and ran the liquid across her forehead and over her flushed cheeks, her eyes fluttering closed in bliss as the water wiped away the sweat that had pervaded her body in the night. She lifted her hair, and unhurriedly drew the sponge across her skin, sighing at the coolness, shivering slightly as drops escaped and slid beneath her gown to caress her back, bottom, and legs before ending their journey in the fibers of the rug upon which she stood.

She glanced in the mirror at the dark puffy circles beneath her eyes and sighed wearily again. The nightmares were getting worse, and she could only attribute the disturbing clarity to her illness, for never before had her dreams been so vivid, nor even remembered. Now, the disturbing clarity and horrifying events unfolding in her mind made her wish she could forget. Each time she dreamed, it was if a story were playing out in her mind from a book. A novel she had never read. A very dramatic, lifelike story, in which she was the main character. Never did the story loop or repeat, nor were there moments of hazy obscurity. The dream always picked up where it left off, as if placed on hold from the dream before. Had she remained in her dream state more than one night, she knew that she would easily discover what the dreams were trying to tell her.

She wondered if the dreams would ever have made an appearance, had she not contracted pneumonia. Perhaps the pneumonia had so deluded her, that even in sleep, it had heightened the sensitivity in her mind, creating a more lifelike situation in her dreams; situations she could easily recall upon wakening.

She only wished that she was able to dream about something other than frightful creatures with jagged teeth that wanted to eat her for dinner.

She slid the sponge down the front of her nightgown, caressing the sweat from her breasts, sighing as the water slid down the front of her body. She closed her eyes and let her mind relax, taking in deep calming breaths, she felt the tension drain away. All was right again, until she opened her eyes and caught sight of her reflection once more. The pneumonia and the dreams were taking their toll.

You look awful, her mind observed. She winced, but for once, she had no witty retort to supply. Her mind was right. She did look awful. Her appearance, once vibrant, was now colorless—dark circles invaded the space beneath her eyes, and lines of strain troubled the area around her mouth and creased her normally smooth skin. She looked closer to thirty than her true age.

"All I need is some sunlight to add a little color to my face and I'll be right as rain," she said unfalteringly, conversing with her reflection—a habit her mother had scolded her about, more than once. Still, there was no one about with whom she could talk freely—except herself, and, on occasion, Chin Woo. Still, her mind tended to argue with her far more often than she'd prefer. Like now.

Liar, her mind taunted. The fact that her mind talked back, was even more cause for concern for her mother, than her. Christina just smiled when scolded, and replied that her mind was the only living entity that truly understood her. It was said in jest, but her mother would scoff and lecture and scoff some more. No matter the continued reprimands, Christina didn't plan to change her inclination. She enjoyed conversing with herself too much, and saw no harm in the habit.

"Well, I've recovered enough to be out of bed, haven't I? If I'm out of bed that means the pneumonia is as good as gone; and that means that I'm well enough to go outside and get some fresh air!" She shot back at her mental adversary. Oh, if only her mother could see her now, she envisioned, she probably wouldn't hesitate to have her committed as she was always threatening to do.

You may be out of bed, but if you stay out too much longer, they're going to have to pick you up and put you back there, her mind snapped back.

"I'll have you know," she continued combatively, "that other than a little weakness, I feel perfectly fine." The sound of her mother's past criticism crashed to the forefront of her mind lecturing that a mental institute was for those who carry on one-sided conversations with themselves.

Of course, her mind teased, shoving other memories back to their recesses, *you're so 'fine' that you're carrying on a one-sided conversation with your brain.*

Oh, great! Christina sighed inwardly. *My brain* is *my mom.*

"Oh, do hush!" She chastised her reflection, knowing she could never talk to her mother in such a fashion. "I simply cannot stay in that bed one second longer. Are you telling me *you* can?" Her mind met the issued challenge with silence. "That's what I thought. Now let's get outside and take in some of that fresh air. It really will make a world of difference. I know it will."

The sound of an approaching horse drew her attention, but by the time she reached the window on the far side of the room, it was too late to see who was arriving. Well, whoever had come calling was not her concern. She had another agenda, and it did not include the entertaining of guests.

Slowly she dressed, and then made her way out of her second-story bedroom, but soon had to rest against the balustrade as a bout of dizziness struck her. She shook her head slowly to clear her mind and then continued descending the stairs. Without a doubt, her body was still weak but her determined will won any battle her tired body waged. When she reached the bottom landing, she sighed deeply.

"A few more steps and I'll be there." The little pep talk was more for her tired limbs, as she recalled a sermon from a couple of Sunday's past about the spirit being willing but the flesh being weak. Nothing was closer to the truth at this moment.

"Mirabelle?" Christina called. The housekeeper, who was standing near the front door cleaning the stained-glass French window, turned at hearing her name. Christina saw a hummingbird outside that window and smiled, "Spring isn't too far away now," she murmured quietly. It was her favorite time of year.

"You called me, Miss?" Mirabelle stopped her cleaning and hurried to stand beside Christina. "Are you sure you're well enough to be up and about, Miss?" The housekeeper's worried glance made Christina sigh in frustration because she could hear her brain siding with Mirabelle. In an act of childish defiance against her mind, she shoved her body away from the balustrade and smiled bravely.

"Actually, I look much worse than I feel. Have you by chance, seen my mother this morning? I want to let her know that I'm stepping out for a few hours."

"Most assuredly, Miss. She's in the solarium, entertaining with your father."

"Ah, the guest that arrived. Do you know who it was?"

"I'm sorry, Miss. I don't know."

Christina's gaze went to the solarium doors and as usual, she felt her curiosity rise. "You may get your wish, mind," she murmured dejectedly, "since we may end up staying indoors for a spell."

"What's that you said, Miss?"

"Oh, nothing. I was just trying to decide whether to step out for some air, or see who's come to call."

"Oh. Well if I might be saying so, sitting in the solarium may be safer for you than traipsing about all over the place by yourself, especially since you're still recovering."

"I know, and I do thank you for your concern. It's just that I don't necessarily want to be stuck entertaining Old Man Michaelson and his wife."

"They are coming around a great deal, aren't they?" Mirabelle agreed, leaning against the staircase.

"That's because they want me to marry their son, David." Christina shuddered as images of the Michaelson's son flittered briefly through her brain. It wasn't that he wasn't a decent fellow, as store clerks went, he just seemed such a weakling that she was terrified he wouldn't know what to do with a wife even if his parents did manage to procure one for him.

"Well if it will make you feel better, I don't think it's Mr. and Mrs. Michaelson today."

"I thought you said you didn't know who it was?"

"I don't," Mirabelle defended. "It's only, I've just started cleaning the windows in the foyer here, you see, and I happened to notice that there was a lone horse tied to the front post, not the Michaelson's carriage. Of course, it could be David Michaelson come to call."

"That would be rather courageous now, wouldn't it?"

Mirabelle giggled, and then quickly straightened her demeanor. "Yes well, he is rather…" she started, but let the sentence hang.

Christina glanced sidelong at the downstairs housekeeper and wondered if she simply had difficulty completing the sentence, or if she could not describe David Michaelson with any success. Probably the latter, she decided after a moment. Even she had difficulty describing him successfully. "Well perhaps I could step inside to see who it is. Wouldn't want my parents thinking they'd raised me without manners now, would I?"

"I don't think they'd ever question your manners, Miss."

"Thank you, Mirabelle. You'd best be getting back to those windows before the day gets away from you. I'm sorry I pulled you away from your duties."

"It's perfectly alright. A break is always welcomed," Mirabelle said and curtsied slightly. "Can I be getting you anything?"

"Oh, that would be lovely. Some toast with orange marmalade and tea with sugar from Hyacinth, if you wouldn't mind."

"Yes, Miss."

"Do you by chance, know whether my parents and their guest have had any refreshments as yet?"

"No, Miss."

"Ask Hyacinth, and if not bring something suitable for everyone. I'm sure that refreshments would be in order."

"Yes, Miss." With a quick bob, Mirabelle turned, leaving Christina to play tug of war with her mind: outdoors, guest, outdoors, guest.

CHAPTER 4

"I too have seen this woman in my dreams, but not as you
have seen her and not as the journey you have taken," Fire Dreamer
said quietly, knowing the reason Baying Wolf sought his counsel this
night. He merely smiled at the incredulous look on his nephew's
face and continued speaking. "This white woman has much danger
awaiting her, but from where this danger comes, I cannot see, for
her troubles do not come to me as clearly as they do to you." Fire
Dreamer narrowed his eyes knowingly. He stopped speaking for a
moment and looked intently into his nephew's eyes. When he spoke
again, it was with a certainty that annoyed Baying Wolf. "You know
nothing of the danger this woman faces, yet you answered the call of
the Great Spirit and went to her as your spirit animal. Why?"

"I cannot disobey the commands of the Great Spirit," Baying
Wolf replied without conviction.

"Pah!" Fire Dreamer laughed. "I have known you all of my life,
and you *never* readily obey anyone's commands. Speak true nephew,
for it is you who sought out my counsel. If it is counsel you seek,
then you must be willing to speak your heart." Fire Dreamer's smile
widened, as did his nephew's eyes. *How many more years would pass
before Baying Wolf realized that I see most everything?* Most *everything*, Fire
Dreamer wondered tacitly. "I did not see what happened to the
young woman, so tell me what it is that disturbed you so that you
need to seek my counsel before the sun rises this day." His uncle
leaned forward slightly, stirring the dying embers in the fire bed.

Baying Wolf began to speak slowly, trying to piece together his
vision. "She was walking among the wild grasses of the prairie. I was
watching her. She was not in distress. She was merely lost. It made
me wonder again, why the Great Spirit would take me from my
sleep and send me to her. Then, I watched from the trees as a great
white beast rose up from behind her. It was taunting her, but she
did not leave. She seemed too afraid to run. I knew then that this
threat was the reason that the Great Spirit sent me to her, so I leapt

from the trees, hoping to frighten the beast away. I guess I frightened her also. At least the panic in her gaze said so. Her fear angered me."

"Because you were there to help her, and she could not see this," Fire Dreamer added.

"Yes."

"Perhaps it was fear of the beast that you saw. Not fear of you," Fire Dreamer supplied.

"I do not think this to be so," Baying Wolf muttered.

"Perhaps you are right. Perhaps she felt you meant her harm as well. Still, should you blame her too much? After all, she was under attack by one beast and another, equally deadly, appears eager to join the feast. Would you not expect to see fear?"

"If I meant her harm, I would have helped that beast tear her apart and then joined in the feast upon her bones! I would not have stood in the trees and just watched."

"Your anger is great, my nephew, and I think it is misplaced. Why *are* you so angry? Surely not because a white woman fears you."

"I'm angry because the Great Spirit should never have told me of her in the first place, because she belongs to the white man and a white man should be the one to help her; because she is in a danger that I know nothing about and yet I feel compelled to help her."

"Your anger clouds your visions, so you come to me seeking answers that I cannot give. You must find the answers on your own; however, this I will tell you—to walk along the dream path to another is an arduous task. It takes a great strength and determination, yet you did this with little thought to your own safety. Apparently, you felt the need to listen to the Great Spirit this time, so you somehow feel, as I do, that the Great Spirit has linked anything that happens to this woman to you. If this were not so, the Great Spirit would not tell you to help her. I think you know this already, so what is it that I can do for you?"

Baying Wolf sat with his head lowered, but did not attempt to speak. Fire Dreamer watched him carefully across the low-burning fire and decided to wait. Many things were troubling his nephew and it would do neither of them any good if they could not find a solution. After a moment, Baying Wolf raised his head, the lack of sleep evident in the dark circles forming beneath his eyes. "Death is surrounding her," he said in a whisper.

CHAPTER 5

Christina waited until Mirabelle rounded the corner before turning and facing the solarium. She may have been bent on going out of doors, but her curiosity always seemed to get the better of her. Perhaps she could find out who was visiting without her parents dragging her into a drawn-out social call. She dreaded those.

She looked around again to make certain she was alone, and then pressed her ear against the chilly wood paneling of the solarium door. If the visitor was nothing to her, she could forgo knocking and simply make her way out of doors. However, no matter how hard she willed it, the voices on the other side remained unintelligible.

Pressing her ear more firmly against the surface, she refused to feel any guilt over eavesdropping. *It is simply my right, she argued tacitly, to know who it is my parents are entertaining and whether I really want to entertain them myself.* The little devil with the pitchfork—also known as her mind—spoke up and tried to convince her that the hushed words she heard spoken on the other side of the door were about her. It also told her that she shouldn't feel at all guilty with trying to find out what they were saying—about her.

"If you really want to know whose behind the door, then knock," a voice mocked from behind her.

Christina jumped and spun quickly on her soft-soled slippers, her hand flying to her chest. "Thomas, you scared the living daylights out of me! What are you doing sneaking up on folks like that?"

"I was hardly sneaking, sis. I made enough noise to wake the dead. If there were any dead around here," Thomas replied, grinning slyly. "You were just concentrating on your spying too hard to take notice."

"I was not spying," Christina snapped indignantly.

"Truly. Then what do you call leaning against a door attempting to hear what is being spoken on the other side?"

"If Mother is in there, I need to tell her something, that's all."

"A plausible explanation. A lie nonetheless," Thomas laughed.

"Looking for my mother is not a crime," Christina hissed defensively. Her skin took on a flushed appearance, belying her justification.

"Well, I'm almost certain she's in there, but there's only one way to know, now isn't there?" Thomas moved around his sister, raised his hand, and knocked sharply on the door.

"Thanks a lot, brother," Christina muttered only seconds before the door flew open. Carlotta tugged Christina forward into her embrace. Over her mother's shoulder, Christina spied the visitor and stiffened.

"Oh, my darling girl," her mother cooed dramatically, pulling back and looking worriedly into her daughter's pale face. "Are you sure you should be up and about?" Christina felt a hand press against her forehead, and heard her mother's voice, but the words and the actions seemed muted as her focus locked onto the man leaning against the fireplace mantle, his demeanor arrogant. "Well, you feel as if you're okay, but you're still much too pale for my liking."

Christina couldn't relate that her sudden paleness had to do with her irrational dislike of their visitor. Her mother would never understand that. Carlotta led her daughter to the sofa and gently encouraged her to sit. "Are you certain you feel okay, my dear?"

"I thought I did," Christina answered woodenly, her gaze never leaving their visitor, "but now I'm not as certain."

"Well come along, darling," Carlotta coddled, "and I'll escort you back to your room. We'll discuss the wonderfully good news another time."

"Good news?" Christina asked perplexed, halting their departure. She tore her gaze from the smirking face of their guest to her mother's happy countenance.

"Of course, child..."

"Perhaps I should speak with Christina alone," the caller interrupted quickly. "I'll be certain that she isn't distressed and will see to it that she returns to her room immediately after our visit."

"Certainly, my boy," Charles Carthington boomed. He turned to Carlotta. "I do not see how any harm can come from it. After all, she managed to make it down here, so a few more minutes certainly can't hurt."

"I don't know, Father..." Christina started, but the visitor interrupted her

"I won't keep you long," the gues fairly purred, causing the hairs on Christina's arm to bolt upright. Before she could utter a serious protest however, her mother and father moved to depart. If her mother's implication of 'good news' hadn't raised Christina's curiosity, she would have departed also. *Damnable curiosity*, she thought.

Her mother stopped by her side, placed a light kiss on her hair, and then dabbed her eyes with a handkerchief dramatically. With a hand placed lightly on Christina's shoulder, she said, "You just sit quietly and we'll leave you two lovebirds alone for a bit. No shenanigans, though, you hear? We wouldn't want you to have a relapse. Pneumonia is a serious thing, you know."

"I'll take good care of her," Jeffrey said, reassuring Christina's parents. Christina reddened, but could pose no objections as her mother quickly shooed her father out of the room, shutting Christina in with a man she barely knew and, for reasons she never fully understood, distrusted immensely. She suddenly wished most fervently, that the caller *had* been David Michaelson. Whereas David elicited no emotional response at all from her, this man somehow managed to make her feel physically ill. Not a good thing for someone just recovering from a bout of pneumonia.

Why in heaven's name, does he want to speak to me alone? She wondered, when his visits usually consisted of a five-minute wait in the corridor while her brother, Thomas, rushed to put on his overcoat.

She shook her head, trying to put a finger on the dislike she felt for Jeffrey Buchanan, and then it hit her like the proverbial bolt of lightning, as certain and vivid a reality as her dreams had been of late. Her dislike of this man had to do with her brother.

Every time Thomas stepped out with Jeffrey, trouble returned. It often made her wonder why her parents were so fond of him, when trouble seemed his permanent escort. A fact her parents seemed oblivious too, if the cryptic comments of "good news" and their lively demeanor when she'd entered the room were any indicators. Both of which had alarm bells ringing in her head.

Still, her infernal curiosity had prevented her trailing after them. Somehow, this visit concerned her, and she needed to know why.

CHAPTER 6

Christina waited just long enough for the doors to bump softly into one another, before turning back to face her surprising visitor. "Would you mind explaining what all that was about, Mr. Buchanan?" She stated curtly, sitting straight upon the couch with her hands pressed tightly in her lap. It was a position she'd seen her mother use when displaying her displeasure. The effect was always effective, so she emulated it in the hopes that Jeffrey would take her own displeasure seriously. He didn't.

"Call me Jeffrey, please."

"No, thank you," she responded tersely.

"As you wish," he replied, his brow knitted in obvious displeasure, and Christina watched with internal delight the struggle he was having to regain his composure. It didn't take as long as she'd have preferred. She wanted him imbalanced, wanted him to feel what she was feeling at this very moment—irritation and annoyance.

"It's nice to see you out of your sick bed. I heard that you were very ill. Although you look less peaked than a few moments earlier. Recovering rapidly, it would seem."

She sighed loudly over his chitchat games, that social banter that always left her feeling phony. Still, to get answers, she knew she would have to participate. "I am a little weak, but feeling much improved. Still, I would like to return to my room in all haste, so if you could be so kind as to answer my question, sir?"

Jeffrey grinned lopsidedly; a gesture that Christina had no doubt would send many women into a fit of the vapors, but not her. To swoon over a man, she felt relatively certain a woman needed to find him attractive, and Jeffrey Buchanan was anything but attractive to her. He simply made her skin crawl. Her gaze flickered over his features and she wondered, if not for his unwelcome association with her brother, if she would feel differently.

He was a good-looking man, she admitted reluctantly; a man

she could see women swooning over—with his bronzed skin, a stark contrast to his near-snow-white hair. On any other man, prematurely white hair might make them look aged, but not Jeffrey. The stark white hair, combined with his manner, only served to lend an air of distinction.

Yeah, but appearances can be misleading, her mind interjected.

Her gaze settled on his, and the chill returned as if a winter's wind blew through the French doors. Instinctively, she glanced at the French doors as if seeking to determine whether there was indeed an alternate reason for her chills. Neither stood ajar, confirming that the coldness in Jeffrey's eyes was that which made her uneasy. Those cold, gray orbs. She'd seen eyes that shade of color before—on a snake. It had crawled across her leg one day as she lie stretched out on the grass, gazing at the sky.

The snake's eyes bore a striking resemblance to Jeffrey's. Both emotionless and penetrative. The sort of gaze that stared deep inside a person, but hid its own essence from view. Mirrors reflecting outward, not inward. Yes, that was Jeffrey's eyes. Soulless. The snake, with eyes as cold Jeffrey's, turned out to be harmless; however, she had yet to determine the sort of damage that Jeffrey the snake, was capable of inflicting. As with any dangerous beast, it was always best to approach with caution. A fact she had a difficult time persuading her mind to agree upon.

"It's nice to see I'm pleasing to look at," he drawled. "Would you like me to stand here a bit longer? If not, I'm getting stiff and would prefer to sit." He was laughing at her perusal. Although Christina was well aware of this, she refused to allow Jeffrey to bait her.

"Sit, if you please, but you never did answer my question."

"I intend to, but thought we might just sit and talk for a short spell." Jeffrey settled into the armchair beside the fireplace and pulled out a cigar.

"I'd prefer you not light that." Christina's color rose as he blatantly ignored her and struck a light against the sole of his obviously expensive boots.

"Sorry, my dear, but I never could take the request of a lady over the taste of a good cigar." Jeffrey took a long draw and blew a cloud of blue smoke toward the chimney. "I will however, try to keep the smoke away from your delicate senses. Fair compromise?"

"As I am still recovering from a serious illness, I would prefer not to be bombarded with ill-smelling cigar smoke, so no, it isn't a fair compromise."

"Well, since I'm not of a mind to ruin a perfectly good and rather expensive cigar, perhaps we can simply discuss the reason behind my visit, and try to pretend you don't mind."

"It you had been a gentleman in the first place and not lit it, your precious, expensive cigar would not be in danger of imminent ruin; and as I will not be subjected to either cigar fumes or ill-mannered guests, I will take my leave. Good day, Mr. Buchanan." Christina stood and started toward the solarium doors.

"Do you always treat callers this brusquely, my dear?" Jeffrey called, and Christina turned abruptly on her heels.

"When I didn't ask them to call, yes. When my parents shut me in a room under enigmatic circumstances with a man that I barely know, yes. When that caller is rude in his manner, yes. When I ask questions and receive no answers..."

"Point well taken."

"Good. Then I'll bid you good day."

Jeffrey sighed loudly, exaggeratedly, "I will ruin my perfectly good cigar, unless you've decided you aren't interested in those enigmatic circumstances."

Christina removed her hand from the doorknob and turned, "So, you intend to answer my question then?" Her tone suspicious.

"I said I would. I'll let you have that little battle." Jeffrey leaned forward and smashed the cigar into the ashtray. "Perfectly good waste of an expensive cigar, if you ask me," he muttered. "There, woman, it's out. Now sit."

"Are you planning to remain this discourteous throughout our conversation?" Christina asked, stubbornly remaining near the solarium door. She certainly wasn't going to remain in a room in her own home and allow a man she disliked to verbally harass her. Especially when she didn't want to remain in his company in the first place. Damnable curiosity.

Jeffrey took a deep breath, the color of his skin deepening to a dark red beneath the collar of his overly starched shirt. The exertion to forfeit his arrogant stance was evident in his jaw, clenched and grinding. So tightly clamped, that his words ground out from between his lips with effort. "I do apologize. I'm not around ladies much, except of course, ladies of the evening, so I find it difficult to bow to all of the requisite and tedious courtesies."

Christina closed her eyes and shook her head in disbelief. It was an apology, as apologies went, and she supposed it explained his lack of decorum...she sighed audibly and returned to her seat on the couch. "If you would be so kind as to explain all of the strange goings-on this morning, in all haste, I would be forever grateful. I find that my head is in dire need of a pillow."

"I took the liberty of stopping by to discuss a certain matter with your parents, and at the moment of your arrival, your father had only just given his consent, which would account for your mother's reaction and willingness to leave you and me alone in the same room without a chaperone."

"Your propensity to mince words is very trying indeed. You have said much, but revealed nothing. Why can't you simply answer my question?"

"Which was?"

"Do you mock me, sir? Do you find it amusing to toy with a woman not long recovered from sickness?" She asked through clenched teeth.

"I do regret your distress, but a little tit for tat was in order, after your less-than-lady-like dressing down of my own person. If we both concede that we will not tolerate the others lack of comportment, I will endeavor to answer all of your questions fully? Agreed?"

"Very well, Mr. Buchanan. Do proceed."

Jeffrey crossed his legs and settled more comfortably in his seat. Without preamble, he stated, "I came here this morning to offer for your hand in marriage, to which your father readily—and most graciously—granted approval."

"I do beg pardon?"

"Oh, come now! I thought that was a very direct, clear, and concise answer to your question as to what had transpired here this morning. Don't tell me that my affianced is too dimwitted to understand the meaning behind one simple sentence. That would be so disappointing."

"You *do* toy with me. I find it highly unlikely that my parents would accept an offer of marriage from a man who has not even deigned to call upon me; and whose only interest to date has been to see what sort of mischief he can get my brother into. Since you seem unwilling to clarify why it is you and I are even conversing, I will take my leave of you." For the second time that morning, Christina made her way to the door only to be stopped short by her damnable curiosity.

"Your brother is the reason why I never felt the need to court you, my dear." Jeffrey's tone made it plain that he was playing with her and truly enjoying himself. It also revealed that, while he may not know her from personal contact, he somehow knew her well enough to know her curiosity was her most powerful foe. When she turned to face him, his expression revealed that he knew she wouldn't leave—not until her curiosity was completed sated. He had her trapped by her own need to know.

"What has Thomas to do with all of this?" She asked, her feet firmly rooted next to the solarium doors."

"Return to your seat, and we'll continue with our conversation, my dear," Jeffrey purred, and Christina winced. She sensed that whatever he was up to would not bode well for her. She forced her legs to return her to the couch, but as unwilling as they were to move, her mind was even more distraught over the turn of events.

Don't be daft. Leave now and find a way to talk your parents out of this farcical situation, her mind kept yelling at her, making it hard to focus on Jeffrey's words.

"As you mentioned, Thomas and I have become rather well-acquainted. Spending many a night enjoying the company of women together and the often-occasioned game of chance. To which your brother has less aptitude than with the women, I must say. So poorly is that aptitude that he's gotten himself into rather a tight spot with some unsavory and violent brigands. Circumstances of which I have the ability to right, with the proper incentive."

"That being?" Christina queried cautiously.

"Again with the dimwitted comments. I thought for certain that my choice was a sound one, but just conversing with you these short minutes has me concerned that you have less than half a brain and are far more churlish than is to my liking. We will have to remedy both sooner rather than later. With that being said, I will again make my point clear and concise. You and I are to wed, because I have determined that you are the woman for me. If you refuse me or try to prevent our marriage from proceeding as I have planned, I will see to it that your brother does not escape his debt unscathed; or your father."

"You expect me to sit here and take your word for all of this? You really must believe me to be a dolt. Well, I'll disabuse you of that notion immediately. I am not dimwitted, nor will I become engaged under threat of harm to my family; especially when you've provided me no such proof..."

The papers that Jeffrey threw at her feet stopped Christina's tirade in its tracks. For the second time that morning, she sensed she'd crossed paths with a snake. That if she bent to retrieve those papers, they would somehow come alive and strike at her very heart, destroy her security and way of life. She stared down at them, refusing to budge.

"Pick them up, Christina," Jeffrey cooed. "Read them."

Christina sat immobile, her gaze transfixed on the pages scattered at her feet. She saw Jeffrey in her periphery as he reached down and scooped the pages up, but still her gaze did not falter. She was immobilized with terror, just as she'd been in her dreams, when confronted by the white beast. Only this wasn't a dream from which she could awaken. The was real.

"Very well, I will read one to you. They are all about the same after all. Except for the monies owed." Jeffrey cleared his throat dramatically, and began reading:

I.O.U. James Witt $200, this the 5th

day of January

in the year of our Lord, 1861.

Thomas Carthington

"Do you need me to read you another one? I have nearly twenty of like content," Jeffrey purred.

"How?" Christina whispered in dazed shock.

"How? Easily enough and I can assure you, totally by design. I have been visiting here for over two years now, allowing the debt to mount, purchasing the IOUs for a song, waiting for the right moment to arrive. The precise moment when I knew you would be unable to deny me, because you love your family too much."

"Why didn't you just call on me? Why go to so much effort to destroy any hope of affection I may have developed for you?"

"I didn't think you'd accept my pursuits. You always seemed oblivious of my existence, and those times you did acknowledge me, I saw the disdain etched on that pretty face of yours. Like when you came in here tonight. You didn't know why I'd come, and though I attempted civility, you still stared at me as if I had somehow intruded into your perfect little world. So, I used Thomas to wheedle my way into your family's life. I made certain that *they* approved of me. After all, a gentleman needs but the consent of the father to wed his daughter, right? Besides, I refuse to grovel at any woman's feet, to play the courting game to attain that, which is no more than what I deserve. Enter Thomas, with his poor aptitude for cards, and I acquire a winning hand. So, you see my dear, the simple fact of the matter is—you will marry me, on my terms, and in my time, or I will destroy your family."

"You'd do that, too, wouldn't you, you snake?" Christina whispered harshly, feeling the noose slowly tighten around her neck, constricting her breathing.

"Call me what you will, my dear, but if it gets my ring on your finger and your body into my bed, then I'll do what I must."

"None of this makes any sense. I must be dreaming," Christina groaned and closed her eyes. The feel of his hand upon hers, startled her into opening them again. She looked down in horror as Jeffrey slid a garnet ring upon her finger.

"No," she cried quietly. "This isn't real. It isn't happening."

His hand gripped her chin and raised her face so that he could look her in the eyes, "It is real, so get used to it. You belong to me now, Christina."

"I think I'd better return to my room now," she whispered, feeling close to fainting. She couldn't comprehend any of it and wouldn't be able to until she got away from Jeffrey. Jeffrey's hand moved from her chin and clasped onto her elbow. He gently led her toward the solarium door.

"You do look rather pale, my dear. Perhaps you should have dinner in your room this evening."

"Stop!" Christina hissed, and pulled her elbow free from his hand, his soothing words snapping her from her shocked doldrums.

"Stop what, Christina?"

"Stop acting solicitous. It's fake, just like this engagement." Christina started toward the door, but Jeffrey stepped in front of her.

"Oh it is very real, Christina, just as real as my threat to destroy your family if you give me any difficulties with my plans. Understand?"

"I understand all too well, Mr. Buchanan."

"Don't you think under the circumstances, that you should call me Jeffrey?"

"That's never going to happen. If it were up to me, you'd never call me by my given name either."

"Very disagreeable," Jeffrey replied angrily, "and definitely unwise. See to it that you aren't this way in the presence of your family or others. Is that understood as well?"

"I understand you, but you understand this," Christina said, straightening her back and clenching her fists at her sides, she labored to keep the tremors from her voice as she spoke. "You've left me no choice right now but to consent to this farce of an engagement. Since I don't fancy the notion of my family's destruction, I will give you no difficulties. If I could envision winning a fight with you, I'd beat you insensately this very moment; however, I'm not dimwitted enough to try. You will however, never have my respect, love, or friendship, and I will be praying fervently every night that the good Lord will strike you down before allowing this mockery of a wedding to take place, and if He doesn't see fit, I may just end up doing it myself." With that, Christina shoved past her betrothed and fled to the security of her room.

CHAPTER 7

"I don't have to dream about white beasts," Christina raged, stomping around her room, "when there is one right downstairs in my own house." She flopped onto her bed and sprung up again, unable to settle long in her agitated state. "How dare he blackmail me into marrying him?" She continued to rail at the walls. "Marriage is supposed to be a sanctified union sprung from love, not this— this—oh, how dare he?" Her energy was quickly waning, but she couldn't quiet her nerves. This level of upset, so soon after recovering from pneumonia, she didn't need. Weakness finally overtook her, exhausting her efforts to remain animatedly livid, so she sat on the bed for a moment, head in hands, trying to calm her breathing. If she didn't relax, she could very well have a relapse. Still, she was having difficulty calming her jumping nerves. When she felt a modicum of composure return, she left her room, slipped from the house and went straight to the barn. She needed to ride, needed to feed from her horse's strength and power. She reached the stables and had to rest against the doorjamb again as a bout of dizziness struck her.

"Where's you is a goin' Miss?"

The voice startled her and she stumbled from turning too quickly. A hand shot out to stabilize her, and then detached quickly. "You shore yous able to be outside?"

"I'm fine, Moses, thank you. Just want to take Shooting Star out for a brief jaunt. He's been neglected during my illness. Would you be kind enough to see him readied for me? I'll just sit and wait on that bundle of hay over there." Christina smiled, but her attempts did not erase the concern from the stable hand's face.

"I'm fine, Moses, really. Besides, Shooting Star will be doing all of the work, since I plan to give him his lead. I'll just be going along for the ride."

"If'n you say so, Miss," Moses accommodated; however, her mind was far less accommodating.

You're not using your head if you think you're strong enough to take this horse riding, it scolded.

"I simply haven't a choice. I need to get out of here. Find a place to clear my head," Christina replied, moving to take the horse's reins, and leading him from the barn.

Who's going to be dragging you back here, when you fall off, her mind retorted, *'cause I can't crawl out of your head and do it, that's for certain.*

"Oh, would you please be quiet for a moment and let me get my strength back?" She sighed and leaned against the barn door.

I'm tired and your body's tired. Shouldn't that be a clue that we need to go back to bed, not go traipsing about the countryside?

"Where exactly you be headed?"

Christina quickly pushed away from the barn and raised her hand to shield her eyes from the brightness of the sun. She peered in the direction the voice had come. Her gaze fell upon the outline of Hyacinth standing in the kitchen door, wiping her large hands on a dishtowel. She didn't need to see her to know she was scowling.

"I'm going for a ride, Hyacinth," Christina called, trying to lighten her tone and hide the tiredness she felt.

"Does your mama know you be outside?"

"I couldn't find her," Christina lied, "but I'll only be gone a couple of hours."

She *had* seen her mother, but Jeffrey's intrusion prevented her discussing her intent.

"Well you best be gettin' back here at a decent hour. Supper ain't gonna be awaitin' on you. And what your momma gonna say 'bout your being gone when you done just gotten over being sick?"

"I'll be back before supper, and I'm feeling much better, I promise. I just need to get some fresh air is all."

"All right then, but where Moses is? A lady don' mount no horse by herself."

"I told him that I'd manage," she called, placing her foot in the stirrup and hauling her weak body onto the saddle. By the time she'd positioned her derriere and had her feet planted in the stirrups, she was sweating profusely, making her wonder at her decision to leave, but only momentarily. She couldn't think straight cooped up in her room. Only one place provided the peace she needed to think, and there was no greater need than now to get there. She desperately needed to rid her mind of the clutter created by Jeffrey.

Christina turned her horse and spurred Shooting Star through the gate, beyond which lead a glorious expanse, and much-sought freedom.

A short while later, her horse slowed instinctively.

"You know where we are, don't you?" She murmured, stroking her horse affectionately. "It does lift the spirit, doesn't it?"

As they turned the last corner, Christina reined Shooting Star in. This was something she did every time before climbing the hill to her favorite spot. Her gaze took in the grassy hilltop, surrounded sporadically by tall pines.

It was here, atop this knoll overlooking a long winding stream, that she came when she was upset, as today, or when she just needed time to be alone. It was to this place that she ran to, as a child, when her brother hurt her feelings; to this place she came as a young lady, when Hyacinth would reprimand her for being too active for a girl. Lately, she came as a young woman to sort out her future.

Now Jeffrey Buchanan was taking those dreams out of her hands, threatening her into a marriage of which she had no desire to be a part.

"Oh! How I hate that man!" She snapped and dug her heels into Shooting Star's flanks. The horse leapt forward and closed the remaining distance quickly, and within a few moments, Christina pulled her stallion to a halt, slid off, and was lying on her back in the grass, heedless of the stains that always found their way onto her clothing. She rolled onto her belly and plucked a blade of grass, a sigh escaping her lips. She picked some more grass and began weaving them distractedly.

"If only I could see past my anger to find a solution," she murmured, her fingers abstractly working with the long narrow blades. "The only solution that seems reasonable to me right now is to drive a knife through his heart, and that just won't do at all. I don't exactly relish the notion of spending my entire youth behind bars. What do you suggest that I do, Shooting Star?"

The beautiful chestnut mare bobbed its head. Then shook it violently as if in understanding. Christina smiled faintly, but her heart remained heavy.

"You're lots of help," she snapped playfully.

As if just realizing that she had been doing something, she glanced down at the blades of grass still in her hands. She had hoped that this place could calm her turbulent deliberations enough to present a solution to her dilemma, as it had always done. Instead, she found that all she'd managed to accomplish was to make a nice little green grass bracelet for her wrist. She dropped the little bracelet and closed her eyes, the warmth of the sun lulling her into a less-than-blissful sleep.

CHAPTER 8

Christina eyes fluttered open. She glanced at the clouds passing overhead and mentally shook herself, wondering why she was laying prone, tall wheat-like blades of grass swaying around her body in a mystical dance.

The sound of distant growling brought her situation crashing back and she shivered in abject terror. She wanted to lift up to see what was happening, but she was afraid of drawing attention to herself. Still, she couldn't stay here and wait for the victor to claim the spoils.

With determination, she carefully lifted her head just above the tallest stalk and watched in fascination the battle that was about to take place.

The wolf had emerged from the shadowy tree line, insinuating itself between her and the beast, baring its razor-sharp pearly whites and emitting a growl that seemed to issue from deep within its chest.

While she was grateful that the arrival of the wolf had temporarily distracted the beast from attacking her, she knew it was just a matter of time before the victor of the upcoming fight claimed her for its next meal. If only she could use the distraction and escape.

She looked over her shoulder and wondered just how far she could make it before either of them noticed that their afternoon snack was getting away.

I need to wait until they are at each other before moving, *she thought. She willed the fight to begin, so that she could depart, but the two beasts just stood there growling and snapping, neither appearing eager to make the first move.*

The sun glittered off the teeth of the wolf, and the thought of those jaws tearing at her tender flesh, spurred her into action. She turned onto her hands and knees, unmindful of the prickly grass that stabbed at her through the thin material of her skirt, or the rocks that jabbed painfully at the palms of her hands. All she could think about was escaping.

She crawled as fast as her clothing would allow, cursing a blue streak at the impediment of her skirts, which continually wrapped annoyingly around her legs, making her movements rigid and slow. If she didn't find those wagons soon, the survivor of that fight would surely find her.

She crawled faster.

Christina awoke with a start.

She glanced at the setting sun and stood reluctantly, mounted her horse, and made her way home. Hyacinth would skin her alive if she were late getting to supper.

Christina turned Shooting Star over to a stable hand, too dejected to brush her horse down as she usually did. When she reached her room, she flopped on her bed.

"Maybe I should stay in my room tonight," she murmured, flipping onto her back. She was suddenly more tired and extremely reluctant to get up to dress. "As sick as I've been, no one is likely to argue. I truly do feel out of sorts."

Without a doubt, she knew that Jeffrey would be at dinner tonight to announce their engagement, formally, and she was worried that her overzealous tongue might go off and give Jeffrey the ammunition he needed to destroy her family.

"I wonder if he actually *would* destroy my family if I defied him," she pondered aloud and then shuddered as a dreadful feeling crept down her spine erasing all doubt that he would do just that. Somehow, someway, she was going to have to reach down deep into her reserve of strength and find a way to deal with this. Although the way things were going, she was going to have to deal with it alone.

It would appear that Jeffrey had her entire family duped. If not that, then they were all blind, and she knew it wasn't that. Her parents especially seemed happy with the arrangement. She supposed they felt she was ecstatic about the prospect of becoming Mrs. Jeffrey Buchanan, but nothing was further from the truth.

What stymied her even more was how to pretend affection for a man she so despised. If she didn't, he would surely become angry, and that anger would likely drive him to ruin her family. Then she would have to live with the guilty knowledge that her inability to act destroyed the people she loved most.

"Well, I've seen actresses on stage in the city, and it doesn't seem to be that hard," she reasoned.

Yeah, well they're professionals remember? Her mind argued with irritating logic.

"Maybe they are, but it still doesn't seem very difficult," she countered. "Besides, Dad is always telling us that we can do whatever we want, if we put our mind to it."

What if I don't want to participate? Her mind argued.

"Well, you are just going to have to, and I don't have time to debate the point with you any further. I need to ready myself for dinner."

I thought we were going to skip dinner.

"Well, I just decided it's better than sitting here arguing with myself all evening."

"Christina, who is it you're you talking to?" Carlotta's voice brought a sudden halt to Christina's one-sided conversation.

"No one, Mother!" She responded, raising her falsely cheery voice so that her mother could hear her through the thick oak door.

"May I come in, dear?"

"Of course." Christina sheepishly pulled the door open, blushing as her mother placed a light kiss on her cheek. "Sorry, mother. I should have let you in immediately. I guess my mind's a bit preoccupied."

"As well it should be, dear." Carlotta went to the bed and sat genteelly on the edge, patting the area invitingly beside her. "Do come sit, dear. I want to talk to you a moment before going down to dinner."

Christina sat demurely, folding her hands in her lap as her mother taught her, and waited quietly for her mother to speak. Carlotta sat a while, looking intently at her daughter's profile.

"Are you feeling up to coming down for supper, my child?" She asked finally, laying a hand gently on her daughter's stiff one. "You still look a little peaked for my tastes, but I suppose if you can ride away on that horse of yours, then you can manage to join your family for a quiet meal, correct?"

"Yes, mother. I plan to join the family for dinner," Christina murmured, suitably chastised. Obviously, her mother wasn't pleased when Hyacinth told her about Christina's foray so soon after recovering from her illness.

"I wasn't quite certain, since it would appear you have not tried to ready yourself, yet dinner will be ready within the half hour." Carlotta's gently reproving tone caused the color in Christina's cheeks to deepen. "I'm glad you are feeling up to coming down, especially since your fiancé will be joining us." The tint on Christina's face intensified, and Carlotta smiled. "There is a great deal I will need to discuss with you before the wedding; however, time is limited right now as you need to ready yourself." Carlotta stood abruptly and headed for the bedroom door. "I'll send Victoria to help you, so you won't be delayed further."

"Thank you, mother."

"You're welcome, child."

The door shut quietly on its hinges, mimicking the very person that shut it. Christina relaxed her demeanor, but sat wishing that she were more like her mother. Carlotta Carthington was quiet and demure. The epitome of a lady. Even when she was chastising her for riding Shooting Star after recovering from pneumonia, or for not preparing for dinner, her voice was always soft and gentle. Christina knew that her grandparents had never reprimanded her mother as a child for being too active or getting dirty, as she herself had.

Another thing she knew about her mother that Carlotta was unaware, was that she didn't love her husband. Yet, she still managed to please him and serve him with grace. Her parents had an arranged marriage between them. A business arrangement, much like Jeffrey detailed for her pending marriage to him. She mulled this over in her mind, wondering whether she could accept her fate with as much grace and civility as her mother had with her father.

She decided not. "The major difference is they have respect for each other. Even if it isn't love, theirs wasn't a marriage founded on blackmail," she murmured, "Oh, why can't I talk to mother about this?"

Because she likes Jeffrey, and wants to see you properly wed and settled before you get too old and burdensome, her mind supplied. Her stomach flip-flopped and she wanted to scream. There had to be someone she could talk to, someone who could help her through this dilemma.

An idea popped into her head, but she pushed it aside, as improbable and impractical. After all, what would *he* know about women and relationships?

Maybe nothing, but at least he can listen to your whining, her mind teased.

"I'm not whining about this. I'm simply desperate—yes, what is it?" Christina asked as a timid knock came at the door. The door cracked a fraction and a black, curly head peered in.

"I come to help you get ready, Miss."

"Come in, Victoria. As you can see," Christina sighed, "we'll have to keep it simple tonight. There's just no time for anything elaborate."

"I got jes the thing, Miss. Perfect hairdo and perfect gown. You jes leave everything to Victoria."

"I'm all yours." *Except my mind,* she added silently and mentally detached herself while Victoria quickly brushed out her long tresses. Again, she started to speculate on whom she could turn to for help. She was going to need all the help she could get to get out of her present predicament.

Could her old friend, Chin Woo, really help her? After all, he was just a man. He may actually side with Jeffrey. *Nah! Not him,* she thought. Perhaps he could just listen to her. That, alone, may provide relief from her mental anguish. Who knows, that philosophical old Chinaman may just have an answer for her. Although an unlikely candidate, he was one person she could confide in right now.

Victoria interrupted her musings when she leaned around Christina and replaced the brush on the vanity. Christina stood and surveyed herself in the floor-length mirror and smiled. "You are a miracle-worker, Victoria. Thank you."

"You very welcome, Miss. You go down now, and I clean up."

Christina made her way out of the room. Her spirits were low, but her determination was high. Tomorrow she would go to the mercantile and have a chat with her dear friend, Chin Woo.

She paused at the bottom of the stairs, the sound of voices drifting to her ears. With a huge effort, she straightened her back, and with determined resolution, marched into the dining room. Her knees were knocking so loudly that she half-expected someone to announce a visitor at the front door. Fortunately, no one did.

CHAPTER 9

Jeffrey walked over to where Christina stood—her back stiff as an iron rod. "It's nice to see that you could join us, my dear." Jeffrey's smile did not reach the warning in his eyes. He placed a light kiss on her cheek, and Christina had to force herself not to flinch.

As Christina took her seat, she looked over to where her brother, Thomas, sat and saw by the alternating look of anger he aimed at Jeffrey and the guilt-ridden look he gave her that he knew some of what had transpired. Had Jeffrey threatened him into silence as well? Exactly how much Thomas knew about her current situation, she would have to decide later, for now her father was standing, wine glass in hand, a beaming expression on his face.

"I have some good news to announce," her father boomed, and Christina felt a sweat break out along her upper lip.

He is not even going to wait until after dinner to make the announcement, she judged silently, bitterly. Her stomach began to somersault again, and she suddenly had serious doubts about keeping any food down. Her hands gripped tightly to the rim of her chair and her breathing slowly, deeply, in and out.

Stay calm! Her mind shouted. *Do not give him the satisfaction!*

"As you are well aware, Jeffrey has asked for Christina's hand in marriage," her father continued, unaware of the discomfort in his own daughter, "and she has joyfully accepted." He paused dramatically, raising his cup in preparation of the toast to come. "I just want to say, Jeffrey, that you are like a son to me, and I'm very pleased that you've taken my own son and treated him like a brother. Now, you'll be taking my daughter from me, so I trust that you will love and take good care of her. I bid you welcome to our family."

Christina drank deeply from the white wine brought from her father's private stock in celebration of the joyous news. She looked across the table at her brother. He had downed his wine just as quickly, and was raising his glass for a refill. His eyes quickly met hers and shifted away.

You hope to bury your guilt in your cup, I see, Christina observed angrily and turned her gaze away. It came to rest on her mother who was wiping her eyes daintily with her handkerchief.

Oh, mother, how could you know me so little that you cannot see the misery in my heart? Her eyes moved again, and settled on her father. He met her gaze and smiled affectionately, obviously pleased with his choice for her mate.

You, I understand least of all, Father. Do you not see the snake you have promised your daughter to?

While her mind raged, she kept the fake smile plastered to her face, but she wasn't even able to maintain that when her father stood again and stunned the room with his next announcement.

"I'm sorry, Jeffrey. I was hoping to save the next bit of news until after dinner; however, I feel as if I have ants scurrying around in my pants, and can't stay seated long enough to enjoy the meal, so I feel I must declare the news now. Then perhaps we can relax and eat. Maybe even discuss what's to come? What say you? Any objections to my speaking now? After all, it was partly your idea, wasn't it, lad?"

"Go right ahead, Mr. Carthington. I'm sure if you hadn't spoken up, my excitement would have gotten the better of me." Jeffrey smiled that charming smile and Christina shook her head in wonder. He could charm a snake, which would make him worse than one. No, even certain types of snakes can charm other snakes. He's just more deadly than others.

Christina shot a quick glance at her mother and watched her eyes widen. *So, even Mother is in the dark.* Although she had to give her credit for maintaining her decorum. Still, whatever her father was about to announce, only Jeffrey seemed aware of it. What did that tell her about her father? Did he really care more for Jeffrey than the rest of his family? Judging by Thomas's face, they had not even brought him into the loop, and he was his father's son. His dejected look told her that he was thinking the same thing. This made her almost want to forgive his disastrous gaming habits—almost.

"Opportunities abound beyond the Mississippi River," her father began. He'd obviously rehearsed this speech several times before dinner, for he spoke as if to a grand audience, not simply his family. "People have been heading west in droves since the gold rush began back in '49. Even my own brother managed to strike it rich. He used that fortune to amass a greater fortune, selling the very cattle us Easterners place on our dinner plate each night."

Christina's head pounded and the somersaults in her stomach grew stronger and more frequent with each word her father spoke. She squeezed the chair arms harder as she tried to focus on what he was telling them.

"So, it is with much deliberation, that I've decided that we too must stake our own claim and head west, before all the opportunities for growth are gone. Right now, the country is ripe for the picking. Miners have barely tapped the gold mines and the land is literally ours for the taking. The government is willing to front land to any able-bodied man willing to work it. I think that Jeffrey, Thomas, and I are more than able."

"Still, Charles. This is our home," Carlotta whispered, her agitation at the news only apparent in the way she violently twisted the napkin in her lap.

"I know, dear." Charles patted her cheek in a way that Christina perceived as patronizing. "We're young enough to build a newer, grander home."

"This is the only home I've ever known. I don't want to move to a hostile land and start over." Carlotta's voice raised enough to send eyebrows rising around the table. She lowered her gaze in embarrassment. Charles coughed, his own color rising. His wife had obviously never questioned his decisions before.

"Be that as it may, the decision is mine and it's been made. I've already cut a deal with Jim Baker, our local banker, for buying our home and all its furnishings for a fair sum. We leave in a month." Charles plopped heavily into his chair and downed his wine. He looked deflated, and so he should. Those sitting at the table did not receive his news as well as he hoped.

"I think I'll retire to my room for the evening. I'm suddenly not very well," Carlotta whispered and left the room.

All eyes followed Carlotta as she left the room. Christina waited until her mother was out of earshot before turning and facing her father again. "Oh, father, why couldn't you have asked your family before making such a huge decision? Or are we not important enough to you to ask our opinion?"

"Watch your tongue, child."

Christina was beyond caring about the consequences of her actions. The stress of the day had been simply too much. "I can't do that father. What you've done is wrong, and I have a sneaking suspicion that someone has bamboozled you into it, someone that's trying to destroy this family." Christina stood abruptly and with a whirl of skirts, fled to her room, and launched herself face-first onto her bedding, tears streaming unchecked down her cheeks.

CHAPTER 10

"Please tell me it isn't true, Thomas?" Christina cried softly, knowing instinctively when he came into her room, though she heard not a sound above her own sobs. When she finally spent all her tears and rolled over on her bed, she found him sitting in the chair beside her. She promptly launched herself from the bed and wrapped her arms around his neck, crying all over again.

After a while, she straightened up and blew her nose with the handkerchief that magically appeared in her brother's hand. "Tell me this isn't happening?" She whispered again, returning to sit on the edge of her canopied bed. She waited for an answer to her question—a question, Thomas knew, sought not only answers regarding her father's announcement, but that would hopefully discount Jeffrey's claims about his gambling; however, she realized that there were no adequate answers, for no matter how Thomas explained his or father's actions it would not erase the fact that they were turning her and her family topsy-turvy.

Christina's anger rose again, but quickly waned as she looked into the helpless expression on her brother's face. The struggle playing across his features was clear: righteous indignation to helpless rage, finally settling into deep remorse. His impotence to act caused by his own weakness to gamble, and his inability to settle his own debt made him heartsick, and Christina knew it.

"Oh, Thomas!" Christina whispered on a heavy sigh, and placed a hand gently on the crown of his head. After a moment, she removed her hand, and slid back against her headboard. Her temper soared again when it dawned on her that, in a month, she would never sleep in this bed again. Her vexation over this realization caused her to wonder whether she would ever have control over her tumultuous emotions again.

She breathed deeply and let loose another sigh, "So, you know he blackmailed me into marriage using your markers and is using my love for my family to keep me quiet about it. What about you? Is he threatening to throw you in jail if you tell Mom and Dad?"

"Yeah," Thomas murmured dejected, but then suddenly slammed his fist into the palm of his other hand. "How could I have been so stupid? I should have seen this coming, but I wanted to be a man and learn to gamble..."

"You wanted to grow up, Thomas, too fast, and play with the big boys," Christina interrupted. "The problem now is you have to pay the price like a big boy. I just wish you and Jeffrey hadn't dragged me into it. I didn't much care for Jeffrey when he was visiting you, because of what he was doing to you, but now..."

"I know," Thomas sighed, "I hate him too."

"To make matters worse," Christina continued, her voice reflecting all of the disgust she felt inside, "Father is acting just as juvenile. How could he do this? How could he just up and sell everything without telling anyone? And you, gambling my life away. What's gotten into this family?" She finished her tirade and instantly regretted her outburst.

Thomas shook his lowered head slowly, trying valiantly to get a handle on his own emotions.

"Well, we probably cannot do anything about Jeffrey presently, but perhaps we can talk some sense to Father," Christina said hopefully. "After all, what could he possibly know about cattle farming or gold mining?"

"Ranching, Sis."

"Ranching, farming. The wording matters not, Thomas," Christina argued. "My point is, Father hasn't the first clue about how to raise cattle or mine for gold. He's a merchant, for heaven's sake, he has been since before we were born. I can't recall a day that he's endured hard labor, can you?"

"Well, whether he has the knowledge or not, he's convinced that he could pull this off." Thomas lifted his head; glad the topic had changed from his own foolish behavior to their father's foolish decision. "He's like a little boy right now. His enthusiasm is that of a child at Christmas. I tried talking to him before coming to check on you, but it was pointless. What he doesn't know, he's certain he can learn from Uncle Peter and as far as the gold mining thing, I don't think he's seriously considering that."

"Just because Uncle Peter made a fortune out west, doesn't mean that Father can. Besides, Uncle Peter headed out west when we were just a gleam in Father's eye. There's no way that Dad has the stamina for an endeavor of this size."

"I know it doesn't make a heck of a lot of sense, Sis." Thomas rubbed a hand tiredly over his young beardless chin. "Jeffrey really did a song and dance on him."

"I don't understand. What do you mean?"

"I said that Jeffrey..."

"I heard what you said. What did you mean?"

"Oh, you didn't know?"

"Know what?" Christina demanded, exasperated.

"This move was all Jeffrey's idea."

"It was? I knew that Jeffrey was aware of the move, but I had no idea that he was directly involved in the decision. Why would he want us to move west?" Christina asked incredulously.

"Not really certain. Jeffrey told Pa that he's heard rumors of a war coming and that he wanted you out of here before all hell broke loose."

"Me?"

"Yep. He wanted to move you out west, after the marriage, and then convinced Father to move along also, so you wouldn't be too far from family. He's convinced that he could do better for you out there, and he wouldn't have to worry about all the fighting that's bound to happen in these parts. Convinced Father of the financial benefits too."

"I take it he's not planning to join the army then?" It was a rhetorical question; still, Christina couldn't help poking fun at her fiancé's obvious cowardice.

"Reckon he isn't. Not that I could really see Jeffrey fighting for anything. Except you."

"I get the distinct impression that his only love is himself."

"You and I know that, but not Dad. He played Dad like an

expert violinist. Add to that the possibilities of striking it big out west and...well let's just say Dad didn't require much persuading."

"I see," Christina murmured thoughtfully, but she didn't really see at all. From what little she had heard, cattle ranching took a lot of hard work. Gold prospecting also. It was work that she just couldn't see Jeffrey sullying his hands doing. It just didn't make sense. Unless he truly did want to leave before war broke out and this was his way of avoiding having to enlist.

"Listen, Sis," Thomas said, and lowered his head again to avoid his sister's gaze. He felt the need to apologize for his behavior of late, but it was still damned hard on his young pride to have to do so. Still, if it wasn't for him, his sister would probably have had a chance at a happy marriage, "I'm really sorry about getting you into this mess," he said finally, his voice barely a whisper.

"Oh, Thomas! If you had a problem, you should have gone to Dad. Surely he could have helped."

"Yeah, he'd have helped, all right. With a beating in the tool shed, he'd have helped." His head snapped up and his cheeks reddened at the image of a confrontation with their father. Christina did understand. Charles Carthington was not the warmest of men, and his answer to everything that Thomas did wrong was to strap welts onto his tail end.

"Well, maybe that's exactly what you needed. As it is, I have to bail you out by marrying a man I cannot stand to be within a few feet of, and I'm none too pleased about the prospect!"

"Oh God, Sis! I'm truly sorry."

At that moment, he looked so much like the sixteen-year-old that he was and not the man that he tried desperately to be, that her heart went out to him. "It's all right, Thomas," she whispered assuredly. "I can take care of that snake. Right now, we need to figure out what he's really after."

"I don't understand, Sis. I thought we figured that out already."

"No, Thomas. We decided why Dad wants this move, but what does Jeffrey get out of it?"

"You."

"Me," Christina agreed. "I just wish I knew why he wanted me so much." She scratched her head for a moment, deep in thought.

"Well, you are beautiful—for a sister."

Christina slapped at Thomas's arm playfully, but then grew pensive again. Thomas watched his sister and smiled. It was as though he could actually see the gears inside her head turning. "Thomas. Let me ask you something?"

"Sure."

"We know that God didn't equip Dad, physically, to handle hard labor, but what about Jeffrey? Have you ever seen him do a hard day's work since you've known him? Have you actually seen him work at all, for that matter? What does he do for a living, anyway?"

"I think he's in the import-export business. At least I think I heard him say something like that once. Not certain though. Of course, that doesn't take brawn. He's a dandy if I've ever seen one. I think the very notion of dirtying his hands would send him into a fit of the vapors."

Christina giggled, "He's not as bad as all that. He is physically strong, but as far as hard work   if he is into import-export, that wouldn't require a lot of hard labor. Working a ranch takes a lot of strong-muscled, backbreaking, sweat-causing work. Am I right?"

"So why do it?" Thomas concluded, warming to the subject. "Especially when he seems to be faring so well here?"

"Precisely."

"I don't know, Sis. Maybe, despite all of our suspicions, his motivations are pure and honest."

"Perhaps, but I highly doubt it."

"Well, until we know for certain, why not try to see it as the adventure father does. After all, we are moving and there's not a blasted thing anyone can do about it."

"From what I understand, Dad has reached an agreement with the banker for the sale of the house already, but what about the mercantile, doesn't he need to sell that? Or has Father already arranged to sell it."

"I think he's already done so."

"So fast? To whom?"

"Andrew Michaelson."

"David's dad?"

"Yep. One and the same."

"Well, I guess that's the logical choice. They've been competing with each other longer than I can remember."

"That's what Dad said. Said he couldn't have found a more suitable buyer."

"How's Mother?" Christina asked suddenly.

"I don't rightly know," Thomas said softly. "I haven't seen her since dinner."

"I'd better go talk to her," she said, slipping off the bed and donning her slippers. "Then I'll go talk to father."

"Sis?"

"Yes, Thomas."

"You know it's not going to do any good, don't you?"

"Yes, I do, Thomas." Christina turned to leave.

"Sis?"

Christina held her frustration in check, and turned to face her brother again. "Yes, Thomas."

"If I could take it all back, I would."

"I know," she whispered, her heart full of love for her impetuous brother. "Everything will be all right, Thomas. It just has to be."

However, her words were not to prove prophetic.

CHAPTER 11

"Chin Woo. Are you in there?"

Christina knocked again on the tiny cabin's door and waited, her impatience evident in the continual tapping of her booted toe upon the small wooden porch. The day had dawned brilliantly with colors splashed across the sky like a painter who'd discovered that his palette held a myriad of hues he'd never seen before, and decided to experiment with today. Christina's heavy heart however, could only see gray as she slowly rode Shooting Star across the meadow to the small clearing where Chin Woo lived. She raised her hand to knock again, but Chin Woo pulled the door open, startling her.

"You try to hit me?" He asked, his left eyebrow arched in question as only he could do. It made his face look lopsided to Christina and she giggled slightly despite the heavy burden that weighted down her spirit.

"Can I talk to you for a few minutes, Chin Woo?"

"We always talk, Cookie, but never you come pounding at my door in early morning."

"I'm sorry, but it's somewhat important."

"The worry in your eyes says so. Come in. I make tea. Then we talk." Chin Woo stepped aside and let Christina enter. She stopped just inside the entrance to allow her eyes to adjust to the dim interior before taking a seat at the small table that took up most of the floor space. She'd visited with him often on the days that he escorted her home from town, but she'd never actually visited his house. The shadowy interior and sparse furnishings were a stark reminder of the differences in their status in life.

Chin Woo was a servant for her father, just like Hyacinth, Mirabelle, and the rest. Standing in his home, shed more light on those differences. Differences before to which she'd turned a blind eye. Now, standing amidst the poverty of his small abode, she had difficulty ignoring those differences, which suddenly increased her nervousness.

Perhaps this had been a mistake; perhaps she'd read more into their relationship than was there. After all, how could a real friendship develop across the imaginary master-servant lines? What if Chin Woo simply tolerated her because he worked for her father? The reflection was so disconcerting, that Christina shook her head violently to dislodge it. No! Chin Woo had always treated her more like family.

When she refocused her vision, Chin Woo was watching her intently. "Is okay for you to be here," he assured her with intuitiveness that bordered on scary. "You never visit me here, so I know what you need say must be important." Chin Woo set about making tea at a small stove that sat in the corner of the one-room cabin. "You tell me why you upset. Is it because Father is leaving this place?"

"Partly." Christina breathed a sigh of relief and brushed the remnants of the disturbing speculation from her mind. Chin Woo was her friend and she shouldn't allow her father's prejudice to become her own. She wouldn't. She'd never treated the household servants with disdain or as if they were beneath her, so why shouldn't she be friends with Chin Woo.

"Is easy to see this," Chin Woo said over his shoulder as he pulled two tin cups from the one cupboard above the stove. "I know you like this place. This is your home, but I can see more worry in eyes than just sadness to leave."

"Your perception never ceases to amaze me, Chin Woo."

Chin Woo put the tealeaves in the cup and turned to face Christina, while he waited for the water to heat.

"What are you going to do when we move?" It was a change of subject, but Christina needed a moment to collect her senses. Asking another man about her fiancé was a sensitive issue and she needed to approach it delicately; besides, she was curious. She'd known Chin Woo since she was a young lady of thirteen; and though it was a rather odd friendship, it was a friendship nonetheless.

He'd even taken to calling her Cookie; a nickname that he came up with because she ate far too many of them in her father's mercantile. Of course, Chin Woo did nothing to discourage her obsession with cookies, especially the coconut ones with chocolate on top.

In fact, each week when she would visit the store, her father would enlist Chin Woo to see her escorted safely home. On those days, Chin Woo would invariably have a cookie or two stashed in the pocket of his Yukata robe, paid for with his hard-earned wages. As she grew older, she objected to his wasting his money on her, but he merely smiled and said, "I like to see Cookie happy". That, of course, had led to her many tutoring lessons in correct English.

"A cookie can't smile," she reprimanded gently, but Chin Woo simply explained, "No, but cookie make you smile. You my Cookie, child, and you make me smile."

That left Christina speechless, and a little uncomfortable, until Chin Woo explained about the loss of his wife and child. That's when Christina realized that to him, she was more than a friend, she was like a daughter.

"Your Father no tell you?" Chin Woo interrupted her musings, and it took a moment for Christina to realize about what they'd been talking—Chin Woo's plans after they moved.

"I haven't had much opportunity to speak with Father since his *big* announcement to move west," Christina responded with a touch of sarcasm. "You've obviously spoken with him however, since you know about the move."

"Chin Woo knows only yesterday. I talk to Mr. Carthington then. He tell me I good worker and, since have no family here, he ask me to come to live with him and work with him some more."

"Are you telling me that you're coming with us?" Christina asked, her troubles temporarily forgotten in her rising excitement.

"That is what I say, yes," Chin Woo confirmed. Christina jumped up from the chair and launched herself at her friend. She wrapped her arms around his neck, squealing in delight. "Oh, Chin Woo, that is so wonderful!" She laughed. "I thought I wouldn't have any friends where we were going, and now—oh, it's simply wonderful!"

"I glad that Cookie happy," Chin Woo croaked, "but would very much like to breathe now, please." Chin Woo refilled his lungs in one deep dramatic intake of breath, and then grinned at Christina, who stood near the table, a blush creeping into her cheeks.

"I'm sorry, Chin Woo," she whispered in embarrassment. "I guess I just got excited."

"Is okay," Chin Woo said, smiling, "I not hurt, and I glad my Cookie happy. Is good to see smile after seeing frown on face when you come in." Chin Woo turned to the stove and removed the whistling kettle from the fire. Slowly, he added the scalding hot liquid to the tin cups and stirred the contents. Holding the cups gingerly with his fingertips, he quickly closed the short distance to the table and put them down. He blew on his fingers, and then took the only other available chair at the small table. "Cookie might wait a minute before picking up cup. Is hotter than I make usually."

"So I see," Christina giggled.

"So, I glad Cookie happy again, but something tell me you not stay happy long when explain other reason you come. You maybe hope I can help some way. That why you come?"

"I was selfishly counting on that." Christina took a deep breath. She looked at the tea leaves slowly drifting to the bottom of the cup and sighed. "You know Jeffrey Buchanan, don't you?"

"Sometime I see him when he come to town. He not very good man, I think."

"You think right. According to my brother, Jeffrey's the one who talked Father into selling everything that my family holds dear to start over in a strange and possibly hostile new land. On top of that," she continued in a rush, "he spent the last couple of years getting Thomas into so much trouble it's truly inconceivable, and now he expects me to bail Thomas out by marrying him. If I don't go through with it, he'll bury us all."

Chin Woo sat and mulled over everything for a minute, his eyes taking in his friend's tense body and clenched fists. *No one should be this worried,* he judged silently, sadly. Right now he wanted to take this man, who had caused so much distress to his friend, shackle him to a board and drip water into his eye—one slow, irritating, agonizing drop at a time. "I no understand what Cookie mean when she say Jeffrey bury family. How he do this thing? And what is trouble that young Thomas has?"

"I'm sorry, Chin Woo," Christina sighed, forcing her words to come more slowly, and to forgo use of idioms. "I forgot that I need to measure my words better, but it is just so nice to have someone to talk to about this. I guess my exasperation got the better of me. It doesn't help that this whole situation agitates me, and when I get agitated I talk faster than I should."

"Is all right, but Cookie need calm mind before explain. Tea is cool now. Cookie drink, then talk."

Christina sipped quietly for a moment, trying desperately to calm her frantic nerves. Chin Woo was right. This whole situation had her too frazzled. She hadn't really known how tightly her confrontation with Jeffrey wound her nerves until she started dumping her misery on her friend. Collect her wits. That's what she needed to do before continuing, or she probably could not explain anything coherently.

"The tea is good, Chin Woo," she commented quietly, her finger running circles along the rim of the tin cup, but Chin Woo didn't comment. He knew she was collecting her thoughts and needed no interruption. Finally, she looked up from her cup and started again. "Jeffrey has been coming to the house for more than two years now."

"I not know this. He come see Cookie?"

"No actually, he didn't. I barely even knew he was around, unless he and Thomas came staggering in late in the evenings after a night of carousing and gambling."

"I not know Thomas gamble."

"He didn't. Not until he met Jeffrey." Christina's eyes narrowed as she remembered Jeffrey's smug announcement yesterday that he held the markers to Thomas's massive gambling debt. "It seems that Jeffrey used Thomas to get to me."

"You lose me again, Cookie. Try to remember my English needs much work. I no understand when talk too fast or when use words that are confusing."

"Jeffrey introduced Thomas to the gaming tables and then watched as he lost time after time. Then he came along and bought up his markers so that he could hold them over my head. He used those markers to blackmail me into marrying him," Christina said, speaking exaggeratedly slow, enunciating each word carefully so that she wouldn't have to explain again. Reliving yesterday's confrontation was having more of a negative effect on her nerves than she thought it would, and if she had to explain it any more today, she'd probably have a nervous breakdown.

Chin Woo watched her talk, but took no offense at her slow manner of speech. He knew she meant no insult. Still, as she spoke each word, agony apparent, his anger increased towards the man that caused his Cookie so much distress. "He one slippery snake," Chin Woo commented as the light of understanding dawned. He sat rubbing a hand along his hairless chin.

"An apt description that I've used several times over the last couple of days too."

"What if Thomas win at gamble?"

"Oh, Chin Woo, I'm not particularly fond of what if games. You know that. Besides, the fact is, he was poor at playing card games. Had he not been, I'm sure that Jeffrey would have simply found some other means by which to blackmail me. He seems determined to have me for his wife. Why, I don't know. I do know however, that I'm equally determined not to *be* his wife."

"That why you need my help?"

"That's exactly why I need your help. I don't have anyone else to turn to. He's got my whole family duped."

"This no easy thing, Cookie."

"I know, but if I have to marry that man, I will die," Christina whined unnaturally.

"I say no easy," Chin Woo smiled, "I no say is impossible."

"You mean you have an idea? Already!" Christina laughed happily and pulled her chair around to sit next to Chin Woo. "Tell me, but bear in mind that we have to keep any plan secret because if he even suspects that I'm plotting against this marriage, he'll strike at me and my entire family."

"My father once say that best way to beat enemy is learn defense of oneself."

"Ooh, sounds intriguing, but do you mind explaining what you just said in the English that I taught you, please?" Christina teased.

"Many enemy strike because they know prey too weak to defend against. Tomorrow I teach you special gift that will teach you to be strong. Strong mind, strong body, will make you not weak. You not weak, you not victim of enemy any longer. Strong mind, strong body, you able to fight anything that tries harm you. Understand?"

"I don't want to fight him, Chin Woo. I simply don't want to marry him."

"I not know how stop marriage." He picked up the cups and made his way to the small barrel of water that served as his sink. He quickly rinsed them out and set them on the cupboard to dry. "Is only gift I have to give to my Cookie," he said quietly, leaning heavily against the stove. "Is all I know."

"I'm not sure what you have in mind, Chin Woo," Christina sighed dejectedly, "but surely you wouldn't expect me to fight a man Jeffrey's size and win? Even if he is a dandy, he's still a very large, very strong dandy." Christina didn't know how to take his offer of help. *Self defense?* It certainly wasn't what she'd been expecting.

"Learn defense of oneself. Clear mind and spirit. Help think better. Maybe then able to find solution how to get out of marriage. If not, at least have strength to keep husband from hurting you."

"Well, it's better than what I came up with on my own," she conceded reluctantly, "which was nothing. Perhaps while we work, an answer will come on how to be rid of that slimy snake, and then I won't have to worry about learning this self-defense of which you speak."

"Come back in morning, before sunrise. We start then. Today I prepare."

"But..."

The abruptness with which their conversation ended startled Christina. She wasn't ready to leave. There was still too many things she felt she needed to discuss with him.

"Go, Cookie." Chin Woo so bewildered Christina that she didn't protest when he tugged her up from her chair, ushering her out the door. He then abruptly shut the door in her face. She walked thoughtfully to where Shooting Star grazed nearby and mounted, her mind still in a whirl. "I hope he knows what he's doing, because if this doesn't work, I may very well have to spend the rest of my life in jail for murder."

CHAPTER 12

The next morning, Chin Woo began meticulously instructing a hesitant Christina in the art of weaponry, and every day for the next two weeks, Christina argued the necessity of it all.

"How is this supposed to prevent my marriage?" She asked continually, her frustration growing daily, but Chin Woo would simply smile and say, "To defeat snake, you must learn to defend self."

It made no sense to her, but every day she trained and every day her skill and confidence grew. She still worried about the upcoming trip, scheduled to take place in just two more weeks. Added to the worry over the move, was the concern she had about the haunting, pervasive dream that tormented her sleep. A dream that wasn't so much a dream as it was a story that ceased upon waking, and then began where it left off each night when she closed her eyes. Not repetitive. Foretelling. Just what it was trying to tell her, she had yet to determine, but she no longer doubted that her dream was more a premonition than anything else; however, if the subject matter was any indicator, she wasn't certain she wanted to know its meaning, for it held a darkness that frightened her.

Even through a worried and sleep-disturbed night, she still managed to face each new dawn with a determination and purpose, which she hadn't possessed until now. Although she complained often about Chin Woo's methodology, deep down she was grateful for the peace their daily workouts gave her, leaving her with a feeling that she could conquer the world. If that were even remotely possible, then defeating Jeffrey would be a piece of cake. She grinned. Perhaps Chin Woo's tactics were bearing fruit. She had not yet felt remotely capable of defeating Jeffrey. Now she was envisioning it as a probability, thanks to the strength and courage imparted to her by Chin Woo.

She only wished that she'd been able to transfer some of her newfound strength and courage to her mother, who hadn't left her room in the two weeks since Father's autocratic announcement.

Every afternoon after training, she would visit her mother's room, coaxing, pleading, and even demanding that she snap out of her doldrums. Nevertheless, Carlotta would just stare at her with a lost look that frightened Christina even more than her dream did.

With only two weeks before the move, and her strength waning daily, she wondered if her mother could leave her bed, much less climb aboard a schooner to travel an undetermined amount of time to her Uncle Peter's ranch.

Her father was not much help. He spent most of his time locked away with Jeffrey making plans, so she was unable to tell her father of her concern for his wife's failing health. In a short span, her family's life would change for better or for worse and Christina was the only one that was thinking with a clear head. She wondered vaguely if her clarity was due in part to Chin Woo and his strange ways. He did say that clearing her mind and spirit would help her think better.

"How de missus today?" Hyacinth asked, as Christina came through the door, carrying her mother's lunch tray.

"Pretty much the same. I have to threaten to spoon-feed her like a baby to get her to eat. Still, she only nibbles. If we don't do something soon, she's going to waste away to nothing." Christina handed the tray to Hyacinth, plopped wearily onto a nearby chair, and laid her hands tiredly on her arms.

"I hate to be de one sayin' dis chil', but I think your mama's tryin' to kill herself." Hyacinth set the tray on a counter, wiped her hands on a dishtowel, and sat across from Christina. She instantly regretted the reaction her words wrought, but she had no choice but to bring it to Christina's attention. If someone didn't do something about Mrs. Carthington soon, she absolutely *would* waste away to nothing.

"I can't believe you actually said that, Hyacinth," Christina hissed incredulously. "I doubt that mother would ever consider taking her own life. That's a sin worse than divorce."

"Right now, chil', being right or wrong be de last thing on dat woman's mind," Hyacinth retorted. "She jes been told dat she be a losin' everything she hold dear, and she ain't thinking straight. If'n we don' do something to help take her mind off de move and give her life purpose again, she jes might up and die."

"I still don't think that mother is so distraught over this move that she'd actually let herself die because of it, but I do agree that we need to do something to make her feel useful. Any suggestions?"

"Well, I does have one thing dat might jes do de trick, but you probably ain't gonna like it none."

"What might that be, Hyacinth?" Christina asked cautiously.

"You can start plannin' de weddin'."

Christina sighed and slumped further into her chair. "That won't do it, Hyacinth," she sighed. "Mom already told Jeffrey that she was in no mood to plan a wedding, especially since we wouldn't have time before the move to plan a proper one."

"Well, dat be true enough," Hyacinth conceded, "but perhaps der be something else dat ya'll can work on, so dat de weddin' will go smooth after ya'll get to your Uncle Peter's home."

"I don't exactly want things to go smoothly, you know."

"I know dat chil', but right now you got to be thinking about your mama," Hyacinth urged, "and der ain't nothing dat's more important to a mama dan to see her baby girl get hitched. Even if she can't see dat de baby girl don't want to get hitched."

"You're right, Hyacinth." Christina leaned forward and propped her chin on her hands. "I may not want to get married to Jeffrey, but planning the wedding doesn't necessarily mean that I'll actually have to marry him, now does it? So if it will help mother, then...well okay, but if she doesn't feel up to planning the wedding, what do I do then?"

"Jes start slow."

"What do you mean?"

"Talk to her about what de weddin' dress should look like, and see how dat works," Hyacinth offered.

"And if it doesn't?"

"We be crossing dat bridge when we get to it. Now skedaddle. I's got a meal to be planning."

"Thanks, Hyacinth."

"You're welcome, chil'."

"Hyacinth?" Christina paused just inside the kitchen door.

"Yes, chil'?"

"Just one more question. How is it that you can readily see that I don't want this marriage to take place, but my own parents are blind to it?"

"Don' be too hard on your momma and daddy, chil'," Hyacinth said softly, "dey means well, I be shore. Its jes dat sometimes parents can be short-sighted when it comes to der child, and even though I be lovin' you like you was my own, I have a good deal better sight dan your momma because you isn't my own flesh and blood."

"Then you see people for what they really are better than someone who doesn't care to see."

"Dats right, chil'," Hyacinth said softly, "and afores you says it, I already knows dat Massa Jeffrey be a wolf in sheep's clothing and I's praying every day dat God gives dat man what for, for de heartache he be a 'causin' you."

"Bless you, Hyacinth."

"No chil'. Yous de one dat needs de blessin'. Do you want to tell me whys you marryin' de man when it be obvious—to me, leastways—dat you don' care to none?"

"Another time perhaps," Christina said, "Right now, I have to go try to coax Mother into leaving her room, with talk of picking out a wedding dress."

CHAPTER 13

"So because the white beast left the fight, and you were unable to destroy it, this is why you are angry?" Fire Dreamer asked, stoking the embers in the fire pit. After Baying Wolf's revelation of the unknown danger surrounding the mysterious white woman in his dreams, they had sat for hours saying nothing, each lost in thought.

"No," he said simply.

"If that does not anger you, perhaps it is the woman's fear of you that makes your anger great?"

"No," Baying Wolf sighed heavily, continuing to shake his head. "I'm angry because I care, but I do not understand *why* I should care. I'm angry because the Great Spirit is asking me to help this woman and because I know nothing. I feel helpless. That is why I'm angry."

"Why did you not destroy the beast? Though he did not want to fight you, you could have still attacked. If you had done so, your task would have been satisfied and you would not be here with me now, a danger still lurking over this woman's head."

"I saw her crawl away," Baying Wolf said softly, petulantly.

"What?"

"I said that I saw her crawl away," Baying Wolf repeated, more forcefully.

"I do not understand," Fire Dreamer replied, truly perplexed.

"I went there to help her. I stood guard between her and her enemy to let her know that I meant her no harm. I engaged the beast at risk to my own self, and when I glanced up, she was slinking away on hands and knees."

"And this angered you so that you..."

"Left," Baying Wolf finished. "I forgot about the beast, and brought my spirit animal home."

"A decision you now regret?"

"If I had not allowed her to affect me so, the beast would be dead and my commitment to her finished. Now, the Great Spirit summons me to complete a task for which I haven't the heart to finish."

"If the Great Spirit is speaking to you, do you not see that the woman must be very important to our people? This woman is not of The People, not of us, but the Great Spirit has interwoven her life with yours in a way that I cannot explain. Her life is important to The People as is the water to the lands, and she is in your hands. You will seek her out."

"I mean no disrespect, Uncle, but how could a white woman be so important to The People? How could she be anything to us?"

"Sometimes you should not question the whys. The Great Spirit is to be merely obeyed."

"I cannot blindly obey!" Anger flaring, Baying Wolf jumped up from his mat, his tiredness forgotten. "Why should I care if this woman dies? She is but another intruder on our lands. She is my enemy and I will push all thoughts of her from my mind. I will never dream of her again and I will never seek her out—in my mind or otherwise! If the Great Spirit wishes to send another, then the Great Spirit can do so."

Fire Dreamer gave his nephew a sharp glance and gestured for him to return to his mat. "I thought for a moment that you had learned to listen to your elders, but your anger, I see, still guides your tongue; however, this day, you will heed my words and speak no disrespect toward the Great Spirit. Do you really dare to question the Great Spirit, nephew?"

Baying Wolf sat sulking across from his uncle. As angry as he was however, he chose not to reply, nearly afraid to speak. He had angered his Uncle, and, in turn, it was possible he had angered the Great Spirit.

"You will go to her. She is more to The People than you can see, or are willing to see right now," his Uncle said, trying to maintain his own calm. *The youth of the day*, he mused silently, *are too angry and stubborn.*

"I'm confused," Baying Wolf interjected softly, "and it is a feeling I do not like. Can't you tell me why I must go? What must I do when I find her? I have asked the Great Spirit these things, but every time I ask, I receive no response. Will you be the same?"

"You will know once you find her."

"No answer from the Great Spirit, and a riddle from you," Baying Wolf scoffed. "You wish me to control my anger, but silence and riddles do not help. Can you at least tell me how I will find her? I do not know where she is," Baying Wolf argued. He knew it was a weak argument that would not stand, still he fought against what he sensed was his destiny.

"When the moon is full, you will begin your journey. Let the eagle be your guide."

"More riddles old man?"

Fire Dreamer picked up his pipe and began to draw deeply from it. He handed the pipe to Baying Wolf who did likewise. "We will talk no more this day," Fire Dreamer said. "Too much anger clouds your mind and you cannot see reason. Still, clouded or not, when the day arrives for you to go, you will do as the Great Spirit bids."

CHAPTER 14

Christina left the house early the next morning, making her way to the training area. She knew it would be sometime before Chin Woo arrived, but her dream had again jarred her from sleep, and she simply couldn't return to a peaceful slumber. She hoped the clear, crisp morning air would clear the fog from her mind, but it remained a jumbled mass of torment.

A little while later, she heard the faint patter of soft-soled shoes and turned. She raised her hand to shade her eyes from the glow of the morning sun and smiled as the shadowy outline standing beside her became more distinct.

"You stay here long time."

"Yes, but how did you know?"

"I come early today," Chin Woo said, taking a seat on the springy grass. "I see you sit here, so I go away and come back."

"So, why were you here early?"

"You destroy targets last time. I need fix new ones."

"Oh, sorry."

"Is okay. So, why you here early?" Chin Woo's voice was soft with concern. Although he was not an emotional man, he had taken a liking to Christina and treated her like a protective father.

"I was just thinking, is all," she sighed.

"Thinking 'bout what?" He asked.

"The last few weeks, this trip, Jeffrey's cunning, Father's disregard, Mother's failing health, my disturbing dream" she listed, and then stopped as she felt the ever-present weight of her situation bearing down on her shoulders yet again.

"Not me? I not on your mind?" His teasing coaxed a smile from her down-turned lips, and she physically shook her head to break free of the mental blues that seemed always to be lurking just near the surface of her brain the past few weeks.

"Afraid not," she answered sincerely. "I just feel so lost sometimes, Chin Woo. Have you ever had an overwhelming feeling that something terrible is waiting to happen, but you can't prevent it because you don't know exactly what that something is?"

"No."

"Well, that's the way I feel about this trip and Jeffrey's motivations for convincing Father to move."

"Hmm, the Snake," he replied thoughtfully.

"Precisely. The Snake," she confirmed with a slight giggle, feeling the load lift further away as it always did when she talked to her dear friend.

"You know, maybe he really want marry you, but not think you want him. So, maybe blackmail only way he have you. Maybe he love you and want make you happy. Maybe he feel if make lots of money out west and take family with you, you love him back."

"Tell me that you're not defending that viper," Christina rejoined, incredulous over Chin Woo's apparent champion of the man she despised.

"You know, Cookie. Sometime, no able to stop future to happen, good or bad. Sometime must accept," he said slyly.

"Oh!" Christina said in sudden understanding, sighing with relief. "You're playing the devil's advocate. You and I both know however, that Jeffrey's motivations will prove to suit Jeffrey and no one else. Besides, you said the key word—blackmail. You can't possibly love someone and blackmail that person the way he did me! He even threatened bodily harm if I crossed him. No! Jeffrey's motives are not pure, and there has to be a way to stop him, before something happens to my family."

"You no dead yet, Cookie!" Chin Woo laughed. "You no see solution—feel defeat. This okay, but sometime what we see is no what will be. Understand?"

"Not at all, Chin Woo. You're talking incomprehensibly again."

"Here. Now. All seem hopeless. Tomorrow, solution may come. Maybe not tomorrow. Maybe long time. Maybe no come at all. Point is, no give up fight."

"Oh, Chin Woo, I'm so glad you've decided to come with us. I feel safer knowing that you'll be there to look out for me."

"Look out for self. That why learn," he said, slapping his thighs for emphasis. "Now! Target waiting. You sit here so long they grow grass at base. No more lazy! Time wasting! Time learn!"

She gave his arm a gentle squeeze and turned to look back at a mother duck splashing about in the pond, her babies preciously mimicking her every move. She did feel better, but there was still much about training that bothered her, and today she wanted to clear her mind about that. After all, Chin Woo said that clearing the mind was essential to preparing for battle, so she certainly didn't need questions concerning this training weighing down upon her, along with all the other problems surrounding her life right now. "Can I talk to you a quick minute about all this training?" She asked, placing a gently restraining hand on Chin Woo's arm when he tried to stand.

"Sure. I listen," he said, settling back down.

"Well, that's a first. Any other time I've asked you about the training you've merely shooed me back to work."

"I no like waste time on talk, but since we talk now, I listen."

"Ah! So, if I ever want to discuss something important to me, I need to make certain we're in the middle of a conversation and not the middle of training before I bring it up. I'll make note of that for future reference," Christina teased.

"If no ask question, I go," Chin Woo said in mock seriousness, making to stand.

"No! I'm sorry," Christina giggled, "I'll get to my point."

"Good. What point?"

"I agree that what I've learned has given a new self-confidence unlike anything I've ever felt. And, admittedly, I've been able to think about my present situation with much more clarity, even if I've derived no solution from that clarity..."

"That good, but what point is?"

"Well, I've just said what the point is. The point is that although I've been able to think more clearly lately, I haven't really thought of anything at all."

"Now it you who no make sense, Cookie."

"Well, all this clear thinking isn't going to be able to stop our move, right?"

"This true. We still leaving."

"Right, we're still leaving. So, clarity of mind isn't solving that problem. Strike one against this training. Then there's Jeffrey…"

"Ah! That real problem you worry over, yes?"

"Yes! Exactly! I still don't know how to get out of this marriage and time is ticking away from me," Christina huffed, hugging her knees to her chest and laying her chin down. "We're leaving very soon, too soon, and when we arrive in Texas, I'm going to be Mrs. Jeffrey Buchanan. All of this training hasn't helped me figure how to prevent that. Now, I'm feeling even more adrift because I think that by discussing wedding plans with my mother, to help her out of her own state of depression, I may actually be preordaining my own fate, which means all of this training is futile, so that's strike two against training. And, unfortunately, strike three is that this training for clear thinking is doing nothing to prevent those weird nightmares that have been occurring nightly. Do you know what a third strike would mean—metaphorically speaking?"

"No, what mean?" Chin Woo asked, attempting to hide his confusion of her too-rapid speech.

"Well, from what Thomas tells me about baseball, it means I'm out. But in this case, out of my mind, that is."

"I no understand all you say, but some I do. First, we preordain no thing in our life," Chin Woo lectured. "Everything that happen, we make to happen. Second, there is solution to Jeffrey, but only time will provide answer and clear mind will help see answer when it come, and third thing is dreams. They no cloud mind, they try show you something that you no ready to see."

"Wow! That's an intuitive analysis for not being able to understand everything I said," Christina laughed. "You know, I have gotten the sense that the dream has been trying to tell me something for a little while now, although I can't figure out what that something could possibly be. All it's been telling me thus far is that a white beast is trying to eat me; and then there's the giant gray wolf that would like to kill the white beast so that *it* can eat me. Basically, it's about whose next meal I'm going to be."

"I think more to it than that."

"Right now there isn't. Anyway, I guess I'm just worried that I'm wasting precious time on learning a skill that I have no use for, when finding a way to get rid of Jeffrey Buchanan is time better served. Do you understand? And please, don't feel insulted by what I've said. I know that you are trying to teach me a practical and special gift, and I thank you for that from the bottom of my heart, but what I need from you now is more understanding about why I should continue when it's obvious after several weeks that it's not solving my current problems."

"Hmm, good point, and I no have answers," Chin Woo said quietly and looked toward the pond for a moment, then continued softly. "Perhaps the god you pray to will help, and take pest away; perhaps you someday like the snake and have no reason to use skills. Still, good idea to learn. This trip we take to new place, I hear much bad things. Perhaps you will need skills for different enemy, or maybe you never need use. I no able see future, Cookie, but I know must prepare for future and so should you."

"So what you're saying is this training is not only to help me with today, but it's also to help me prepare for any eventuality— now or in the future?"

"Is right. And you say yourself it easier to think now."

"You know, Chin Woo, I'd be lost without you."

Chin Woo cleared his throat and then stood. "Time growing short for trip. Today we work hard, maybe it help if pretend targets are Jeffrey?"

Christina laughed. "Can we work with the throwing stars? I really like them. Perhaps I can embed a few into Jeffrey's—I mean, the target's—heart."

"Today, I give you stars as gift to go with little knife I give you before. They small and can hide in pocket of skirt."

"Another present for me?" Christina laughed and clapped her hands exaggeratedly, like a small child.

"Yes, now come. No give you if no know how to use." He helped Christina rise, then took her by the elbow, and ushered her down the hill. She spotted the targets sitting near the pond and suddenly felt a destructive urge come over her.

"Hand me one of those throwing stars, Chin Woo," she said mischievously. "I feel the need to rip your targets to shreds again."

CHAPTER 15

Silence.

The lack of noise was more terrifying than the sound of pending battle, and Christina stopped crawling long enough to peer back in the direction she'd come. The white beast was lumbering into the trees, and the wolf was nowhere, that she could see. She scanned the horizon all around, but saw no signs of the gray fur amidst the green and brown blades of grass.

Is it out there now, stalking me? *She wondered.* Now that the beast is no longer a threat?

"No, please, no," she cried, returning to her hands and knees. She didn't know which scared her more, the white beast or the wolf. What she did know was that she'd never convince either that a gourmet meal she'd never make. Doubly difficult since she didn't speak either's language.

If you continue crawling away, *her mind said, adding fuel to her fears,* then the wolf can easily catch you. Heck, even that beast is within catching and eating distance. So might I suggest you make a run for it?

Christina braced her hands on the ground and prepared to stand. "I can't," she wailed. "What if they see me?"

Get up! *Her brain screamed.* It isn't like you to cower like this!

"This is my dream, and I can cower if I want," Christina retorted. "It's not as if my fears are unfounded. How would you like it if two horrendous creatures were fighting over your flesh and bones?"

They are, but at least I want to do something about it, *her mind's voice retorted.*

"Fine! We'll run," Christina snapped, "but when one of those two starts gnawing on my body, you'd better not shut down and try to escape the pain, because I certainly won't be able." Without waiting for her mind to respond again, Christina leapt to her feet, hiked her skirt to her knees, and ran as fast as her legs would carry her.

She seemed to run forever, but soon caught sight of the wagons in the distance and slowed her pace. She cried out with joy, but her victory was short lived as a loud roar, which sounded both angry and painful, reached her ears.

She knew it was the beast's ululation, but the thunderous noise seemed too close. Much too close.

Reluctantly, she stopped and peered over her shoulder, releasing an involuntary cry of alarm. The white beast was stumbling in her direction, baying and groaning. It closed the gap faster than Christina imagined an animal of its size could manage. Apparently, it decided that, without the interference of the wolf, it could attempt to regain its prize. Her.

She looked toward the wagons and back toward the beast. Would it dare follow her that far? Did she dare risk her family's safety and the other families as well?

CHAPTER 16

Christina awoke with a start, her breathing labored. She glanced out from her second-story window at the early morning light and sighed. Today they would begin their journey west. She lay back down on her side, drawing her pillow tightly into her embrace, listening to the chaos, which echoed from downstairs. Someone would be pounding on her door shortly, hustling her to get ready. She sighed and thought about the dream, trying again to make sense of it.

"The sequence of events laid out in the dream signifies danger," she said aloud, trying to find reason where there appeared none. She could only feel the permeating sense that danger was lurking nearby; that the dream was foretelling of an unpleasant fate that awaited her, or someone she loved. "There are simply too little details right now, and I simply haven't the ability to translate imagery into reality."

You better develop that ability right quick, her mind supplied, *especially since storybook images appear all you'll be supplied.*

"I know, and that's why part of me wants desperately to get back inside that dream so that I can decide exactly who those animals represent."

What made you say that? Her mind asked.

"Say what?"

Before now, her mind explained, *you were convinced that those creatures were simply desperately hungry beasts that decided you'd make for good eating. Why the change?*

"I don't know," Christina replied hesitantly. "It's just something that came to me, but I feel that I'm right in believing the two beasts in my dream represent human counterparts outside of my dream."

Very astute, Chin Woo number two.

"Yes, it seems that the clouds are lifting, or maybe you're just getting smarter."

I will accept the latter of those two as fact.

Jeffrey's laughter drifted up the stairs and Christina winced. "Do you think that perhaps that white beast could be representative of Jeffrey? I mean, after all, he does have white hair and he has been threatening my family and me of late."

I'd say that's an extremely good possibility.

"We're already trying to figure out what to do about him. Do you think that maybe my dream will provide a solution?"

If I had to hazard a guess, I'd say the solution is the wolf.

"Yet I haven't a clue *who* the wolf is, if it's anyone at all. Maybe Chin Woo?"

Doubtful. I can't see him being that fierce over anything. Even his Cookie.

"Too true, but who does that leave?"

A stranger.

"Why doesn't that thought bring me comfort?"

"Christina, are you awake, my dear?" A voice drifted through the massive door and under Christina's sheltering blanket. "If you are, you really need to get out of bed and start preparing to leave," The voice continued, the lackluster tone revealing the feeling of disillusionment and misery. Hearing that dejection broke Christina's heart, though she tried desperately to maintain a cheery facade as a way to encourage and support her mother.

As she pulled open the door and prepared to give her mother a giant, welcoming hug, she immediately realized that all of her efforts had been for naught. Her mother's weight had dropped dramatically in just four weeks. The dress she wore, once flattering, now hung on her like a sack. She looked much as a child who snuck into her mother's wardrobe to try on clothes that wouldn't fit.

The face however, was anything but childlike. Her cheekbones jutted from sunken flesh and her eyes, usually vivacious now sat dull and lifeless in their sockets. Her flaming locks, although coiffed by her maid, had lost its shine, and the curls hung limp from the partial bun atop her head. Christina was appalled, but remained determined to be a well of strength from which her mother could draw her own strength.

"It's good to see you out of your room, mother," she said in a cheerful voice that she hoped would hide her unflattering thoughts.

"I wish I could say it's good to be out," Carlotta said quietly, "but I've finally come to the conclusion that, short of barring myself in my room and staying there forever, I really haven't much choice in my husband's decision."

"I know it's upsetting, Mother, but can't you at least try to adjust?" Christina asked hopefully.

"If I were prepared to adjust, dearest," Carlotta said, "I would have done so weeks ago. I simply have no desire to start over, and if it wasn't for your pending marriage, I'd find a way to stay here." The tone in her mother's voice was just portentous enough to confirm Hyacinth's earlier statement that her upcoming wedding was probably the only thing keeping her mother alive, for it looked as if she was already walking hand-in-hand with death.

"Oh, Mother, please don't say that!" Christina cried, drawing her mother into the room, then tried again to force a cheeriness to her tone that she didn't feel. "I'm certain as I can be that once we get to Texas, you'll find reason to love it."

"No, dear, I will not, but don't worry, I'll do what I can to present a cheerful veneer at your wedding. It will be, after all, the last joy in my life."

"I love you, Mother, you know that, and I know this probably sounds selfish, but can't you at least try to be strong for Thomas and me?"

Carlotta smiled sadly, and placed a hand gently on her daughter's cheek, "No, I won't pretend any more to be happy when I'm not. I haven't been happy for quite some time, but I've made due because of my children. Now, you and Thomas are grown, and you'll be starting a family of your own one day soon. So, now I get to be selfish. I don't wish to uproot at this stage of my life, and it's wrong of your father to have decided matters without consulting me—not that he ever has discussed anything with me. Do you know that he's not made the slightest effort to check on me during these past weeks because preparations for this move have consumed him? I could've remained in bed and wilted completely away, and he'd never have known. Well, no matter. I've decided to move, and hopefully God will grant me a little more strength to make the journey as I do hope to see you marry." Carlotta scrutinized her daughter's face for a few minutes before speaking again. "You've always been strong-headed, which is something I've tried desperately to correct, but now I wonder if it won't hold you in good stead through the remainder of your life." Carlotta's smile was weak, "Well, enough talk now. You need to get dressed and help the men folk pack up the wagons."

Christina wanted to refute her mother's words, wanted to argue and rant. Anything at all to get an emotional rise from her listless voice, but all she could think about was how dry and cold Carlotta's lips were as they brushed across her cheek before turning to leave.

CHAPTER 17

When Christina finished dressing in her traveling attire, she made her way downstairs to the kitchen, seeking a temporary escape from the pandemonium around her. Deliberately ignoring her mother's dictate to help pack.

Hyacinth was already in the kitchen preparing the last meal that she would ever make for their family, her sadness evident in the handkerchief that she gripped tightly in her fist. Occasionally, she would raise it and hastily swipe away a stray tear as she hurriedly packed baskets already overflowing with meats, cheeses, and bread.

"Good morning, Hyacinth," Christina said with the same forced cheerfulness she'd used with her mother.

Hyacinth quickly wiped away another tear and laid the tissue on the counter before turning to face Christina, a smile on her face that did not reach far enough to eliminate the sadness in her eyes.

"Morning, chil'. Don't know whether it be good or not, though. Why ain't you out der helping your folks wit' de loading and such. Der's lots to be done, chil'."

"Nag, nag." Christina deposited herself on a stool and glanced curiously inside one heavy-laden basket. "You planning to feed everybody in Georgia with this?"

"Gotta be somebody a caring what you be eating out der."

"It won't keep for more than a day or two." She eyed the abundant amount of sliced meats and cheeses critically.

"Well, dat be jes fine. You be eating good for dat day or two. After dat, you alls gonna be living on God's good graces, and you's gonna be a wishin' dat I done gone with ya." Hyacinth's dark gaze traveled over Christina's slim form. "You gonna be a wasted away to nothing, you is. Maybe dat's a good thing. Maybe Massa Jeffrey not be wantin' to marry no scarecrow."

"Oh, I do wish that would happen. If I thought that would be a deterrent to him, I'd starve myself to death."

"Now don't you be doing nothing foolish chil'." Hyacinth

waved a freshly baked loaf of bread in Christina's direction for emphasis, her scowl deepening.

"Don't worry, Hyacinth. I'm many things, but foolish isn't one of them. Not that I'm aware of, anyway." Christina snatched a piece of cheese from the basket and popped it into her mouth.

"So, is you ever gonna tell ol' Hyacinth why you be so dead set against hitching yourself to ol' Lucifer in disguise?"

"Isn't that reason enough?" Christina laughed at the description, but it quickly faded when she remembered what he'd done, and with a sigh, she told Hyacinth from where her anger stemmed. "He blackmailed me into it, Hyacinth."

"You joshin' dis ol' woman!"

"I'm afraid this isn't something about which I'd josh."

"And your ma and pa's allowing de weddin' anyway?"

"They don't know, and as you said earlier, Mother can't know."

"I ain't never said dat your mama shouldn't know about nothing, chil', so don't you be putting no words into dis here mouth o' mine, ya hear?"

"Sorry, Hyacinth, I didn't mean that the way it sounded," Christina apologized quickly. "I only meant that Mother and Father like Jeffrey, and with Mother's health as frail as it is, it wouldn't do her any good for me to upset her further."

"But de man's done you wrong, chil'. Surely dey be understanding dat."

"If I even attempt to tell them, Jeffrey has threatened to ruin Father and he'll see that the local magistrate tosses Thomas in jail."

"It must be something powerful strong he got against you."

"Yeah. It's called 'love for my family'."

"I's real sorry about all dis, chil'." Hyacinth's shook her head, her jowls quivering with the motion. "If'n it would help any, I can always sit on him. Squish him like a bug."

Christina started laughing again—glad to have another person to talk to about her situation, "If only that would work."

"Ain't der nothing dat you can be doing?"

"Chin Woo's been teaching me how to defend myself. I can

now shoot a rifle, throw a dagger, fire a pistol with incredible accuracy and he's even shown me how to use a special weapon from his own country called a throwing star," Christina whispered, afraid of being heard by someone passing by the kitchen.

"What in de name of de Lord is he doing dat for!" Hyacinth yelled loudly, obviously unconcerned about eavesdroppers.

Christina cringed at her housekeeper's outburst and paused in her explanation, thinking the reason was obvious, and then recalled that the reasons weren't obvious to her either, when Chin Woo first explained. "To protect myself," she said simply, certain that said it all.

"Who's you protecting yourself from, chil'?"

"Jeffrey! Didn't you hear what I said? He's threatened me with bodily harm if I give him any trouble."

"Well, I might be jes a ignorant housekeep, but I don't see how no knife, gun, or whatever it be you training with, gonna help you none if'n dat man takes it into his head to take you to task. You looked in de mirror lately chil'? You a sprite compared to dat man. He's jes as likely to yank whatever it be dat you threatening him with right outta your hands and den break you like a twig. An he will to, if'n you go wavin' a knife or some such under his nose."

"There's more to the training than protecting my physical body. It is also providing me with a way to think clearer and giving me an inner peace that I've lacked for so long. So besides just physical training, it's also a mental discipline that is supposed to help me face unpleasant circumstances with a calm and rational assurance."

"I's been in some mighty sticky situations chil' and calm and rational don' work none when you faced with danger, I promise you dat. Minds don' work right when a body is 'bout to get hurt."

"I hope you're wrong, Hyacinth, because this is all I have to work with right now, and will be all I'll be able to depend upon should danger cross my path. Chin Woo is certain it will be a benefit to me."

"Chin Woo dis. Chin Woo dat. Chin Woo ever stop to think

what be happening to you if all dis training don't work. No! Never mind. Don' answer dat, cause I can see dat you think it be a good thing and I guess you know what you doing, chil'." Hyacinth threw her hands up in disgust, and then returned to packing the picnic basket.

"I'm not sure that I do know what I'm doing, Hyacinth, but I do know that I'll do whatever is necessary to keep that man or any man from hurting me. Like you said, I'm small. I have to have an added advantage—and this is it."

"Well, I not be arguing with you no more about it. If'n you think dis is best, then so be it. I think you needs to be spending your energy finding a way out of de marriage, instead of finding ways to keep his hands off'n you *after* you's hitched, but dat be all I going to say on de matter. Oh, and your mamma sent me ta mail somethin' dis morning."

"What was that?" Christina accepted the change of subject, not wanting to leave Georgia with Hyacinth upset with her.

"De order for your weddin' dress. Appears you done took my advice about dat. She showed me a real purdy picture of it in dat fancy catalog of hers and den told me to mail off de order. She was still a might bit sad, but at least her mind was on somethin' other dan the movin' for once."

"I tried to get her to wait to have the dress made when we reach Uncle Peter's, but she insisted it be mail-ordered. That way it will be there upon our arrival. She's absolutely convinced that the west is uncivilized and that she would never be able to locate a decent dressmaker to make me a dress. Honestly Hyacinth, from where does she get her notions?"

"De papers, chil', dats where. Dey don't be painting no purdy pictures about dat place out der. Leastways, it got her doing something 'sides moping about."

"Well, I'm just glad Dad talked Jeffrey into stalling the wedding until we reach my uncle's place. Maybe, just maybe, before we get there, I can find a way out of this mess."

"And if'n you can't?"

"I can't think about that."

"Why not you jes tell your mama and papa what Jeffrey done and de consequences be damned. 'xcuse my language."

"That thought has crossed my mind, but another thought was only seconds behind that one, convincing me that if Jeffrey was capable of blackmailing me into marriage, he's capable of far worse to prevent interference with his plans. I can't put my family at that kind of risk. Leaving their fate in the hands of a mad man? I may as well just shoot them all myself."

"I reckon. If'n it was me, I'd do nothing less."

"Thank you, Hyacinth. I still wish you'd reconsider going. I could use another ally. Is the newspaper accounts the reason why you aren't joining us?"

"Well, dats for one I 'spose." Hyacinth stopped her task and lowered her heavy bulk onto the chair beside Christina again. "I is certain dat your dad's brother done got all de house help he done need..."

"We won't be staying with Uncle Peter forever, Hyacinth," Christina interrupted, "just long enough for us to build a place of our own. Don't you think we'll need you then?"

"Makes no never mind, chil'. You can be finding new help when you be needing it, but your papa done give me my freedom papers and I gonna use 'em to make my way up north. Got me some kinfolk up dataways. Sides which, I done told ya dat dis ol' bag o' bones ain't got de strength to be trotting halfway cross de world in no rickety wagon. 'Sides, if you so desperate for house help, why you not taking Mirabelle, Victoria, and Moses?"

"They just don't want to go, so Dad found them employment elsewhere."

"I see."

"I've known you all my life, Hyacinth," Christina smiled sadly, taking the large woman's hand into her petite one. "You're like family, and I'm sure going to miss you."

"Well, don't be gettin' all choked up on me, chil'. I gonna be missing you too." Hyacinth removed her hand and stood to resume her task. "Now skedaddle, so I can be about my bus'ness. You be leaving soon, and I still got packing to do."

"Ok, Hyacinth, I'll skedaddle. I'll always hold you close to my heart, and wish you all the happiness in the world." Before Hyacinth could respond, Christina fled the kitchen.

"God go with you, chil'," Hyacinth murmured to an empty doorway. "Somethin' tells me you is gonna need Him a sight bit more dan I will."

CHAPTER 18

Christina emerged into the foyer just as Jeffrey was walking up the front steps. She had avoided his company since the day he'd forced his ring upon her finger and wanted nothing more than to never spend one minute alone in the same room with him—ever. She most certainly didn't feel like dealing with him today.

Making a beeline for the stairs, she hoped to find seclusion in her room, something she'd done more often than not when he came calling. She thought she was secure when she'd made it halfway up the staircase, but Jeffrey summoned her, drawing her up short.

"Christina, I'd like a word with you." His commanding tone grated on her nerves and, for a moment, ignoring his bidding was a huge temptation. The last thing she needed or wanted however was for him to follow her to her room. Something she didn't doubt he would do if she ignored him. She descended the stairs and reluctantly followed him into the solarium.

"It will be an adjustment for both of us, but I'm sure we'll do okay, won't we?" He began, turning to face her as she strolled grudgingly into the room behind him.

"If you're seeking assurances from me, Mr. Buchanan, you'll get none."

"I was kind of hoping that a month without my company would have softened your temper and your obvious dislike of me. I can see that it hasn't." When she didn't respond, he continued, "If you continue to glare at me in such a distasteful manner after we are married, my dear, I will have to restrict you to our bedroom. After all, I can't very well have anyone realizing your true feelings for me."

"I don't particularly care, Mr. Buchanan. Now is there a reason that you wanted to see me, or might I take my leave of you?"

"I want you to reconsider marrying me..." Jeffrey stopped speaking as a look of hope spread across her face. "It would appear that I didn't start that sentence correctly, so I'll try again." Jeffrey grinned as the look of hope faded from her face and felt a surge of power run through his veins. The knowledge that he could control her very transparent emotions, worked on him like an aphrodisiac. "What I meant to say, darling, is that perhaps you'd reconsider marrying me before we leave, instead of waiting until we reach Texas."

"We're leaving this afternoon, so that's not likely to happen."

Jeffrey reached into his coat pocket and pulled out a folded piece of paper. "This here, my dear, is a special license that will enable us to marry at this very moment. All we have to do is send someone to bring back the minister."

"My father has already determined that we cannot plan a proper wedding on such short notice, Mr. Buchanan, so it's not likely he'll agree to a wedding that takes no planning at all. I'm his only daughter, and I'm certain that, as his only daughter, my father will want to throw me a grand wedding. Besides, I'll gladly wait until we reach Texas. Until then, there's always the chance that something untoward will befall you."

"Or you, my dear," Jeffrey grinned. "That brings me to my reasoning. Your welfare and that of your family."

"My welfare means nothing to you!" Christina took a deep breath and tried to reign in her rising anger. "And you aren't threatening my family again, are you? Because if you are, that will truly be the last straw. I will simply not live with threat after threat hung over my head."

"Are you quite done, my dear?" Jeffrey cooed, and Christina nodded, unwilling to trust herself to speak again until her pulse returned to normal. "Good. Now, all I was trying to say is that should anything happen to your family, you may very well be forced out of the train by the wagon master, as it's my understanding that they frown heavily on single women traveling alone. Causes all sorts of problems."

"I sincerely doubt that all three members of my family will fail to make this journey safely, so as far as your proposal to wed early is concerned, I don't think it will be necessary."

"Anything could happen, sweetheart. The bodies of the dead

litter the trail west. For whatever reason, the poor souls simply could not complete the trek. Engaged or not, if something should happen to your family, the wagon master could very well force you out. He could desert you anywhere along the trail and then you'd be begging for my protection as your husband."

"That's the second time you've mentioned something untoward possibly befalling my family, which sounds suspiciously like the threats you claim you aren't making. You aren't planning a little accident for them, are you?"

Jeffrey laughed, "Don't fret, my dear. My creative skills do not extend to murder. I only mention it, because accidents happen all without my help. Or don't you read the newspaper, dear?"

"I try to avoid trash, and I'll say it again, nothing is likely to happen to me or my family so the answer to your proposal remains a resounding no."

"Maybe I should explain my reasoning to your mother and see if maybe I can persuade her to my way of thinking; perhaps she'll even settle for the marriage now and a mock wedding when we reach our destination."

Panic filled Christina, and the desperation she'd succeeded in pushing aside the past few weeks came crashing back with a vengeance. If he did approach her mother, and explained things like that, then her mother could very well change her mind and agree. Of course, if he was entirely sure of his reasoning, why hadn't he already done so?

No, her brain supplied, *he wants to see if he can push you into it first. He really isn't certain he can convince dear old Mom to give up the big wedding in exchange for her daughter's safety.*

Well, Christina thought grimly, *I simply won't acquiesce. I just can't.*

"I can see the wheels turning in your head, my dear," Jeffrey purred. "Does that mean that the idea holds some merit, perhaps?"

"Not at all. I am curious though. We'll be married when we reach Texas, so why the push to change the plans Mother has approved?"

"Because if I don't claim you now, it's possible that you and that conniving Chinaman, that you call a friend, are just likely to devise a scheme to end our engagement." Jeffrey laughed sharply at the incredulous look that appeared on Christina's face. "That's right, Christina. I know all about how the two of you have tried to devise a scheme to rid yourself of me over the last few weeks. It's a disgrace, the way you hang all over that yellow barbarian. And yes, Christina, I know all about the early morning meetings, and the weapons that Chin Woo gave you. Are you trying to make a laughing stock out of me?"

"How..."

"Did I know?" Jeffrey finished for her. "I don't give away trade secrets, my dear; however, I will give away this one: when we're married, I will beat you within an inch of your life if you go anywhere near that pint-sized oriental yellow dog again. Too bad I can't do so now for it would give me great pleasure to take you both to task," Jeffrey said, watching with pleasure as the color rose in Christina's cheeks.

"You are a sick, disgusting..."

"Be that as it may, my dear, I do find myself in a quandary," Jeffrey interrupted. "Do I allow my fiancé to keep the little stash of weapons that her Chinaman gave her, or does she turn them over to me?" Jeffrey held out a hand toward her, palm up, in an obvious attempt to prove his control over her.

Funny, but he really expects me to comply, she thought.

When she remained immobile, Jeffrey moved closer, bringing his face to within inches of her own. "Are you sure you are making a decision that is wise, Christina?"

"You are not taking my weapons from me, Mr. Buchanan. Those were gifts from Chin Woo to protect me from wild animals and such," Christina lied with more bravado than she actually felt.

"Sure they are."

"You can't have them," Christina persisted stubbornly.

"Very well, Christina," Jeffrey said, and then moved to whisper in her ear, "but if there ever comes a day you decide to use one against me, you'd better make sure I'm sleeping when you do.

Otherwise, there will be hell to pay. Do you understand well enough?"

"I understand all too well, Mr. Buchanan." Christina wondered who had been spying on her and why she'd never seen the little rat before.

"Perhaps now that you know that I have someone watching your every move, you'll reconsider your schemes with that little yellow nuisance."

"Devising a scheme and actually seeing it through to fruition are two different things. Why don't you just relax, Mr. Buchanan? If I'm really meant to marry you, it will happen," Christina explained in a patient tone that belied the panic she felt in her heart. "Meanwhile, I will continue to scheme, and pray for your demise, and you may continue to sweat and wonder whether you'll actually get me for your wife. Good day to you."

With a whish of her skirts, Christina whirled about and fled from the solarium. Her heart felt as if it was about to burst by the time she reached her room. With a sob, she flung herself across her bed and cried.

"Oh, Chin Woo! It didn't work! All that training was for nothing, because now he knows what we're up to and he'll be on his guard. What am I going to do now?" There was, of course, no response, but somewhere in the recesses of her mind, Christina thought she heard a wolf howl.

CHAPTER 19

Christina decided to remain in her room until it was time to leave, but watched from the window as Jeffrey and her father loaded their belongings tightly into their wagons. A movement below caught her attention. Thomas was lugging a trunk toward the wagons. She saw him glance toward her father and Jeffrey. His tension was apparent in the stiffening of his spine. He lowered the trunk and stood there. To anyone else watching, he may have simply been resting, but Christina knew better. In fact, if she could see his eyes, his gaze would most likely be shooting daggers into Mr. Jeffrey Buchanan.

After a moment, he flopped heavily onto the trunk and Christina smiled. His tired state was a ruse, she knew. He was simply avoiding Jeffrey. She didn't doubt that when Jeffrey moved away, Thomas would resume moving, and laughed aloud when her theory proved right.

She wondered how much longer it would be before everything was loaded. They had been at it for several hours already, and their packing didn't even include the bulk of the furniture that her father was selling to Mr. Baker. She couldn't say she was eager for the packing to conclude, for that would signal their departure. Apparently, her mother was hiding away also, as she hadn't seen her since the loading began.

She inquired after her mother, when Mirabelle dropped lunch by her room. Mirabelle informed her that her mother had been wandering aimlessly around the house the whole time, saying a tearful goodbye to every little item that was remaining.

Christina sighed heavily over that news, but decided that their course was laid out, and she might consider it the adventure Thomas suggested.

She watched as her brother hefted yet another large trunk into the back of their wagon. Thomas explained earlier that the schooner, the smaller of the two wagons her father had obtained for

the trip, was where she and her mother would be bedding down.
She had her doubts however, as the men shoved more things into
the back.

Of course, she should be grateful to have a place to bed down
at all, or to simply sit and rest for that matter. From what Thomas
told her, most of the families would not even have that luxury. The
Wagon Master allowed only the families with two or more males to
bring more than one wagon, so it didn't matter as to one's wealth or
lack thereof. If a family had but one driver, they had to cram all
possessions into their one wagon, which inevitably meant that the
family members—men, women, and children—would have to walk
the entire distance, cram all persons onto the small board seat at the
front, or simply dispose of all their acquired possessions.

Christina shuddered at that thought. Adventure or not, it was
going to be a difficult enough journey for those allowed to ride but a
little, but for those having to walk the whole way, it would be hell.
She felt selfishly thankful that she wasn't going to have to be one of
those walking. She was also thankful that her mother didn't have to
walk at all, for she was almost certain she'd never make the trip if
forced to do so.

Christina indeed felt fortunate, at least in that regard. She also
felt privileged that she wouldn't have to be bedding down on the
cold hard ground like the men folk would be doing, something that
displeased Jeffrey a great deal, but that which displeased him,
thrilled Christina no end.

She took pleasure in thwarting him or simply bringing a little
misery into his life. She received even more pleasure when those
around her managed to make his life miserable for her, leaving her
with plenty of energy to gloat.

A movement in her periphery caught her eye, and she glanced
over toward the side of the house. Her breath caught and tears
threatened at the sight of her mother openly weeping over the
flowerbed. To anyone watching, it may have been a wretched sight,
but Christina understood her heartache all too well.

Her eyes strayed to where her father was standing on the lawn talking to Mr. Baker, who had finally arrived. She wondered what he would do if he turned and saw his wife making a spectacle of herself over the lilies that wouldn't bloom for many weeks yet, or rose bushes that still lay dormant after the winter cold.

Would he understand her heartbreak, as did she, or would he reprimand her for behaving in such an unladylike fashion? Christina could only wonder. Perhaps if her father hadn't taken leave of his senses, all because of Jeffrey's scheming, they would be sitting to luncheon right now, enjoying a sherry with their meal and, most importantly, her mother would be healthy.

Christina rose languidly from the window seat and walked slowly to the front door. Her gaze fell upon Chin Woo, who was struggling to climb onto the schooner, and she almost laughed. She walked down the walkway and nimbly climbed next to him.

"Look at the bright side, Chin Woo," she said with a smirk on her face.

"From where I sit, there is no bright side," he answered in an obviously disagreeable mood.

"You could be driving the Conestoga," she continued undaunted, nodding at the much larger wagon.

"Why that make me feel better, Cookie?"

"Well, you only have to handle two of these foul-smelling beasts. Jeffrey has to handle six."

"Ahhh. That make me feel much better." One beast chose that moment to raise its tail and leave its smelly mark on the street, erasing any smile that she'd achieved. She grinned when he began cursing up a blue streak in his native language.

Christina pulled a handkerchief from her sleeve and pressed it over her nose to keep out the smell the oxen had left, laughing at the miserable expression on Chin Woo's face.

"I chose a poor time to talk to you," she laughed and then grew somber again, remembering that what she wanted to tell Chin Woo was no laughing matter.

Chin Woo noticed the sudden change in his friend and stiffened slightly. "What wrong, Cookie?" He whispered, looking around to see if he could find the cause of his friend's distress. Christina was looking around also, to make certain that Jeffrey was nowhere within hearing distance. She spotted him standing on the lawn near her father, laughing at something that the banker had just said.

Christina lowered the handkerchief, shoving it angrily back up her sleeve—the memory of her confrontation with Jeffrey fresh in her mind.

"Jeffrey knows everything," she blurted out in a harsh whisper. She saw Chin Woo's eyes widen with understanding.

"I so sorry, Cookie. I know you not want him to know and now he do. How he find out?"

"He's had someone spying on me, but at least I stood my ground about the weapons." Christina felt a renewed sense of relief about that little victory.

"What mean?" Chin Woo looked at her quizzically.

"That means that Jeffrey didn't take the weapons away from me, even though he tried. I wouldn't let him." Christina kept talking with one eye pinned on Jeffrey. "He asked me for them, but I told them that you'd given them to me to protect myself against wild animals."

Chin Woo wanted to laugh, but his heart was too heavy. "I tell you something now, too, Cookie." Chin Woo stopped and he bent his head, in embarrassment. "I know that what I teach you not work," Chin Woo started and then stopped again, rubbing a calloused hand across his dusty face. "You a woman, and woman no made to fight. Still, you come to me for help, and I feel helpless in my heart like nothing I feel before. I no help to give you, so I give you only help I know. The same help my father give me as a boy when bullies try to hurt me."

"Oh, Chin Woo, you are so wrong," Christina cried, placing an arm around her friend's bent shoulders. "Yes, Jeffrey knows, and no, I probably cannot use the weapons against him. Still, the gift you gave me was more than just a knowledge of weapons; it was a strength of mind unlike anything I've ever known before." Christina paused to pull the handkerchief from her sleeve again, handing it to Chin Woo who'd begun to sniffle lightly. "Do you think that I could ever have stood against Jeffrey's demands this morning, had you not taught me to be strong?"

"Cookie always strong," Chin Woo whispered proudly.

"You're wrong. I'm a coward, and I'm scared to death of what my future holds now that Jeffrey is a part of it. Thanks to you however, I could probably withstand Jeffrey's bullying without the need of weapons."

"Cookie really believe so?" Chin Woo asked hopefully.

"I know so, Chin Woo. I really do." Christina patted her friend lightly on the hand. "Besides, we may really, and truly, encounter some horrible beasts on the trail, and your weapons may indeed come in handy, right?"

"Right," Chin Woo smiled brightly. "So, I did maybe help Cookie?"

"More than maybe," she assured her friend. "More than you'll ever know."

The sound of weeping caught her attention and she turned to see her mother still kneeling by the bed of flowers that she'd never see bloom again on a warm spring day. Her silent cries had turned into full-blown sobs drawing everyone's attention. "Excuse me, Chin Woo, but I think my mother needs me."

Without waiting for a reply, Christina jumped unassisted from the wagon. She had been trying to see this inevitable trip as the adventure that Thomas and her father did, and truly sometimes, when she wasn't dwelling on getting rid of her affianced, her spirits lightened and she wondered what lay ahead. Then she'd hear her mother weeping at night, or she'd have the nightmare that bespoke of danger, and her spirits would wane. She was only partway to where her mother knelt, when her father brushed passed her and lifted her mother by the elbow, whispering softly in her ear.

Well, at least he seems to care, she thought bitterly. Tears fell down her cheeks as she watched her father lead her mother gently to the rear of the schooner, whispering something in her ear. Christina wondered at what he was saying to her, not that it would matter, for her mother appeared not to be paying attention to him. Her eyes held a glazed look as if seeing beyond here and now.

Christina turned her back on the scene. Her gaze fell upon the house she'd called home for seventeen years. Sadly, she turned and headed back to the schooner that she would call home for the next month or more. After her arrival in Texas, she'd call her Uncle Peter's place home. She wondered bitterly if she'd ever have a place of her own to call home again. Any house she shared with Jeffrey would never feel like a home to her, and her sadness turned to anger. While Jeffrey remained in her life, she'd never have a place to call home, which made her want to damn his hide to Hell repeatedly.

Her father called to her, and soon the wagons were moving down the main street of town. Christina raised her face heavenward and closed her eyes in supplication for a safe journey. When she opened them, her regard fell upon the moon competing in the sky with the setting sun. It was a full moon. "What is it that Chin Woo told me about full moons?" She wondered. "Is it supposed to be a good omen or a bad omen? Well," she whispered, "time will soon provide the answer to that question."

CHAPTER 20

Again the warriors returned from the hunt, but the buffalo was growing scarce, and the efforts to feed The People were becoming more difficult. It used to take one hunt to feed his people, now it took several long and tiring journeys, which only added fuel to the anger that the young warriors felt toward the white man. They held the white man accountable for their current suffering. If not for the needless slaughter of their main food supply, the women, children, and elderly would have full bellies instead of worrying over where the next meal might come.

It also angered the young warriors that the effort of the hunt made them too tired to enjoy the celebrations that the women held upon their return, and many of them sought their beds early. Baying Wolf was one. He lay atop the animal pelts, staring at where the support poles crossed near the top of his teepee. The last vestiges of light filtered through the hole near the top, lending an eerie quality to the paintings lining the walls.

He leaned over and doused the flames; however, it mattered not how tired he was, his mind refused to allow his eyes to close and claim his enervated mind. The white woman was back. He sensed her presence in his mind, just as if she were standing beside him. His anger mingled with a wary shock to know that he no longer needed sleep to find her; that she was there in his mind continually and he could sense her there.

He wondered vaguely if she could sense him in the same way he could sense her. If so, was she trying to shake him free as he was trying to do with her? No matter how hard he mentally shook himself however, thoughts of her clung tenaciously, making him even more foul-tempered than usual.

He gazed into the increasing blackness, willing his drooping eyelids to stay open, for he knew that if he could sense her while awake, then his mind would definitely seek her out in his dream state. He had no desire to see her again.

Sweat issued from every pore in his body, but he didn't know whether this resulted from the warmth of the embers emanating from the recently doused flames, or from his attempts to fight the natural inclination to sleep.

In frustration, he sat up and yelled angrily to the Great Spirit. "Why do you seek my help? Why can you not find one of her own kind to help her? I foolishly tried to help her before, but all she did was to run from me like a frightened doe." He did not truly expect a response, so when thunder crashed, rending the silence of the evening sky, it startled him.

He leapt from his mat and pushed open the flap to his teepee to appease his curiosity. He had not seen storm clouds brewing upon his return, but the weather changed quickly on the prairie. He needed to console himself that the thunder he'd heard was not the Great Spirit, but merely the weather.

He lifted his eyes toward the sky and froze. There before him was the very sign he was unprepared to see—a full moon rising in the waning twilight and an eagle soaring high above.

"Your eagle guide has arrived and so has the time for you to depart, my nephew."

Baying Wolf spun at the sound of the voice behind him and looked into the smiling face of his uncle. "You have a secret, old man, that you will not share with me," Baying Wolf said, barely able to contain his anger. "You know why I must go to her, don't you?"

"I will overlook your disrespect because you need to go prepare for your journey." Without receiving the answers he wished, Baying Wolf stalked back to his teepee, mumbling angrily under his breath.

When his things were prepared, he mounted his horse and lifted his eyes to the eagle soaring above. "Great Eagle," he murmured reverently, "guide me to where I need to go. Even if I do not wish to go there."

"You will understand soon enough, my nephew." The mysterious tone in his uncle's voice as he approached Baying Wolf's horse, confirmed Baying Wolf's suspicions that his uncle was withholding information from him.

"So you say, but you will not help me understand and I cannot see..."

"You cannot see," Fire Dreamer interrupted, "because the anger in your heart has clouded your vision."

Without responding, or waiting for further comments from his uncle, Baying Wolf dug his heels into his horse's haunches and took off at a gallop. The last time he went to aid this female, he remained ensconced in his tepee, his journey a mental one. Now however, The Great Spirit was forcing him to leave his home to seek her out.

He slowed his horse to a trot and, again, lifted his gaze heavenward, "Why must I be the one to go to this woman?" As before, he received no reply. "Not even a crack of thunder," he mused, glancing at the cloudless sky. "Very well," he sighed heavily, "I will go because you wish it, but in my anger I'm not certain how I will treat her when I find her."

A clap of thunder sounded loudly at this proclamation, startling Baying Wolf and his horse. "Now, you listen and answer," he mumbled, spurring his horse into a gallop again.

CHAPTER 21

Christina pulled the handkerchief further up the bridge of her nose. The dust kicking up from the wagons ahead of theirs was making it difficult to breathe, and the handkerchief covering her nose and mouth did little to help. Also inhibiting her chance for a cheery disposition was the unbearable heat, which the thick canopy overhead did little to diminish. Christina felt an absurd affinity with a chicken roasting over an open fire, and if it were a live chicken, she had no doubt it would empathize with her.

Dirt and grime clogged every pore in her body. She reached up self-consciously and touched her hair, pulling it quickly away when she felt the oil and filth that had built up in only a few short days. For someone who was used to bathing on a daily basis and washing up at least three times a day more, the filth was beginning to weigh heavily on her. She cursed under her breath their wagon master's display of stubbornness in not allowing them the luxury of a bath during their short stops. He may not mind stinking like a horse's behind, but she certainly took objection to it. "I smell as poorly as the beasts pulling the wagon," she muttered under her breath.

"What was that you said dear?" Her mother lifted her head and stared at Christina tiredly.

"Nothing, Mother. You just keep resting."

Just then, the wagon hit yet another rut and she let go another string of violent thoughts, all directed at the men in her life, except Chin Woo of course. If it weren't for them, she wouldn't be on this blasted contraption. Her next sense of affinity was for a sack of potatoes. She certainly knew what it felt like to be tossed and jostled without regard for bruising.

The thought of bruised potatoes brought to mind her derriere, which had been subjected to more bouncing and jarring than an entire year in a saddle. Her body and mind screamed for rest. Still she bore the suffering stoically, except for the occasional unintended outburst, as she didn't want to disturb what little rest her mother was getting. Her mind, however, ranted and railed continually, daringly using unladylike vernacular she'd reserved of late for thoughts solely related to Jeffrey.

She leaned her head out of the front of the wagon and propped it on the seat, looking into the dense forest on either side. She imagined that she could reach the lush foliage if she were to stretch forth her hand, so close it appeared.

Stop imagining that, or you're apt to do it, and end up getting scratched severely because of that infernal curiosity of yours, her mind warned.

She was about to rebut, when Chin Woo interrupted her thoughts.

"How Cookie doing?" He looked over his shoulder and grinned at the grimy face glaring at him, obviously disgruntled.

"About as well as you, if your face is any indication. Mind if I join you up front? It really is unbearably hot back here."

"It only going to get hotter after crossing Mississippi River. There, no trees for shade."

"Ugh." As Christina climbed over the seat, her skirt caught and tangled around her legs. She fought with the material for several minutes, finally tumbling over onto the seat and almost off the wagon. It was a very unladylike display, which brought laughter from her brother, riding nearby on his horse.

Chin Woo grabbed the back of her skirt and tugged, unable to prevent laughing.

"Stop laughing, you big galoot. It's not my fault I have to try to maneuver around in these gosh-awful skirts." When she got her skirts arranged and was seated comfortably, Christina squinted against the dirt that the forward wagon kicked up. To make matters worse, the beasts pulling the wagon gave off an even stronger pervasive odor that her handkerchief couldn't block. "How can you possibly suffer through all of this...muck!"

"I quit seeing and smelling two day ago." Chin Woo tugged at his own bandana that kept threatening to slip down his nose. Christina would have thought he was joking had the scowl on his face been absent.

"How many days before we take the lead?"

"We start six wagon back. We travel three days. We take lead in three more day," Chin Woo explained with a loud sigh.

"Yuck!"

"Yuck, muck," Chin Woo grunted.

Christina grinned, "We may have three more days to suffer this dirty onslaught, but Jeffrey has four more." Chin Woo let go a genuine laugh at that observation, and even her pessimistic mind let go of a giggle. Seemed everyone loved hearing anything in which Jeffrey suffered.

"I think last night to ask you question" Chin Woo said, as if mention of Jeffrey jarred his own memory, "What you know about Jeffrey?"

"I'm not sure I understand."

"What you know about him?" Chin Woo repeated. "Where he from? What drive him to marry you?"

Christina thought for a moment, but could not provide a ready answer. "I can only say he started coming around to collect Thomas for a night on the town, a couple of years ago. Since he never did more than nod in my direction, we never conversed, so I never really got to know him. I do know that his nods always made me feel ill at ease, which is another thing I can't fully explain—my reaction to him. How can I hate a man that I never really met before last month?"

"You have good instinct. Still, you ever think how he know *you*? He know you so good he make you marry him."

"What do you mean, Chin Woo?"

"How he know you so well? How he know you marry him to save family?"

"Well, he's been around the family enough to have discussed me, I suppose, and to see how close we are. Surely if he'd shown an interest, Thomas would have said something. If he knew Father and indicated a desire to get to know me, surely Father would have let me know. It all made little sense before, but makes even less sense now. So, how does he know I'll marry him to save my family? I haven't the faintest idea. Why do you bring this up now?"

"To defeat enemy, one must know enemy."

"You're starting to wax philosophical on me again, Chin Woo," Christina teased gently.

Chin Woo snorted, "My father once say that if you want to defeat enemy, you must first know enemy. If you do not know Jeffrey, how you supposed to know how to get out of marriage? I think on this long time, Cookie. I try teach you be strong of mind. I try teach you fight like man. What I forget was most important lesson my father teach me. Before battle, learn everything about enemy. This so to uncover weakness to use against them. Understand? If you know nothing about Jeffrey, where he from, what is weakness, how can you make plan to defeat him and get out of marriage? And that is best I can explain."

"I'm following you." Christina thought for a moment and then suddenly burst out laughing.

"What Cookie find funny?"

"Jeffrey sent spies to keep an eye on me to prevent us from doing the very thing that we are still doing."

"What thing?"

"Putting our heads together to try to devise a plan to prevent this marriage. To be honest with you, Chin Woo, when you told me the other day that all that training had been for nothing, I'd pretty much consigned myself to marrying Jeffrey. Now here we sit, trying to concoct yet another scheme to get me out of this mess."

"I no quit thinking how to get Cookie out of mess. It just took me long time to think what next step should be."

"Have you figured it out yet, other than getting to know him, that is?"

Chin Woo lowered his head and shook it dejectedly, "Next step to know Jeffrey not seem big step, but we have much steps to take before Texas? Yes?

"Yes. Thank the Lord above, but we'll have to tread softly. Jeffrey's spy could be lurking about anywhere."

"He very smart man, but since I no see spy inside ox's tail-end," Chin Woo said, motioning toward the ox in front of them, "I think is pretty safe to talk right now."

"Oh my, Chin Woo, that was a very disgusting observation." Christina tried to wipe the thought of a pair of legs dangling from an ox's rear-end out of her thoughts. When that didn't work, she redirected the subject back to their original conversation. "I think that perhaps I need to have a heart-to-heart with Jeffrey when and if our wagon master finally allows us to stop. What is it with this man, anyway? Does he have to drive us so hard?"

"I not know. I tired, too, but it be worth being tired to get where we are going."

"Not if it gets me down that aisle faster than never, it won't. Sorry, I shouldn't complain. If you take away the dirt, the mode of transport, and the foul-smelling team pulling our wagon...well, the view is rather beautiful."

"I agree. But if you do talk to Jeffrey, promise be very careful."

"I promise; and Chin Woo, remind me to thank your father if I ever meet him."

"Why you want thank father?"

"Well, if he hadn't taught you all of those tidbits of wisdom, I'd probably be a very unhappy Mrs. Jeffrey Buchanan in another month or so. As it is, I have more faith, as time passes, that we'll find a way out of this trap."

"Just be careful that trap doesn't spring before you out of its way."

"Well, with you, and your father's help, we could probably spring a trap of our own on Jeffrey Buchanan."

CHAPTER 22

The wagon master called a much-needed halt the next evening in a beautiful little clearing that allowed the wagons to form a circle. The perimeter of dense, breathtaking forest provided just enough space in the center for everyone to build a fire and prepare their first decent meal. For this, Christina was extremely grateful, since they'd finished all of the pre-prepared supplies yesterday that Hyacinth packed for them.

In the distance, Christina could hear the babbling of a brook and couldn't wait to get dinner underway so that she could join the other women that had already left for a cool bath.

"You speak Jeffrey now?" Chin Woo passed by carrying the large pot that Christina would use to cook the vegetables she was busily chopping.

"No," Christina said, wiping a dirty sleeve across her sweaty forehead. "I'll wait until this evening when everyone has bedded down. Right now, I need to finish cutting these vegetables and then I'm going to take a much needed bath."

"The water is here," A voice called from a few feet behind. Christina looked over her shoulder to see Thomas hurrying up to them, two large buckets filled to overflowing with spring water. "Why don't you go on down and wash up, Sis, while Chin Woo and I get the fire started and the water on to boil? By the looks of it," he said, giving his sister a quick once over, "you are in dire need of a thorough wash."

Christina punched her brother playfully on his arm, causing the water to slosh on his pants. "You shouldn't talk, Baby Brother. The only part of your face still white is your teeth," she rejoined, "and even those are questionable."

"Well, the faster you women finish primping, the sooner us men can get down there and wash the smell of oxen and horses off of our bodies."

"Thanks, Thomas, but I need to finish chopping these

vegetables first, or there won't be anything to put in the water when it starts to boil."

"You don't think that Chin Woo and I know how to wield a knife? We're men, remember? We're the ones with the skills. I can easily handle that knife better than you, so turn it over and head on out."

Chin Woo and Christina exchanged amused glances, but didn't dare share their secret. Of course, Christina couldn't hold back the giggle that escaped when she thought of her brother's expression should he know she *could* wield the knife better than he could, and with deadly accuracy. The poor vegetables actually stood a better chance of surviving in his hands than hers.

"Oh, all right then, Baby Brother," Christina stood, stretched the kinks out of her back, and tossed the knife at her brother.

"Hey!" Her brother yelped, taking a step back, "Watch where you toss that thing!"

"Catch it next time," Christina teased.

"Catch it. Yeah right," Thomas muttered, stooping down to pick up the now dirty utensil.

"Hey, maybe I'll see if Mother wants to bathe," Christina said, turning toward the rear of their schooner.

"Mother's already down there," Thomas said. "Didn't you know?"

"She is?"

"Yeah, she left shortly after we stopped."

"That's great! Maybe she'll snap out of her doldrums when she sees how beautiful this place is."

"I don't know, Sis," Thomas said, suddenly somber, "she didn't look all that well and only gave me the barest of smiles when I greeted her."

"Oh, well, maybe a bath will change all of that." Christina turned and quickly retrieved some fresh clothing from her trunk and flounced off. When she reached the brook, she glanced around at the women playfully washing, looking for her mother's diminutive form. She spotted her about fifteen feet away, washing her dirty clothes on a rock, her long brown hair still hanging wet across her shoulders.

She stood, watching for a moment, and said a short prayer of thanks that her mother had finally taken the time to bathe; to care for herself at all. Still, her worry would not abate completely, until they arrived at Uncle Peter's, and her mother regained her weight and her spirits. As it was, her mother was not taking this trip at all well. She'd barely spoken two words since they'd left Georgia, and she still refused to leave the back of the wagon unless necessary. Not that the wagon master had afforded them many opportunities for that purpose.

In fact, over the last three days, this was the first time that they'd stopped for the entire evening. All other stops had been brief and only for an hour or less. She'd heard other families talk about the danger imposed with the constant traveling, especially during the night, but no one had the bravery to confront the wagon master; and it was no wonder, as he was a burly man with an equally surly temper.

Christina made her way toward her mom, careful to watch her footing so that she didn't slip on the moss-covered rocks. "Mother?"

Carlotta Carthington looked over her shoulder at her daughter and smiled dimly. "I'll be along shortly to help with dinner. I just wanted to get all of this grime off of me, wash my clothes, and change into something fresh."

"I understand, but there's no rush," Christina said, forcing a cheerful tone into her voice. She took a seat close to her mom and hugged her knees to her chin, "Thomas and Chin Woo are starting for us so that we can relax a bit."

"How kind."

"How are you feeling, Mother?"

"I don't think you truly want me to answer that, love," Carlotta said softly.

"But of course I do," Christina protested. "You're my mother and you are obviously going through a difficult time. So much so that you've allowed yourself to become ill. So, when I ask how you're doing, I'm not just being polite. I sincerely need to know that you're okay."

"I wish I could reassure you of that, but, in all honesty, I feel as if my life is over," Carlotta whispered. At her daughter's gasp, she quickly tried to explain. "I've spent a lifetime in the home we just sold. I've raised you children there, entertained there, and built my life there. My mother and father passed away in that very house and we buried them in the small cemetery down the street. Did you know that? Of course you did. So you see, my dear, that house is more to me than just a home. It was the center of my entire world. It was mine, so I should have had a say in whether we sold it. For your father to selfishly take it all away without so much as a by your leave, drag me halfway across the country to a strange and hostile land—well it has broken my heart into more pieces than may be repairable at this late time in my life. Now, did you really need to hear me express those thoughts?"

"I knew that you felt betrayed by Father, but I didn't realize how deep your sadness went over losing the house." Those were the most words her mother had spoken since the beginning of their trip, but Christina was more concerned at the content of the little discourse than the fact that she'd actually spoken. "But now that I do understand, isn't there anything I can do to reassure you or to help mend your broken heart? After all, you still have Thomas and me to think of, right? And if you try to think positively about building a grander home, instead of dwelling on what you've lost, then maybe your health will improve."

"I'm sorry to disappoint you dearest, but this move has shattered my heart, along with any desire to start over. Still, I have a wedding to look forward to, if nothing else."

Christina didn't have the heart to tell her that she did not intend to marry Jeffrey. "Perhaps Jeffrey and I should postpone our nuptials until you're feeling better, and are fully recovered from this move. I mean, after all, celebrating a wedding when you're out-of-sorts about the move would be selfish, and to ask you to fake happiness as you suggested wouldn't seem at all right. And since I'm certain that you'll adjust splendidly once you've gotten over the circumstances behind the move, then there's no need to rush things, is there?"

"Well, at least I know you're not pregnant," Carlotta said softly.

"I do beg your pardon, Mother, but what did you say?" Christina gasped, wondering whether the sound of the nearby rushing water had impaired her hearing.

"Well, a mother does worry over that sort of thing, you know, especially when the fiancé tries to pressure the parents of the girl to wed posthaste instead of waiting for a proper ceremony. But your desire to postpone the wedding for my sake tells me that Jeffrey's eagerness to wed stems from his love for you and not worry over some indiscretion."

"Oh, dear me," Christina said, her face matching the color on the feathers of a nearby cardinal. "I would never—that is to say that I never had any intention—I mean, truly Mother, just the thought of sleeping with Jeffrey…"

"Calm yourself, my dear," Carlotta said softly. "It's a natural thing for you to want sleep with the man you love. Not that I'd know about that first hand," she murmured with a trace of bitterness.

"Mother, please! We haven't slept together," Christina protested.

"Oh, well, that's all well and good too," Carlotta said, patting Christina's cheek lightly. "But it's nice to know you'll go to your wedding still a virgin. It means that we didn't totally fail you as parents."

"You know Mother," Christina sighed in exasperation, "I think I liked it better when you *weren't* talking. Now that you are, you are blathering on in a senseless manner that, I must confess, is rather disconcerting."

"Truly! I rather thought I was speaking plainly, and aren't you a surprise speaking to me in such a manner."

"I'm sorry. I didn't mean any disrespect," Christina apologized.

"I guess this situation is more stressing to me than I let on as well."

"It's okay, dearest. Now, go. Join the other women. Of course, you might want to hurry or you're going to be the only one left down here. I'm just going to finish dressing and head back to the wagon."

Christina looked over to where the other women were and noticed that a majority had already made their way onto the bank in preparation of heading back to camp. "I think I'd rather stay here with you."

Carlotta's eyebrow arched at the declaration, "Really! I thought after the discomfiting conversation we just had that you'd jump at the chance to exit my company, or was it not you that I was speaking with only moments ago," Carlotta said, only half teasing. "And since I've completed my ablutions and you've not yet begun, I'd catch my death sitting on these cold stones waiting for you to finish. Besides, I'm tired, and wish to rest, so shoo."

"All right, Mother, but I won't be long. Surely you can sit for a few minutes more, maybe enjoy the scenery, and think things over. Then we can walk back to camp together?" Carlotta merely smiled as Christina moved gingerly toward the other women.

The jovial atmosphere at the brook was contagious and soon Christina found herself laughing and splashing with those women that had chosen to remain behind a short while longer.

She scrubbed her scalp with the lye soap she'd taken from her mom, ducked her head in the swift moving stream, and then started again. At last, after a third scrub down, she ducked her head in the water and felt the dirt and grime rinse completely away, along with the tension she'd felt since before the journey began. She even forgot Jeffrey during her short bath.

After she'd gotten her hair satisfactorily clean, Christina ducked into the water, lathered soap into her hands and set about scrubbing her body under her shift and pantaloons. Of course, if anyone knew she was touching herself in such a scandalous fashion, she may find herself ostracized from the wagon train.

Well, hopefully nothing that dramatic, she laughed silently. Still, she had clean undergarments awaiting her on the bank and she was definitely *not* going to put clean undergarments on a dirty body. That, and she simply couldn't stand the gritty feeling clinging to her entire body a second longer.

When she finally finished scrubbing her body down, she realized that only two women remained at the water's edge and neither of them was her mother. In a panic, she began wading quickly to shore, looking frantically around for any signs that her mother was waiting for her. She wasn't worried so much that her mother might have accidentally fallen into the water unnoticed and drowned. Her concern was that she might have deliberately fallen unnoticed to take her own life.

Shame welled inside her for thinking that her mother would consider suicide, but she thought it nonetheless. Now she needed to assure herself that it hadn't happened. Of course, if Hyacinth hadn't planted the notion that her mother would maybe do such a thing in the first place, she probably wouldn't be wading desperately toward the bank now, searching for a drowning female. Hyacinth had been right about Carlotta Carthington—she wasn't a strong woman, mentally or physically, so the strain of the move could very well send her searching for an easy way out of her current situation.

She reached the bank completely exhausted and had to stop for a moment to regain her breath. She bent over and placed her hands on her knees, drawing air deep into her depleted lungs, but her heart refused to slow its furious pounding.

"Excuse me," a quiet, timid voice whispered from behind her, causing Christina to jump nearly back into the water. "I'm sorry," the woman continued with a giggle, "I didn't mean to startle you."

"That's all right." Christina eyes continued scanning the area for her mother.

"If you're looking for your mother, that's why I'm here," the lady continued quickly.

Christina stopped looking around and brought her gaze back to the woman standing before her. Her already rapid heartbeat quickened still faster, and she dreaded to ask what it was the woman was there to tell her. She forced herself to remain calm and said a prayer that the news she bore was not ill.

"I'm Margaret, but my friends call me Maggie. What few friends I have," she murmured shyly. "You are Christina, aren't you?"

"Yes, yes," she said, trying but failing miserably to keep the impatience from her voice. "You said you have something to tell me about my mother."

"Oh that! I'm sorry," the woman giggled again. "I tend to be a bit scatter-brained sometimes. At least that's what my husband says, but I'm not really. I just get a bit off track."

"Well, it's nice to meet you Maggie, but you were going to tell me something about my mother," she repeated more firmly.

"Yes, she said to tell you that she headed on back and not to worry about rushing. She'll probably be asleep by the time you get there," Maggie finished quoting the message with a smile of self-satisfaction and Christina breathed a huge sigh of relief. "Well, I have to be getting back before Stephen misses me," Maggie said suddenly, turning to leave. "Have to get dinner finished for the men folk."

"Could you possibly stand watch a moment while I change into some clean clothes, and then I'll be happy to walk back with you?" Christina asked.

"Not at all," Maggie replied.

Christina could tell by the constant glances over her shoulder that it was an inconvenience, so she did her best to pull her clothes over her wet body quickly. "If you have to get back now, it's no bother," she offered.

Maggie waved a hand at her, "It's no bother. It's just that I waited for you as I gave your mother my word I would, and I'm just a little concerned that I will be delayed preparing dinner."

"I'll help you get it going, if you like," Christina offered, shrugging into her shirt. "It's the least I can do for helping Mother like you did."

"No, no. It's no bother, really."

Christina could see by the way Maggie fidgeted with her hands that *something* was bothering her, but to her credit, she did her best to pretend that nothing was amiss.

"You know, I wish the wagon master would stop more often and allow the women to spend more time together. I mean, I've spent so much time in the company of my men folk that I'm beginning to talk just like them, and they've got the worst vernacular of any human being I've ever met." Christina laughed when she realized that Maggie was right. It had been a pleasant time, short though it was, with the women joining to bathe and talk. Something the wagon master had not afforded them since leaving Georgia.

At least Christina had her mother and Chin Woo to talk to. Well, with her mother, she did more of the talking of late, but it was still better than keeping company with two uneducated men that normally wouldn't stop to give a woman the time of day.

"Are you married, Christina?" Maggie asked suddenly.

"No. Engaged to someone, who I rather wish would drop off the face of the earth," Christina answered truthfully. "I'm ready. Are you ready to head back?" She stooped to pick up her belongings and fell into step next to Maggie who had already started at a surprisingly fast gait upon her announcement of being dressed. "Are *you* married?" Christina reciprocated the question, picking up her pace to fall in alongside Maggie.

"Me? Yes. My marriage is a farce. Stephen is not the man of my dreams, that's for certain. Not to mention having to put up with his uncouth brother. At least you have a chance to end your engagement before it becomes official."

"I'm sorry to hear that, but my situation isn't any better. Jeffrey has a noose tied snugly around my neck and he's just likely to tighten it and strangle me before letting me out of our engagement."

"Ouch, sounds painful."

"It is."

"Hey!" Maggie broke the short silence that had fallen. She stopped walking and turned to face Christina, her eyes twinkling as if she'd just thought of something extremely conspiratorial. "Why don't you come to my wagon for dinner tonight?"

Christina tried hard not to laugh. That was what had gotten Maggie all excited? A simple dinner invitation? She really must live a sheltered life and miss the company of other women.

"My husband says I'm a gosh-awful cook," Maggie whispered, sounding suddenly uncertain, she seemed to retreat within herself, "so you don't have to accept if you don't want to get poisoned."

Christina's heart went out to the woman standing before her. Her life was difficult and unpleasant, and she suddenly wondered whether she would become the same unsure, pitiful creature after a few years of marriage to Jeffrey. She shuddered at the thought. "I'm sure that your cooking isn't all that bad," She said in an attempt to be encouraging. "It most certainly couldn't be any worse than mine."

Maggie smiled shyly, "Well, I'm not actually cooking since we're having canned beef and canned beans."

"Well, how about if I bring some of my gosh-awful rice to have with your gosh-awful beef and beans? Sound all right?"

"Sounds delightful."

A booming voice sounded in the distance, startling both women. Maggie seemed to wither right before her eyes, "That's Stephen. He's waiting on supper," her voice was a mere whisper, "so I'd best be getting back now."

"I'll be there in about half an hour. Does that sound okay?"

"Just fine," Maggie replied, and then turned to leave. She was halfway to the wagon when she turned around again. "Christina?"

"Yes, Maggie?"

"I'm very glad your mother gave me the message to deliver to you."

"I'm glad too," Christina smiled. "Now I have a new friend."

CHAPTER 23

Christina's arms stood extended from her sides, the small pot of rice in her right hand weighing it down so that it was uneven with the left. She tilted her head back on her neck as she spun slowly in a circle, her gaze soaking in the multitude of stars that lit the early evening sky. She sighed as a peaceful feeling stole over her, wrapping her in its warmth, like the down quilt she used to wrap up in on cold winter nights.

"Hey, Sis!" Thomas called, running toward her. "You're going the wrong way. The Bishop's wagon is the other way."

"I know that, silly goose." Christina lowered her arms, the peaceful moment shattered. "I just thought I'd take the long way around. It seems so much quieter on this side of the wagons, doesn't it?"

"It's also going to be really, really dark in a few minutes, making this side of the wagon extremely dangerous."

"It's not as if I'm going into the woods, Thomas. I'm simply walking the perimeter, right next to the wagons. What could possibly happen to me here?"

"More than you could possibly know, Sis," Thomas whispered dramatically, his eyes scanning the dense forest. "A wild animal could come, drag you away, and eat you *and* that rice you're carrying. Or yet, a wild Indian could catch a glimpse of that red head of yours in the firelight and decide to haul you off and make you his slave..."

"Oh, Thomas!" Christina laughed. "You really are something else, you know that?"

"Are you going to turn around and head in the right direction?"

"No! I'm going to continue my nature walk in this direction," Christina replied stubbornly.

"Want me to join you?" Thomas persisted, equally stubborn in his protection of his sister.

"Not in the least. This is the first time I've had a chance to be alone in many days, and I fully intend to take advantage. Now go away."

"All right, but you have to promise to yell really loud if something happens."

"I give you my word," Christina answered in mock solemnity, "that if man or beast tries to drag me away, I will yell as loud as my tiny lungs will afford—that is if they don't somehow seal my lips with magic powers first."

"Smarty."

"Thanks for caring, Thomas, but I'm sure that nothing untoward will happen between here and Maggie's wagon. Okay?"

"Fine." Thomas ran off again and soon disappeared around the corner of their wagon. She loved her brother, but was happy to watch him leave. She wasn't joking about needing the time to herself. She couldn't think of a more pleasant way to spend it than here in this rugged country under skies so clear that every star in the universe seemed visible; where all she could hear were the sounds of God's creatures singing His praises.

The chatter on the other side of the wagons seemed far away and she felt a peace within herself as she'd never felt when she'd lived near town. Maybe this was God's way of telling her that she belonged here in this wild country. His country.

She heard a noise beside her and stopped suddenly, catching the lid on the rice pot when it threatened to fall off. She stepped into a nearby shadow and remained motionless. Her gaze scanned the growing darkness of the forest beyond and stopped when they fell upon a doe delicately sniffing the air. She smiled at the sight, wanting to reach out a hand to stroke the satiny fur that shined in the moonlight.

"If I had my shotgun, we could have deer stew tonight."

She watched in growing anger as the deer started and bounded off into the woods, and then turned to face the intruder. "You're a heartless cad, Mr. Buchanan," she accused, and then started walking away. When he fell into step beside her, she snapped. "What are you doing out here anyway?"

"I came to talk to you. Maybe form a truce of some sort."

"A truce?" She asked, suspicious. "You make it sound as if we're at war."

"I feel as if I've been doing battle with you since we announced our engagement." Jeffrey's soft admission brought Christina to a halt. She was angry with him for disrupting her peaceful walk, but hearing him speak in a tone that made it sound like their problems were a result of her stubbornness and had nothing to do with him, made her ire elevate quickly.

"Don't you mean since you *blackmailed* me into this engagement?"

Jeffrey sighed in exasperation. This wasn't going at all the way he'd hoped. He saw her leave camp and followed, hoping to persuade her into marrying him without her brother's markers hanging over her head. When he'd seen her twirling in the evening light, his breath caught in his throat. She looked so beautiful and so alive, and he wanted nothing more than to have that same vibrant spirit in his life, his home, and his bed. If he forced her into this marriage, he had no doubt she'd make things as difficult as possible for the remainder of his life.

He cursed himself repeatedly for not being able to let her go, to let them both out of this living hell that he'd created, but he'd wanted her for too long to let her walk away. She would be his, with or without a truce; and if that meant forcing his husbandly rights on her, then so be it. *That particular struggle just may prove intriguing*, he thought.

His body's infantile response to her presence angered him, especially when he didn't seem to have any effect on her at all. While other women sought his company, she ignored his very existence. While other women swooned at his feet, Christina stomped on his heart. He could snap his finger and bed any woman within hearing range, but what he wanted more than anything was Christina.

"Perhaps I made a mistake by coming out here this evening. I thought perhaps we could be friends and start again, but I see that you'll never let that happen."

"The only way we could ever be friends, Mr. Buchanan, is if you forget this parody of an engagement and return those markers to my brother. Let us all go free."

"I bought those markers to keep your brother out of jail and to keep those men from doing something foolish, like killing him; and the day we say our vows is the day I will destroy them."

"And you'll call them in and ruin my family if I refuse to say those vows," Christina added. "How could you possibly think that I could be anything but your enemy, Mr. Buchanan, with a threat like that hanging over my head? I want nothing to do with you and will not rest until I'm free."

"Then the battle rages on," Jeffrey said philosophically.

"And I intend on winning."

"The victory will be mine, Christina, have no doubt about that, and there's nothing you or your little Chinaman can do about it. Short of killing me, that is."

"We'll think of something. Short of killing you, that is," she mocked.

"By the time you do, we'll have said our 'I do's' and then it will be too late. You'll be my wife and I'll show you how a proper wife is supposed to behave."

Christina stiffened and turned to walk away.

"Have you ever noticed, my dear," Jeffrey called to her as she retreated, "that you're constantly running away from our little chats?"

"Good night, Mr. Buchanan."

"Just you remember, darling," Jeffrey shouted, determined to have the last word, "that there will come a day when running away will not be an option. That's a day I'm looking forward to."

Christina continued walking, refusing to accept that he might just be right. She laughed shortly as it dawned on her that she'd missed her opportunity to talk to him and find out more about him, but any time she found herself in his company, he provoked her temper. Well, perhaps she could control her anger more effectively should the opportunity arise for her to speak with him again later.

CHAPTER 24

Christina absentmindedly combed out her hair for the night, stroking perfunctorily, her mind on the meal she'd shared with Maggie and Maggie's men folk earlier in the evening. She'd arrived at Maggie's wagon a few minutes late and realized instantly that something was amiss. The chatty lady she'd befriended earlier at the brook was gone, replaced by a silent, sullen recluse who spent the entire meal in near silence, face averted.

It hadn't taken Christina long to deduce that Stephen had beaten Maggie, but the why was a mystery. Probably for her presumptuousness at inviting Christina to dinner without seeking her husband's permission first. *That ill-bred buffoon!* Christina thought angrily.

She'd wanted to talk to Maggie privately at some point and time, to try to find out the real reason behind the beating; however, Maggie had withdrawn into herself too far and her husband, Stephen, had shadowed her every movement ensuring that she stayed that way. The glances that he aimed at Christina during the meal left her little doubt that he blamed her for his wife's supposed defiance. It also spoke volumes about how much he'd delight in delivering a few punishing blows in her direction as well, if he thought he could get away with it.

It was the most solemn meal Christina had ever attended. When it ended, she bid a hasty farewell, and quickly returned to her own wagon, the empty pot in hand. *Well, at least the rice had been a welcome addition to the meal,* she thought bitterly, *because I most certainly wasn't.*

Her family was sitting by the fire when she'd returned to her camp, and even though they'd asked her to join them, she begged off, feigning sleepiness. She placed the rice pot by the fire and promised her father she'd rinse it out first thing in the morning. After a quick peck on his cheek, she climbed into the rear of the schooner.

Before reaching for her nightclothes, Christina peered over to where her mother lay and gave a sigh of thanks that she was already asleep. Carefully, she reached over her mother's sleeping form and grabbed her brush.

Now, a short while later, she still sat combing her hair, trying to fathom everything that had happened earlier in the evening with Maggie, without much success. She had no doubt that the change in Maggie's demeanor was the direct result of her surly husband; but had he hurt her, or did his presence merely intimidate the poor woman so much that she couldn't function around him? The fact that Maggie averted her face during the entire night spoke volumes.

A noise beneath her wagon brought her thoughts back to the present and she perked up. Voices from underneath told her that it was her dad and brother bedding down for the night. The time she'd waited for had arrived. She would simply have to puzzle out Maggie's difficulties later; for right now she had a snake to charm.

She gave her hair a few more strokes and waited to hear them snoring, which usually didn't take long. With the wedding only a short time away, she needed every minute to find a way out, and as Chin Woo said, she'd have to get to know Jeffrey better if she were to find a way to defeat him. A task to which she wasn't exactly looking forward. She berated herself again for allowing her temper to ruin a perfect opportunity earlier for speaking to Jeffrey, which left her wondering whether she'd be able to do so now with better results.

There they go, she thought with a smile, *snoring in unified harmony*. She laid her brush down and moved to the rear of the wagon, glancing again to where her mother lie. *Still sleeping*, her nervous mind assured her. She lifted the rear flap and leaned out as far as she dared without tumbling out. A glance around the side revealed the family fire still burning. A sigh of nervous relief escaped when she saw that Jeffrey hadn't joined the men folk in bedding down. A few other fires still roared nearby, which meant that she wouldn't have the privacy she wanted, should their discussion become heated, as often happened.

She would just have to be careful not to lose her temper yet again. With her father and brother snoring fitfully only a short distance from the fire, it wouldn't take much to wake them. Perhaps she could find a way to get Jeffrey off alone. The thought made her skin crawl and she came close to forgetting the whole blasted idea; however, Chin Woo's words reverberated in her mind and she knew she needed to try. Unpleasant though it may be, she had to find a way to speak with Jeffrey alone. Long enough to discover what she needed to know.

"God, give me extra strength tonight." She sought steadiness in the short pray, but her fluttering nerves refused to still. With an added mental push, she strengthened her resolve, nervously straightened her dressing gown, and patted the dagger that lay in the pocket, its weight a reassurance to her addled brain. As quietly as she could manage, so as not to cause the wagon to squeak, she slipped down from the back and quickly peered beneath to make sure she hadn't alerted the men folk to her presence. When she was fairly certain that it was safe, she tiptoed around the side of the wagon to where Jeffrey sat, a cup of steaming coffee grasped in both hands, apparently deep in thought.

"Jeffrey?" Christina whispered softly, and then jumped back a step when he bounded up off the log he'd been on, coffee sloshing onto his shirt and pants.

"Damn and blast!" He wiped the front of his shirt with his hand, glaring at Christina for the intrusion. "What in blazes do you want, woman? I thought you made it perfectly clear that my presence was not welcome in your company!"

"I've come to apologize for this afternoon," she hurried on, afraid that if she didn't get it out, she'd turn and hightail it back to the safety of her wagon. "I was hoping that I could talk to you for a short while."

"Talk? You also made it abundantly clear that you never wished to speak with me." He stared at her suspiciously, waiting for the insults that she was bound to hurl. He could not believe that she'd actually approached him with the intent of having a civil conversation.

"If you would lower your voice please. I don't wish to wake everyone."

Jeffrey looked at the few men that remained seated beside their fires, and then glanced about at all the sleeping bodies strewn everywhere. None appeared to have noticed his short outburst, and if they did, they seemed content to ignore it. He glanced at the wagon where Christina's family slept, seemingly undisturbed, and sighed. "What is it you want to talk about?" He turned to sit back down by the fire.

"Wait! Don't sit!"

Jeffrey halted in mid-bend and looked up at his fiancé, "What do you propose I do? Stay squatting like this all evening?"

"Certainly not," Christina laughed shakily, determined to hold her tongue, and her temper. "I thought perhaps we could walk a ways to talk privately."

Jeffrey straightened suddenly, the suspicion returning to his eyes, "Planning a little ambush?"

"What?" His comment took Christina aback.

"Well, why else would you suddenly be so eager to walk privately with me?" He continued, certain he'd pegged her motivations. "First, you approach me after nearly everyone's abed, fairly begging for my company. Then you nearly trip all over yourself to ensure that it's a private walk away from prying eyes. And don't think it escaped my notice that I'm suddenly 'Jeffrey'. Why is that Christina?"

"Really, Jeffrey, you are the most insuff—" Christina quickly reigned in her tongue and temper. She took several deep, calming breaths, and reminded herself that this conversation was vital, even if strangling him was more appealing. "We're supposed to be married in about a month and yet I know nothing about you, except of course that side which I don't like."

Jeffrey continued to stare at her, obviously not satisfied with her explanation.

"Anyway, I thought that since I probably could not find a way out of this, I might ought to get to know you better."

A sudden gleam lit his eyes making Christina more than a little nervous. "Let's walk, my dear." He turned and headed toward the sound of the stream where she'd bathed earlier in the day. Without benefit of a lantern, staying directly behind Jeffrey was the only option, an option that left her feeling horribly uncomfortable. How Jeffrey managed to make it all the way to the brook without colliding with a tree, tripping over a root, or stepping in a hole, she didn't know. He did however, and within a few minutes, they were standing on a rock beside the brook, the moon shimmering off the surface like a hundred dancing lights. The sight enthralled Christina, so much so that she nearly forgot that Jeffrey was standing close. Almost.

"What is it you wish to discuss?" Jeffrey asked and started to sit on the rock, stopping halfway. "May I sit?" He asked mockingly.

"Of course." Christina sat beside him, careful to keep as much distance between them as the small rock allowed. "I guess what I'd like to know," she began, "is, well, there's so much really, I'm not sure where to begin. Where are you from, for starters?"

Jeffrey snorted ironically, "You really don't have a clue, do you?"

"I'm not sure why that would amuse you. I already told you I didn't. Thus, our conversation."

"Do you remember the blacksmith's son, by any chance?" Jeffrey asked.

"Not really, but how does the son of a blacksmith relate to you?" Christina was truly puzzled.

Jeffrey snorted again, beginning to enjoy this, "Because I was that son."

"Truly! I never..."

"Knew?" Jeffrey finished for her. "Of course you didn't. That's because you were too busy entertaining that Chinaman to notice anyone else around you."

"I'm not following you, Mr. Buchanan."

"Ah, we're back to standing on formalities again, I see. I

wondered how long the familiarity would last. Long enough to lure me away from camp, as I first suspected. China-head around here somewhere, hiding?"

"No," Christina said, "I just don't feel comfortable calling you by your given name. It suggests an intimacy that doesn't exist between us."

"Except when you want something from me?"

"Can we get back to our conversation perhaps, before either of us says something offensive and we cannot continue talking civilly? After all, the point of all of this was to try to gain a little peace of mind over this engagement."

"Is that why? Well, no matter. Now, what were we talking about?"

"You were the blacksmith's son, but wouldn't we have met when father brought me with him to shoe the horses?"

"The first time I saw you, I nearly collided with you in front of your father's store. It was also the same day you met the Chinaman."

"He has a name, you know."

"I don't give a damn! To me he's a Chinese servant and nothing more. Certainly not worth all the time you've spent with him."

"I was thirteen when I met Chin Woo. Dad hired him as a clerk and he barely spoke a word of English. I took pity on him as any young girl might do and decided to take him under my wing to teach him English. In return, I've gained an invaluable friend. I remember that much about that day, but I truly forget meeting you."

"That's because you were so enthralled with *him*, that I warranted no attention. Even though I nearly knocked you over, you just waved me off and didn't even look me in the eyes."

Christina could see that Jeffrey was quickly losing control on his temper and prayed that she could part company with him quickly. "I was enthralled with you as much as you were of that Chinaman. You reminded me of a doll somehow. You had your hair all primped and you had on a beautiful blue velvet riding habit."

"I remember that." Christina quickly grabbed hold of the diversion in the conversation. She just needed to keep the conversation going on an even keel. She sighed inwardly, and thanked the good Lord above for his help in controlling her wayward tongue. "My mother was hesitant to let me ride into town," she continued, "with only my younger brother for an escort, but I finally talked her into it. She said that if I was going to go into town that I had to dress properly; like the young lady I was."

"I don't recall seeing Thomas with you," Jeffrey said in a calm conversational tone that brought hope back to Christina's wary mind. *Perhaps he won't blow up after all*, she thought.

"That's because Thomas took off the minute we hit the edge of town. He figured I could find the stable and the store without much difficulty, so he headed over to the Michaelson's mercantile to get some candy."

"Why not simply go to your father's place? Why go to another mercantile that was a direct competition?" Jeffrey asked perplexed.

Christina laughed shortly, "Because Andrew Michaelson would always give Thomas a little bit more candy for his money than Dad would. Andrew used to tease that he'd drive father out of business, one penny at a time."

"You mean your father used to make you and Thomas *pay* for your own candy?" Jeffrey figured that they would get whatever they wanted free, and that, of course, used to upset him since he got very little and had to pay dearly for what little he did get.

"Of course. My father used to tell us that we had to learn the value of money, and since he had to pay for the candy that we ate, we'd pay him back for it before we put it in our mouths." Christina smiled at the memory, but then the smile faded. "Now, of course, we have nothing but the money Father got for the sale of the store, and the house. I still can't understand why you had to talk Father into this harebrained scheme of moving out west when we were perfectly happy with our lives the way they were?"

"You probably haven't heard about the talk of war, being a lady and all and living on the outskirts of town the way you did, but it seems that the plantation owners are a mite bit upset because people up north are none too pleased with the fact they make their living on the backs of slaves."

"Actually I heard a little. So do you think it will come to war then?"

"Yes."

"Is that why you wanted to move west?" Jeffrey looked at Christina for the first time since sitting to talk with her. "It's why I wanted *all* of us to move west," He emphasized. "I didn't want to see my fiancé and her family hurt or killed by some marauding Yankees. Of course, had I known that your father was going to invite that friend of yours..."

"What is it exactly that you have against Chin Woo?" Christina asked, knowing that she was returning the conversation to dangerous ground. Still, if she were going to clear the air, she would have to get rid of this cloud hanging over their heads.

"Like I said earlier, before we got off on a different path, my father saw me staring at you all bug eyed. I guess he took pity on me, if you can call it that," Jeffrey snorted again, 'Son,' he said, 'you've a better chance of bedding every whore between here and Texas than you do of getting near that one. She's way above your lot in life'."

"I never thought of you that way."

"You never thought of me at all, Christina," Jeffrey said. "Anyway, my father gave me one of his hard-earned pennies and shooed me off after you. Told me to go buy you a piece of candy. Maybe impress you a bit. Of course, had I known that he was laughing at me the entire time I was running down the street like a lovesick puppy, perhaps I'd have maybe held onto my dignity a little longer. By the time I arrived at the mercantile, you were already leaving on the arm of that Chinaman. You and I nearly bowled each other over, but you didn't even look me in the eye. Merely straightened your skirt, mumbled a quick apology, took the Chinaman's arm again, and walked away, laughing stupidly at something he said to you. How you even understood him, I don't know."

"I wasn't actually leaving with him. My father merely had him escort me back to the stables," Christina explained patiently. "He felt that I would be safe in his company, and I always was." She looked at the moonlight bouncing over the tranquil water, and then what he'd said dawned on her. "Is that why you said what you did at the house, about why you didn't call on me? Something about women falling all over you of their own volition? It was because you didn't want to put yourself in a position of being humiliated again, the way you did when you chased me to my father's mercantile?" Christina tried not to feel pity for this pitiful man. "If you abhor the idea of courting me, why bother with me at all? Do you really dislike me so much because I didn't notice you when you were but a boy?"

"Dislike you? I've literally dreamed about you from the moment you brought your horse into Father's shop to get it shod. I've waited patiently for a chance to get closer to you, so that maybe one day, you'd look at me with even half the affection as you do your yellow servant. Instead, you never showed any emotion for me at all, and now the only emotion you have for me is contempt."

"How could you expect different? Maybe if you'd taken the time to get to know me. Maybe if you'd put your pride aside and courted me like a regular..."

"No!" Jeffrey yelled suddenly, slapping his hands on his thighs. "I will not chase you like a lovesick puppy. I'm a man damn-it, well-off and exceeding fair to look at. You should be lucky that I chose you to be my wife."

"Lucky?" Christina's own temper rose at that absurdity. "How could I feel lucky when you've blackmailed and threatened me since the day we *officially* met. All you have accomplished, Jeffrey Buchanan is to solidify my disdain for you."

"I did what I had to do," Jeffrey said simply, shutting himself off from further reach.

"No," Christina murmured sadly, "you didn't have to. You could have chosen a different way, but you didn't, and now you'll never be anything to me. I want nothing to do with you."

"Perhaps if I paint my face yellow, you'll view things differently."

Christina's palms itched to slap his arrogant face. "You know, I came out here tonight to attempt a civil conversation, which you're making extremely difficult."

"You're right, of course." Christina could tell by Jeffrey's tone of voice that his acquiescence was insincere, and the smirk on his face only confirmed it. "It's just that I get a little riled thinking that Chinaman may have touched you only as I should. He's the only one I could never find a way to dissuade."

"What do you mean 'dissuade'? Christina asked the question, but wondered if she truly wished to hear the answer.

"Didn't you ever wonder why none of your suitors ever came to call a second time? Even David Michaelson had his mother and father come call on you for him."

Enlightenment dawned and suddenly Christina could control her anger no more. "You've attempted to control my life, long before you were in my life? You are beyond despicable, Mr. Buchanan. You are a—a—a—snake!"

"Yes, well, I'll be *slithering* into your bed in just a few short weeks, and there won't be any more room for your Chinaman!" Jeffrey's head snapped sharply to the side when Christina's hand contacted his cheek. He rubbed his stinging flesh and glared at Christina. "You look rather attractive when you're riled," he murmured, continuing to stroke the side of his face, while his gaze traveled from Christina's heated countenance to her heaving breasts. "You have a lot more power in you than I imagined as well. Never figured you could wield that kind of force."

He emitted a short, humorless sound that may have been a laugh, but if he saw humor in what she'd done, it didn't reach the blaze emanating from his eyes. Anger had turned his normally gray eyes into a much darker charcoal, but more disconcerting than the anger directed at her was his lack of action. She may not know much about Jeffrey's past, but what she knew of him recently revealed he didn't sit idly by and let himself get assaulted. Yet there he sat, simply glaring at her, as if undecided with how best to proceed. His lack of immediate action unnerved her more than had he retaliated with immediacy.

She wanted to stand up to leave, but the rock they were sitting on was not large enough for her to pass Jeffrey, not that she seriously believed he would allow her to walk away without payback. A shiver ran down her spine. Payback. She glanced at the water only a few feet away from where they sat and began to doubt, seriously, whether she was going to make it back to camp at all.

Don't think that way, her mind said, trying to calm the runaway thoughts that barreled through her head.

"Jeffrey," she began quietly, but the look he gave her silenced her.

"Trying to soothe the savage beast, my dear?" Jeffrey said softly. Too softly.

The shivers running along Christina's spine spread out to encompass her entire body. "I think you know that I cannot allow what just happened to go unpunished," Jeffrey announced, after what seemed eternity.

"Jeffrey, I..."

"Speaking now will only anger me more, Christina."

"And I'm not entitled to be angry over your baiting comments," Christina argued, her ire rising again. She was scared, more scared than she'd been in her entire life, but he'd been wrong too, she decided, and he needed to know that.

"You'd attack me over a Chinaman?"

"You know that this wasn't because of Chin Woo..." Christina started, but Jeffrey cut off her defense when his hand snaked out and latched onto her wrist. With a sharp tug, he pulled her onto his lap. "What are you doing?" She squealed, struggling to release his strong hold. She squealed louder when he twisted her arm around behind her, effectively pinning her chest against his own. The move drew her face mere inches from his.

"The China-face was such a good lover that you'd go to battle for him? Is that it?"

"Jeffrey, you are insane," Christina hissed. "Now let me go…"

"Or, what? You'll hit me again. Unlikely," Jeffrey smiled wickedly, twisting her arm tight. Christina moaned. "Perhaps if I snap your arm off that would prevent any more hostilities toward me in future. What do you think?"

"Jeffrey, please."

"Now this is more like it," Jeffrey said, releasing the pressure only slightly. "If you would submit yourself to me like this, then we wouldn't have any difficulties at all, now would we? Of course, something tells me that pain may be the only thing to which you respond. I did tell you that I would enjoy meting out punishment, didn't I? And believe me, I'm truly enjoying myself right now."

"Let me go, Jeffrey," Christina hissed.

"No," Jeffrey snapped. "In fact, I think now is a good time to sample what you've been giving the Chinaman."

"I haven't done anything with Chin Woo. He's like a father to me."

Jeffrey lowered his face closer to hers, "If I ever find out that he did touch you, I'll kill you both." His mouth descended in a harsh kiss that bespoke of all his years of pent-up frustration and anger. Christina struggled furiously, but couldn't shake free of his iron grip.

Hyacinth is right! Her mind cried. *You can't defend yourself against him.*

He released one of her hands and clasped her hair in his fist, drawing her closer and tighter against his chest. The pressure against her lips increased and she tasted the blood that slid through her compressed lips and into her mouth.

Her free hand frantically searched for the pocket of her dressing gown and the dagger hidden within, but it was an exercise in futility. Between her thigh and Jeffrey's thigh, her pocket was simply inaccessible.

After what seemed eternity, he raised his head. The maniacal gleam in his eyes terrified her. "I could take you right here and no one would be the wiser."

"I'll kill you before I allow you to lay a hand on me."

Jeffrey's sudden laugh startled her. "I do believe you would try, but don't worry. I'm not going to assault your virtue—tonight. Not nearly enough privacy, or rope, available." He let his statement hang in the air and was delighted to see her blush. "Besides, I think I made my point rather clear, wouldn't you say?"

"When I tell my father what kind of man you really are, he'll…"

"What, Christina? Do you honestly think he'll believe you, especially when I tell him that you instigated the whole thing?"

"I did not! I simply wanted to have a civil conversation with you and you assaulted me. He'll believe me. I'm his daughter…"

"…and I'm his son," Jeffrey interrupted again. "Maybe not in name yet, but I'm his son. He'll believe me over you, my dear, simply because I can be quite believable when I so choose. You know it's true." He released her so suddenly she almost fell into the brook. Regaining her balance, she moved back to the rock she'd occupied only moments earlier. She rubbed her wrists to restore the feeling that his grip took away, and glared at him. She hated that he was right; hated it more because she had to admit he was right, even if she didn't acknowledge it aloud. It was still a thorn in her side to concede victory to him in any manner. "Besides," he continued, "if you tell him anything that makes him think we're not a happy couple, I'll have Thomas thrown into the first jail we come to, so you might do well to think twice."

"I may just escort Thomas to jail myself, if it means not having to marry you," Christina said, without realizing she'd spoken aloud until Jeffrey responded.

"I doubt very seriously you'd want to see your brother jailed and your father ruined, so don't try to bluff me Christina. You aren't good enough."

"I despise you Jeffrey Buchanan!" The hated conviction behind those five small words, gave Jeffrey pause, but he recovered quickly.

"I don't particularly give a damn," Jeffrey replied with a grin. "Like me or hate me, it won't change the fact that you'll be my wife before long and we'll have the opportunity to finish what we just started."

"This isn't over." Christina stood and moved to pass. Jeffrey remained seated, forcing her to sidle precariously around him. If she lost her footing, she'd wind up taking a midnight swim. She sighed when she returned to more stable footing, and then picked up her speed as she started back through the trees, his laugh taunting her as limbs slapped her face, and root after root snagged her feet. When she finally reached her wagon, angry tears glistened in her eyes and she knew, come morning, that she would look a fright.

What made her angrier was the fact that her attempt to get to know her foe nearly cost her virtue.

CHAPTER 25

Christina looked back at the beast slowly closing the distance. She had a decision to make and soon. If she headed for the wagons, the men could probably take it down, but if she was wrong and it overpowered her loved ones, she'd be responsible. She couldn't live with that possibility.

Anger, resulting from a feeling of helplessness, overwhelmed her. She rounded on the beast, her fists clenched at her side.

"What do you want with me?" *She screamed.*

The beast stopped moving, lifted its head, and roared loud enough to shake the ground beneath her feet. She shuddered, trying to control the fear that threatened to consume her.

"Listen," *she said, deciding to try reason,* "I haven't enough meat on me to make a decent meal, so I'm not sure why you're so adamant about pursuing me. There are animals hereabouts that would be much more appetizing. Take that bunny with antlers that I was chasing before I got lost. It was almost as tall as I was and I've heard that rabbit meat is rather tasty."

The beast roared again, and Christina felt a mild sensation of confidence sneak beneath the veneer of fear. If nothing else, her talking to it was keeping it from approaching further.

"If you like, I could have my brother set a trap. Maybe that will provide you with a decent meal."

The beast howled loudly as if outraged by her suggestion, returned to all fours, and started ambling in her direction again, its head swinging back and forth, a continual growl emanating from deep within its barrel chest.

"Uh oh!" *Christina whispered to herself.* "It would appear that attempting to bring in outside help is a no-no." *She was about to reassure the creature that her idea held merit and that she'd set the trap herself, if need be, when another noise reached her ears. She glanced at the beast to see if he'd heard it as well.*

He had. He was standing, sniffing the air. He shook his head, glared at her, dropped back to all fours, and began moving as quickly as his bulk allowed—away from her. If she didn't know any better, she would have thought that the creature was afraid, and it didn't take long to figure out from where the fear originated. Out of the shadows of the tree line, a band of coyotes strolled, sniffing the air in search of prey.

"Not again," she whispered. *"Am I never going to be safe in this land?"* She had just decided that hiding would be advantageous, when something powerful struck her from behind and knocked her to the ground. She shook her head slightly to dislodge the stars circling her periphery, wishing her attacker had knocked her unconscious.

The sound of panting left no doubt that the wolf had returned, and was now sitting on top of her back. She froze and felt a new terror grip her when the panting changed to breathing, and the paws to hands. The weight shifted slightly to the side, and then she felt his hands on her waist, shifting her so that she was lying on her side, facing him. Her eyes widened in astonishment and she tried to control yet another bout of fear that threatened to suffocate her.

"Do not fear me, white woman," he said softly, *"I'm here to protect you."*

"Christina." A hand lightly shook her and Christina gladly gave up her dreams for the world of reality. "It's time to get breakfast on, dear." Christina cracked open an eye and saw her mother move away. No light shone through the rear of the wagon and Christina moaned dismally.

That was one thing, among many, she hated about being on the trail, the fact that she and her mother were required to rise before all to prepare a decent breakfast. Of course if they wanted to eat hardtack and gruel, they could sleep in at least until dawn, but that wasn't good enough for the men. They wanted real food and it was up to the women to get it ready for them, and in sufficient time for them to eat at their leisure before the wagon master yelled, "pulling out".

Still, she felt a little better knowing that the men had to get up shortly after they did to prepare the wagon, horses, and supplies for the next stretch. If she hadn't wakened so grumpy, she would readily agree that neither sex had the better part of the bargain on this journey.

Christina felt her swollen lips and winced. Come daybreak,

everyone in her family was going to know that Jeffrey had been kissing on her, but would they think anything untoward or would they merely grin knowingly?

Maybe Thomas and Chin Woo would question it, but her parents wouldn't. To acknowledge that Jeffrey was not right for their little girl would mean their judgment had been wrong and that was something her parents would never admit.

CHAPTER 26

After breakfast, Christina watched Jeffrey walk away from the campfire with her father, her eyes narrowing in renewed anger.

One of these days, Jeffrey, she thought angrily, *someone more capable than me is going to wallop you good!*

After they were out of sight, Chin Woo and Thomas settled in on either side of her.

"Are you all right this morning, Sis?" Thomas's gaze scanned Christina's scratched face and swollen lips.

"Why would you ask that, Thomas?" Christina asked in mock ignorance.

"You no funny right now, Cookie," Chin Woo chastised lightly. "We see face and know something not right."

Christina's eyes misted. She ran her fingers through her hair, "I'm sorry, it's just that if I allow myself to feel sorry for my circumstances, I'll break down and never stop crying, so I cling to the sarcasm and the anger like a shield. I appreciate your concern though. Thanks." She patted both sets of hands that lay on hers and smiled at each in turn.

"What happen?" Chin Woo could see that Christina was reluctant to answer, but he was also equally determined to get answers.

"Please, tell us, Sis. Maybe we can help."

"Oh, Thomas! You know there's nothing that can be done. If there was, I wouldn't be in this mess to begin with."

"Jeffrey did this to you?" Thomas asked.

"Who else would have?"

"But the scratches?" Thomas looked at her face confused.

"Oh, those are courtesy of the tree limbs that smacked my face last night when I was leaving Jeffrey's delightful company, but this," Christina gingerly felt her swollen lips and winced at the tenderness, "is definitely courtesy of Jeffrey Buchanan."

"The snake. Is my fault," Chin Woo sighed and lowered his

head, rubbing his hands through his hair in agitation.

"It's no one's fault, Chin Woo," Christina assured him. "Jeffrey would have found a way to make his claim on me noticeable even if I hadn't gone to speak with him last night. I really don't think the man is all that balanced mentally."

"That another reason is my fault," Chin Woo said in self-derision. "I should have seen he no stable, but I no see and now he hurt my Cookie."

"I'm not hurt, Chin Woo. I'm angry and humiliated, but not hurt."

"Maybe Chin Woo and I should take Jeffrey Buchanan for a little walk of our own."

"No, Thomas! I don't want either of you touching him, do you understand?"

"He can touch you, but we can't touch him?" Thomas argued.

"I want both of you to be able to finish this journey with me. If you lay a hand on Jeffrey, he's just likely to have you arrested for assault. Then he will have you stuck in some backwoods jail cell for Lord knows how long," Christina argued back. "So, I want your solemn oath you'll steer clear, just as I'm planning to do. Okay?"

Both men reluctantly nodded their agreement, and Christina smiled encouragingly. "Can you fellas handle the dishes this morning? I want to pay a visit to Maggie."

"Sure, Sis. We can do that. Right, Chin Woo?"

"You go, Cookie, and visit friend. We take care of everything here."

"Thanks," Christina said. She stood and made her way back to the wagon, calling for her mother, but her mother didn't respond. She stuck her head in the back flap and noticed that her mother was asleep yet again; and, yet again, she'd failed to eat her meal.

This trip must be more tiring on her than she lets on, Christina thought. *Best to let her get her rest, I guess.*

She smiled sadly at the sleeping form, and then headed to Maggie's wagon.

CHAPTER 27

"She's indisposed, as you fancy-pants folk like to say." Stephen lit into Christina the moment she stepped into camp and asked after Maggie.

Yeah, you probably beat her senseless for something stupid, you big clod, Christina thought hotly, but was determined not to do anything that might make him lash out at poor Maggie.

"If I stop by later, do you think my visit will improve her disposition somewhat? I'd really like to talk to her."

"Listen. Why don't you just be staying near your own wagon and your own folks, and be leaving my Maggie alone? She don't need to be around your uppity manners no ways."

"Uppity? Me? Hardly!" Christina tried to keep the tone of the conversation light.

"You folks with your fancy clothes and your fancy talk, think your better'n us plain folks, and you be giving my wife ideas. Making her think and such. It ain't good for a woman to think 'n such."

"Listen, I promise not to be giving your wife ideas if you will allow her to ride with me on my wagon on occasion, so that we can gossip like all women like to do. I mean, we may not be able to think, but we sure do love to talk."

"Is you making fun of me, woman?"

"Absolutely not!" Christina said in mock indignation. "I'm just trying to help you see that women need companionship just like men do. Only difference is, men like to drink and carry-on and women just like to talk. There's no harm in that, now is there?"

Stephen scratched at his beard that had grown scraggly over the last week, all the while eyeing Christina with suspicion. Christina stood stock still, trying to look as innocent as a newborn babe.

She hadn't realized she was holding her breath until Stephen spoke, "Don't suppose so," he said. "Might be good to get her and that li'l brat away from the wagon every now and again."

"Brat?"

Christina received no answer to her query, since Stephen was already yelling for his wife. "Maggie, get your scrawny backside out from under that wagon. We got company, woman. And bring the brat with you!"

Christina's breath caught in her throat when Maggie crawled from beneath the wagon bed. By the look in her eyes, she'd known all along that Christina had come to call, but was too frightened to move from her place beneath the wagon.

Christina smiled encouragingly, and then drew in a sharp breath when a small dirty child, no more than four or five years, scrambled hesitantly from beneath the wagon, on the heels of his mom. She gave them both a reassuring smile, but her gaze kept going back to the young boy that hid timorously behind his mother's skirts.

"You gonna be riding with this here woman every day now, so get what you need to be a getting and go on with her. The wagons gonna be pulling out soon."

Maggie smiled widely, but quickly wiped the smile from her face when her husband looked at her again, "You still here, woman?" His tone was so hateful that even Christina cringed. "That beating you got wasn't enough to clean out them ears of yours?"

Maggie turned quickly and scampered into the rear of the wagon. Within moments, she returned carrying only a worn, faded shawl and a dirty handkerchief to cover her face. She passed her husband with lowered eyes, but he drew her up short with a sharp tug on her arm. "Just you remember, woman, to be back over here fast when the wagons stop. I don't want my meals held up for no body. Understand me?"

Maggie simply nodded and waited with learned patience to move only after he removed his painful grip from her arm. Stephen smiled in a mixture of satisfaction and disgust, and then shoved his wife away, "There was a time, when you was entertaining. Now you're just a weak-minded simpleton that provides relief for me when the need arises. Get on outta here!"

He watched her back up a little and smiled grimly. She didn't even give him many reasons to strike at her physically anymore, simply stared at him vacantly. "Get gone!" He watched her walk away, and determined he'd have to find more ways to entertain his self, even if it meant cutting loose on her more often, just for the hell of it.

"Why do you put up with that?" Christina asked, as they walked back toward her wagon.

She glanced at Maggie when she didn't answer immediately and realized that she was merely pondering the question, her hand abstractly stroking the red marks that was still present from last night's smack.

"I don't know. I guess I just decided that giving in was better than having my body battered regularly, and there's my baby to consider," she said, glancing down at the small boy in tow.

"But he still beats you, you can't deny that."

"No. I don't deny it, but since I quit fighting him, the beatings are less, and a lot less brutal, too. I don't think he sees me as a challenge no more." At Christina's look of confusion, Maggie laughed harshly. "When we first got married, I didn't put up with his drinking and carousing and didn't mind saying so. It seemed to give him some sort of perverse thrill to get my dander up. One day, I guess I went too far and embarrassed him in front of some company and he lit into me, right there in front of three of his drinking cronies. Beat me and then raped me, just to give them a show. The life just went out of me after that. I don't think I'd ever suffered as much humiliation in a lifetime as I did that day. The devil took over my husband that same day, 'cause he beat me for what he called 'ever little defiant word' that came out of my mouth after that. It got to where I didn't even talk when I was around him. He finally lost interest, I guess. Now he only beats me when I forget myself and do something stupid."

"What about your son? Does he hurt him too?"

"Joseph? He used to," She said, and pulled the young boy closer to her side. "Broke his arm once, then took him to a quack to get it fixed, 'causin' he didn't want to be spending a whole heap of money for a real doctor. Don't know if you've noticed or not, but Joseph's arm is twisted funny-like."

"No, I didn't," Christina whispered past the lump in her throat and the hurt in her heart.

"That's because Stephen makes him wear long sleeve shirts. Even in the heat of summer, he's not allowed to play without a shirt. Can't bring no shame on Stephen, no sir. A boy with a twisted arm is a shame he can't bear. Matters not that he's the one that broke it, and refused to pay for proper care so that it could set right. Anyway, he hardly bothers with him now either. Guess he doesn't want to risk breaking any more bones and forking out any more money to have them set. Course when he's older, he'll probably start in on him again. Heard him tell his brother, Michael, that the boy will be needing a few good whippings when he grows up to keep him from becoming a momma's boy. Lord, but I hate him so. I know he's my husband, Christina, but he's just no good."

"Christina, Mrs. Bishop!" Christina jerked at the sound of Thomas's loud call. "Hurry up and climb on board. The wagons are moving out in a minute!"

Maggie hefted Joseph into her arms and picked up her pace, following Christina into the Carthington's campsite. Christina's gaze met Jeffrey's briefly and she frowned at him angrily before climbing into the rear of the wagon.

Maggie caught the look. *Lord, please don't let Christina end up like me,* she prayed. She hefted little Joseph aboard, and then took the hand that Thomas offered in assistance. "Thank you," Maggie whispered.

"Welcome, Mrs. Bishop," The tone in Thomas's voice was so polite, it made Christina smile. "Nice you can join our merry little family." Maggie smiled and shimmied aboard. Her eyes adjusted to the dimness inside and she spotted Christina's mother laying off to one side.

"Are you sure it's okay for us to be in here? We don't want to disturb your mother's rest."

"She's just overly tired, is all." Christina checked on her mother and sighed. Although she was almost certain a herd of cattle moving straight past their wagon could not disturb her mother, Christina still kept her voice to a whisper. "She isn't taking this trip well, but I'm sure that when she wakes up she'll be happy for the company."

Christina settled on a rolled blanket and pointed to another area for Maggie to sit with her son. Joseph promptly laid his head on his mother's lap and fell asleep. "Guess my mother isn't the only one exhausted," Christina said, smiling toward the little boy.

"It's all the walking we've been doing. It does take its toll on a body." Maggie's face registered relief at the chance to sit again. Both women held on as the wagons jerked into forward motion.

"It's stuffy in here though, isn't it?" Christina wheezed after breathing in a lung full of stale air. She scooted back to the rear of the wagon and stuck her head out. "Thomas!" Thomas pulled the reins on the horse and directed the stallion toward his sister.

"What ya need, Sis?"

"Could you raise the flaps on this side of the wagon? It's terrible in here."

"Kind of hard to do while the wagon is moving, but I'll give it a try." Thomas nudged the horse closer to the rear of the wagon and threw the reins toward his sister.

"Hold the horse for me, will ya?" Without waiting for a reply, Thomas stood in the stirrups, accustomed his body to the rocking motion of the horse, and then pulled himself to a standing position on the saddle. Without a second thought to his safety, he leapt from the saddle and grabbed hold of the top of the wagon, pulling himself up to lie prone on the wiry frame.

Christina gazed in awe at the acrobatics. She didn't realize how much skill her brother had with horses. A moment later, she heard him shuffling about atop her head and felt a moment's regret at asking him to do something that was difficult and potentially dangerous.

She heard a grunt and saw one of the side flaps pull up slightly. Another grunt and it rose even higher, until light filled the inside. After a few more grunted efforts, he managed to get the sides completely up and tied down.

When it sounded like Thomas was going to try to raise the other flap, Christina called up to him. "That's all right, Thomas. We can breathe easily now."

She heard shuffling again, as Thomas made his way back toward the rear of the wagon, "Sure, Sis?" Thomas breath was coming in short gasps, but he was smiling none-the-less.

"More than sure. Are you going to be able to mount from up there?"

"Nothing to it. Just pull on the reins a little and position him closer to the side for me, okay?"

Christina did as he instructed. Thomas steadied himself on top of the wagon, his arms out by his side, concentration evident on his young features. After another moment, he leapt from the wagon and landed with precision on the rear of the horse. The horse whinnied at the sudden jolt, but adjusted quickly.

Christina tossed the reins back to her brother, who was grinning as widely as she was. She applauded softly, "Bravo!" She cheered.

Her brother tipped his hat and laughed. He pulled on the reins and took up his previous position.

"Wow!" She shuffled back to her position on the rolled blanket, shaking her head in wonder. "I didn't know my brother had it in him."

"I saw some of it from my position here," Maggie commented. "It was impressive, but you don't think the light is going to disturb your mother's rest, do you?"

"She has her face averted, so it shouldn't. Besides, the fresh air will do her some good as well."

The two ladies settled into a comfortable silence, but Christina couldn't help wondering about her companion and soon broke the silence with a question. "How old are you, Maggie? I'm sorry, you don't have to answer that," Christina retracted, embarrassed by her noisiness.

"I'm nineteen." Maggie blushed abashedly when she saw

Christina's look of astonishment. "I know I look a lot older than that."

"No, no. It's just that..."

"You thought I was a lot older than nineteen," Maggie finished for her. "How old are you?"

"Seventeen," Christina smiled. It amazed her that the woman before her was only slightly older than herself.

"Wait until you've been married two years to an abusive husband, and have a baby. Of course, by the look of your face, right now, Jeffrey hasn't even waited to put a ring on your finger before leaving his mark," Maggie stated solemnly. "Anyway, in a couple of years, you'll probably look as haggard as I do, I'm sad to say." She looked at the little boy whose head rested on her lap, then added softly, "Little Joseph makes it worthwhile though. I don't think I'd make it if it wasn't for him."

"I'm sorry that things are difficult for you, Maggie." Christina wished she could change her friend's circumstances, as well as her own.

"So, I was wondering," Maggie began, deftly changing the subject, "what the noose is that Jeffrey has so snugly around your neck?"

Christina looked perplexed for a moment and then remembered their conversation by the wagons earlier in the week. She glanced over to where her mother lie to ensure she was sleeping before daring to answer. She sighed in relief when her mother's gentle snoring reached her ears. Still, she couldn't bring herself to talk above a whisper. "Jeffrey coerced me into marrying him by threatening to have my brother thrown in jail because of some gambling debts; and since Father doesn't have the money to bail him out, it falls to me to see he doesn't go to jail to begin with."

"That's simply awful! Why can't you just tell your father? Maybe he'll take Jeffrey into the woods somewhere, tie him to a tree, and let the wolves feed on his no-good hide. Something I wish my daddy had done to Stephen before we married."

Christina laughed softly, "I wish it were that simple, but

unfortunately it isn't. If I was selfish and didn't give a lick about my family, then threats or no, I would tell Jeffrey to take a running leap off the nearest cliff; but I do care too much and he knows it."

"I'm sorry for you. I can say that and mean it, since I have a no-good man for a husband too, but you know what's funny? Well, maybe not funny, but—well funny—you know?" Maggie stumbling over her words was funny to Christina, but she was polite enough not to say so. "What I mean by funny is that Jeffrey just doesn't seem violent. I saw him from a distance and he carries himself like a well-bred gentleman."

"It's an act he has down pat. Believe me, I've seen the true Jeffrey, and it isn't gentlemanly."

"He gave you the bruised mouth, didn't he?"

"Yeah, when he attacked me last night," Christina said and Maggie gasped. "Don't worry, he didn't manage to assault my virtue, just my mouth."

"You seem like a very nice girl, so I can't figure why he would treat you so poorly. He isn't going to win your affection by mistreating you."

"I don't think he cares too much how I feel about him. He just seems to want to take possession of a prize. Besides, you of all people know that it isn't necessarily a woman's character that makes a man's character go bad. You can't tell me that Stephen is nasty to you because you're a bad woman, can you?"

"No, I'm not," Maggie asserted, "and Joseph isn't a bad boy. Stephen's just an abusive bounder. Oh, Christina, I'd really hate you to end up like me. Isn't there anything that can be done?"

"Chin Woo and I haven't given up trying to find a way out."

"Chin Woo?"

"The man up front, driving the wagon. Jeffrey thinks a conspiracy is in the works between Chin Woo and me…and he's right."

"So because he thinks you two are conspiring against him, he assaulted you?"

"More that he was angry and trying to prove a point."

"That's the other thing I can't figure. I mean, you're a beautiful girl, to be sure, with that flaming mane of yours and those emerald eyes. You kind of remind me of a lioness, but there are plenty of beautiful women in this world, so what is about you that makes Jeffrey so determined to have you?"

Christina blushed, unable to find anything to say about her Maggie's complimentary description. "I kind of think he's a little unbalanced, to be honest. I mean, why else would he be so obsessed with me?"

"I'll tell you a secret. When I first saw him, I thought you were the luckiest woman on earth. He's such an attractive man. Of course, now that I know him for what he really is, just the thought of him makes my stomach churn. I can only imagine what he does to yours."

"My stomach does somersaults every time he comes near me."

"Normally somersaults would be a good thing."

"Not these. These leave me nauseous."

"Kind of like what my husband does to me."

"I suppose so. Gee, Maggie, I'm really sorry things are so rough on you," Christina repeated.

"You've got to find a way out of this Christina, or in a few years you're going to end up a bedraggled old woman before you're twenty. Do you want to be that way, like me?"

Christina wanted to refute that being like Maggie wasn't such a bad thing, but she couldn't. Not that Maggie was a bad person or unattractive, really. It was more her situation that left Christina's blood cold. A situation closely similar to her future with Jeffrey.

Both women fell silent, thinking about the hand life had dealt them, and then Maggie broke the silence and they forgot their depressing circumstances for the moment, "How long do you think it'll be before we reach the Great River?"

"The Mississippi?"

"Yeah, that's it. I forgot the name of it."

"Well, I heard the guide tell Father that it would be at least another week or two, depending upon the weather and the trail. We

are traveling a lesser known route to Texas, you know? It's
supposed to help us arrive more quickly, but truth be told, I'm not
in all that great a hurry what with that noose getting more snug by
the day."

"What do you think it will be like?"

"The Mississippi?"

"No, Texas."

"My Uncle Peter likes it well enough, at least that's what Father
says. It's more arid than Georgia though."

"What's 'arid'?"

"Dry and dusty."

"Oh! Well, after being on this trail, I guess we'll be used to the
taste of dirt by then, don't you think?"

Christina's laugh caught in her throat as she stared into the
distance, through the clearing of trees, "Now that resembles my
life."

Maggie's gaze followed the turn of Christina's face, "Looks
awful dark and gloomy out there."

"Yes, it does, doesn't it?" The words came out in a strained
whisper that had Maggie looking at her curiously.

"You okay, Christina?"

"Of course. I'm fine. I guess I just feel that my life of late is
like that approaching storm—dark and gloomy—threatening to
snatch away my joy." Christina smiled weakly when she saw concern
light in Maggie's eyes. When she spotted the guide riding toward
their wagon, she muttered a polite "excuse me" and shuffled closer
to the front where Chin Woo sat so that she could hear what he had
to say—whether it be about the approaching storm or hostiles,
anything was better than the disquieting conversation she'd been
having with Maggie.

"Afternoon," he said, speaking to Chin Woo. He tipped his hat
respectfully in Christina's direction then turned back to address
Chin Woo, "Do you speak English?"

Chin Woo nodded, and the wagon master continued, "We'll
have to hole up here. There's a serious storm a blowing that'll

probably reach us within the hour. It'll be too rough to attempt to ride through. Have the flaps lowered on the wagon and secure them tightly."

When Chin Woo acknowledged his instructions, the wagon master spurred his horse to the next wagon in line. Christina scooted back to where Maggie sat and explained that they were in for a serious storm.

"Hey, Sis!" Thomas called, as the wagons slowed to a crawl and then inched to a halt. He pulled on the reins and positioned his horse next to the open flap on the side of the wagon. He tipped his hat courteously toward Maggie and then brought his attention back to Christina, "It's probably best if Mrs. Bishop heads on back to her wagon to settle in. Storms gonna hit any time now. I'll wake Mother and climb up to lower the flaps."

"All right. It's a shame that we have to disturb Mother. Can't we just let her sleep through it?"

"Not likely to be able to anyway once the storm hits us. Besides, we'll need everyone sitting or there isn't going to enough room in the back for us all to squeeze in."

"I see. Well, I'll walk Maggie and Joseph back to their wagon, then I'll join you in ours."

"Fine, but you'll need to hurry."

Christina took little Joseph from Maggie's arms, and then watched with pride as her brother jumped from his horse to help Maggie alight. Of course, Christina was just his sister so Thomas did not afford her the same courtesy.

She handed Joseph down to the waiting arms of his mother and then alighted with ease, jabbing her brother playfully in the ribs for not obliging her also. Her brother smiled sheepishly, a blush creeping into his boyish cheeks.

When they reached the Bishops' wagon, Christina waited while Maggie and Joseph settled on worn blankets beneath. She wished that she could have them stay with her wagon during the storm, but understood that there wouldn't possibly be any room left for them in the already cramped interior. Still, the thought of Maggie and

Joseph, left to the elements, huddled beneath their meager shelter was enough to make her want to cry.

She fought back tears and stooped down beside them so that she could talk to Maggie for a few more minutes, "Your men folk should be along shortly, Maggie." She didn't really know whether that thought would bring Maggie reassurance, but she supposed any company was better than being alone—or not. "I probably need to get back to my wagon soon, but I'll wait for a little while until they show up."

"All right."

"Are you going to be okay?"

"I'm just a little nervous is all. Those clouds looked eerily dark."

"The storm will blow over quickly. You just try to relax. It's important for Joseph that you do. I heard it said somewhere that a child can sense his mother's nervousness and it makes them cry. Remember rain will only get you wet." Christina instantly regretted that statement especially since the likelihood of getting wet was a near certainty.

"I wish we could stay with you in your wagon, but I know that there isn't enough room. I'm glad, though, that we get to spend more time together now," Maggie continued. "You know, I caught myself talking like Stephen the other day and it startled me," she teased, referring to their earlier conversation about certain men's language deficiencies.

"Ouch! That is bad." Christina realized that Maggie was trying to lighten the tension and joined in, "I don't think either of those men ever received any sort of formal education. And, if you start swearing too much, I'll have to move you into our schooner permanently, just to keep you from turning into an uncouth heathen."

Maggie laughed and hugged Joseph closer, "I'm all right Christina. You go on and get to your schooner before the storm breaks."

Christina smiled again and turned from the wagon. She

sprinted back to her family's schooner, nearly colliding with Stephen on the way.

"Maggie's already waiting at the wagon!" Christina called in passing, though she was near certain that he couldn't care less about his wife's whereabouts, unless it was mealtime. Not surprisingly, he ignored her and continued his way.

She reached her own wagon in time to see Jeffrey crawling inside. Her steps faltered and she hesitated, not wanting to spend, what could very well be a few hours, in such proximity with him.

"Hurry and climb aboard, Sis." Thomas took Christina's elbow and ushered her the remaining few feet toward the back of the wagon, "Dad has already ensured everyone is crammed inside, and look, I do know how to be a gentleman."

Christina turned when she'd climbed aboard, "Thomas, do we have any extra ponchos or anything?"

"What for, Sis?"

"Maggie and Joseph are going to have to ride out this storm with meager shelter."

"So are we, Sis."

"I meant they have to huddle beneath the wagon, and that's going to provide almost no shelter at all. They're going to get drenched."

Thomas saw the worry in his sister's eyes and gave her arm a quick squeeze, "I've got just the thing. I'll be back in a flash."

"Thanks, Thomas."

Christina turned around after her brother sprinted off and paused just long enough to locate a place to settle down. She moved near the space next to Chin Woo.

"We've left that spot for Thomas, dear." Her father's voice brought her to a halt, "Your place is over here, near your fiancé. Where did Thomas run off to, anyway? Storms going to hit any minute."

Christina felt a strong urge to keep going and plop defiantly down beside her friend, but didn't want to raise suspicions. "Thomas went to give my friend some covering. He'll be back in a moment." She turned and crawled over to the cramped space left available beside Jeffrey and squeezed in. Thomas hadn't been kidding when he said it was going to be a tight fit. It was uncomfortable, crammed shoulder-to-shoulder with everyone.

"We saved this space," her mother whispered tiredly, "just in case you need his support."

Christina forced a smile for her mom's sake, but it didn't reach the coldness in her emerald eyes. She adjusted her position, careful to keep as much distance between them as possible. "How are you doing, Mother?" Christina whispered into her mother's ear.

"Just tired, dear," Carlotta's said, her voice so soft that Christina had to strain to hear her response, "I don't think I'm sleeping all that well."

Christina was about to counter that she was sleeping more than she should, but her gaze was drawn to the rear of the wagon as the flap was drawn back. Thomas pulled himself on board just as a wall of hail and rain approached them with a kind of menacing determination of its own. It took only a few minutes to reach their wagon, shaking it with an explosion of wind, rain, and hailstones.

"Blasted!" Jeffrey shook his head violently from side-to-side, spraying the occupants with the water that dripped into his white hair. "The cover's sprung a leak!" He shouted over the din, scooting closer to Christina.

"I see what you mean!" Thomas raised his hand to catch a stream of water as it poured down steadily in front of him.

"Looks like we're all going to get a bit wet," her father yelled, as another leak started. "Chin Woo, reach behind you and see if you can't reach those blankets. Maybe we can keep the women dry enough, if we cover them." Without consent, Jeffrey threw the blanket over their heads. Christina immediately broke into a sweat beneath the suffocating wool. After a moment more, her breathing grew shallow as she fought against inhaling the musty stench that the old blankets exuded.

"When do you think it will end?" Christina raised her voice so that they could hear her above the pounding rain. She hugged herself tightly against the chill that penetrated, even under the heavy blanket.

"I don't know, but it better be soon or the ground will be too muddy to continue," her father yelled back.

"I don't think I can survive under this blanket too long. I think I'd rather take my chances with the rain." She struggled to lift the blanket over her head, but a strong pair of arms pushed them down and away.

"You'll survive until the rain passes, my dear, but you might not survive if you catch another case of pneumonia. Best to keep the blanket on until this passes," Jeffrey said, removed his hands from hers and shifted on his uncomfortable seat.

"I can't bloody well breathe under here, imbecile." Christina thought she'd spoken in a whisper, but her mother heard her.

"Christina! Such language to use with your fiancé!"

"I'm sorry, Mother, but it's so danged uncomfortable."

"Well, like Jeffrey said," Carlotta patted Christina's knee reassuringly, "it's better to suffer a little of this than to come down with another bout of pneumonia that may very well kill you."

Perhaps pneumonia and death are preferable to marrying Jeffrey, she thought. "I'll try, mother, but even you have to admit, this dank odor is a bit more than any nose should have to endure. The rain isn't helping things any." Even to her own ears, she sounded whiny, but she just couldn't feel anything but disagreeable when she was this close to Jeffrey Buchanan.

"It will be over soon," Carlotta assured her again.

"I hope so."

The rain continued for another half hour and then came to an abrupt halt.

"Do you think it's over?" Christina's voice sounded too loud in the sudden quiet, although she had spoken in no more than a murmur.

"It's over." Thomas shook the remaining water from his hair, and then scooted to the edge of the wagon to look around.

"Good," Jeffrey said, rubbing a hand through his drenched

mane. "Let's just hope that it didn't wet the ground as much as it did us or we may be in a world of trouble."

"What do you mean?" Carlotta asked. Pulling the blanket from her head, she took a deep, grateful, cleansing breath.

"Well," Charles Carthington continued for Jeffrey, "if the ground is too wet, the wheels wouldn't be able to pull free of the mud. We'd be stuck here until it dries out."

"Can't we just drive through the mud?" Christina asked.

"It's not as easy as all that, Christina," Jeffrey said. "If the ground is too wet, the wagon wheels will sink from the weight of the wagons and the suction will hold them there. Try to pull 'em free, it often makes matters worse. Sink deep enough and you have to abandon your wagon. It's best just to wait and see how wet the ground is. Hopefully it dries quickly."

To their detriment, the pounding rain had left the ground saturated forcing the wagon master to call a halt to their travels through the remainder of the day. During that time, the air cooled for a short while, but then the heat returned to scorching degrees. Even though they were able to set off the following afternoon, the rain, heat, and humidity had taken its toll. Property was dried or destroyed and disposed of; stuffy-nosed misery spread rapidly through the occupants; and within another week, people suddenly began to get deathly ill.

CHAPTER 28

"From the dust of the earth were these bodies created, oh Lord, and in death will these bodies return to the dust, but the spirit of these good people lying here today will soon join you in your heavenly kingdom."

Christina stood listening to the minister drone on, her heart heavy and her eyes burning with unshed tears as she stared at the three graves before her. Two were members of the Flaherty family. The third was unknown to her. She hadn't known John and Eileen Flaherty or their thirteen-year-old son, Matthew, very well, but still her heart went out to the young man whose mother and father now lay dead. The look of uncertainty in his eyes and the pain of loss etched on his young face caused her heart to lurch, but like her, he seemed unable to cry.

His lack of tears, she reasoned, probably stemmed from the sudden shock of the loss of his parents, but once the shock wore off, he would shed many tears, she had not a doubt. She wished she could claim shock for her lack of tears, but she couldn't. She simply hadn't known these people. Not well enough to shed tears for their loss.

Maggie, on the other hand—bless her soul—was weeping for the loss as if they'd been her own family. Not merely strangers. All Christina could do, was think about was how fortunate she and her family were that fate did not count them among the sick and dying. She knew it was a selfish thought, but she thought it nonetheless.

She glanced toward the two wagons that the doctor was using as a sick bed for the remaining six people who'd contracted the sickness. She wondered whether the men would be digging six more graves by day's end, or if the doctor could save their lives. She did hope that they would make it. She didn't know if she could stand and listen to more words of death given under the guise of comfort, or whether she could stand to see more bodies lowered slowly into the cold, unfeeling ground.

The doctor had called the sickness that was spreading around 'dysentery'. He blamed it on the standing water and the swarms of flies that had descended during the layover after the rains earlier in the week. Still, she never knew that a sickness could strike and kill in so short a time. It made her realize just how fragile a human life was, which made her think of her mother, who'd been too weak herself to leave the wagon bed to attend the funeral services.

The doctor tried to explain that those who'd contracted the sickness were the ones whom the journey had already weakened, and those that died simply had no strength to combat the ravages on their defenseless bodies. Christina looked over toward the wagon where her mother lay, still sleeping, and wondered why she hadn't contracted the sickness as well. The journey had undoubtedly left her severely weakened, as was evident by her constant need for sleep. She supposed that her mother's self-imposed seclusion had prevented her coming in contact with the more infectious areas of camp.

She glanced again at the wagons holding the sick, wondering about the meeting the wagon master wanted everyone to attend. He wanted it held immediately after the funeral. It didn't take a fortuneteller to know that his meeting was going to be about the delay the sickness was causing in their travels. Already they were a week behind their intended schedule. At last, the minister said 'Amen' and two men moved in to shovel dirt over the bodies.

When done, everyone made their way wearily to the front of the wagons to hear what the wagon master had to say. "I know this isn't the most appropriate time to bring up the subject," he started, raising his voice so everyone could hear him, "but we need to take a vote about whether to continue without the sick or to have everyone wait it out."

At the uproar that followed, the wagon master quickly raised his hands for silence. "Now I'm not saying to abandon them, folks, so don't go mistaking my meaning," he said, then waited for the uproar to die down before continuing. "I'll leave a scout here so that he can bring those able on through. The doc has done all he can for them, so it's up to their own sense of determination to survive and God's good graces to pull them out of it. If they don't, then the scout will give them a proper Christian burial."

When it looked like there was going to be another outburst, the wagon master quickly raised his hands for everyone to be silent. "Before ya'll go and get riled up again, hear me out," he yelled, then waited a moment to make certain that everyone's attention was focused on him again. "Now, barring any future problems, and some hard traveling, I can get you to Texas inside three more weeks. As promised and paid for; however, if we have to continue stopping for every little thing, then it could be over a month before this journey is through," the wagon master said, watching the faces around him for reaction. "Again, don't go mistaking my meaning. I didn't mean it to sound as if death is a small matter, but we have to put these little distresses behind us quickly and keep moving or we're never going to reach our destination. Now, I'm not trying to upset you folks and I know it's been a rough haul; however, I do have a schedule to try to adhere to because I make my living transporting you fine folks out West. If I don't get back to Georgia sooner than later, I'm going to be losing out on getting hooked up with the next group waiting for a guide. I miss out on earning my living because you fine folks can't stomach hard travels...well, you'll be making up my lost wages between you."

Outrage turned to stunned silence as everyone tried to take in what the wagon master was saying. Christina shook her head, appalled at the wagon master's lack of chivalry. Her ire rose further when a voice shouted from behind her.

"I say we leave 'em!" Christina scanned the crowd and recognized the voice as belonging to Stephen Bishop, Maggie's husband. *No surprise there.*

"You heartless excuse for a man!" A woman shouted from beside her.

Anger again replaced disbelief as people slung hostile words back and forth. "How can you possibly consider leaving those poor sick folks alone in this defenseless country with no one to tend them?"

"Then you stay!" Bishop yelled again.

"Lou Anne is right!" Another woman jumped into the fray. "We can't just leave them poor folks here. There's no telling what might happen to them."

"Then you stay too! I can't afford to pay this man extra to get me where I need to go, and we'll never get there if he abandons us all." Stunned silence returned as Stephen Bishop's words sunk in. The thought that the wagon master might actually desert them if they were unable to pay more money for his time, never really occurred to any of them. To them, the threat was merely a bluff to keep them moving.

When the crowd turned in silent unison seeking confirmation that he wouldn't do such a thing, the wagon master shrugged his shoulder and lit a cheroot. "It's your folks decision, but those going with me, need to be ready to pull out within the hour." Without another word, he jumped down from the tree trunk he'd been standing on and sauntered back toward his horse.

After that abrupt exit, the crowd broke up quietly and meekly returned to their wagons to prepare for the next leg of the journey. Each family contributed some of their food store and fresh water for the sick—and for Lou Anne and her husband, who decided to remain.

The Flaherty's son, Matthew, decided he'd stay as well. "Maybe I can help pull some of these folks through. Especially since I wasn't much good to my folks." Christina overhead when he was talking to Thomas. Christina felt her heart turn over and she said a quick prayer that he'd make it through safely, along with the others that had decided to stay, as well as for those that were still sick.

An hour later, only seven of the original ten wagons pulled out.

CHAPTER 29

For four arduous days and nights, the wagon master led them over seemingly impassable trails, determined to make up the time lost. The travel through nighttime hours was the worst, and no matter how hard the wagon master pushed, he simply could not get them to move quickly enough to suit him.

No matter how irritable the wagon master got, or how hard he drove them, caution reined when the sun went down, especially since no one fancied driving their oxen into a gully or worse. Finally, after the third night, the wagon master simply let them be since any movement at all was better than none.

On the fifth day, the Mississippi River finally came into view and everyone breathed a collective sigh of relief, exhaustion clinging like a shroud. When the wagons slowed to a halt, Christina climbed from the back and stretched the kinks out of her aching body.

"Mom, you need to come down to stretch." When her mother didn't answer, Christina peered into the dim interior, and realized that her mother was still asleep; had been for nearly the entire time. It was as if she sought escape from the demanding journey in her dreams.

Perhaps it's for the best, she thought. *Maybe the rest will help her body regenerate its strength.*

Christina turned away from the wagon and gasped.

"What's wrong, Sis?" Thomas pulled his horse to a stop beside her and jumped down, looking in the direction of his sister's stunned gaze.

"I didn't know it was this big," Christina murmured in awe.

"Is that all? Man, Sis. If you're going to scare a body, make sure there's a good reason for it, will ya?"

Christina snapped out of her semi-trance and laughed, "Sorry, Thomas." She looked back toward the bank and saw several large rafts tied to poles sticking from the reddish-colored water. "Are those rafts the ones we'll ride across on?"

"Those are them."

"It doesn't look safe. How are they going to manage to go straight? That current looks mighty strong to me."

"See the huge rope spanning the river?" Thomas pointed, and Christina squinted against the sunshine blinding her sight.

"Now I do."

"Well, there are men on each side of the bank. They pull the rafts back and forth using those ropes."

"By themselves!"

"Using horses, silly."

"Oh."

"Anyway, the ropes keep the rafts on course."

"Since when did you get to be so smart anyway?" Christina teased.

"Since I already asked one of the guides. Well, gotta go."

"Thomas, what are we supposed to do while you men folk are transporting the wagons?"

"Well, you can't fix anything to eat, since we can't pull anything out of the wagons to use. But I sure am mighty hungry. Got any suggestions, Sis? I'm getting extremely tired of jerky," Thomas grinned.

"Well, we can always start a fire and roast a rabbit on a spit," she said, then snapped her fingers, "Oh, darn. I forgot to shoot a rabbit."

"I'll see what I can rustle up."

"I was just joking, Thomas," she said.

"Well, I wasn't. I'm sick to death of jerky, so see what firewood you can collect. I'll just turn these horses over to Dad, and then take Chin Woo to see about hunting some food." She watched Thomas lead his horse to where the other men were already heading, and then started toward the bank. As she got closer, she stared in awe at the expanse. A sudden feeling of predestination flooded her heart and mind, and she knew that whatever destiny had in store for her lay across that river.

"The water looks red, doesn't it?" Maggie queried, running up beside her.

"Maggie, you startled me!"

Maggie just giggled. "Come on, I told Little Joseph that I'd let him look at it up close," she said, and then sprinted off at a pace that only a mother with a child understands, Joseph running unsteadily beside her.

Christina smiled at the pair, and was glad that Maggie had some moments of happiness with her baby boy. It gave her hope for her own future, should she find no way to prevent her marriage to Jeffrey and end up with a child. Maybe that would give her something to live for as it seemed to do for Maggie.

Christina joined them at the riverbank. She started to splash Little Joseph with the water. The young boy laughed, throwing his hands up to ward off the droplets of water that kept hitting him in the face.

"I'm gonna get you," Maggie said, grabbing playfully at her son. Joseph squealed with delight and toddled away, racing up the hill toward the wagons, as fast as his young legs could carry him. His high-pitched laughter drawing smiles on the faces of those whom he passed. "I'll be back in a moment," Maggie said, smiling at Christina. She bolted up the hill after her son, playfully threatening to get him and tickle him. Christina smiled and leaned toward the water, splashing the cool liquid on her face. The sight of the water tempted her to find a place along the bank to bathe, but with so many people tromping about, privacy would definitely be an issue.

They'd be stopping temporarily once all the wagons crossed. The women were thrilled to hear that the delay would afford them time to bathe. She'd also wait until then to cook any meat that Thomas and Chin Woo caught. Having to cook twice would be pointless, after all. Especially when the other women were relaxing and socializing.

She stood and glanced over her shoulder, spotting Maggie a short distance away, chasing Joseph, who was still squealing. She smiled and stretched her back, then sat on the grass. Leaning back on her elbows, she dropped her head back on her neck, letting the warmth of the day relax her muscles.

She heard another delighted squeal and opened her eyes. A laugh escaped her, as she watched Little Joseph barrel past her and a quickly-tiring mother chasing him down. The game was over for her. "It's time for your nap, you little heathen, now come here!" She scolded, rolling her eyes and grinning when she saw Christina watching her.

Christina lifted her head and scanned the bank on the other side, the sense she'd had earlier that her destiny somehow lay across the bank of this mighty river, returning. For all of her distress over leaving her home, she somehow felt that this place was where she was to be; that something important was waiting for her on the other side.

A movement in her periphery drew her attention a little way downstream. She turned her gaze in that direction, hoping to see an animal indigenous to the region. An animal she'd never seen before. Her dream flitted into mind and she shuddered briefly, "Of course, I'd prefer it not be a giant rabbit," she said softly to herself, half in jest.

She sat up straighter; trying to peer into the shadows, suddenly wishing the sun was behind her, not shining directly in her eyes. She silently willed the animal on the opposite bank to move from the trees and step closer to shore, but it remained stubbornly hidden in the thick mass. Her gaze pinned to the movement as the outline of its shape passed directly in her line of sight. She thought it would continue moving upstream, but when it was immediately in front of her, it stopped as if sensing her presence, as if wanting her to notice its presence.

"Well, if you want me to see you," she whispered, more to herself than to the animal, "then step out of the shadows." She didn't know what she expected the animal to do, but compliance wasn't it, so when it moved from the tree line and into the sunlight, she blinked in astonishment. Alert wariness quickly replaced the astonishment. It was a wolf, and it was standing there, watching her.

"It's just coincidental," she murmured to herself. "There's no way possible that you could be who I think you are. Could you? No. That's just plain silly."

Then why is it watching you so intently, like it knows you? Her mind asked.

Indeed it was. It sat staring at her, as if it was waiting for her to say 'hello' or something, perhaps somehow acknowledge that it was the wolf from her dream. Its tongue was lolling to one side, and she could see it was panting heavily as if it had run a long distance to be there.

She could also see that, if this was indeed the same wolf, her dream had not exaggerated its massive size, for even from this distance she could tell that it would probably stand as high as mid-thigh next to her.

"You don't look like you want to eat me," she whispered, unable to look away from the huge dog. "In fact, you're quite a beautiful thing, aren't you, fella?" She smiled as the wolf yawned widely and stretched its back. Then sat and scratched its ear. Her smile widened and then vanished. She sensed, rather than saw, another movement near the wolf, still cloaked in the shadows. She squinted, her gaze attempting to penetrate the shadows again.

"Bring company?" She asked, the hairs on the back of her neck standing erect. She didn't see anything, but something told her that the wolf had not journeyed alone. There! Something to the left of the wolf was making the branches sway. She brought her focus to bear on the area, squinting with all her might. There was something there, but what or who?

Christina stood and instinctively brushed the rear of her skirt, and then moved closer to the edge of the river. She lifted her hand and shielded her eyes from the sun. "So, fella," she called to the wolf, trying to shake the nervous feeling that had suddenly draped over her like a cloak, "you travel with your girlfriend? Is that who's hiding in the trees, hmm? Is she too shy to come out and say hello?"

The wolf stopped panting and sniffed in her direction, making her smile. "Not so fearsome outside of my head, are you?" Christina said softly. "Or is it that I'm just more brave with so much water separating us, huh?" The wolf started panting again, and then moved to the water's edge. After a moment's hesitation, which had Christina's heart rate increasing slightly, the wolf dipped its head down and began to drink heartily. "Scared me for a moment," Christina said, a shiver running down her spine. "Thought you were going to swim across and eat me after all."

She let loose a nervous laugh and was about to turn away, when the trees fluttered again and the other animal she sensed moved forward. Only it wasn't an animal. Her breathing became shallow, and sweat popped out from every pore on her body. The wolf, having drunk its fill, returned to stand next to the new arrival, and there was no longer any doubt that her dream was becoming a reality.

CHAPTER 30

Even from across the half-mile expanse she could see both the man and the wolf, staring at her, watching her intently. Although her mind assured her that neither of them could harm her from so far away, her heart refused to slow its frantic pace. If it had been just the wolf, she could have coped, but to have the man join the animal; to know that they were now following her; to have them both standing there, staring at her; to discover that her dream was no longer just a dream, but somehow prophetic. It was far too much for her tired mind to assimilate.

She swallowed hard and tried to force herself to breathe normally, but it was an uneasy task. She shouted at her mind to operate, to make her eyes shift and her limbs move, but neither would listen. She stood rooted as if the man and beast across the banks of the mighty Mississippi wielded a special power over her.

"Wow! What a task that was!" Maggie huffed, coming to a halt next to her friend. "I think putting a child down for a nap has to be the hardest thing in the world," she continued, unaware of her friend's distress. "Just wait until you have one of your own and you'll know exactly what I mean. Of course," she whispered, "we both hope those children will be with someone you love, right?" As if just realizing that her friend wasn't listening to her, Maggie turned her head, her brow creasing with worry. "Christina, are you okay? Your face is as white as a snowdrift!"

When Christina remained immobile, Maggie moved to the front of her, unwittingly breaking the eye contact that Christina had with the man on the opposite shore. Christina blinked rapidly.

"Are you okay?" Maggie asked again.

Christina stood mute, drawing in deep breaths, trying to bring her rapid heartbeat under control. Unfamiliar with western ailments, Maggie feared her friend might have contracted a deadly disease similar to the one that had killed so many others on their train. She sprang into action. Taking Christina by the arm, she turned her toward the wagon, prodding her along gently, speaking comforting words in her ear. When she was certain that Christina wasn't going to collapse at her feet, and since she continued walking trance-like on her own accord, Maggie rushed ahead calling for Christina's dad to fetch the doctor.

Christina turned her head and looked over her shoulder. Man and wolf were gone, but the feelings they evoked remained, gripping Christina's heart like a vise. Thomas heard Maggie's shouts and came rushing to Christina's side. When she failed to respond to his concerns, he scooped her up into his arms and hastened toward the wagon. He moved quickly, depositing her on her makeshift bed moments later. The activity awakened her mother and she rolled over groggily.

"Hey, Sis! What's gotten into you?" Thomas patted her hand frantically.

Christina could only shake her head, her mind too numb to send the message needed to make her jaw move so that she could answer him with any manner of coherence.

"What's happening?" Carlotta struggled to a sitting position and scooted over to her daughter's side.

"I don't know, damn-it!" Thomas snapped before he realized to whom he was speaking. "Sorry, Mom."

"You should be, young man," she snapped with far less bravado than in times past, "now go fetch the doctor!"

"Someone already has and I'm not leaving her side." Thomas saw the startled look in his mother's eyes at his tone of voice. "I didn't mean to snap at you. It's just that I've never seen Christina acting so strange before, and I'm worried. This isn't like her."

Carlotta placed a weakened hand on her son's head. "She'll be fine. She's a strong girl."

A few minutes later, the doctor pushed through the crowd that had gathered and ducked inside the Carthington's schooner.

"She can't breathe with so many people crowding 'round her. And for God's sake, raise the flaps on this gosh-darned contraption so we can get some air and light in here. How in blue blazes am I supposed to treat this girl if I can't see her, or if I can't breathe from the stifling heat," the doctor continued ranting. "Now, both of you get out so I can have a look see!"

"I'll be staying beside her, Doctor," Carlotta announced in a quiet tone that brooked no argument. "Thomas, you go ahead and raise the flaps on the wagon. That will give the doctor room to work and the light by which he needs to see." Thomas reluctantly did as his mother bade and scooted past the doctor. He started to climb aboard the schooner and raise the flaps, but Jeffrey beat him to it.

After a short examination, the doctor climbed from the rear of the wagon and pronounced Christina fit as a fiddle. "She seems to be suffering from a mild case of shock. Could be a delayed reaction to the move? Hell! I don't know. All I know is, she ain't sick or dying. I've given her a sedative that will help her rest tonight, and we'll see how she's feeling in the morning."

"Can they move her?" The wagon master asked in his usual tactless manner.

"Certainly!" The doctor exclaimed. "She's in shock, not suffering from any broken bones, nor, as I said, is she on death's door."

"Good," he proclaimed, obviously satisfied that there would be no more delays. "All the wagons should be across by nightfall, so the trip can continue without further hindrance."

"You mean we're not stopping to rest for the night?" Thomas asked, not that the revelation that should surprise him. They hadn't stopped for the past four nights, so he wasn't certain why tonight should be any different.

"The animals will have received enough rest on the crossing. I see no need to rest further. After everyone has had a chance to down a good meal, we'll start again." Without allowing any additional comments, the wagon master spurred his horse into motion and rode away.

"Well, at least we can eat the rabbits that Chin Woo and I caught," Thomas muttered to himself, and then climbed back aboard the schooner. He fought for a position next to Christina, as his mother, father, Chin Woo, and Jeffrey took up nearly all of the space provided. Jeffrey acting the devoted fiancé. It sickened Thomas no end.

The crowd dispersed, leaving the Carthington's alone. Only Maggie and Joseph remained, maintaining a silent vigil just outside. From the opposite bank, Baying Wolf observed the activity as they carried the white woman to a nearby wagon. He had not a doubt that it had been his appearance, and not that of his wolf, that had caused her sudden distress.

Again his angered flared. Even though he'd just taken the time to visit her dreams recently, she still feared him. Did he not tell her that he meant her no harm? Could the white woman not understand English? He knew he spoke it clearly enough. He took a deep breath to calm himself, and looked down at the wolf. "Since the Great Spirit knows what he's doing, why can't he enlighten me and the white woman? Maybe then she wouldn't be so afraid of me and I wouldn't be so angry with her."

The wolf yelped and panted. "You're right," Baying Wolf said, patting the wolf on the head. "That would be too easy. Come! We'll rest for the night and be ready to follow them out at first light." As he led his horse toward a campsite, he was unaware that at first light the wagon train would be nowhere in sight.

CHAPTER 31

Christina lie motionless. She knew that the man beside her was Indian. She'd seen enough of the civilized variety walking the streets of Savannah, but this Indian was of the savage sort that she'd read about, as was apparent by his state of attire, although he did appear to speak English as well as those she'd met back East. If not for his strange clothing, she might think him civilized.

She watched him warily, thoughts of escape flitting through her mind, as he lifted himself high enough to see above the grass. Curiosity over what was happening overshadowed her fear of the man and she made to rise. It also helped her calm that he hadn't attempt to scalp her yet.

"Stay!" *He commanded, pressing a hand firmly on her shoulder and forcing her to return to the ground.*

"I want to see what's happening," *she replied in desperation. She heard savage noises in the distance and attempted to raise up again.*

"You do not listen well," *the Indian said, glaring at her.*

Christina lowered herself back down, a shiver passing through her at the anger she saw aimed in her direction. She instinctively reached toward her pocket and the knife inside.

"Do not fear me. I will not hurt you," *he said, his tone gentle, belying the anger in his gaze.* "I'm only here to help you, but if you do not heed my words, then I cannot protect you."

"Protect me from what?"

"I do not know this, but the coyote coming from the trees are a sure threat."

"No offense, but there are a large number of those animals out there, so how could you possibly defend me?"

"I will have an easier time if you listen. Besides, they have found their prey."

"The white beast," *Christina asked intuitively.*

"Yes. It lies beneath a mountain of snapping teeth and slashing claws."

"Then the beast is dead."

"If not. It will be soon. We need to go."

"Go! Where?"

"I will try to get you back to the wagons. Perhaps your men can defend against the attack."

"Attack?"

"They are many in number, and so will consume that meal quickly. We need to get you to your wagons and warn the men there before they turn their attention in that...it's too late." *Baying Wolf heard the signals, which signified the end of feasting. He lifted his head briefly to confirm his conclusions and growled.* "They are coming. Stay low and follow me."

Christina did as he bade, but maneuvering in a half-squat when she was in a long skirt wasn't easy. The man in front of her didn't seem to have any problems at all, but the look he shot over his shoulder every few seconds displayed his frustration at her inability to move faster. The pounding of the four-legged beasts reached her ears and she shivered.

They were getting closer.

She stopped suddenly, and strained to hear their approach. When their wails reached her hearing, she immediately noticed there was something different about it.

She glanced over at the Indian. He must have noticed as well, for he turned his head slightly, and she could see his brow, furrowed in concern. When Christina raised up a bit to see what was happening, the Indian didn't try to stop her, but before her mind could fathom what her eyes were seeing, the Indian dove for her, pressing her down; shielding her body with his.

"My family!" *She yelled above the new sound of battle cries.*

"We are too late!" *He whispered harshly, close to her ear.* "If we move now, they will see us and we will surely die."

"But my family," *she whispered, struggling to move from beneath his heavy weight.*

"I am sorry."

"Noooooo!"

CHAPTER 32

A loud moan pulled Christina from her dream. She blinked several times, wondering whether it had come from her mother again, whose moaning woke her a few times a night, or if the moaning issued from her own throat this time. She shivered as the dream replayed in her mind. Surely, her dream had not been a premonition, but merely a nightmare. Her family couldn't be in danger.

Another moan reached her ears and she groped around in the blackness, searching for the candle and matches. Her hand brushed against the candle, and she set about trying to light the wick in the dark. On the third strike of the match, their darkened wagon erupted into light and Christina turned back to face her mother who lay in troubled slumber. As softly as she could, she lifted her mother's hand, stroking the aging skin. She sought to coax her mother from her unrest with words of strength and encouragement, silently praying that some of her own strength would transfer to the fragile body lying beside her.

Her mother's restlessness tempted her to lean out of the wagon and call to her father or brother, but decided it would be pointless. They couldn't help her mother sleep any better, and the wagon master wouldn't be pleased if she called a halt over something as minuscule as an apparent nightmare. She was a little surprised however, that no one had heard her mother's disturbed moans and come to check anyway.

Even though the doctor had sedated her earlier, she vaguely recalled wakening at least four times throughout the night, sitting with and reassuring her mother until Carlotta returned to a peaceful sleep. Perhaps if her own sleep had been more restful, she too would not have heard the moans.

"Is everything all right in there, Sis? I see the candle lit," Thomas whispered loudly through the lowered canvas.

Christina released her mother's hand and shuffled to the rear of the wagon. "Mom's just having a hard time sleeping, Thomas," she whispered back.

"Anything I can do?" Thomas asked, seeing his sister's head peer from the rear flap.

"I don't think so."

"Maybe I can ride over and get another sedative for Mom to take. Maybe help her sleep a little better?"

"I don't think that will be necessary, Thomas. It will be daylight in a few hours. Too late to take anything now. Besides, Mom doesn't really need any help sleeping; she's been doing enough sleeping to make up for all the sleepless nights of everyone in this wagon train."

"It does seem that way, doesn't it?" Thomas concurred. "You think she's going to make it all the way to Texas?" He asked worriedly.

"Of course she is," Christina answered with more conviction than she felt, for Thomas had voiced her own concerns. "And when we get there, we'll get a good doctor to look her over and maybe hire someone to nurse her back to health."

"Sounds good," Thomas said, "if you can convince Father to part with the money it'll take for that."

"It's his wife, for heaven's sake! Of course he will part with the money." Another loud moan drew her attention. "Mom's sleep is restless. I'm going to go back to sit with her."

"Okay, but let me know if you need me for anything."

"I will, Thomas. Thanks."

"And Sis? How are you feeling? Looks like you've gotten over whatever shocked you, although you still look a bit bedraggled."

"Just lack of sleep," she said, not mentioning her encounter, or her brother's observations over her current appearance. She lowered the flap and returned to her mother's side.

"Want me to raise the side flap?" Thomas asked a second later. She thought he'd already ridden away.

"No," Christina responded in a loud whisper. "We could use the fresh air, but I don't want the noise to disturb Mom."

"Let me know if you change your mind," Thomas yelled softly, but Christina didn't respond further. She watched her mother's head toss restlessly from side to side and sighed. Looking down into her gaunt face, she wondered, yet again, what they were supposed to do about her rapidly deteriorating health. She slept so much that she barely ate, and even when they could rouse her long enough to eat, she merely nibbled at the food. Unbelievably, she'd lost even more weight. The clothes that had started hanging on her body before they left now looked like a potato sack hanging on a scarecrow.

Sitting quietly, she watched her mother's labored breathing and wondered just how many days she had left in her. Would she even be strong enough to make the last two weeks of the journey so they could get her much-needed medical attention?

As the hours ticked by, Christina continued to whisper words of strength and encouragement, and hour by precious hour, Carlotta's spirit faded. Even in repose, there was a sadness surrounding her, which no amount of encouragement could ease. It was as if her decision that this move wasn't for her, was causing her body to shut down; as if she were taunting the angel of death to come and claim her body. Christina felt a shudder run through her mother's body and tightened her grip slightly.

Looking into her mother's disturbed features, she reflected again, on just how different she and her mother were. Her mother was physically and mentally incapable of dealing with the unpleasantness that life sometimes dealt, having been too sheltered. Even giving birth had been an ordeal for her, a duty to her husband through which she very literally suffered. She'd given her husband two strong children and had nearly died trying to give him a third. The child died instead. She was done. There would be no more children, but she wasn't perturbed by the notion, for she'd performed her wifely duty.

Traveling to this barren land was also no more than a wifely duty, one she had endured stoically, but as with the birthing of her third child, it was killing her; however, this time she appeared disinclined to fight death, but seemed to welcome it. As the sun rose in the Eastern horizon, Carlotta Carthington drew her last breath nestled in her daughter's arms. It took a moment for Christina to realize that the rise and fall of her mother's chest had stopped, and she simply sat watching the still figure. When it registered, she lifted her mother's head and laid it on her lap, gently stroking her hair, tears of sorrow trailing silently down her dusty cheeks.

She knew that she should call out for her father and brother, but was temporarily unwilling to share her grief. When she could cry no more, she lowered her mother from her embrace and crawled stiffly to the back of the wagon. Thomas knew immediately, by the stricken look on her face, that something was wrong.

"Call a halt to the wagons, Thomas," Christina's voice cracked and she had to stop a moment before continuing.

"What's happened?"

"It's Mother. She's passed on."

The wagons slowed to a halt. The doctor came by and officially pronounced that a severe case of malnutrition had caused Carlotta Carthington's death, but Christina knew that she'd really died of a broken heart.

So again, the trip was delayed just long enough to bury another from their dwindling few in a simple unmarked grave, in a strange land, far away from the home she loved. Christina stood by the open grave. Angry tears fell unchecked down her face, one hand tightly gripping Thomas's, the other clinging to Maggie's.

This wouldn't have happened had we stayed in Georgia, her mind shouted. Her gaze lifted and locked onto Jeffrey's. *This is your fault,* her narrow, angry gaze accused, but his cold blue eyes merely pierced hers as if to say unconcernedly, 'I told you this could happen'.

She lowered her eyes and stared blankly at the dried, caking mud that clung to her shoes.

I know you'll be watching me from heaven, Mother, she said in her mind, *so you will probably know soon enough that I don't intend to marry that cold-hearted bastard standing across the way. I only hope that you can forgive me in death, as I know you would never have been able to in life. I do love you so. I always will, and I pray that you find true peace and rest now.*

CHAPTER 33

Baying Wolf awoke with a start, a sudden despondency enfolding his heart like a death shroud. He shook the remaining cobwebs from the corners of his mind and looked around. In an instant, he was on his feet. He ran through the trees to where the wagons were supposed to be, but were not.

"Why did you not wake me?" He yelled to the eagle above. "How can I protect the white woman if I cannot even keep up with where she is?" With swift angry movements, he returned to his camp and dressed swiftly. Leaping onto the back of his great stallion, he gave the eagle one last look of discontent, and then spurred his horse into a gallop. Ardently, he beseeched the Great Spirit that the feeling of foreboding that clung to him this day had nothing to do with the white woman's safety, or the dream they'd shared.

CHAPTER 34

"Not even you can be that cold!" Christina's anger temporarily replaced her grief, as she again locked horns with Jeffrey. As callous as she'd discovered him to be, she never really expected that he'd take advantage of her mother's passing to attempt use of the special license still tucked inside his coat pocket. She fought back the tears that threatened to fall.

"I told you before we left that the trail was difficult. I cautioned about marrying beforehand lest something untoward befall your parents," Jeffrey lectured. "What will it take before you realize I'm right?"

"Leave me alone," Christina implored, rubbing the sides of her temples with her fingertips. "I have no desire, nor the strength, to do battle with you today."

"Perhaps I'll speak with your father. Certainly he'll see reason now."

Christina watched in relief as Jeffrey stomped off. She was simply too weak and tired to do combat with him. The wagon master had called another halt, this time near the Red River, to allow time to bury her mother. Shortly after, he announced that they would be staying the remainder of the night. If she hadn't been so downhearted, she would have joined in the shouts of glee—but her heart just wasn't up to rejoicing, anymore than it was up to battling with Jeffrey. She glanced at all of the food nearby, that the other families brought by after the funeral, but could not find her appetite. Jeffrey had stolen it with his aggressive confrontation and dogged determination.

"If going to fight Jeffrey, you need to keep strength up," a voice said softly beside her as if reading her thoughts. She turned and weakly smiled at Chin Woo.

"You're right, I suppose," she said. "Besides, I did promise Hyacinth that I wouldn't do anything foolish, like attempt to starve myself to death. Of course, the closer to Texas we get, the more the idea holds merit," she said, shooting an evil look in Jeffrey's direction. "Anything would be preferable to becoming Mrs. Jeffrey Buchanan. I'd even prefer that a savage spirit me away and force me to become a slave. Okay, maybe I'm not *that* desperate to get out of this marriage." She felt a shiver crawl up her spine.

"I would no let Cookie do anything foolish, so eat." Chin Woo stooped in front of her and tried to hand her a small plate of food.

"Do I really have to eat, Chin Woo? I'm not all that hungry."

"You need strength." Chin Woo shoved the plate under her nose. "I like your mother, Cookie. She treat me nice..."

"Oh, Chin Woo, she barely even knew you existed," Christina sighed.

"Yes, but she no mean to me," Chin Woo grinned.

Christina shook her head, "You are something else, Chin Woo."

"What I say?"

"Nothing."

"Anyway, I no want you die like she because no eat."

That snapped Christina out her depressed state. She brushed the remnants of a stray tear from her eye and took the plate from Chin Woo's outstretched hand. "I can't help thinking," she said through a mouthful of food, "that she wouldn't have starved herself to death if it hadn't been for this move."

"Too late to look back now. Mother make mistake. She die. Must go forward," Chin Woo gently said. "You argue with Jeffrey about marriage again?"

"He's trying to take advantage of Mother's death, and her not even a day in her grave."

"He really putting pressure on." Chin Woo nodded in understanding.

"You heard what he said?"

"I hear some. It hard not to," Chin Woo muttered. "Let just hope father not cave to pressure," he said, nodding toward where Jeffrey and her father stood in heated debate. She couldn't hear what Jeffrey was saying to her father, but his pacing and flailing arms were an indicator that he was losing yet another battle.

"Why you not go bathe. I finish putting food away," Chin Woo offered gently and then added with a sly grin. "You need bath real bad. No smell very good." His attempt at humor brought a small smile to her face. Something he hadn't seen much of all day.

"Honestly, Chin Woo," she sighed in exasperation, "between you and my brother's comments, I'm going to start feeling less than beautiful."

"Right now, you no look beautiful," Chin Woo responded with a smile, "but look beautiful again after bath."

"Do you think if I stayed this way, it might discourage Jeffrey from wanting to marry me?"

"The Snake no marry you for beauty." Chin Woo was suddenly serious again. "He marry you for to control you and break you. Now go, so I clean up. We not stop for too much more time." Chin Woo turned away, effectively bringing an end to the conversation, but Christina continued to dwell on what they'd talked about and quickly reopened the exchange.

"I just wouldn't feel right about taking a bath."

"Being clean not feel right?"

"No." Christina shook her dirty head. "Taking a bath on the day of my mother's funeral doesn't feel right."

"You no think your mother want you be clean?" Chin Woo knew the rebuttal was silly, but he had to snap Christina out of her doldrums. The trip was a hard one and she needed to be alert and healthy to survive it. She needed to put her mother's death aside quickly and move forward for Chin Woo realized, even if Christina did not, that if she allowed depression to bog her down, pulling free would be very hard. And he didn't want to see that happen to his Cookie, or she may end buried along the trail as well. He told her as much, but she just shrugged her shoulders.

"I just feel I'm being disrespectful somehow."

"I no think your mother standing in heaven wagging her finger at you for wanting be clean. She probably laughing that you think staying dirty okay. Now go! Leave me to clean and no bother me more."

"Thank you for being a good friend, Chin Woo. I'll be back before dark. Thanks for cleaning up the food, too. I know it should be me doing it, but right now, I only have the mental fortitude to feel sorry for myself." Chin Woo only nodded. He knelt down and began collecting the leftovers that would also serve as their evening meal.

Christina smiled slightly and sighed heavily. She turned toward their wagon and crawled into the rear, a bout of depression striking her again as her gaze fell upon her mother's meager personal belongings. She quickly gathered her soap and a clean change of clothing and left the wagon, fighting back the tears that seemed to threaten to overwhelm constantly today.

She walked with leaden steps toward where the other women splashed noisily about, and then stopped. Observing their playful gaiety was too much. She simply couldn't participate in the revelry. Not that they would probably expect her to, but if she went down there, her mood may very well put a damper on their joy and she wouldn't feel right about that. She glanced to her right, down some ways from the other women, and saw that Maggie was busily bathing Joseph. Although it would appear by the water on them both that Joseph was giving Maggie more of a bath than the other way around.

The sight brought a smile to her face, but it didn't last long. She liked Maggie and loved little Joseph dearly, but the thought of spending time with them was even less appealing than bathing with the group of laughing women.

Maggie had been a pillar of strength during her mother's funeral and she would be forever grateful for her newfound friendship with the woman, but sometimes a person needed solitude. This was one of those times. Spending time with anyone right now was something she didn't want to do; neither did she particularly want to bathe. *Chin Woo is right*, she thought, catching a whiff of her malodorous self, *I definitely need a bath*.

She scanned the area in the opposite direction, but could see no one through the trees near the bank. The word 'privacy' jumped into her head and she latched onto it tightly. She eyed the distance to the water's edge, trying to decide whether that was within the realm of safety that the wagon master had laid out for them; however, after only a moment of thought and hesitation, desire for aloneness overshadowed common sense and she headed away from camp.

She glanced over her shoulder to make sure no one noticed her and picked up her pace a bit, her mood suddenly lighter at the thought of a luxuriant bath and time alone. It took her longer than she thought it would to reach the area, and when she glanced back over her shoulder again, she couldn't see the wagons. Her dream flitted through her mind and she felt her heart skip a bit.

Calm yourself, her mind advised. *You couldn't possibly have wandered far enough away to get lost.*

"You're right, of course," she responded quietly, "my dream has me flustered, is all. Still, just to be on the safe side, I think I'll just..." she paused her one-sided conversation and started maneuvering her way through the trees the way she'd come. When she spotted the wagons not a minute later, she let out an audible sigh of relief and returned to the water's edge. She started to undress and then stopped. A shiver of remembrance ran down her spine and she shot a look at the opposite bank. She squinted, staring into the shadows of the tree line, but could spot no suspicious movement. She also didn't sense any presence nearby as she'd done earlier in the week when the man from her dream appeared in the flesh.

She let the breath go that she was holding, relieved that neither man nor wolf was observing her with their spooky intensity. She tore her gaze away from the other bank and stared into the crystal clear water only a few feet away. With another quick look around, she unbuttoned her blouse and flung it over a nearby branch. Her skirt quickly followed, but she stopped short of removing the remainder of her clothes. She may be relatively sure of her privacy, but something about being unclothed tended to invite prying eyes, and someone may just show up unexpectedly to enjoy the show.

Although she didn't sense that the Indian was nearby, she still couldn't shake the sensation that someone was not too far away, keeping an eye on her.

"Get a hold of yourself, Christina, or you're going to end a nervous wreck," she said to herself. She shook the tension away and moved to the inviting water. Unlike the Mississippi River, this water was clear and steady, until she stepped into it, then the water around her became a dirty brown.

"Disgusting." She used her hands to wipe off what grime she could, and then reached on the bank for her lye soap. With another exclamation of disgust, she dunked her head in the water to wet her hair. She flipped it back over her head, spewing dirty water in all directions, and then dipped the lye soap in the water. Twisting the soap around and around in her hand, she worked up a thick lather and began the long and difficult task of cleaning.

CHAPTER 35

Jeffrey watched, sullen, as Christina made her way toward the distant bank, his agitation at having his plans thwarted again, driving his temper higher until his vision blurred.

Why couldn't he make them see reason about the marriage? He thought. Carlotta had died at an opportune time, to his way of thinking, but trying to convince Christina's father to entrust his daughter into his safekeeping, had been a wasted effort. In fact, it had been downright disastrous. He hadn't anticipated Carthington's strong sense of protocol. There would be no wedding for at least the next six months, not while he was he was alive and kicking, and most certainly not while his family was in mourning.

Six months! Jeffrey's mind railed. In their less than ten minute conversation, Carthington had delayed the wedding—originally scheduled for sometime next month. *Damn his hide! Carthington couldn't do this to him,* his mind screamed. He'd waited too long, patiently biding his time, scheming and planning, until he'd finally been able to entrap Christina. Now, he felt it slipping from his grasp because of her mother's death.

"Maybe this trip hadn't been such a good idea," he griped petulantly to himself. "If we'd remained in Georgia, Christina would be my wife now. Still, if her mother hadn't insisted on a fancy wedding, we could have married before leaving. Damnation! Her parents have created one hindrance after another!" He stomped his foot as would a little child denied a particular want. He felt himself coming unglued, but maintained just enough presence of mind to realize he needed to regain control. He rubbed his fingers in circles on his throbbing temples trying to reign in his runaway temper.

There has simply been too much clouding my vision and too many setbacks standing in my way, he assured himself, *but all that will change soon enough. It has to.*

Staring at the stand of trees that Christina had long since vanished within, a plan formed in Jeffrey's mind. A plan he was certain would convince Carthington to hand over his daughter on a silver platter in no more than two months. Not the demanded, irritating six. With a sigh, he felt himself come back on an even keel, his emotions evening out like a ship in the wake of a storm. He turned with a renewed determination and headed back toward the Conestoga. He was going to need some rope.

CHAPTER 36

Christina hummed softly to herself as she ran the soap back up over her arms. It was the third scrubbing each body part received and although her skin was red from the effort, she couldn't seem to shake a sense of filth lingering on her body, so she continued to scrub. "I know what's wrong." She stopped work on her arms and looked around. With careful steps, she moved further into the depths, and then lowered herself as far into the water as possible.

With another glance in all directions, she lifted her camisole and rubbed the lye soap on her belly, moving her hands quickly over her breasts and up toward her neck. Changing hands, she rinsed the soap free and sighed. That's why she hadn't felt clean. There was still dirt clinging to her body beneath her clothes.

Without a second thought, Christina stuck a lathered hand down the front of her pantaloons and washed the grime away from there as well, and then stretched further until she reached mid-thigh. Her spirits lifted as she spied the dirt washing away downstream. When she'd finished rinsing, she pulled her hand free and bent at the waist. Lifting her chin to keep her head above water, she tugged at the band of the bottom of her pantaloons and pulled both as far up her legs as she could, which was just above her knees.

"There doesn't seem to be a place on my body that an inch of grime doesn't cover." She lathered the lye soap, lifted a leg from the water, and scrubbed, balancing precariously. "How in heaven's name," she continued her one-sided discussion, "all this dirt manages to find its way under all my clothing is beyond me." With a huff of completion, she lowered herself back onto both feet and started wading toward shore. She looked up at the sky and noticed that the sun had noticeably shifted position. It was apparent that she had taken more time to clean than she'd intended. Still, it was worth the time just to be clean again—physically—for the relaxation had affected her mental state as well and she felt rejuvenated.

She reached the bank and pulled herself up. Yanking her dirty clothes from the nearby tree limb, she laid them out on the grassy bank, and then stretched out atop them. The water washed the grime away, and now, while she had a moment of peace, she determined to allow the sun to cleanse away her stress, drying her underclothing in the process.

"Besides, the meal Chin Woo threw together is probably cold anyway, so a little more time isn't going to make that much of a difference." She closed her eyes and allowed her body to relax, and her mind to drift on a cloud of nothingness.

Jeffrey observed her from his vantage point behind a tall pine, glancing toward camp every now and again to make certain he was out of sight. After all, if his strange behavior did draw attention, someone could very well come down to investigate, and he wanted Christina all to himself.

When Jeffrey first stole his way out of camp, it had been his intention to jump her and assault her; take care of the thing with quick efficiency; but when his eyes scanned her scantily clad form, his carefully laid plan took a flying leap from his brain, replaced with an overpowering lust. The wet camisole hid nothing from his prying eyes, and he felt his groin tighten in anticipation. To him, this was better than the burlesque shows that he'd frequented in Georgia.

When she pulled herself onto the bank, he knew that his time was running short. His action would have to be swift or his opportunity could well pass by; but then she'd laid herself out on the shore, as if in invitation, and his heart skipped a beat. He fantasized that she knew of his scrutiny and was waiting for him to join her. Ready for him.

His practical side knew better however. He held no delusion that she would allow him to bed her willingly, but bed her he must. If she became pregnant, which is what he was hoping for, that would be all it would take to force her father's hand and make him forget his damned protocol. It wouldn't put him out to wait a month to confirm a pregnancy, especially since it was far better than waiting for the passing of a six-month mourning period. He slid from behind the tree, silently, and knelt beside her still form.

She seemed to sense his presence then, for her eyelids fluttered open. She tried to scream; however, all she managed was a squeak as his hand pressed down on her mouth, effectively cutting off any further sounds of protest.

Jeffrey's assault stunned Christina into momentary immobility. The sight of him kneeling over her was more frightening than having an Indian accost her. At first that's what she thought had happened, but it was definitely Jeffrey's smirking face that was above her own. Even though the sun was behind his head, leaving his features mostly in shadow, there was no mistaking that snow-white hair.

When her mind finally managed to register her predicament, she began to struggle in earnest, her legs flailing in an attempt to dislodge the hand pressed across her belly, holding her firmly to the ground.

Jeffrey chuckled and lowered himself so that he could whisper in her ear, like a lover. However, the words he murmured were not ones of passions, but of promise. "I told you that you would be mine," he whispered softly, "and I think now would be a good time to take possession, wouldn't you agree?"

Christina felt close to fainting. The hand that he clamped down on her mouth was cutting off her air supply. She tried to turn her head to the side, but he merely pushed harder making her wince and moan.

"Be still and I won't have to use so much force." She quit struggling instantly in the hopes that he would lessen the pressure. With an inward sigh of relief, Christina felt his hand lifting slightly. He didn't remove it, but it provided just enough space for her jaws to shift, open, and bite down hard on the fleshy part of his palm. Jeffrey pulled his hand away with a cry of outrage, but recovered swiftly, and before she could yell for help, his fist slammed into her jaw. Stars erupted around her head like a halo and Christina fought to stay conscious.

"I warned you about defying me, Christina." He shifted his body so that he straddled her, and then slapped her again. "You don't take to lessons very well." Incognizant, he struck her again, his indignation dominating his actions. "Perhaps by the end of our session today, you'll be more adept at learning."

Christina clung to consciousness by a mere thread, but her body felt like lead and her head ached violently. She knew that she needed to scream, but couldn't seem to find the strength to move her already bruised and rapidly swelling jaws.

Jeffrey slid off Christina and looked at her battered face, not with regret, but with satisfaction. He wasn't exactly happy that his first time bedding her, she looked like they'd spent an hour in a boxing rink, but it had been unavoidable as he feared it would be. She watched through a haze as Jeffrey removed a coil of rope from around his belt and stretched it taut. "I couldn't assault your virtue before, remember?" He said, his tone taunting. "We were minus a rope. Do you think we'll still need it?"

Christina didn't respond, but the glare in her eyes gave Jeffrey all the answer he needed. He grabbed her limp wrists, binding them securely together, then slung the loose end of the rope around a sturdy branch nearby and tied it tight. He looked at his handiwork and smiled. Reaching cupped hands into the river, he retrieved a good amount of water and flung it in her face. She sputtered as some liquid found its way into her mouth. "Sorry for that, my dear," he smiled solicitously, "but I just wanted to make certain you were fully lucid, since you have said nothing since the little attitude adjustment."

Christina's seething anger increased. He knew she was awake; had thrown water in her face deliberately to bait her further, but she wouldn't bite. He would get no satisfaction out of her. Not with words or sounds.

He reached out, stroked her still damp hair, and let his hand drift across her face already turning purple. His hand continued its journey down her neck and across the rapid rise and fall of her breasts. "As much as I'd like to draw out our love-play, time just isn't a luxury we have right now, so foreplay is out of the question. It's a shame, since I think you'd probably appreciate my abilities if we had the time to spend."

Christina clamped her lips tightly together, as if trying to prevent her fear and anger from escaping. He stretched himself out beside her and kissed her bruised cheek with a tenderness that belied his earlier actions and words.

"I don't have to hurt you, you know." His hand roamed freely over her scantily clad body. "All I ask is that you do as I wish." He looked down the length of her, following the movement of his hands. "You are even more beautiful than my imagination ever envisioned," he whispered almost reverently, and lowered the straps of her camisole, revealing her breasts to his sight.

The thought of him touching her was almost her undoing, and she fought to keep the bile down and her emotions in check. If she gave him a sign of encouragement or provoked him in any manner, the abuse would start again.

I think I may just prefer unconsciousness, she thought. Her body seemed to sense her reticence and squirmed slightly.

Jeffrey's hands reached out and grasped her hips, forcing her to remain stationary. "You are not going anywhere, love, so you might as well resign yourself to the fact that you and I will join. Holy matrimony can come later." His free hand reached down and ripped her wet camisole from her. He looked at her mouth, swelling rapidly, and then at the damp material crumpled in his fist. "I just can't take the chance." He lifted her head and wrapped the remains of her camisole round her mouth. "Not too tight, is it?"

Christina narrowed her eyes in anger, but her anger soon fled when Jeffrey turned his attention toward her pantaloons. Tears sprung forth and blurred her vision when Jeffrey tugged at the waistband. Pulling sharply, he stripped away the only barrier between him and her virginity.

So much for not fighting, she thought, blinking the tears away rapidly. She glanced at the ropes tying her hands. *No way to free myself,* she thought, and then yelled at her brain to start formulating a solution.

He skimmed her naked form greedily. With a wink, he stood

and started shedding his own clothes, and Christina saw an opportunity to act. His pants dropped around his ankles and Christina lifted her legs. She struck Jeffrey's thighs as hard as she could. With absurd inner glee, she watched as he tumbled into the Red River, his arms flailing like a windmill as he tried to regain his balance.

She knew however, that if someone in camp failed to notice him fall, or hear him yell, then it would be all over for her when he regained his footing. If someone failed to notice, he would return to her to wreak havoc on her defenseless body.

CHAPTER 37

"Hello Chin Woo, is Christina around?" Maggie stopped near the fire. Her son was clinging to her skirts in his normal fashion. "Stephen said that coming for a visit would be okay."

"She still at river, bathing," Chin Woo answered automatically.

Thomas's head shot up and he looked toward the bank, devoid of human forms. "There's no one down there, Chin Woo. Are you sure you didn't see her come back?"

"No. I here whole time. I not see her." Chin Woo stood and scanned the late afternoon horizon, concern etched on his face. "Maybe she come back when I not see and go sleep in wagon."

Thomas jumped up from his sitting position and ran to the rear of the wagon. He stuck his head in and let his vision adjust to the dim interior, but there was no sign of Christina. "She's not there."

"Maybe she's gone visiting with Jeffrey and your father," Maggie offered helpfully, when she noticed neither of the men were present in camp.

Chin Woo and Thomas looked at each other, both knowing that Christina would never go anywhere willingly with Jeffrey and wasn't exactly thrilled with her father's company either.

"Chin Woo, you head up that side of the bank," Thomas instructed, pointing westward, "and I'll head downstream. There's always a risk that she might have fallen and hurt herself, or that the current carried her away."

"I'm coming too. She may need me," Maggie said, hoisting Joseph onto her hip.

Chin Woo nodded and started in the direction that Thomas suggested. Maggie tagging along as quickly as she could. He was halfway to the bank when he heard a splash further down. He turned his head in time to see a man fall into the water. His pants were down around his ankles and he was cursing up a blue streak.

If the man had been anyone other than Jeffrey Buchanan, he probably would have overlooked the man's strange behavior, but his gut told him that Christina was in serious danger. Not wasting any time, he turned back toward the wagon to collect his weapon. He may know how to fight, but Jeffrey was a much bigger man and he was wise enough to know that additional help would be a good thing to have. As he ran past Maggie, he yelled at her to go find Thomas, but his strange and rapid speech was lost on her. Still, the splash that alerted Chin Woo also drew her attention, so she continued walking. Perhaps she could provide assistance; perhaps the splash had been Christina. When she reached the bank however, she was completely unprepared for the sight before her eyes.

CHAPTER 38

"You arrogant woman!" Jeffrey snarled, crawling from the river sputtering. "You will pay dearly for your insolence. That I promise."

Christina continued swinging her legs, making it difficult for Jeffrey to get on the bank. He slid down the muddy embankment again, as her legs flailed and struck him in the forehead. Christina smiled grimly behind the camisole covering her mouth. If she weren't so afraid, she'd be having the time of her life.

Jeffrey gripped the muddy surface again, spitting water from his mouth.

Let's see how you like drinking river water, Christina thought smugly.

"What's going on here?" Maggie shrieked. Christina's legs stopped moving in midair, and Jeffrey froze in water up to his knees.

"Nothing that concerns you," Jeffrey snarled, snapping out of his momentary shock. "Christina and I would like a little privacy, if you please, so go away." Christina's shook her head in agitation, moaning loudly. She prayed that Maggie would not allow Jeffrey to intimidate her. Surely, after having dealt with the likes of Stephen, she'd know a bully and not risk leaving her with Jeffrey in her current state of distress—and undress.

Jeffrey started toward the bank again, and Christina started her kicking. "Stop that, woman!" Jeffrey howled, when a blow from Christina's heel contacted with his shoulder.

"You leave her alone, Jeffrey!" Maggie shouted. "You're not going to hurt her anymore!"

Jeffrey stopped trying to climb ashore again, and sent a piercing gaze at Maggie. "And you are strong enough to stop me?"

Maggie put Joseph down and knelt beside him. "Don't move from this spot, sweetheart," she whispered in her sternest mother's voice. Then she moved toward Christina's bound hands.

"Get away, you hag!" Jeffrey snarled, and hurled himself toward the bank. Christina's legs again began to flail, but Jeffrey's blinding rage made him oblivious to the blows that she landed. He reached out and snared her ankles, slinging them aside. Then landed with a thud nearly atop her. "I will deal with you in good time," he snapped, hauling himself upright. He kicked his pants free from his ankles and stomped toward Maggie. She began backing away, eyes wide with fright.

When the sound of a hammer cocking reached their ears, Jeffrey froze, Maggie smiled and Christina starting crying. It was over! The cavalry had arrived in the form of Chin Woo and Thomas.

"You all right, Sis?" Thomas asked. The strain in his voice was evident and it made Christina want to cry. The feeling intensified when he averted his eyes for her modesty's sake. Because of his kindness however, he forgot she was unable to answer from behind the gag.

She moaned, looking at Maggie. "Is that a yes?" Maggie asked and Christina nodded. "She's not hurt too badly," Maggie said, scanning Christina's swollen features, "but if you fellas don't mind, I'll leave Jeffrey to you, so that I can get her unbound and covered."

"Thank you, Maggie," Thomas said, keeping his gaze averted. To Chin Woo he said, "if he tries to interfere, shoot him."

"Where you go?" Chin Woo asked.

"I need to go get Father and some men who'll bear witness so we can take this slime bag into custody. You know what—Maggie, leave Christina tied."

"What?" Chin Woo and Maggie said at the same moment, but Jeffrey understood all too well Thomas's strategy and wanted to throttle him.

"Cover her, but I want witnesses to attest to her unwillingness. I don't want him getting off on a technicality. You can remove the gag though."

"You'll regret your interference. All of you." Jeffrey glared at them, his face still flushed with anger.

"You only man who gonna have regret."

Maggie sidled past Jeffrey, and went to Christina's side. She tugged the clothes from beneath her friend and draped them across Christina bare body.

"We'll get you untied when Thomas gets back, okay?" Maggie said, tugging at the still-damp camisole covering her mouth. A loud bang startled them both and they jerked around in time to see Jeffrey jump at the rifle in Chin Woo's hand.

Somewhere in the sane recesses of Christina's mind, she knew it was an absurd struggle, since they had already fired the rifle and it was now empty. Of course, there was still the possibility of clubbing someone with it.

Christina twisted her head, trying desperately to keep up with the movements of both men. They shifted out of her line of sight for a minute, and Christina felt a moment of panic.

"Maggie, move! What's happening?" Maggie shifted slightly and Christina gasped. In that minute, Jeffrey managed to wrestle the rifle away from Chin Woo, and swung it with deadly force at Chin Woo's head.

"What's taking Thomas so long?" Christina said, struggling to free her bonds.

"I hear them now," Maggie said, placing a comforting hand on Christina's shoulder. "Lie still. I'll do my best to shield you from prying eyes, until we can get you untied." Maggie moved to Christina's head and knelt down, but Christina couldn't care less about prying eyes. Someone needed to help her friend.

Jeffrey took another swing, and Christina winced. *That was too close,* she thought. In his growing agitation at being unable to hit Chin Woo, Jeffrey swung with all his might. The rifle missed, but the momentum pulled Jeffrey too far to the right, exposing his left side. It was all Chin Woo needed.

Before Jeffrey could regain his footing, Chin Woo leaned on his left heel, lifting his right foot in the process. He spun his body around to the left, driving his right foot into Jeffrey's kidneys. Jeffrey went down with a grunt of pain, just as a crowd of people broke through the trees. Chin Woo swiftly walked through the crowd, drew a sharp blade from the back of his pants, and sliced the ropes tying Christina's wrist with one powerful blow.

Christina gratefully pulled the bonds from her hands, started to sit, and suddenly remembered her state of undress. She lay back down on the grass, rubbing the feeling back into her chafed wrists.

"How are you holding up?" Thomas asked, while a crowd of men surrounded Jeffrey, binding him hand and foot.

"I've been better. Let's see how he likes being bound," she said, nodding toward Jeffrey's prone body. "Can you get rid of them soon though? I've had enough of being unclothed."

"I'll see what I can do. Can you give her a hand, Maggie?"

"Sure."

"Thanks," Thomas said. "I'll go help with Jeffrey."

"Don't do anything foolish that will land you in jail."

"Don't need to worry about me Sis, but Dad is another matter."

Christina glanced toward her father, his face red with the exertion of trying to pull free from two men clasping tightly to his arms. She heard one of them trying to calm her father with assurances that Jeffrey would be taken care of, but her father wasn't listening. It wasn't until Thomas went to him that he stopped his struggles, and gave the men his word that he'd leave Jeffrey alone. Securely bound, the men dragged Jeffrey away, the crowd following until only Thomas, Maggie, and her father remained.

"He'll stay trussed up like a Thanksgiving turkey until we reach the next town. Then we'll turn him over to the local law until a trial date can be set," Thomas said over his shoulder, while Maggie helped Christina dress.

"We'll find a way to keep you from having to come back and testify, darling. You've been through enough already," Charles Carthington added.

"My clothes are on now," Christina said, and both men turned quickly, rushing to her side.

Charles knelt in front of his daughter. He felt an outrage swell in him like nothing he'd ever felt before as he scanned her battered face, and he had a sudden overwhelming urge to take the law into his own hands. If he weren't such a God-fearing man, he'd do just that—tear Jeffrey Buchanan apart with his bare hands. "I can see that he did a lot of damage to you, Pumpkin, but...well...did he *hurt* you?"

Christina knew what he wanted to know: was her virtue still intact, or had he stripped it away from her? Her cheeks flamed with renewed humiliation, but she managed to reassure her father with a slight shake of her head.

"Why don't we go back to the wagon and let you rest." Maggie suggested, placing a comforting arm around her shoulders. "Maybe the doctor can give you something to help you sleep for tonight."

"No," she replied quickly. "I know this sounds strange, especially after what's happened, but I'd really just like to stay here and be alone for a while."

"Absolutely not!" The sudden outburst gave everyone an unwanted jolt. "You are not going to stay here alone and that's final!"

"Father, please."

"I said no!"

"Father," Thomas interrupted, "why don't I just sit close by and stand guard over her. It's not like Jeffrey is going to get loose and come after her."

"I stay too," Chin Woo said, standing off to one side.

"I don't know," he ran a hand wearily through his graying hair and felt suddenly old and tired. Tears stung his eyes as he tallied the losses brought on by this damnable trip. The last thing he wanted to do was add his baby girl to that growing list. Sometimes he wished that he could turn back the hands of time and return them all safely to their home in Georgia.

Christina closed her eyes and cried silently, her emotions, mingled with those of her father, threatened to choke her. Seeing her father weep unabashed, was almost her undoing. She drew her knees to her chest and lowered her head, which had started to ache, and let the tears fall freely down her bruised and swollen face.

Her father whispered comforting words in her ears and laid a hand of comfort on her head. When she looked up a short time later, her tears expended, she was alone. For a minute, panic seized her, but then she spotted Thomas and Chin Woo sitting a short distance away, chatting and she relaxed.

Curled up into a tight ball, drained and exhausted, she let sleep take her.

CHAPTER 39

They were gone.

She knew they were, long before the silence reached her ears. What's *happened to my family? She wondered.*

It was too quiet, by far.

She opened her eyes and saw the Indian watching her intently, a look of sadness in his opaque eyes. He opened his mouth to speak, but she raised a hand to stop him. She didn't want to hear him speak, didn't care to receive the comfort he freely offered.

She stood on shaky legs and started to walk toward camp, but stopped. She looked over her shoulder toward the carcass of the white beast.

It lay unmoving a short distance away. Dead, she had no doubt. On legs stiff from squatting so long, she walked woodenly toward the creature, an irrational need to see it; to be certain it was dead. She also needed something—a distraction—until she found the strength to go into camp.

The first thing she noticed as she approached was the fur. It was gone. Replaced by tanned flesh. The second thing she noticed was the face, bloodied and nearly unrecognizable. Nearly.

The white hair and gray eyes left no doubt. Jeffrey's sightless eyes stared into space.

Christina should have been shocked or appalled, but she felt nothing but pity for the man that had tried so hard to make her his. Instead, his selfish efforts had cost him dearly. The price was his life.

Of course, his efforts hadn't left her unscathed. She had lost her home, her mother, and nearly lost her virginity.

She turned away, shaking her head sadly.

She stumbled as she started toward camp. She really didn't want to go, but she needed to know.

"You do not need to go," *the Indian said, stepping into her path as she drew nearer to him.*

"Yes, I do."

"I will go with you."

"I'd rather go alone."

"I will be here," *he said, moving to let her pass.*

CHAPTER 40

Christina awoke abruptly to the sound of distant thunder crashing in her ear. Forgetting where she was for a moment, she sat upright and instantly regretted the suddenness of the motion when a dizzy spell threatened to send her spiraling into oblivion. Hands unsteady, she reached up and pressed the palms against her temples, attempting to steady the swirling stars that clouded her vision.

After a few lung-filling breaths, her vision began to clear, but the thunder, which had awakened her, continued to increase in volume. She glanced at the sky. Not a cloud was in sight. Something didn't fit. It was then she felt the vibration beneath her, creating a tingling sensation in her legs. She placed her hands on the ground, and the tingling sensation slid up her arms. Something was wrong. She sensed it, long before she heard the shrill cries in the distance. The shrill cries startled her. She'd heard it once before—in her dream.

Oh my God, my dream! The attack foretold is becoming reality.

She struggled to shake the vestiges of sleep from her head as she rose from behind the tree. She had to help her family. The Indian in her dream had prevented her from helping, and they all died. She couldn't let that happen again. She saw Chin Woo and Thomas still sitting vigil nearby, heads together in concentrated conversation. She raced up to them, startling them with her sudden appearance "It's happening! Why are you just sitting here? We've got to do something."

"What's up, Sis? You nearly scared the pants off us?" Thomas snapped. Only then did Christina realize that the only sounds penetrating the silence of twilight were the animals that used the cloak of darkness to hunt their prey.

"Didn't you hear?" Christina exclaimed. "We were under attack!"

"As in attack by Indians? That sort of attack?"

"Yes."

Thomas scanned the horizon, but saw nothing. "Are you feeling alright, Sis? You've suffered some severe trauma over the past two days, which could be affecting you poorly."

"I thought I was," she whispered. She cast a glance at Chin Woo who was looking at her, his gaze full of concern. He knew she was having a specific dream, but never had that dream disturbed her waking hours. Until now.

"Perhaps you dreamed it?"

Christina looked over at Chin Woo and shook her head in bemusement, "I don't doubt that, it just seemed more real than it ever has before." Thomas' brow knitted in confusion, but Chin Woo nodded, comprehending, as Christina droned on. "It was as if it was really taking place—now—and the images were no longer representations, but appeared in true form."

"Ok, Sis, now you're scaring me. Would you like to go back to the wagon? It's getting late and none of us has eaten anything all day. Maybe that would account for your...um...strange dream?"

Christina sighed and settled on the ground. "I'll stay a bit longer. I need to clear my thoughts, and I'm not hungry yet."

"You don't come back with us, Dad is going to get very agitated."

"I'll trust you to work your charm on Dad, and I promise I won't remain long. I'm just not ready to be around people yet."

"What are we then? Chopped liver?"

"You are, but Chin Woo is Szechuan Beef."

Thomas grinned, feeling a little better at knowing his sister hadn't completely lost her mind. Her face, however, had lost all of its beauty, and that wouldn't be rectified until the swelling went down and the bruising subsided. He felt another surge of anger towards Jeffrey, wanting to pummel him as he'd done Christina. He sighed instead, "I'll let Dad know that you're closer to camp and should be okay by yourself for a short bit longer."

"I stay," Chin Woo offered, but Christina did not want company at that moment, and said as much. She needed to be alone for a while to try to discern what these waking visions meant. After all, dreaming about the future without living it first was scary enough. Both men conceded and made their way up the hill.

Thomas stopped and turned, looking at his sister gazing out across the river's expanse. "Christina?"

Christina looked at Thomas over her shoulder, and Thomas flinched at the look in her eyes. She looked haunted. She looked older than her seventeen years. "Yes, Thomas?"

"If you aren't back to camp in half an hour, I'll be back; and I'll drag you back to camp if I have to. Understand?"

"Yes, brother. I love you."

"I love you too, Christina."

Christina turned and refocused her gaze across the river, wondering when the attack would occur; wondering where her protector was at that very moment.

CHAPTER 41

An attack was going to happen. She knew that with as much certainty as she knew her own name. But when? Could the reason for the waking dream be a warning that it was going to happen soon? She sighed, uncertain of what to make of it all. All of this prophetic dreaming was new to her, and for all she knew it could still be but a nightmare—with no more connotations of reality than dreaming about heaven. She closed her eyes and brought her fingertips to her temples, gently rubbing in circles, attempting to ward off the headache that threatened to engulf her brain. All of this attempted dream interpretation was taking its toll. She had to relax or her head would explode.

Keeping her eyes closed, she began to breathe deeply, in and out, allowing her body to go limp, and her brain to cease all form of thought. It was another of Chin Woo's tricks and it had been extremely effective when thoughts of Jeffrey intruded and threatened to stress her overwhelmingly. He called it meditation.

After a few minutes she did begin to relax, the throbbing in her head subsided, and the fog vanished from her brain allowing clearer thinking, but all of that mattered little because the vibrating thunder and shrill cries had returned. This time, louder than before, and this time when she was fully awake.

She shook her head violently, trying to dislodge the irritating dream, forcing herself to breathe normally. This was getting beyond ridiculous. It was bad enough suffering through the dream when she closed her eyes, but she didn't know how she would survive if it started haunting her days as well.

She grew concerned when the noises didn't abate after a moment more, rather continued to intensify; and then the screams of terror joined with the shrills of assault—the dissonance reverberating around her like a pitiable operatic aria.

She looked toward camp and her eyes widened in alarm. She blinked, and then blinked again, and then pressed her eyes together and squeezed tight. When she peered from beneath her lashes, the attack was well under way. The dream had ended. Reality was now brutally asserting itself.

Arrows flew through the air like birds after small prey, striking whatever was in their path—and everyone was in the path of the assault. Her gaze fell on a lone figure racing toward her. Thomas! He was returning to see her safe. "Christina!" He yelled, getting closer. "Get behind those trees! Now!"

"No!" She screamed.

He reached her side, grabbed hold of her arm and pulled her back toward the riverbank. "Come on!"

"No! Thomas, I can help!" Christina cried, trying to release his hold on her arm.

"No, you can't," Thomas screamed in return. "Now either stay here and stay hidden, or I'll tie you to a tree myself. Do you understand? I'm not going to lose my sister to these savages!" Christina stopped struggling and threw her arms around her brother's neck.

"Do you think I want to lose my baby brother?" She asked, trying not to cry.

"You won't. I like my scalp right where it is, but this is a man's fight, and if I let any more harm come to you, I wouldn't be able to call myself a man; and if I'm not a man, I may as well let them kill me, because I won't be worthy of this fight. Do you understand?" Thomas said, pulling Christina's arms from around his neck and looking at her intently.

"I promise not to get killed," Christina said softly, a lone tear streaking down her bruised face. Thomas kissed her cheek softly, and then turned away. In a moment, he was gone, throwing himself amidst the fray with a yell of resolve.

"Please don't die, brother," she whispered, as she watched the near-naked Indians surround the wagons—firing arrows as quickly as they could pull one from its sheath. She'd never witnessed such accuracy, deadly delivering blow after blow to the people running about, gripped by panic; but needing common sense. One of the equestrians slowed near a pit, the fire still burning, and lowered an arrow into its midst. When he withdrew it, the tip was ablaze. He loaded the arrow into the bow, took aim, and watched as it met its mark, igniting one of the wagons nearby. The wagon became a deadly inferno, the flames chasing the fleeing occupants. He let out a shrill shout of victory, and then pulled another arrow from its sheath. By the light of the fire, she saw men and women huddling beneath the wagons. The men raising rifles to begin their defense, but it seemed too little too late. A rifle fired and an Indian screamed, but none seemed to see the Indian near the fire pit, preparing to rein more conflagrating terror down upon their heads. But she did, and her promise to remain hidden, and safe, fled. She had to do something!

Stooping as low as possible, she skirted from tree to tree, stopping only long enough to make certain none of the Indians noticed her. She ducked behind a tree and peered around the side, pulling back quickly when an Indian rode by close enough to touch. She had not realized just how close she'd moved to the wagons, but now that she was here, she determined to do something to help. She pulled the pack of throwing stars from her pocket, opened it, and looked at the shiny metal with the sharp tips. If ever there was a time to put into action all that Chin Woo had taught her, helping to protect her family was as good a place as any to start. She spotted the native next to the fire pit, laughing as he watched yet another wagon go up in flames; preparing another arrow with deadly flames of destruction.

Christina closed her eyes and said a quick prayer that every skill she had learned would help her family now. She wiped her hands on her skirt, took a deep breath, and then peered from behind the tree again. The Indian had set the next arrow and was drawing back the bowstring, preparing to fire at his next target. She stepped from behind the tree, cautious to remain hidden in the shadows, eyed the Indian as she did the wooden targets Chin Woo erected for practice. Inhaled and exhaled to steady her hand, and let loose the star.

She quickly ducked behind the tree, and peered out, waiting

with bated breath as the star soared straight and true. She forced herself not to let out her own yell of victory, as the points embedded into the Indian's arm, forcing him to drop the flaming arrow at his horse's feet. The horse reared, dropping the Indian onto his rear. She grinned at the mixture of pain and confusion spread across the Indian's face. He glanced at the star, and then yanked it free with a cry of anger, tossing it aside.

Christina had struck a blow, but she had hoped for a deathblow. If she were going to do more than anger the attackers, she was going to have to make each throw count. That wasn't going to be easy, since her practice targets never moved. She peered from behind the tree again. The Indian she'd stabbed was no longer on the ground; was nowhere in sight. She sighed. That left those on horseback, racing circles around the wagons. She would just have to throw her stars and pray some fatally struck her targets.

She stepped into the shadows again, and aimed at one of the moving targets. She threw the star and groaned in frustration as it flew past a rider and collided with the ground beyond. She sighed and pulled another star.

So much for making each shot count, her mind snapped.

"Not now!" She hissed. She let loose her third star and was pleased when a rider jerked in surprised pain, but as before, he did no more than yank the star free, look at it in confusion, and toss it aside.

Christina moved back behind the tree and leaned against it, closing her eyes in frustration. She simply hadn't received the training needed to defend herself or her family against such an onslaught—"and why hasn't the Indian from my dream shown up to assist?" She hissed irrationally. With a cry of anger, she stepped out again and hurled the star, not bothering to take aim.

She laughed, near hysterical, as it embedded in a rider's neck, knocking him from his horse. She watched in awe, as the native stood, pulled the star free, and then realized his mistake. The blood began gushing inexorably from the wound. He was a dead man, and Christina felt momentarily vindicated. She couldn't stop them all, but she wasn't so helpless as to stop at least one.

As the sun lowered on the horizon, the flames from the wagons became her only source of light. It also made it easier to see the massacre unfolding before her. She simply wasn't providing sufficient help. While she'd managed to kill one murdering heathen; the heathen's had managed to kill dozens—and the rampage was far from over. Rifles continued to fire, but the number of reports decreased as more arrows found the marks, leaving the huddled mass of women and children, widowed and orphaned. Christina peered around the tree again, ready to take on Indian number two, but the warriors had stopped circling and had dismounted.

It was then that Christina heard it. A silence more terrifying than the horrible battle cries from moments earlier. That could only signify one thing—the threat was gone. The men were dead.

Thomas! Chin Woo! No! Her mind screamed in denial. *No! It's not possible. Thomas promised me he wouldn't die.*

The sound of whimpering and sobbing reached Christina's ears and she forced her misery aside. She peered around the tree and her blood ran cold. The dismounted warriors were closing ranks, moving toward the surviving women and children. By the leers on their faces, their intent was obvious.

A feeling of despondency draped over her and she felt tears of frustration trace a path down her battered face. How could she possibly defend those helpless victims against so many? Her weapons were limited, designed for use at a distance, and hand-to-hand combat was definitely *not* an option. The only thing she would accomplish should she step from behind the tree was to commit suicide. From there, her thoughts turned to Maggie.

She peered around the tree again and scanned the heads of the huddled mass; however, none had Maggie's coal-black hair or a little boy of Joseph's size wearing a long-sleeved shirt. That meant one of two things: she escaped and was hiding, or she and Little Joseph already lay among the dead or dying. She shuddered at the thought and then shook it away.

She turned from the sound of shrieking women and children.

She could do nothing now, but weep for their pain and pray for
their souls.

CHAPTER 42

With a heavy heart and leaden steps, Christina turned from the horrible sounds and made her way back toward the banks of the Red River, praying along the way. All she could do now was wait until the savages departed and then see if she could aid anyone who might have survived. Survivors. She clung to that one word.

A movement to her right drew her attention and she turned, startled; worried that one of the Indians might have caught sight of her and decided to take her scalp for a trophy. Her fears eased a bit when she determined the movement to be a good distance away, and although it was dark, the light from the flames revealed enough of the person fleeing the ravages of the camp to discern that it was a woman, not an Indian. But why would she flee with her belongings?

Christina wanted to yell at her to drop her load; that no amount of earthly possessions was worth her life, then the possession lifted its head and Christina gasped. There was only one woman with a child that young—Maggie.

She's alive, but for how much longer? Christina wondered, as another figure left the area of the raging infernos that was once their wagon. The light was close enough to this one to see that the crouching figure was half-dressed and carrying something shiny clutched in his hand.

Maggie was apparently unaware that the Indian was stalking her, and the heathen was not in any hurry about catching her either. It was as if he knew that she wasn't going to be able to escape his grasp. Christina could imagine his preying gaze following her every step while he enjoyed the little game of cat and mouse.

"Please, dear Lord in Heaven," she pleaded in hushed tones, "give Maggie's feet wings and me courage." With no more thought to her own safety, Christina lifted her skirt and took off at a dead run, with just enough forethought to stay to the shadows, away from the light. "Run, Maggie!" She whispered harshly. "Run like you've never run before!"

Maggie's lungs were hurting, and having to carry the weight of her child made movement awkward, nevertheless, she was determined to try to save her baby as well as herself. Her foot caught in a hole and she stumbled, sending Joseph flying from her arms. She lay still for a moment and then tried to stand, the pain shooting from her ankle clear up to her hip. She fell again, but refused to stay down.

Resolutely she stood and limped toward her son. He hadn't moved, and even when she reached down and scooped him up, she knew that the fall had rendered him unconscious. She clasped him to her breast, and continued limping onward.

Christina watched her friend struggle, and silently pleaded with whoever would listen, to help see Maggie safe, until she could get there to help defend her. Another cry—piercing and ominous—resounded through the night air, causing the hairs on Christina's arm to stand erect. The sound was emanating from where Maggie was, which obviously meant that the cat and mouse game had ended.

Christina ran faster and tripped over a root. She uttered words she didn't realize were in her vocabulary and then uttered more expletives when she stood and a pain shot from her knees down to her toes, slowing her movements. Worsening the situation, she lost sight of Maggie and her attacker.

Why can't I catch them? She yelled in silent torment. In reality, the elapsed time was no more than a few minutes, but for Christina it seemed an eternity before she wove through the last stand of trees. She came to a sudden halt at the sight before her. The hunter and hunted seemed as one. The only view that Christina had of Maggie was her skirt protruding from beneath her attacker's legs, her own unmoving. She glanced around quickly, but saw no sign of little Joseph either, but she'd have to worry about him later. Right now, her concern had to be Maggie.

Christina jerked, as the warrior emitted a yelp of triumph, grabbing Maggie fiercely by the hair. He raised a blade, wicked in length, and pulled back on Maggie's long, flowing black mane. Then with a quick sawing motion, he sliced the top of her scalp away. The fact that Maggie issued not a sound was a telling sign.

Christina turned and retched. Tears ran down her battered face, tears of sadness and bewilderment, but the victory yells that sounded behind her brought her quickly back to her wits, and her anger rose rapidly replacing her despondency. With another string of atypical curses, she limped as fast as she could toward the Indian, then let out a tortured yell.

He spun around at the sound and stared dumbfounded at her approach. Christina took advantage of his stunned disbelief. With rapid movements and sheer determination, she pulled the pouch from her pocket, tugged open the lid with a jerk and pulled the remaining six stars free, dropping the pouch.

Without pause, she palmed a star and hurled it across the short expanse, palmed the second and sent it flying immediately after the first, then a third and the fourth, until all six stars protruded from his upper body.

The warrior shrieked as the first star hit its mark, but his reaction time remained too slow to prevent the next five from penetrating. Christina watched with detachment, praying that her accuracy proved deadly. He glared at Christina angrily. Her detached interest turned to growing alarm, as the Indian started to pull the stars from his body, his gaze belligerent. To Christina it seemed as if none of the wounds inflicted were serious.

She fingered the dagger in her pocket in preparation of the hand-to-hand combat she so dreaded and slowly retreated. She wanted to turn and run; however, fear kept her gaze pinned to her adversary. Chin Woo had taught her to face the enemy, never turn away—and this heathen was definitely her enemy.

As she looked on, luck swung back in her favor and she paused in her retreat. Her hope rose, as the Indian reached for, and clasped hold to the last star embedded in his body. The star lodged deeply in his throat.

Christina silently urged the star to break its hold, as the Indian tugged, winced, glowered, and tugged all the harder. She wordlessly egged him on, watching his determination with rising anticipation. With a final grunt, the star broke loose, leaving two holes in his throat.

The Indian's gaze widened and he reached up to cover the puncture wounds, struggling to catch his breath. Christina knew that it wouldn't be a quick death; he might in fact survive the injury inflicted, if he could find a way to patch himself, not that she'd give him that opportunity. Still, he posed no threat to her at that moment. No immediate threat.

It was the potential threat that kept her there, her gaze pinned to his. Though she could not risk his survival, she did not intend to see to his immediate demise. He needed to suffer as he'd made Maggie suffer; but if he proved able to withstand death, then and only then would she ensure death was swift.

For now, she would sit and wait until he drew his last breath. Pray that each breath was agonizing.

When the time came, faster than Christina hoped for, the Indian's eyes bulged in the sockets, then rolled back in his head. With a final gurgled cry, he fell backward, his body landing in a heap atop Maggie.

Christina sank to her knees and began to weep. She'd never had to kill before, never really thought that she would need Chin Woo's training to kill a man. A shiver raced up her spine, and then down again and before much time passed, she was shivering uncontrollably.

Minutes passed, and she slowly regained control, but then she heard the victorious cries of the Indians still raiding her camp, and the crying and shivering started again. This time, she cried for the loss of her family, for she knew with certainty that they were lost to her forever. For just a moment, as the tears subsided again, and her gaze, melancholic, turned toward camp, loneliness tempted her to make her presence known, so that she could join her family and friends in the hereafter. A nagging doubt however remained, that one or more of them might have survived the attack, and if that were the case, they would need her to nurse them back to health.

Another nagging thought surfaced to join the first that she was not meant to die; that her destiny was still somehow meant to be fulfilled.

A flurry of activity caught her attention. She scooted behind a tree as the warriors galloped by. *Murdering, savage heathens!* Her mind yelled in helpless frustration. *If I ever come across one of your kind again, he'd better turn and hightail it in the opposite direction or I'll make mincemeat out of him. That's a promise!*

Unless there happen to be more than one of them again, her mind interjected with irritating logic.

"Oh, shut up!" She snapped and then slumped against the trunk. She drew her knees to her chest and laid her head down. It was throbbing painfully. She closed her eyes and tried to relax, but her heart and mind were still racing frantically.

She wanted to jump up and head toward the camp to search for survivors, but she needed to wait a short while to assure herself that the Indians didn't return. She'd heard somewhere that they never left their dead behind, so it was quite possible that when they noticed the one she killed wasn't on his horse, they may just return to search for him.

She slowed her breathing, drawing air in and out in attempt to ease her tension and closed her eyes. When she did, Maggie's dead body took form in her mind. Her eyes flew open and her breathing increased its pace again until it felt like a runaway carriage inside her chest. She was on the verge of panic and she knew it.

She scooted back around the tree and, forcing a calm she didn't feel, began to concentrate on her breathing. Her eyes however, remained stubbornly opened. She simply could not make herself close them; could not force herself to look away from Maggie. After a long while, she felt her body relax and her eyes grew heavy. Shortly thereafter, sleep claimed her enervated mind.

CHAPTER 43

It was well into morning the following day when Christina's eyes reluctantly fluttered open. A shaft of light found its way through the canopy, spearing Christina's pupils. She clamped her eyes tight and shifted slightly, and then reopened them. Her mind was too muddled to recognize her surroundings and it took her mind a moment to register her whereabouts.

Her gaze fell on Maggie and she shuddered, jarring her brain into full wakefulness. A sense that something was different registered, and she shook her head, trying to force her brain to think of what it could be. Then it dawned on her. The Indian's body was gone.

Shock that the Indians that retrieved the body didn't notice her nestled against the tree, so close, bolted through her body like lightening. Perhaps they'd returned in the night; perhaps their attention was only on their fallen friend. Whatever the reason, her shock was replaced with gratefulness, that washed over her like newly fallen rain—grateful that they had already returned to remove their dead, grateful that they had not discovered her; and grateful that she was now able to move about without fear of their return. More than anything though, she was suddenly grateful to be alive.

"Alive? Why should I be grateful to be alive?" She pondered aloud, her gaze settling on Maggie's lifeless body again. In that moment, her gratefulness gave way to anger and she began to question the sense of it all. Why had they allowed her to live, when she didn't have a little boy? Why couldn't they have seen and killed her, instead of allowing her to live with the guilt of survival? Why had they spared her life, instead of Maggie or any of the others?

When she received no reply to her silent pleading questions, she let loose a scream of anguish from the depth of her soul, "Why? Why don't you answer me?"

Because they can give no answer that would satisfy you or relieve your guilt and anguish, her mind supplied.

"You're right," she replied, suddenly weary, "and I'd not willingly accept an answer either—for it would merely be an excuse. An unacceptable excuse." Fighting the urge to remain where she was and die a slow, miserable death from starvation—a justifiable end in her mind—she stood slowly. She looked around, trying to decide what to do next, not that her legs were ready to go anywhere. In fact, it took a huge battle between will and appendages before her legs admitted defeat and started to walk.

She'd only gone a few steps when she stopped again. This is where the Indian had fallen, the grass still crushed where his legs and feet had lain. *Of course, there wouldn't be an impression of your upper body or head, would there, you, murdering savage?* She thought angrily. *Since you had to fall right across Maggie's dead body. No respect given in life or death. Poor Maggie. It just doesn't seem fair.*

The sun glinted off an object nearby, drawing Christina's attention. It was one of her shooting stars. A quick search of the area found the remaining six. The sight of the dried blood, clinging to the sharp tips, startled her and she dropped them. When she realized how silly her response was, she laughed nervously and then bent to retrieve them again. With a sigh, she deposited them in her pocket. As much as the sight of the blood disturbed her, she didn't want to clean them right now. Something about the blood reminded her of what had happened the night before, and it wasn't something she was prepared to forget. The blood would serve as a reminder until she was ready to put it behind her.

"I'll miss you, Maggie," she whispered, kneeling beside her friend. "We didn't really get to know each other as well as I'd have liked, but you were a strong, sweet girl and I'm really sorry to have lost your friendship so soon. You and Little Joseph brought joy..."

Little Joseph!

Christina stood and scanned the area nearby.

Little Joseph lay a few yards away. The caked blood on his temple visible even from where she stood, as well as the flies swarming about his head.

"Oh," she moaned and moved slowly toward the small child.

She shooed the flies away, but they wouldn't go. With a sigh of frustration, she sprinted to the water's edge and collected as many large sized stones as she could carry. Her return trip was much slower and it seemed to her that there were even more of the unwanted pests buzzing around the poor child's head than when she'd left.

She dropped the stones and started placing them over the body, beginning with his head. Determined to take away the pesky flies meal. She didn't have the tools to bury the bodies, but she could provide a grave of sorts to prevent scavengers from taking advantage of them in death. When she covered his face from marauding insects, she hurried back to the water's edge, repeating the process until he was covered—completely and respectfully.

It makes me feel good to do something constructive, she thought, and then went back to where Maggie lay. She wanted to drag her to lie in repose next to her son, but the thought of touching her was almost more than she could bear. Still, it was the least she could do for her. One last act of friendship.

She closed her eyes and took a deep breath, and then knelt and clutched Maggie beneath her arms. The sight and stench of death reached her nostrils and she dropped the body. Stepping away, she leaned over at the waist, her stomach heaving violently. When her stomach settled, she straightened, a shiver running down her spine. She wiped the perspiration from her forehead, and then frowned in contemplation.

She had to get this accomplished. Her friend had died a brutal death, knowing that her son had gone before her, and she *would* honor her by allowing her to lie next to him; she would not insult her by holding her breath as if her stench was too much of a burden to handle. She owed her that much at least for tripping over a damnable root; for not reaching her in time to save her life.

With a renewed determination, she grasped Maggie beneath the arms and dragged her across the grass. Laying her out next to the stones beneath which lay her baby boy, she repeated the process of gathering stones as she'd done for Joseph, until not one sign of her was visible.

"God is waiting for you now, to give you the peace that you never knew here on earth. I'll miss you both, and will remember you forever in my heart. Goodbye, my friend. Goodbye, my little Joseph."

With both bodies seen to, she wiped the sweat from her brow and glanced back toward the shells of the wagons. She shuddered, knowing what would greet her would be beyond unpleasant, should she go up the hill. She also knew that there wasn't any possible way to give them all a decent burial. Still she had to go, had to see if there were survivors.

As she made her way toward the charred remains of the wagons, a vulture swooped down to feast on the bodies she couldn't see, making her empty stomach heave again. It took all of her determination to continue, dread consuming her the closer she moved.

As she rounded the corner of one of the wagons, the sight of the vultures' feasting made her stomach lurch again, and she spun from the sight quickly, gripping her stomach with one hand, holding her mouth closed with the other. She swallowed hard to keep the bile down, and when she'd finally regained control over her body, she continued, deliberately keeping her head turned away from the carnage.

From the pocket of her skirt, she pulled a handkerchief and wrapped it around her mouth and nose to help alleviate the scent of death. Unlike with Maggie, she had no desire to inhale the noxious scent lingering in the air. There were simply too many corpses, which had already started to rot in the ever-increasing heat of the day. The handkerchief however, did little to alleviate the stench.

Keeping her gaze averted, she approached the center of camp, now the center of death, waving her arms wildly, yelling at the top of her lungs. She heard the vultures' wings flapping in departure and a shiver of relief ran down her spine. As they lifted higher, the wind generated by the beat of their enormous wings pushed the loose strands of her hair into her face, tickling her cheek.

They were gone, but she knew that it was only temporary. They'd return the minute she departed. Tears from angry grief slid down her face as she wrapped her arms tightly around herself, swallowing in large gulps. She wondered how she was going to make it through the day when her empty stomach refused to quiet and her legs balked at any movement.

Her mind, usually so strong and capable, now waged a valiant struggle against her reluctant appendages. She questioned just how many battles she would have the strength to win before accepting defeat and yielding to her own desire to die.

After several deep, steadying breaths, she opened her eyes and released the punishing grip from around her waist. She looked up and saw the scavengers circling high above, just waiting for her to leave, so that they'd have the opportunity to return and feast on the slaughtered remains.

"What would you do," she yelled defiantly and nonsensically, "if I simply decided to stay here flailing my arms at you? Hmm? The thought crossed my mind, so why don't you simply go find some other carcass to gnaw on?"

The vultures stayed and Christina sighed. *Obviously, you aren't stupid creatures,* she thought dejectedly, glancing at where they circled tenaciously. It was if they knew she wouldn't hang around too long. After all, they could handle the smell of death, but she couldn't. Not for long anyway. Christina looked hopelessly at all of the bodies strewn around the burnt-out shells of the wagons, knowing that she'd have to turn their remains over to the scavengers sooner than she'd like.

She sighed in frustration when yet another stream of tears started falling unbidden from her eyes. She sniffled loudly and forced her tear ducts to cease their production, for there was simply no time for tears. The renegades could be close by and the vultures could decide she was a hindrance to their meal and decide to attack her. It just wasn't a safe place to be now. Besides, she had to *go* somewhere. She certainly couldn't sit around a graveyard mourning everyone's loss.

She sniffled again, and then turned to make her way through the bodies littering the camp, searching for her family. It didn't take long to find them. Tears and nausea welled in unison as she sank beside the arrow-riddled figure of her father, her brother's inert form laying only a few feet away. All the family she had was gone now. She was alone. The tears she'd fought to control earlier, now fell freely down her contused cheeks, leaving a trail in the dust coating her face. Desolation engulfed her.

"I should have died with you," she whispered. "I shouldn't have stayed hidden behind that tree like a coward, but, daddy, I did try to help. I want you to know that I truly did. But what good did I do? Everyone is dead, but me." She buried her hands in her face as the tears turned into huge racking sobs that shook her tiny frame.

It took a long time before her mind regained control of her body. She reached up to brush the tears away with the back of her hand and winced. She gingerly traced the bruises lining her swollen cheeks, yet another reminder of yesterday that she would carry with her for some time to come. Tracing the swollen path along her face, made her think of Jeffrey, and she suddenly wondered how he fared during the attack.

After a quick, half-hearted search, she spotted him, still tied to a wagon wheel a short distance away. Arrows riddled his body. She felt a moment's pity as she thought about his inability to defend himself, but it disappeared quickly.

"Well, we finally found something we had in common," she said irreverently, moving to kneel in front of him. "Neither of us had a real chance to stand up and fight. The only difference being, I lived and you died. Somehow, I knew I'd find you this way. Dead, I mean. Not tied to a wagon wheel." Christina knew she was babbling, but couldn't seem to find the mental will to stop. "I saw you in my dream," she continued, talking to the dead body staring sightless into the distance, "did you know that? No, I guess you wouldn't. I didn't even know it was you, but I guess I should have, considering it had your personality. Still, somehow I felt that you wouldn't survive this journey. Of course," she laughed in bitter shortness, the tenor of her voice rising with each word, "I didn't know that my family would die, too. What kind of prophetic dream is it supposed to be, if it doesn't give you the whole picture?" She shouted, looking up at the sky.

"Maybe *you* know?" She ranted; addressing an eagle that sat perched on a branch above her head. The eagle screeched a reply and Christina laughed hysterically. "You think that's it, then, do you?" She continued, carrying on her one-sided conversation. "You think that the dream didn't mean to tell me everything? Or do you think I just don't know what the heck I'm talking about?" The eagle screeched again and appeared to eye her wonderingly.

"I don't think I know anything anymore," she murmured, and lowered her head into her hands. "Why did this have to happen? Why was Jeffrey not the only person to die?" A thought struck her and she stopped murmuring, raising her aching head quickly. She stood and turned from Jeffrey's ravaged body and began to search the camp. Her gaze frantically searched the faces of the men, searching for that one face whose skin tone was closer to yellow than brown, whose eyes slanted slightly and nearly disappeared when he laughed, searching for her friend, whose body she'd not seen on her first pass through camp.

"Chin Woo," she called, but received no reply. For nearly fifteen minutes and with rising hope, Christina sought and called to her beloved confidant; her dearest friend. After an extended search, she sighed happily, for certainly that meant he'd found a way to survive as she had. Unfortunately, her happiness was short lived, when she spied a small piece of white material protruding from beneath the huge form of Stephen Bishop, Maggie's husband.

With a small cry, she shoved his massive weight from the body of her mentor. Bloodstains covered nearly the entire front of his robe, but it wasn't possible to determine whether the blood belonged to Chin Woo or Stephen Bishop. Of course, it didn't really matter, since either an Indian's arrow or Bishop's weight could have done him in. He was such a small man.

"Chin Woo?" She whispered, gently shaking his shoulder. "Please, tell me you can hear me?" She pleaded, her hope fading when he remained unresponsive. She'd called this man 'friend', the man who was more like a father than her own had ever been. He had taught her to defend herself, to respect herself, and that quitting was not an option. Never quit. Still, she had quit, and now he was dead. Dead, because she hadn't had the courage to come out from hiding and fight.

He taught you to defend against one, *not* many, her brain emphasized.

"But I know how to use a rifle better than most of the men that died yesterday," she argued. "They died defending their loved ones, so I should have done the same. Instead, I stayed hidden. My attempts to aid my family were just shy of useless," she berated herself.

Could you really have made that big a difference? Her mind asked, *or would you be lying here beside them now? Lifeless. Is that what your family and friend would have wanted?*

"I don't know," she whispered dejectedly. "I just don't know." She leaned over and lay her head on his stiffening shoulder, the only part of his body not caked with blood, and closed her eyes, weary from seeing so many fatalities. So many lives wasted.

"Cookie?"

Christina jerked upright, her eyes widening in disbelief, "Chin Woo? You're alive?"

"No," the voice replied softly, barely audible, "I only wait..." He broke off as a hacking cough tore from his lungs.

"I'll find you some water," Christina said, but Chin Woo lifted a hand to stop her. It was then she saw the blood that was draining from his mouth.

"No," he said, when the coughing subsided. "Water no need. Need only know my Cookie alive. Now I rest."

"Chin Woo," She whispered urgently when he closed his eyes again. "Please don't go. I need you."

His eyes fluttered open again and Christina sighed in relief.

"I'll help you," she smiled encouragingly. "I'll find a way to make it all better."

"I no need help and you no need me," Chin Woo said, his voice growing fainter with each word he spoke. "You strong. You live. I proud my daughter, proud..."

"Chin Woo?" Christina searched his face when he stopped speaking, but though his eyes remained opened, the life in them was gone. "Please! Chin Woo, no, please! Don't leave me!" Christina beseeched but soon realized that her pleas went unheard. Her friend was gone.

She knelt down and tenderly closed his sightless eyes. She had shed so many tears since leaving Georgia. So many new, unpleasant memories would haunt her forever. She knelt back, not really knowing how to say goodbye, but knowing that she must. She took a deep breath and sighed heavily. Grieving forever was no more an option than was quitting. Both would upset Chin Woo, should she allow herself to succumb to either. He wanted her to live, to be strong, and for his sake, more so than her own, she would try to do so.

"I just don't know what I'm going to do now," she whispered to Chin Woo's lifeless body, "but I promise you that I won't give up the fight. I'll do what I can to survive using all the skills that you taught me, so that when you look down from heaven you can do so with pride." When she turned to survey the scene a final time, it was with a new determination not to allow this to happen to her. She vowed not to shed another tear for those lost, for it would be a waste of much-needed energy—instead she would use that energy to survive.

A fire started in the pit of her stomach, engulfing her and soon anger replaced her sorrow. A deep burning enmity for the people who had wreaked such devastation on her life.

CHAPTER 44

Fear gripped his heart as Baying Wolf drew closer to the death that he sensed waited over the next rise. He had seen the vultures circling and knew with sudden dread that he had arrived too late to help the white woman. He'd wasted a day searching for the wagons that had gotten an entire night's head start on him. He cursed himself repeatedly for allowing such carelessness, but with so many wagons heading west, tracking a particular one was exceedingly difficult.

No! He railed silently. *I cannot use that as an excuse for my failure. I should have kept her in my sight.*

When he spotted the scavengers overhead, he prayed to the Great Spirit not to let it be her wagon; however, it appeared that his prayer had not reached the deity quickly enough, for his guide was soaring nearby, a safe distance from the vultures, which quickly disabused him of his hope and his heart sank.

His failure was complete! He was a warrior. A warrior that never failed and it bothered him greatly. It also bothered him that the Great Spirit had placed the safety of one of his enemy in his hands, and he hadn't cared enough to try. And if his failure bothered him, then it must surely bother the Great Spirit. He gazed toward heaven, waiting for his god to strike him down, but no bolts of lightning appeared. He breathed a sigh of relief, but could not relax.

He was just now beginning to realize that this white woman was important or the Great Spirit wouldn't have sent him, a great warrior, to protect her. Instead of obeying as he should, he had balked and questioned the deity's motives. He shook his head in self-disgust. He deserved to die. He was unworthy to be called warrior.

His horse flung his head back as if in agreement and Baying Wolf snorted. "I do not need you to agree with everything I *think*, my friend," he grumbled and the horse whinnied. "I guess we better return home," he said quietly. As if in response to his master's command, the horse started forward. "Have we been so long away that you do not remember how to return, my friend?" Baying Wolf asked when the horse continued on the way they'd been heading. "Perhaps you did not understand. Our journey is complete. I have failed the Great Spirit, the white woman, my uncle, and my people." He shuddered again in disgust. Saying it aloud was a painful blow to his pride. The horse whinnied loudly, bobbing his head.

"Nor do you need to agree with everything I *say*," Baying Wolf berated. "Now, let us return home." The horse whinnied, but didn't turn. "It seems I am not the only one with a stubborn, disobedient spirit, hmm? So what is it? Do you wish me to look upon the white woman's dead body so that my failure is more painful?"

As they topped the small rise, the horse halted and Baying Wolf surveyed the slaughter below. It was nothing new to his eyes, but such waste always caused his heart to rage. His people also caused this kind of devastation, and though he wanted no part of the white man in his world, he preferred that they just go back to where they belonged—peaceably; however, he was a man of intelligence and knew that many more whites would come, and many more whites would die. As would many of his own people.

Down there, right now however, was the white woman of his dreams and he needed to find her. Perhaps he could apologize to her for his failure. Maybe that would ease his mind a bit. He nudged his horse forward, and then halted abruptly. Rubbing his eyes, he focused on the vision before him. Stunned in disbelief.

"You are smart—for a horse," he murmured and the horse whinnied.

CHAPTER 45

Christina's resolve to stay determined and strong threatened to flee as she approached the burnt remains of her family's schooner. She climbed inside carefully, eyeing the frame warily. It could fall apart at any moment, but she needed to see if her weapons were still among her things or if the Indians had looted her precious stash.

The tarp, or what remained, lay atop most of their belongings. She lifted the heavy, gray mass and heaved it aside, sighing when her efforts revealed her trunk. The fire blackened its surface, but it didn't look as if anyone had been tampering with it, giving renewed hope that she would find her weapons safely ensconced beneath her clothing.

The relief was short-lived. Her clothes lay disarrayed. Evidence that someone had rummaged hastily through her things. She slung her clothing aside, searching, but to no avail. Her weapons were gone.

Improper language bounded through her brain, and she slammed closed the lid, and then plopped down on top with a heavy sigh. The light reflected off the surface of her mother's mirror and she started as the rays momentarily blinded her. She picked the mirror up to study her face, but decided against it. She wasn't ready to see her reflection yet, to see the damage that Jeffrey had caused to its fragile structure.

She formed a pouch using one of her blouses, laid the mirror and matching brush in it and a change of clothes, then began sifting through the remains of her family's belonging to see what else she could salvage that would be of use to her on her journey. Some of the things she picked up held sentimental value, but she put them aside with a sad heart. She didn't know how far she needed to go to reach civilization; however, she did know that she had to walk to get there, so she needed to take only those things essential to her survival—like food.

She jumped down from the schooner and made her way

toward the Conestoga, praying with each step that the Indians hadn't left her completely without sustenance. As she approached, she could see that the tarp, undermined by the fire, had fallen on the supplies. It was also obvious, the closer she got, that most of those supplies had alighted from the flaming tarp and would no longer be edible. Still, she had to make certain. Her belly rumbled in agreement and reminded her that she hadn't partaken of any food since early yesterday.

Placing her tiny bundle on the ground, she heaved herself onto the much larger wagon, grumbling. She tumbled inside, her skirt raveling around her legs. She struggled with the heavy fabric for a moment, finally disentangling herself with a mighty tug. As she'd feared, the fire scorched nearly all the sacks and ruined the contents. "Bloody savages! If you can't kill me with arrows, you'll do it by starvation, is that it? Well, I'm not going to let you!" She said. Decision made, she jumped from the back of her wagon and lifted her makeshift bag. She moved to another wagon that didn't look in too bad of shape and reluctantly climbed aboard.

A daguerreotype of the Hamilton family stared at her from its broken frame on the floorboards and she shuddered. She quickly looked away, shaking the feeling of guilt that drifted over her for intruding. "I'm sorry," she whispered, "but I hope you'll understand. I'm not really stealing. It's a matter of necessity now."

She took the daguerreotype and slid it in her pocket. She hadn't really known this family well, but since she was collecting reminders of what had happened, at least this was one reminder that wouldn't fade with time, or wash away with water.

Your determination to remember this day is a little on the spooky side, her mind said.

"Yeah, well, you better not try to forget either."

How can you go on with your life if you don't put the past behind you?"

"The past is already behind me," Christina said sarcastically, "but I don't have to wipe the memories from my mind. Not yet, anyway."

Does that mean you'll let me forget eventually?

"Eventually." Christina knelt and started to sift through the charred remains of the Hamilton's belongings.

It's amazing, she thought, *the many things that can be discovered about a person, just by sifting through belongings: a bottle of Jack Daniels hiding in the trousers of Mr. Hamilton's chest. Another in the pocket of his wife's dress. Hmm. Interesting.*

She added that to her small stash, and then jumped from the wagon. There hadn't been any food there, either. Her next stop brought her to the Alston's wagon. Hopefully, she would find some edible food stores soon for her mind was objecting fiercely at intruding in dead people's effects and her stomach kept reminding her, painfully, that she hadn't eaten in many hours. With this stop, she hit pay dirt, for the Alston's had stored their food supplies in a chest rather than burlap sacks.

Apparently, the Indians had tired of opening trunks to find clothing and had stopped looking through them. Otherwise, she was certain that they would have looted this trunk. Either that or they decided it would be too difficult to haul a trunk out of here on horseback. Her mouth watered at the sight before her: bacon (smelled as if it was going rancid, though), beans (didn't have the means to cook those), rice (same as the beans), apples and carrots! Wow! Fresh fruit and vegetables. Okay, maybe not *that* fresh, but definitely edible, and she definitely intended to eat them.

Her mouth watered as she reached in and plucked two of the juicy red fruit and a carrot from the bottom of the chest. She plopped on another chest and ate her precious find, moaning with pleasure. She had the urge to polish off the whole lot, but common sense prevailed. After all, eating everything in sight would be foolish. She needed to have something to take with her.

She picked up the remaining apples, and the carrots, transferring them to her makeshift carrier. The few precious items wouldn't hold her for very long, but at least it was something and perhaps she'd find help before she ran out of supplies. Or she may get lucky and find some more food stores stashed in the other wagons.

Her luck didn't hold however, as a search of the remaining wagons turned up no more undamaged food stores. As with her own wagon, the fire had burned the food supplies beyond use and the few personal belongings that had survived the torching were of no practical use. She had found a revolver and some bullets in one wagon that they had overlooked. That was a fortuitous find and she'd guiltlessly loaded it, and shoved it in her skirt pocket.

The search completed, she now stood on the edge of camp. She looked about her in incertitude. Earlier her determination has been strong, but that was a determination to survive, but how was she supposed to do that? She'd filled her belly, which was a start, but now what? Her initial thought was to head to her Uncle Peter's in Texas, but now she didn't know exactly how she was supposed to go about that. Distance and direction made her pause.

Perhaps we should continue heading in the direction that the wagons were going. We're bound to run into some sort of civilization eventually, don't you think? Surely, someone would come to your aid.

"I suppose so," she responded, a little tentative.

Well, we certainly can't remain here. I mean no disrespect, but I don't want to stay around all of these dead people.

"Ah, so that's where your sudden bravery extends. I should have known. Very well, we'll go." She quickly mapped out a strategy in her head, figuring that if she stayed close to the river, perhaps she might come upon a settlement. If not, at least she knew that eventually she would run across some sort of town. All she needed now was the nerve to head out on her own. She took a deep breath and drew upon her every ounce of courage. If she were going to make this perilous journey, she would need all the bravery she could muster. She turned in a circle one last time, making certain that she wasn't forgetting anything, knowing deep down she was merely stalling.

Her eyes widened, her heart sank, and her resolve fled.

Oh, no! Her mind cried as she stared in dread at the mounted warrior on the hill. The urge to run and flee was strong, but she knew that she wouldn't get far. So she stood frozen, hoping beyond reason that the warrior would ignore her and go about his business.

She fingered the revolver in her pocket and felt tempted to go ahead and shoot. As nervous and tired as she was however, her aim was bound to be inexact; expending all of her bullets before she met her mark. Of course, if she missed, she still had her throwing stars, but he'd have to be a lot closer than he was for those to make a difference.

He spurred his horse and moved toward her slowly. Without a second thought, she pulled the revolver from her pocket and took aim at his chest.

CHAPTER 46

"Why do you pull a weapon on me and not use it? Cowards should not carry guns!" Baying Wolf shouted at her when he'd closed the distance to within shooting range. He was taking a chance at moving this close, but he was hoping that she would recognize him from her dream. To do that, he needed to be close enough for her to see his face.

He quickly looked her over, trying to decide if she was the white woman the Great Spirit sent him to help. It was hard to determine through the bruises and the swelling. Someone had beaten her; battered her face, making it difficult to decide if she was the one.

If it weren't for the red hair, he would turn around and ride away, for that was the only evidence that she was possibly the woman he sought. Of course, taunting her about the revolver wasn't the wisest course of action. Still, it irked him that she would threaten him before even knowing his intention. When it looked like she was only going to stand there brandishing the weapon in his face, he slowly dismounted and moved to the front of his horse. Now less than ten feet separated the two unlikely combatants.

"Are you going to shoot me?" He asked again, raising his arms out by his side, increasing the size of the target.

"I wouldn't be so cocky, Indian." Christina finally snapped from her shock and raised the point of the revolver a notch higher, aiming it at the center of his forehead. "I do know how to use this and will if you don't mount up and ride away, at once!"

"If you wish to shoot me, go ahead! I'm not stopping you!"

Christina started at that. Her intention was not to kill anyone in cold blood; had rather hoped that the sight of the weapon would be enough of a threat to make him leave. Of course, as angry as she was, his invitation was more than appealing. Still, she had a hard time justifying killing anyone without cause. Maybe if he attacked her—no! She certainly didn't want that.

"Well, shoot me."

Christina lowered the revolver and sighed, "I can't. I'm not a murdering heathen like your people; however, that doesn't mean that I'm incapable, so if you want to keep your face intact you might want to mount that horse of yours and go back from where you came."

"I say the same to you," Baying Wolf said, crossing his arms defiantly across his chest. "Go back where you came from, white woman."

"Listen, you ignorant clod head," Christina snapped insensibly, "I've just had a horrible morning coming off a worse night; I buried my mother, buried my dear friend and her son, had to say goodbye to my entire family and all of my friends; so I don't have a home to go back to. And if I did have anyone left to go home to, which I don't, I'd still have to find a way to get there. And how is it that you speak English so well anyway?"

Baying Wolf tried to sort out all that she'd said, but finally gave up trying. He got the gist of it. She was scared. Her courage impressed him, but he refused to allow her to see it. Apparently, she had yet to recognize him. She was still too distraught over her recent loss to realize that he was not a threat to her. And that distress would make it difficult for her to see. He would wait until reason returned to enlighten her, when she was more receptive.

"You came that way, so go back that way," Baying Wolf instructed, pointing a finger to the East. "You will find someone who will help you before long, but you cannot keep going west. You do not belong here."

Christina didn't miss that he'd ignored her question, nor the fact that he was pointing toward the East. "Exactly how do you know where I'm from?" She asked in a suspicious tone.

He sighed and lowered his head, "I have been following you," he said softly.

Christina's eyes widened at that and she took an involuntary step back, lifting the revolver again, "I'm not going to let you hurt me," she said through clenched teeth.

Baying Wolf's head snapped up at the tone of her voice and grimaced when he saw the sight of the revolver pointed at his head again. This time however, her finger was firmly on the trigger and it would take only a small amount of pressure to put a giant hole in his skull. "I do not wish to hurt you," he said gently. "You have already been hurt enough, have you not?"

Christina fell silent, staring at him incredulously. Then it dawned on her that he was referring to her face. She lifted a hand instinctively and ran her fingers along her cheek.

"Who has hurt you?"

"It doesn't matter," she said, "he's dead."

Baying Wolf's eyes widened. "By your hand?"

Christina shrugged, not willing to disabuse him of that notion. Perhaps if he thought her capable of committing bodily harm, he would leave her in peace.

"I'm not here to hurt you," he repeated. "I have come to help."

"Help! Your kind murders innocent women and children, and you expect me to believe you want to help me. More like you want to rape and scalp me!"

"I'm not like those who killed your family," Baying Wolf whispered, trying to keep a tight rein on his temper.

"How do I know you weren't with the ones who killed them, and are trying to trick me into trusting you so that you can kill me too? No witnesses left to point a finger at your people. Huh?"

Baying Wolf closed his eyes and counted to ten, his resolve to control his anger faltering. He counted to ten again and tried to remember that she had suffered great trauma and it would not serve him well to frighten her more. "I would hardly be standing here talking to you if I wanted you dead. How is it you can think rationally one minute and sound so irrational the next? Do you wish to die?"

"I do, but I don't." Christina blurted in a whisper that bespoke of tremendous pain. "At least not in the way your people kill."

Baying Wolf winced at that. "Well, it will not be by my hand. You are safe with me. Do you not know who I am?" He said, abandoning his earlier hesitation at revealing his identity. He stepped closer, but stopped when fear shone in her emerald eyes. It took a moment, but the fear dissolved and recognition took its place, widening her eyes considerably. The reaction, when it came, was not what he'd expected.

CHAPTER 47

"You! You, son-of-a-pig!" She yelled, dropped the gun, and launched herself at him. His reaction time was slow and she barreled into him, knocking him flat on his back. She knelt on his chest, pummeling him with her fist. "Why weren't you here? You were supposed to protect me! That's what you said in my dream—that you were going to protect me, but you didn't. You weren't even here, you—you—you". Christina collapsed against his chest and began crying again. After a moment, it dawned on her just what she was doing and that he was doing nothing about it. She froze. She looked into his eyes, expecting to see murderous rage, but instead saw curious wonder.

"Are you finished, white woman?" He asked, mimicking a pained expression.

"Oh, my word!" She whispered. She rolled off his chest and stood with alacrity. "I—I'm—I don't know what came over me. I didn't...I'm so sorry." Christina's face was red beneath the bruises and she was slowly retreating, as if she expected a horrible retribution for her actions.

"Calm yourself," Baying Wolf said. He stood and dusted off. "You did not hurt me, but you are strong for a woman, and I think there may be a dent or two in my chest now."

Christina eyed him warily. It sounded like he was joking with her. It looked like he was joking with her, but why would he be acting this way, unless he *was* joking with her. Perhaps she whacked him harder than she intended.

"Are you feeling okay?" She asked cautiously.

"I'm not hurt. I understand that you are tired, scared, and therefore not thinking well. If I did not know this, then I might be angry, but I'm not. I'm happy that you are unhurt. That means that I have not failed the Great Spirit after all. Perhaps it was not this tragedy that I was supposed to protect you from, but from something that is yet to happen. Yes, I'm okay. I have not failed."

"And I thought that I was losing it," Christina whispered to herself, and then his words sank in. "I'm in more danger?" She asked. Her fear returning like a punch to the stomach.

"I do not know this. I only know that the Great Spirit has sent me to take you—I do not know where. I am only to ensure that no harm comes to you."

Instead of seeming pleased by his answer, her emerald eyes darkened, and the part of her face not covered with contusions turned a splotchy red. "What kind of god do you have, anyway?" She said through clenched teeth.

"I do not think I understand what it is you wish me to say?" He replied, confused by the sudden hostility emanating from her.

"What kind of god sends you to protect me—one person—but allows the senseless slaughter of so many others?"

"I'm but one man. Even as great a warrior as I am, I could not have protected anyone against so many. Not even you, the one I'm meant to defend." That gave Christina pause. She knew that sort of helplessness, for she had felt the same, but she would not let the topic go.

"Then why could your god not ask help from more than one man? If he knew that there was danger, why did he send only one man and—where is your wolf, by the way?"

"Around," Baying Wolf said, "but you should not be angry with the Great Spirit. He sent only me because *you* must live. I do not question his reasons for this and neither should you," Baying Wolf said, knowing it was a lie. After all, he had questioned the Great Spirit several times about the importance of a white woman to his people. He still could not understand, but the fact that she had survived a massacre meant that someone, other than himself, was watching over her. "Do you blame your God for allowing you to live and your family to die?"

"No, I don't suppose I do," Christina sighed, "but I feel I have to blame someone. The deaths here were—well, it didn't have to happen. We weren't hurting anyone."

"No, but that is not how some see the intrusion of the white man onto our lands," Baying Wolf said. "If there were fewer of you coming here, killing off our food supply simply for the fur, and leaving the meat to rot in the prairies. If fewer of your men were taking our women to make them slaves or simply for pleasure. If fewer of your people were killing our warriors for trying to defend our hunting grounds and our families—it is something that you probably could not begin to understand."

Hearing it voiced in such a manner, reached deep inside Christina, and she somehow did understand—both sides. "It's senseless no matter the justification," she whispered, "whether it's the white man's reasoning or the Indian's. It doesn't justify the slaughter of little children and women. Men shouldn't drag us into their battles, but they do, and we suffer for it. They rape us, kill us, or leave us childless or widowed. But I do understand, unfortunately better than I want to right now."

Baying Wolf listened to her in wonder. He had often felt and thought the same way. She was unique—for a woman, for a white eyes—and intelligent. More than any woman, or most men, than he had ever met. She had suffered so much, yet she was willing to understand his people; she was not allowing anger to cloud her thinking and to blame him for the actions of others. At least, not at this moment.

He suddenly felt small, for he often allowed his anger to cloud his thinking and yet he had not suffered nearly as much in his many years of living as she had done in just the past couple of days. "I cannot tell you why this happened," he said, "but there must have been a reason or it would not have happened, just as you have lived for a reason. You may not feel that the reasons are justified, but when something bad happens, it is best to learn from it and then put it behind you. That does not mean to forget, but perhaps it will make you a better person."

Christina narrowed her gaze and looked at the man standing in front of her. She wanted to believe that he was only trying to help; however, she wanted to shout 'try having your family massacred and see how quickly you forgive and forget'. Something inside wouldn't let her.

Just standing here talking to him had lessened the pain in her heart and she wondered, not for the first time, who this man was and what he meant to her future. She was very certain that someone somehow connected him to her, for her dream gave her that sense, but that didn't mean she was going to entrust him with her future easily. Maybe one day, but not soon. He was a savage, no matter who'd sent him, and savages were not currently on top of her list of those to trust.

"What do I do now?" She asked, leaving his attempted solace unchallenged.

"We will travel together. I will take you where you need to go. I will protect you."

Something in his tone made Christina pause. She smiled wryly. "So, tell me something. Do you actually want to be here?"

The question startled Baying Wolf. *Can she really read me so easily?* He wondered. "Leaving my home to come here was not easy," he admitted reluctantly.

"To help a white woman," Christina finished for him, smiling at the irony of their situation.

"To help a white woman, yes, that is right. I was very angry that the Great Spirit would send me to help one of my enemy, but after meeting you, I can see there is something about you. Something that I cannot explain," he finished lamely, not willing to credit her with too much too soon.

"Do you think it makes me feel great that my enemy is here to help me?" She asked conversationally. "Perhaps, since neither of us wishes the other's company, we should just part ways. You go home and I'll go where I need to go."

"I cannot do this, for the Great Spirit has sent me to see to your safety..."

"Which we both know is a moot point, because my safety is no longer at issue. The massacre is done and I'm alive," Christina said, unable to control the bitterness that crept into her tone.

"I will not leave you alone again. It is my duty to go with you. I will not shame myself by failing a second time. Besides, a woman alone would not last a day here," Baying Wolf declared passionately.

"And if I refuse to accompany you?" Christina challenged. "After all, no matter if I believe you were not involved with those who killed my family, the point still stands that you are my enemy..." Christina stopped speaking, suddenly thoughtful.

"And?"

"What?"

"You were speaking," Baying Wolf said, "but you have not finished what you were going to say."

"Oh! I will go with you."

"You speak in a very confusing way. First, you say you will not accompany me and then you say you will."

"I just remembered that a dear friend of mine once told me that I should keep my friends close and my enemies closer. And since I haven't a clue about how to get to Texas on my own or how to survive in the wild alone, what better way is there to keep you close and get where I need to go also. Might as well take advantage of the situation. After all, you will follow me anyway, won't you?"

"This is so."

"Well, I suppose we should be on our way then," Christina turned and retrieved the revolver where she'd dropped it earlier. She put the weapon in her pocket and picked up her small bundle, throwing it over her shoulder, and then started walking. She didn't wait to see what the Indian would do, nor did she doubt for a minute that he would let her out of his sight. That thought was both comforting and unnerving.

In her heart, she knew that this man, this heathen, would not harm her, but for some reason his nearness bothered her a great deal. It was something she didn't readily comprehend, but did wonder whether the tenseness she felt over his nearness derived from his maleness. And he was definitely all male.

One thing that disturbed her was traveling alone with only a man as chaperone. An Indian male at that. If anyone discovered them together, it would shatter her reputation. Something nudged her firmly from behind, nearly knocking her flat on her face, which jarred her from her musings. She turned, ready to berate the Indian, but instead encountered two large nostrils, which snorted loudly in her face.

"Don't you think it best to ride?" Baying Wolf asked, a grin spreading on his deeply tanned face. "Enemies or not, it will take much longer for us to part ways if you walk all of the way to your destination."

Christina blushed and patted the horse on the nose. She wanted to refuse, but common sense prevailed. Walking would be impractical when she could easily ride, but being so close to this savage wasn't exactly appealing either. She nearly changed her mind when he reached down and hauled her up behind him. She had to wrap her arms around his waist to stay on the horse's rump, which brought back her earlier observation. He was definitely all male, and he most certainly had more of an effect on her senses than Jeffrey ever did. A shiver raced down her spine. *Why couldn't you have been horrid to look at and less appealing to touch?* She wondered in irritation.

"Cold?"

"No!" Christina snapped, determined to control her body's reaction to his body from here on out.

CHAPTER 48

"If we must speak," Baying Wolf said immediately after spurring his horse away from her camp, "then we must do so in a way that is not hurtful to the other. After all, this is going to be a very long journey and offensive words will only make it unbearable. Agreed?"

Christina had agreed, but now, several hours later, neither of them had spoken a single word to the other. Afraid of offending, but more so, still feeling threatened by the other's race. As the silence stretched, the tension mounted, and Christina began to wonder what would be worse, never speaking at all, or guarding every word spoken.

She was about to ask his opinion on the matter, if for no other reason than to hear his voice, when he pulled the horse to a stop and quickly dismounted. It was still hours before nightfall, but already Christina could hear the sound of crickets in the nearby brush. She sighed, a feeling of peace settling over her. She breathed in the warm evening air and closed her eyes for a moment, experiencing the essence of nature. The feeling of belonging returned and she smiled.

"White woman seems happy to be here," Baying Wolf said softly. He watched as tranquility wrapped itself around her and was hesitant to intrude on her inner peace, but he needed to hunt before night fell. Christina didn't respond to his observation, merely sighed.

Forgetting how long they'd ridden, and how long it had been since she'd sat a horse for so long a stretch, she threw her leg over the saddle and slid from the horse's back. Her legs gave way at once and she found herself in Baying Wolf's embrace.

Christina gasped as he pulled her closer, knowing that it was because of her traitorous legs that he was holding her so, not out of desire—or so she preferred to believe. Of course, the gleam in his eyes said quite the opposite, causing the blush in her cheeks to intensify. Adding fuel to the fire, he was not in any hurry to release her, nor did her legs seem to be in any hurry to recuperate.

Christina didn't see how the situation could degrade further, and then he opened his mouth. "White woman not used to riding astride, perhaps Baying Wolf teach," he chuckled. Those were the very words her legs needed to function again. Instantly, she felt a tingle start down her thigh and spread through her calf. Finally settling into her toes. With a shove against his chest, she stumbled away, her nose lifting in an indignant air.

"Just remember that I have a weapon, before you start getting any ideas," Christina retorted. "Is this a good place to stop to hunt?" She asked, deftly changing the subject.

"White woman hungry already?" He asked, teasingly.

"Famished, if you must know," she replied. "I haven't eaten much of anything since yesterday morning."

Baying Wolf smiled shortly, and then turned to retrieve his bow and arrow from the sling hanging across his horse's back. "That is why I stopped," he said, "because your stomach's talking too loud to enjoy the trip."

"You are just full of humor, aren't you?" Christina snapped. "All of it at my expense."

Baying Wolf looked around, "And who else would I tease? There is no one else here?"

"Oh, do hush!"

Baying Wolf laughed, and then turned to leave. Christina realized his intention and made to follow him.

"Where are you going?" He asked over his shoulder.

"With you," Christina replied, moving to stand next to him. "I'm going to hunt for my supper. After all, you are only here as protector, not provider, and it wouldn't be fair of me to make you do for me what I can do for myself."

"Women do not hunt. Men hunt," Baying Wolf said, his tone sounded offended, all trace of humor gone. "If you are able, maybe you can build a fire to cook the food!" Baying Wolf suggested, walking away.

"Touchy, touchy," she murmured, plopping down on a nearby

log. She winced as her tender derriere contacted the hard surface. She lowered her elbows onto her knees and plunked her chin down onto her palms with a sigh. "I may never have hunted before," she huffed, talking to herself, "but that doesn't mean I'm incapable. At least I'd have a better chance of catching a meal than I would to start a fire. I've never started a fire before either, so just how does he expect me to do it. Now, when he gets back, there's not going to be a fire to cook the meat and we're going to end up eating raw food. Yuck!" Christina sighed again.

The women in his village could probably build a fire with their eyes closed. Her mind taunted.

"Oh, without a doubt! Smarty! But I'm not exactly Indian, now am I?"

Well, maybe if you tried, he'll be inclined to help you finish it.

"Well, it's a thought."

She stood and stretched her aching limbs, and then started to forage the surrounding area for whatever sticks she could find. It took a while, but when she was done, she felt a surge of accomplishment and smiled. Her smile vanished however, when Baying Wolf returned from the hunt a short time later and shook his head in dismay.

"You're a useless white woman," he said in a tone that made it difficult for Christina to tell whether he was teasing her again, or not.

"I did the best I could," she grumbled, returning to her seat on the log. "It's not as if my parents raised me outside of civilization, you know. I didn't have the need to build fires every day."

Baying Wolf grinned and bent over the pile she'd collected. He quickly arranged and lit the wood, and soon it roared to life. "Don't you have places for fires in your homes?" He asked.

"Well, yes, but I never actually started one of those either."

"Uh-huh, well, I won't even ask if you can prepare animals for cooking then." He was teasing. Christina sighed. At least his earlier displeasure was gone. She didn't particularly like seeing him glare at her. It scared her silly. Maybe if he weren't a savage, his scowl wouldn't be so intimidating.

"You're right. You'd better not ask."

Baying Wolf laughed, "Well, come here then."

"What for?" Christina asked warily, eyeing the carcasses of two rabbits that Baying Wolf pulled from his satchel.

"So that you can learn to clean and cook," Baying Wolf said as if it were obvious. "After all, I'm doing the hunting, so you can't expect me to do the cooking as well."

"No, no, I don't suppose so." Christina's stomach roiled when Baying Wolf pulled a wicked-looking blade from his legging. "I'll tell you what," she offered, doing her best to keep her bile down, "I'll do the hunting and *you* do the cooking."

"I'd rather eat, now come and I will teach you."

"Very well, but I have to warn you, the sight of blood may make my stomach react in ways which may ruin our food."

"Ah, I see. Well, I will take care of it tonight, but you will have to learn before the trip is over. You claim to be able to hunt, but if you don't have the skills needed to fix the food you catch..."

"I get the idea," Christina whispered, keeping her head averted. She threw her hands over her ears as the sound of the knife whizzed through the air and landed with a thud, severing the head of the first rabbit.

CHAPTER 49

Christina watched as Baying Wolf walked away into the trees a few days later, leaving her again to build a fire for their meal. It had been the first stop since her near encounter with her stomach contents when he'd tried to get her to disembowel a furry little bunny. Since that evening, they'd subsisted on the small stash of food she'd discovered in the wagons before they'd left on the sojourn, some berries, and edible plants that Baying Wolf collected along the way. Her horde was now gone and the further they moved toward the plains, the fewer pickings there were to choose from.

Baying Wolf had finally called a halt and insisted that he go hunting before his stomach shrank into nonexistence. She'd agreed, reluctantly, since she knew it meant he'd expect her to take care of things she was incapable of taking care of, like building fires and dismembering small creatures.

He'd spent the morning instructing her on the proper way to stack the correct-sized sticks for an optimum flame, when all she wanted to do, by the time the lesson was done, was to set his antagonistic tongue on fire.

When he retreated, she stuck her tongue out childishly, and then smiled slyly. Most of the much-needed time of instruction, she'd spent trying to figure out how to avoid the task of skinning poor little dead animals, and she'd finally arrived at an alternative. She'd prove to him that she could catch their meal. Then he could take over the duty of cleaning and cooking *her* catch.

With a quick glance at the area he'd disappeared to, she snatched up the supplies she needed and sprinted the other way. The trees here were thicker, but she was bound to come across something tasty to eat eventually. Hopefully, sooner, and preferably before Baying Wolf returned to camp and discovered her missing. For if he returned to find her gone, he might not be so appreciative of her efforts when she got back.

He was definitely more adept at this hunting thing, but she did know how to use her weapons even if she'd never actually brought down a moving animal with them. A moving man, yes. Animal, no.

"Okay, let's see what there is to eat around here," she said to herself, glancing about the area. After more than an hour, she started to wonder whether if anything actually lived on this side of the woods, or if they all inhabited Baying Wolf's side.

A movement off to her right startled her, and she ducked quickly behind a tree. A moment later, she took a quick peek and her heart stopped beating.

"Oh, my! You fellas are even more beautiful up close," she murmured softly to a deer that was moving toward her, unaware as yet of her presence. She reached as quietly as she could into her skirt pocket to retrieve her knife. It was then that the deer chose to look up and pin her with its mournful gaze.

"I can't do it!" She exclaimed in a whisper. "I can't hurt something so gorgeous."

Well, it's either kill them or skin them. You're not going to be able to get out of one without accomplishing the other, her mind said.

"Thanks for the reminder, but there has to be something around here that I wouldn't mind stabbing to death or hacking to pieces."

I'm sure there is, but would it necessarily be something you'd want to consume.

"I'll tell you what. Don't help me, okay?"

You'd be lost without me. Come to think of it, you are lost with *me! Do you happen to know where we are?*

Christina took a glance around, but could only see trees. "No, I don't, but I'm sure we couldn't have wandered that far from the campsite, right?"

Yeah, right.

CHAPTER 50

Deciding how late the day was getting through the thick canopy overhead was hard. All Christina was certain of, was that it was endlessly dark and that she had been traveling a good while. She was growing more thirsty, tired, and hungry with each step. She'd tripped over so many roots, been slapped in the face by so many limbs, that she feared what her already damaged face might look like now after the added abuse.

She stumbled over yet another root and fell on her hands and knees. She stayed there and hung her head down, fighting back the tears that threatened to fall. Now she could add bruised shins to her list of growing injuries. She plopped onto her rear and wiped a dirty hand across an even dirtier face, listening to the loud grumbling in her stomach.

"My goodness," she groaned, talking to her belly, "you sure are in a disagreeable mood. It's not like you're the only one hopelessly lost, or incredibly stupid and equally scared for that matter." When the grumbling persisted, she tilted her head wonderingly. Her stomach may be protesting loudly, but not that consistently, she was sure. What she was hearing was something in the near distance.

She stood quickly and fell back on her derriere as a sudden bout of dizziness struck her. "I'm going to have to find food soon." She stood more slowly and began making her way toward the ever-increasing noise. As she neared it, her smile widened. She recognized that sound. It was running water.

That meant something to drink and possibly something to eat that she didn't have to kill. Lifting the hem of her skirt, she began running through the woods. The limbs attacking her face and arms were now a small nuisance in her quest to reach the source of the watery sound in all haste. Her smile turned into near-hysterical laughter as a breathtaking waterfall came into view.

Without bothering to remove her clothing, she dove into the crystal pond at the base of the falls and instantly began to sink as the dress rapidly absorbed the water. It felt as if Hyacinth had jumped in behind her and landed squarely on her shoulders, driving her rapidly to the sandy bottom below.

With growing panic, she ripped at the buttons of her skirt, praying with dwindling breath that they would come free before she suffocated and drowned. Someone heard her prayer, and the buttons freed from their holes one at a time, until her skirt fell away. She kicked her feet hard, the edges of her vision dimming rapidly. The black murkiness faded as she swam higher and the water around her turned a bright turquoise suggesting that the surface was nearing.

With her final breath, she broke above the water and gasped. She tried to take in air, but it was too much of an effort. She flipped on her back and lay there, filling her lungs slowly with shallow breaths.

You know, you're going to have to swim back down and haul your skirt...

"Not another word. I'm well aware that I can't prance about half dressed, but if you don't mind, I'd like to catch my breath before swimming down and losing it a second time."

Fifteen minutes later, after another harrowing dive to the bottom of the lake, Christina pulled herself onto shore, dragging her waterlogged skirt behind her. Again, gasping for breath.

"Next time I leap before I look," she huffed, "do me a favor, and actually speak up a little faster. That way I don't try to kill myself so enthusiastically." Her brain protested acceptance of blame, but she barely heard it over the rumbling in her stomach. The stars swimming around her periphery reminded her that she had to find food—and soon.

Standing slowly and carefully, she walked around the lake, searching for anything that would provide sustenance. She spotted a small bush covered with plump looking berries partway around the pond, but hesitated as she knelt before it, wondering whether they would curb her hunger or end her life.

"If I don't eat, I'll die of starvation," she debated aloud; "however, if I eat something like this without being familiar with it, it could very well kill me," she reasoned further. "I suppose I could try to wait to find something else," she continued, struggling with her indecision. "If there is anything else." She tapped her chin, thinking, but the continued grumble issuing from her tummy interrupted her thoughts.

Oh well, her mind interjected with its usual annoyance, *at the rate you're going, you'll likely die out here anyway, so you might as well silence that racket down below. It's giving me a headache.*

"Do hush! *You* are a headache." Forming a pocket out of the hem of her skirt, Christina picked as many berries as she could, and then carried them to the water's edge for cleaning. She ate leisurely, groaning her pleasure with each juicy bite. When she'd quieted her stomach, she lay back, pillowing her head with her hands and stared up at the star-filled sky.

"Perhaps I can find a place to live on my own around here," she dreamed aloud. "It's too bad women can't own land in their own name. I'd build a little house in that small little clearing on the other side."

You don't know how to build anything, her mind teased.

"I know that," she retorted, "but I can dream, can't I?" Her mind drifted to Baying Wolf and she winced as she imagined his expression when he returned and found her missing. Especially since she apparently wouldn't be returning to camp until sometime tomorrow.

"It's a good thing I won't be there to see it. He's probably going to be furious. Of course, he may just be relieved that he doesn't have to watch over me any longer." She stopped her one-sided conversation as something splashed in the water near her feet. Thankful that the full moon provided some light, she peered into the growing darkness toward where the sound emanated.

"Good heavens!" She squealed, her hand flying to her chest as if trying to keep her heart from coming out, as the source of the noise jumped high into the air, flipped its tail and returned to the water with a splash. Christina emitted a nervous laugh when she realized how silly she was behaving. "Just a fish, for heaven's sake," she laughed and lay back down. "Well, Mr. Fish, maybe you and I can arrange to have breakfast together tomorrow morning. Then I'm going to have to try to find my way back to Baying Wolf. I wonder how that reunion's going to go."

CHAPTER 51

It had taken longer than anticipated for Baying Wolf to snare lunch, but he was grateful for the time to be alone to think. The woman in camp was a disturbing enigma. She made him laugh with her innocent ways, but it bothered him that she remained guarded around him. He could still see the uncertainty in her eyes in an unguarded moment when their gazes met. It was not so much fear, but wariness. He just didn't know why it should bother him so much.

He had already told her that he meant her no harm, had proven that over the past days in her company, but still she was cautious. To make matters worse, she was completely helpless. Could not even build a fire or skin a rabbit? How she had thought to strike out on her own was laughable? Still, she had courage. He had to give her that. Most white women of his acquaintance would never have attempted to leave the sanctuary of the wagon train, even with dead bodies decaying all around them. They would sit and wait, hoping that help found them in time. Still, this one was determined to search for help—did not wait for it to come to her.

At least he was here now to keep her safe, not that she saw him as a guardian angel. It was like watching a newly captured colt—eye reflecting unease and nervousness, ready to bolt at the slightest chance or provocation. Still, to her credit, she stayed.

If only he could convince her that his intentions were to help her, not bring her harm. Of course, he knew that was going to be hard to do after what happened to her family. It still surprised him that she didn't shoot him when he first met her. Obviously, she considered him her enemy and felt the need to watch him carefully, but fortunately not eliminate him.

If it had been the other way around, he wouldn't have hesitated to shoot. No, she was definitely unique, and he wondered, not for the first time, if that uniqueness was what the Great Spirit saw in her. Well, she was with him now, and he would see her safe to wherever her destination was.

Baying Wolf retrieved the rabbits and headed back to camp. He was determined to continue treating the woman gently until he broke through the invisible barrier that she had around herself. When he came through the trees and could not find her however, his good intentions fled and his anger flared. Fear over her safety and failing the Great Spirit again foremost in his mind.

"Foolish white woman. When will you trust me?" He shouted to the emptiness surrounding him. The eagle screeched loudly from atop a nearby tree, and Baying Wolf's anger increased.

"I know I have to find her! So why don't you show me where to look? That way I can turn her over my knee and beat sense into that empty head of hers. At least then, she will have good reason to fear me!" As if understanding the command, the eagle rose from his perch and soared off into the distance.

CHAPTER 52

Christina stretched her aching limbs and yawned widely. For the first time in her life, she'd slept alone, in middle of nowhere, and it empowered her and lifted her spirits. Unfortunately, her body was not joining in the celebrations. She yawned again, and stretched, twisting her back and bending her knees in an attempt to work the kinks out of her tired muscles. When she felt certain that her muscles would survive, she lay back and looked at the sun that had started to rise, low on the horizon.

"Hello, Mr. Sun," she greeted warmly, "welcome to my world. It's truly lovely isn't it?" She laughed at her own silliness and then rolled onto her belly, plucked a piece of grass and nibbled thoughtfully. Why she felt so happy this morning, she could only hazard a guess. Could be because she'd manage to survive a night on her own in the wilderness, or simply that she'd finally slept soundly for the first time in months, since the dream was gone.

The nightmares of a white beast and a wolf had disappeared. Her night had been dreamless. She now knew without a doubt what she'd guessed at before. Her dreams were visions and it had been trying to warn her about Jeffrey. Since Jeffrey was now dead, she no longer needed the wolf or his Indian companion's help, which meant that she really didn't need him to finish this journey.

After all, if she were still in any danger, wouldn't she have dreamed it? Started a new vision last night? She shuddered at the thought, but felt uplifted by it as well. She didn't need the Indian any more. She was free to go on her way. So, if she could just find a way to catch, kill, and cook her own food this morning, then she could do just that, and with the confidence that she wouldn't starve before reaching an outpost or her Uncle Peter's home in Texas.

Her heart still ached for those that she'd lost, but at least she knew they would be looking down from heaven with a smile; and when she finally caught her first meal, Chin Woo would undoubtedly laugh with glee. Her stomach rumbled and she giggled.

"Well, I'd best be about proving myself, to my stomach, at least." She stood up and slapped the earth from her skirt, laughing at the futility of the gesture, and then made her way back to the berry bush. She ate a small breakfast and then turned to kneel in front of the lake. "Now let's see about having breakfast with that fish I met last night, and since my *former* companion was kind enough to teach me how to start a fire, I may even get to eat it cooked."

After half hour of slapping at uncooperative fish, she sat back on her heels and decided she might better try another tactic or she may not be eating anything but berries today. She wriggled her bare toes in the water while her mind formulated a plan, but jerked when one of the fish took a nip at one of the wiggling appendages.

"Hey!" She cried, pulling her toes back onto the bank. "Hey, wait a minute!" She rolled back onto her belly and lowered her fingers into the water, wriggling them as she'd done her toes a moment earlier. After waiting only a moment or two, a fish surfaced and took a nip at her pinky. Christina fought the urge to wrench her hand from the water and waited patiently for the fish to return. When it did, she'd be waiting.

Her concentration on the fish was so intense that she didn't readily hear the footsteps approaching until it were too late to hide. A twig snapped directly behind her and Christina pushed herself upright, spinning on her heel.

CHAPTER 53

"Well, well, well," exclaimed an intimidating voice from an equally intimidating-looking man. "What do we have here?" A horrible feeling crept inside Christina's mind as she faced the man directly in front of her. He was very tall, her mind noted. Taller than Jeffrey or her father had been. She craned her neck to look up at him and wished she hadn't.

Hair covered his face like the wild berry bush she'd been nibbling from. Oily dirt clung to the strands matted to his scalp and face, hanging limply over his shoulders. His face was dirty. Distinguishing where the hair lay against it was hard. She wasn't even certain as to his ethnicity. It looked as if he'd never acquainted himself with water. If his appearance wasn't evidence enough of that fact, his smell certainly was.

Of course, she couldn't say all of that much right now. After all, she didn't look any more appealing than he, but at least she was relatively clean; however, it seemed that her lack of hygiene or temporary lack of beauty was not a deterrent to him, for he continued to peruse her with lust emanating from his hazel eyes.

Her breath caught in her throat as two more men appeared from the trees. She wondered if they were relations of the first as all were extremely tall, none had bathed recently, and all were unidentifiable regarding their race; however, that wasn't where the similarity ended. Each man was staring at her in a way that made her wonder whether a woman fell into the same category as water: never acquainted with.

If they had, the woman was either a more frightful creature than she was or their taste was not at all discriminating. Of course, Jeffrey had eyed her with the same look, even after he'd beaten bruises on her face, so this must be the way that all snakes look at their intended victims before striking. Her thoughts shifted inadvertently to her former traveling companion, but the emphasis on 'former' no longer held the appeal it did when she'd awakened this morning.

He had never looked at her in a way that would make her feel uncomfortable. Of course, that could simply be because he was more selective: women with contused countenances not among his preferences. Suddenly she wished that she'd stayed with the Indian, for she didn't have a doubt that he could dispatch these three in a second.

However, he was not here, and all she had to defend herself with was her knife and throwing stars. Looking at the massive amount of hair and clothing on their bodies however, made her uncertain as to the weapons' penetrating ability. Still she had no choice but to try, but if she pulled any of her weapons now, they'd jump her in a second. Somehow, she had to distract them, get them to back away, and separate them. The outlook of her situation was not looking very encouraging.

An idea formed, but she rejected it. It formed again, and she stubbornly shoved it back.

Excuse me!

"Not now!" She snapped.

"Oh, I don't know about that, luv. Now sounds daggum good to me," one of the men said.

I'm trying to give you an idea, so would you mind not shoving it away every time it's presented, if you please?"

The idea popped back into the forefront of her mind and she laughed in derision. "You must be joking," she said under her breath.

You won't be laughing when they take hold of you in about thirty seconds, and since I didn't see anything in here to suggest you had an idea, you could at least give mine a shot.

Christina's eyes widened. Her mind was right. They were closing ranks. Apparently, they were through sizing her up and undressing her with their eyes. Now they wanted to see the wares up close and personal. She smiled shyly, and clasped her hands demurely in front of her skirt, feeling exceptionally foolish. But she probably could not accomplish anything if they became wary of her.

If they did not see her as a threat, perhaps they would be less inclined to assault her.

When the closest one smiled widely at her antics, she could see that his teeth were rotting—what teeth he had. Her smile nearly faltered then, but she kept it bravely in place. When his breath, rank and foul smelling, reached her nostrils however, her lips drooped shortly and she felt as if she would swoon. They didn't seem to notice her reaction, so she quickly replaced the smile, her cheeks hurting in an attempt to hold it in place.

"So what's a purdy little thing like you doing out here in the middle of nowhere," the second man asked. Christina hardly would have categorized herself as pretty at the moment, with her knotted, tangled hair and scratched-up, bruised face, but the wooly mammoth's comment only served to prove his lack of discriminatory taste. "In need of some help?" He asked, lowering his travois full of pelts. "We like helpin' women in need." He cackled at his own wit, showing that he too was missing most of his teeth, the rest simply awaiting a strong breeze to fall free. Christina watched warily as they continued closing in on her slowly. They seemed to sense that if they moved too quickly, she would startle and run like a deer. Not that she had anywhere to run to, she realized, when her back bumped up against a nearby tree. Water on one side, a tree to her rear, and three hairy mammoths blocking the only escape path. Not encouraging. Time to divide and conquer.

"I was separated from my traveling companions," she stated in what she hoped was her most puritanical voice, attempting to sound harmlessly innocent. She was also trying desperately not to gag as their foul stench threatened to suffocate her. If she could only convince them that she was truly a lady, perhaps she could persuade them to help her, instead of attack her virtue. Forget the fact that a lady wouldn't be caught dead in the wilderness alone without a chaperone, or that these men had left all manner of civilization behind a long time ago and wouldn't hesitate to fill their needs on anything in a skirt. Of course, if playing the helpless virgin didn't appeal to their sense of chivalry, she could always play to their greed and offer them some sort of reward.

That's it! She thought with inward glee. "I'm certain," she continued, hoping that the trembling in her voice wasn't too apparent, "that if you *gentlemen* were to guide me to the nearest fort or outpost, or some sort of civilization, the reward would be most handsome."

"Well, now," the apparent leader grinned, "we might jes' be willing to help you out thar little lady," he said and Christina sighed. But when he next spoke, Christina's relief turned to terror, "'course, the reward we would be wanting," he paused for effect, letting his gaze rove greedily over her disheveled appearance, "is you—payable in advance."

Christina's knees nearly buckled and the color drained from her face, but she praised herself inwardly for not cowering in the face of their sheer depravity. She leaned against the tree slightly in what she hoped was a nonchalant manner, drawing support from its massive strength.

Time to go back to plan A. Distract and separate.

"Well, I obviously can't satisfy all of you fellas at once," she bluffed, deliberately emphasizing her southern accent. "So why don't you big boys just stand over there," she said, pointing a good distance away, "and I'll slip out of these here clothes and we can enjoy ourselves some leisurely pleasure. That is, if you fellas don't mind waiting a short spell. After all, it will take a while to remove all the layers, so you might as well enjoy a good show."

"Ladies don't offer themselves up on a platter like that missus," one of the men said with suspicion, glancing over his shoulder as if expecting an ambush, "so either you ain't what you seem, or you ain't alone." He finished his statement with a quick draw of a long-bladed knife from a sheath on his waist. His companions quickly followed suit. "So, which is it?" He asked, pointing the tip of the blade toward her neck.

Christina took a huge gulp of air, forcing it past the large lump in her throat. "You're right," she improvised quickly, "I'm not a lady, but I did get separated from my traveling companion. We were on our way to Texas. There's supposed to be a new house opening where my companion was hoping to find us work."

"So then why..."

"The charade? I was just nervous about entertaining so many at once. I'm rather new at this, so if you'll give me a minute, well, allowing me to undress at my leisure might help me to get over my nervousness." Hoops, hollers, and obscene comments followed her suggestion by two of the men and they quickly lowered their gear and began dancing a silly jig around the tree.

The third man; the man who'd questioned her; the one Christina had pegged correctly as the leader, worried her. He stood leaning a little too composed against the opposite tree, watching her through half-closed lids. Fortunately, lust overshadowed caution for him as well; however, he still seemed to be anticipating trouble, and so she decided that he would have to be the first to die.

Although she didn't much like the idea of killing a man, she really had no choice. It was either them or her virtue, and possibly her life. She knelt down as though to unbuckle her nonexistent shoe, letting her hand slip unseen into her skirt pocket. With a fluid motion, she palmed one of her throwing stars and pulled her hand free.

She must not have been as clever as she thought, because the man against the tree pushed away and moved in her direction. The distance wasn't that great, but it seemed to Christina that the man was taking an extremely long time in reaching her. Her own movements, as she stood and aimed the star at the only spot on the man's head that didn't have any hair, seemed heavy and surreal.

She glanced shortly at the two men still dancing around and prayed that their leader would not call out and attract their attention. When the man had closed to within what Christina considered a reasonable, no-way she could possibly miss distance, she grabbed the tip of the blade and flicked her wrist.

Her breath held and she watched in amazement as two of the five tips imbedded deeply into the front of the man's throat. She quickly palmed one more star and threw it, watching as it imbedded a few inches above his right eye. His good eye bulged in astonishment, and he instinctively reached for the weapons, pulling back his hand with a yelp as another of the tips pierced his palm.

Irritated, the man howled and reached again for the throwing star protruding from his eyelid, ignoring the pain as he pulled it free. Christina didn't wait for him to remove the other star, nor did she plan to hang around to find out if they did any permanent damage. She had a break and she intended to use it.

Turning on her heel, she fled in the direction she'd come yesterday, running as if the hounds of hell were on her tail, which in reality they were, for she could hear them behind her, yelling for her to stop—as if their calls would persuade her to cease her flight. She picked up speed, not deterred by the branches or roots. After all, they couldn't very well cause more damage than she'd already sustained.

She ran, praying the entire way for a miracle. Instead, she ran into a tree. She would have landed in an unladylike heap, had the tree not sprouted hands and grasped her firmly by the upper arms.

Baying Wolf stood glaring down at the breathless woman in his clutches. He could tell that she was frightened, and that she'd been fleeing something was obvious. This pleased him very much.

"Men—three –," she gasped breathlessly. His head snapped up and he quickly pushed Christina behind him, as he heard the men rapidly approaching. She collapsed onto her bruised knees and said a quick prayer of thanks. She definitely needed help, she admitted readily, and she couldn't think of a better answer to prayer than the man standing beside her.

He was such an intimidating figure of a man that perhaps the men on her heels would think twice about attacking her when they got a good look at the fierce expression on his face. It didn't matter much to her, right then, that his expression was a direct result of her disappearance. She lifted her chin and arched her head, listening to the rapidly approaching footsteps. From her vantage point, she saw the Indian's bone-carved knife protruding from the top of his leggings and without a second thought, grabbed it.

Baying Wolf shot her a disgruntled glance.

"I lost mine somewhere. Besides, I do know how to use this," she assured him, pushing herself up to stand beside him, her breath, and her composure, rapidly returning. "Just ask the wounded man through those trees."

Baying Wolf smiled at her, and for just a moment her heart missed a beat. *His face is extraordinary when he smiles*, she judged. "You are very foolish, but brave," he murmured appreciatively, and Christina blushed. She didn't have time to dwell on his comment or his handsomeness as just then, the two remaining trappers broke through the trees panting heavily, and came to an abrupt halt.

"Well, looky here, Ned." The trapper on the right exclaimed between breaths. "It looks like this here lady ain't only a whore, but 'ppears to me she's a squaw to this here savage."

"Yep," the other responded.

"She done killed our friend," the trapper on the right continued, addressing Baying Wolf.

Baying Wolf's eyebrow arched in surprise, but he showed no other sign of acknowledgment. Christina however, had no qualms about expressing herself.

"Good!" She said, standing up a little straighter. "Maybe that'll teach you to try to rape a lady."

"We did no such thing! You offered us a show. 'Sides which, you ain't no lady, so it ain't possible to rape you. Right, Ned?"

"Yep." The quieter man had obviously promoted the man speaking to head man with the death of his friend, and he was doing his best to make a sufficiently intimidating presence.

"Why not you give her to us and we'll take her on to the local lawman. After all, she did jes murderlize our bestest friend without reason." He poked his friend in the ribs, seeking support.

"Yep," his associate responded, but when Baying Wolf failed to respond, the two trappers looked at each other, whispering in low tones.

"— he don' speak English..."

"Yep."

"—can take him?"

"Yep."

Christina wanted to laugh as snatches of their conversation drifted over to where she stood. If it was possible, they had to be the most inept morons on the planet, and the fact they thought they stood a chance against a seasoned warrior, seemed to prove it. Still, she hoped that they would just go on their way and leave them be, since she didn't relish the notion of killing anyone else and she didn't like the idea of the Indian getting drawn into a fight that would cause him to hurt someone. It just didn't seem right that he'd have to kill to defend her honor, especially when he didn't want to be here defending her in the first place.

When the two men broke ranks and separated, their decision was clear: attack from both sides and maybe one of them would live long enough to take the squaw. Well, Christina wasn't going to be responsible for the lives of anyone too ignorant to know when they were out skilled. Baying Wolf seemed to agree with her, for he quickly raised his bow and pointed the protruding arrow at the chest of the man of little words.

Christina palmed Baying Wolf's knife, ready to let it lose upon his command. The new leader flushed in anger, not quite sure how to continue.

"Why not leave off, Injun?" He snarled. "She ain't worth your hide. You don' need no beat up, stinkin' white woman to whore with. 'Specially one that be a murderin' whore. We're happy 'nough to take her off your hands."

"Yep," His friend added.

"This white woman is my property. You will die before touching her." Christina bristled at his declaration, but wisely kept quiet. *Just wait until we get out of this*, she thought. *Property, my eye!*

"Well, leastways we know he talks English."

"Yep." The man of little words agreed.

With no warning, the newly self-appointed leader sprang, his friend quickly following suit. Christina heard the whiz of Baying Wolf's arrow at the same moment she released his knife. Both assailants registered shocked disbelief, staggered about cursing for a few minutes, and within moments drew their last breath. Christina looked at the two men lying at her feet and began to shake violently. It wasn't as if she hadn't killed a man, she'd killed three at last count, but the strain of fighting and defending herself combined with all she'd had to endure suddenly struck with the violence of a gale force wind.

She would have collapsed, had Baying Wolf not wrapped his strong arms around her and held her tightly to his strong chest. "Hush, woman. You did well," he praised quietly into her hair. "Baying Wolf proud."

So that's his name, her hazed mind mused. He continued to speak soothing words to her until her quivering ceased. When she looked up at him through red-rimmed eyes, he smiled, and then his earlier words returned to the forefront of her mind and her irritation returned. Did he really see her as his property? Was she not more to him than just another horse or a newly carved bow? And who was he to declare that she was property to begin with? She hadn't consented to be his woman, had not allowed him the privileges of a mate. She pushed hard against his chest until he released her, and then spun on her heel and stomped off through the woods.

Baying Wolf watched her go, and then turned to look at his knife protruding from the second man's chest. She suitably impressed him.

CHAPTER 54

When Baying Wolf caught up to Christina a short while later, she refused to stop at his bidding, or speak to him. He grabbed her arm and spun her around. "Do you have berries in your ears so that you cannot hear me speak?"

"Yes, I can hear you speak, and yes, I am deliberately ignoring Baying Wolf," she said, seemingly oblivious to the lack of circulation where his hands gripped her upper arms. "That *is* your name, isn't it? You could have introduced yourself properly when we met, you know. I shouldn't have had to discover it when we were under attack."

"I am sorry that I did not reveal my name to you. Will you now cease your foolish behavior?"

"And stop calling me foolish. I am not foolish, nor am I your property. Now, if you'd be so kind as to release my arm..."

"You are angry, not because I did not tell you my name, but because I declared you my property?" Baying Wolf laughed softly.

"I suppose you think that I should be honored that you declared me your property. Well, I'm not. I'm not your stallion or your weapon. I'm a person, just like you."

"You are nothing like me," Baying Wolf grinned, his gaze raking over her womanly curves in appreciation.

"You're impossible!"

"I am sorry that I did not tell you my name, and that I called you my property. Now will you cease your fool...I mean, irrational behavior?"

"Oh, irrational is much better than foolish."

"Good. You are irrational. But did it not occur to you that I called you my property so to offer reason for my defense of you?"

Christina cocked her head in incredulity. "How could telling those two buffoons that I'm your property possibly provide defense of my person?"

"Were you not my property, I would not have come to your

rescue."

Christina saw the mischief in Baying Wolf's gaze and shook her head, "You're unbelievable, and I'm done playing at words with you. I'm going back to camp."

"Can you find your way without getting lost?"

She would have thought he was joking, but the glimmer of amusement no longer lit his eyes. "Aren't you returning also?"

"I need to hunt or we will not eat tonight."

"Didn't you go hunting earlier?"

"I caught rabbit, but I doubt it is still in camp, since scavengers can smell death miles away, and I had to leave the kill to come in search of you." There was no disguising his renewed irritation, and Christina blushed. "Now I need to know if you can you find your way back to camp?"

Christina wanted to assert that she was quite capable, but that *would* be foolish, so she merely shook her head, embarrassed at having to declare herself truly unfit for living in the woods; embarrassed at revealing her reliance upon Baying Wolf for every little thing—including directions.

Baying Wolf let out a shrill whistle and within moments, Wolf appeared to stand next to him. Baying Wolf knelt beside the giant animal and spoke in his native tongue. Wolf panted and moved to Christina's side.

"It's as if he understood you," Christina said in awe, petting Wolf on the top of the head.

"He did," Baying Wolf said simply, and then turned to leave.

"Thank you, Baying Wolf," Christina said softly. She didn't expect he could hear her, but he turned and smiled at her.

"You are welcome, White Woman."

As soon as he disappeared into the thick of the trees, she turned to look at Wolf, "Well, boy, lead the way."

Wolf turned and headed back to camp, a grateful Christina sprinting close behind.

CHAPTER 55

When daylight turned into night, Christina began to worry, glancing nervously into the trees beyond their camp. She had long ago made a fire with the instruction that Baying Wolf gave her; had long ago stockpiled sticks to keep the blaze alight, but after several hours, her stockpile was decreasing rapidly and her nerves were becoming ever tauter. Especially since she wasn't about to go into the darkening woods to collect more.

She hoped that Baying Wolf hadn't met with danger, because she truly did not relish the notion of taking off on her own again. A noise to her right startled her and she breathed a sigh of relief when Baying Wolf stepped into the campsite. Following closely on his heels was Wolf.

"Well, I was wondering where you'd gone off to," she said to the wolf. With obvious delight, the wolf bounded over to where Christina sat, and then knelt before her, evidently waiting for her to lavish more affection upon its head. Christina didn't disappoint, rubbing the gray fur lovingly, "Who's a good boy, hmm?"

Baying Wolf smiled slightly, "Do not spoil him," he said without conviction. "I see you prepared the fire. It is a good fire." He slid the string holding his latest kill off his shoulder and laid it on the ground. There were five rabbits, their lifeless eyes staring into space.

"Why were you gone so long?" Christina asked, trying to keep the accusatory tone from entering her speech.

"I needed time to think. I am sorry if I worried you. And finding food toward evening gets much more difficult. Most animals go to bed when the sun starts to sink in the sky. What comes out at night to hunt is not very good for people to eat," he said with a teasing grin. She didn't reply, instead she sat eyeing the rabbits with nervous dread. It was her turn to skin and cook now, and she wasn't looking forward to the upcoming task.

"Well I suppose we'd best get to it, shall we?" She gave a small, nervous smile when his head shot up. He was looking at her quizzically. He already unstrung the rabbits, laid them out, and with a knife in hand, readied to butcher them for cooking.

"I did not think you were going to do it."

"I didn't either, but I suppose that if you hunted for the food, the least I can do is my part and help cook them."

"Come," Baying Wolf extended a hand in her direction.

Christina nodded slightly, and then stood and moved over to where he was kneeling. "I will do my best, but I can't make you any promises. What I end up doing to those carcasses may make them unfit for human consumption."

Baying Wolf laughed softly, "Since I am hungry I will prepare the food tonight. You watch and learn." Several times, as she watched him skin and spit the five bunnies, she wanted to turn away and retract her offer to learn; however, what he'd said was true. If she ever found herself in a situation where she needed to fend for herself, she'd need to know how to do this. Her stomach however, wasn't as convinced of the necessity of the lesson and threatened to spill what little contents remained.

Later, as the smell of the roasting meat collided with her nostrils, her stomach, no longer nauseous, grumbled in anticipation.

"We will eat soon," Baying Wolf smiled, eyeing her noisy belly. Christina blushed, and then turned the conversation to a different subject.

"So, where is it exactly that we are going, Baying Wolf?" She asked.

"If you let me eat before we talk, I will be happier to answer your questions." Christina blushed slightly and Baying Wolf smiled. "Would you get the plate from the satchel on my horse?"

"You have plates?" Christina realized belatedly the insult in that outburst, but figured it would do more damage to try to retract it. Baying Wolf looked at her and shook his head slightly.

"One plate," he answered, but did not comment. By the look in his eyes, she figured he thought it best to leave it alone as well. "Which I will let you borrow, if you go to get it." She retrieved the metal plate and was pleased to see his supply also included a fork, which she brought along as well.

"Are you certain that you don't want to use these?" She offered in a conciliatory tone.

"No, we heathens are used to eating with our hands."

"I didn't mean..." she began, but he raised a hand to silence her. He pulled the stick holding the bunnies from over the fire and slid one of them onto her plate, and then placed the others between two rocks beside him. With his hand, he pulled the meat from the bones of one of them, eating hungrily.

"Aren't you going to give any to your wolf?" She asked, casting a glance at the wolf curled up near the fire, sleeping soundly. When she said 'wolf,' it's ears perked up and it's eyes opened. "Is that its name then?" She asked.

"Yes, I call him "Wolf" and no, he will not eat with us. He is a hunter. To feed him will hamper his skill."

"Oh, I see." However, she didn't really see at all, since she'd never encountered a wild animal before.

"Do not concern yourself. He will not go hungry. He will probably eat better than we will. Is the food not good to eat?" He asked finally, noticing that she hadn't started eating yet.

"Oh, I'm sure it's fine. I guess I'm just used to saying grace before eating. Would you mind terribly much?"

"What is this 'grace' that you wish to say?"

"It's simply a prayer to thank God for the food that we're going to eat."

"I have already said a prayer of thanks to the rabbits for allowing us to nourish our bodies with their own."

"You prayed to the rabbits?"

"It is our custom to say thanks to the animals that we kill before eating them. That way they will know they did not die without cause; so that they will know that it is because of their death that we can live and fight another day. Does this not please you?"

"I didn't mean..." Christina started, embarrassed yet again at her ignorance, but was cut off by a wave of Baying Wolf's hand.

"Say the prayer you need to say, before the food is too cold to enjoy."

Christina wasn't sure she could utter a prayer on command, but felt tried. "Dear Lord," she began, closing her eyes, "thank you for this food that we are about to receive. May you use it to strengthen our minds and bodies, so that we will be able to serve you. Amen."

"Now may I continue to eat?"

"Yes, thank you." Christina dug her fork into the rapidly cooling meat and tugged. The tender flesh pulled easily away from the bone and she thrust it eagerly into her mouth. She closed her eyes and moaned as the meat dissolved quickly. She swallowed and moaned again, when the meat hit her empty belly.

"You sound more as if you are being pleasured in bed rather than eating a meal."

Christina's eyes flew open wide and she found herself blushing again under the scrutiny of Baying Wolf's heated gaze, his own meal temporarily forgotten. Baying Wolf laughed at her discomfort. She really was a strange woman. "Eat, woman. And be quiet if you can," he teased mercilessly, returning his attention to his own meal. Christina thankfully returned her attention to her food, trying desperately not to make another sound. By the time the meal ended, she was over her embarrassment and ready to continue their conversation, but before she could open her mouth, Baying Wolf spoke up.

"Clean the plate and fork first before talking again."

Christina looked around to try and find a source of water, but didn't see or hear anything remotely resembling the clear liquid. "Clean them with what?"

Baying Wolf sighed heavily and stood. "How do your women survive when you know nothing?" He didn't mean to sound so harsh, but her helplessness scared him. He wondered what would have happened to her today, had he not come upon her running from the trappers. She probably would have ended up dead.

He took the plate and fork from Christina, picked up some dirt from the ground, and wiped it across the utensils. He repeated the gesture several times, and then pulled a leaf from a nearby tree and wiped the remaining dirt from the surfaces.

Baying Wolf saw Christina cringe and sighed again, "Water is precious," he explained as patiently as he could manage. "When we reach an abundant source of water, we will clean the plate and fork as they need to be cleaned, but until then, this will get rid of the scent of food that may draw wild animals to our camp. Then we would risk becoming their food. Understand?"

Christina merely nodded and sat with her hands clasped in her lap, feeling foolish. She thought about the opinion she'd formed of him simply because the color of his skin was different from her own. Then her mind drifted to Chin Woo and her shame increased. Chin Woo was as different from her as this Indian was, his culture just as strange, but she'd never treated him with anything but regard.

Yeah, well it wasn't Chin Woo's kind that slaughtered your family right before your eyes either, her mind argued, defensively, *so you shouldn't be so hard on yourself. He doesn't seem to hold your skin color against you though.*

"I'm sorry if I was a little short with you. Do you not wish to talk to me now?"

"No. I mean, yes," Christina blundered. "What I mean to say is, yes I'd like to continue our conversation, but I'd also like to apologize for my behavior. It's just difficult for me to sit here with..." Christina stopped when she realized that she was about to blunder into another embarrassing statement, but Baying Wolf picked up what she was about to say.

"A savage?"

"No. That is not what I was going to say," Christina murmured. "You've been very kind and helpful to me and I fear I've let my tongue run amok on occasion."

"You have had a bad time, white woman," Baying Wolf conceded. "I understand this and know that sitting and eating with me is difficult for you. Knowing that people like me destroyed everything that you love. It would be hard for me and I am a warrior."

"It would?"

"Yes, it would, but you must try to understand that I'm not here to hurt you. I'm only trying to help. Can you understand this?"

"I'm trying to, yes."

"Then I will answer your question from earlier. You did not tell me where you wanted to go," he said, then lie down on his back, and shielded his eyes from the light of the fire with his arm. The other arm he propped behind his head for a pillow.

It took Christina a moment to realize what question he was referring to, but then enlightenment dawned. "Are you telling me that if I tell you where I want to go, you will take me there?" At his grunt of what Christina could only assume was an affirmation, she plunged on. "Well, why didn't you simply tell me this before? I assumed that you would take me to the nearest form of civilization and dump me there."

"Is it possible for you not to speak?"

"What did you mean by that, anyway?" She pursued, refusing to be baited.

Baying Wolf removed his arm from his eyes and stared at her, "The Great Spirit has commanded me to guide you to safety. Dumping you somewhere, as you say, would not be obeying. The only way to keep you safe is to take you somewhere that you know."

"You still could have told me this earlier."

"While we have tried to be civil to each other, white woman, you still harbor in your heart mistrust. I could have told you that I would take you to safety, but you would have looked at me with the same suspicion as you do when I tell you that I mean you no harm."

"Fair enough, so do you happen to know a rancher named..." Christina began again, but a command from Baying Wolf cut her off in mid-sentence.

"Come here!" He ordered softly and Christina froze as a deer caught in the light of a flame.

"No, Baying Wolf!" She answered with more bravado than she felt. "and I won't allow you to intimidate me into going over there either."

"I simply want you to come here so that I can teach you the

pleasure of silence." When she remained seated, Baying Wolf grinned. "Perhaps you are willing to bargain?"

"Bargain?" She asked suspiciously.

"I will talk to you for a little while if you will come sit here beside me." The twinkle in his eye cautioned Christina that he was being mischievous, but she didn't think he was joking with her. He was definitely up to something.

"I don't think so," Christina said nervously, twisting her hands in her skirt. "I think I'll wait until tomorrow to talk to you some more. I'm more tired than I thought anyhow."

"White woman coward."

"I am not!" She replied hastily.

"Then bargain," he challenged.

"Fine, but the bargain will simply be that I'll sit next to you if you'll talk to me a little longer. Deal?"

Baying Wolf shrugged his shoulder noncommittally, and then nodded to a place next to him. Christina stood on shaky legs and walked over. She sat on the ground beside him, adjusting her skirts under and around her like a shield. *A very weak, ineffective shield,* she thought, when she caught the glint in his eyes. "Now we talk," he grinned widely. "Tell me, white woman. Where did you learn to throw a knife like that?"

Christina sighed in relief. Perhaps he did simply want her to sit next to him to talk. Nothing more than that. Boy, she really had to get over this unnecessary prejudice she had against him simply because of the color of his skin. "A very dear friend taught me. An elder oriental man. He was one that died by the hands of—Indians."

The slight hesitation in her voice brought a smile to his lips. "So, you do not blame *my* people any longer?

"I don't suppose so. After all, you really weren't there, now, were you?"

He laughed shortly, "but you still blame me for not being there."

"A little. Somehow, when I saw you in my dream, I guess I started to rely on you more than I should. When I realized that my dream was really visions of my family, I looked around, and I honestly thought you would be there as you were in my dream. I don't know if that makes much sense."

"I'm sorry that I was not there," Baying Wolf said softly. "I found you easily enough and then I grew careless. I did not expect that the wagons would continue their journey at night. If I had remained watchful, then I may have been there to help you. In that, I failed you."

For the first time, Christina realized that he was hurting too, in a way. He was a warrior and not used to unsuccessfulness. By not being there, he had let her down. He felt he had neglected to aid her in her time of crisis, and that was a great weight on his shoulders. No wonder he was so adamant about helping her again. The thought of failing a second time would be too much for him to handle—or his ego.

"I don't think you would have done any better than I did against so many," she conceded.

"Thank you," he said softly.

"You're welcome," she acknowledged, her voice a mere whisper. Silence fell between them as the sun lowered further on the horizon.

After a while, Baying Wolf spoke again, "so, can you shoot that revolver you carry as well as you throw the knife?"

Christina smiled devilishly. "Let's put it this way, had you known how well I can shoot, you probably wouldn't have gotten so close to me, especially with me so angry and the gun cocked."

"Would you really have shot me?" He asked.

"Only if you'd given me reason."

"Hmm, I appreciate knowing that being Indian is not sufficient reason."

"Yes, well, about my earlier question. If I tell you where I'd like you to take me, you'd really take me there?" Christina asked deftly changing the subject. She was uncomfortable with the tone he'd used with his last statement, not to mention the fact that she really didn't want to dwell on the massacre of her family right now.

"You doubt Baying Wolf?"

"No. I just..."

"Talk too much," Baying Wolf finished for her, and then reached up and grasped her neck with his hand, drawing her down to him. "Now no more talk. Learn pleasure of silence." This kiss was different from the one Jeffrey inflicted on her and she felt sparks ignite in the pit of her stomach. He kissed her slowly, exploring her lips. Nipping. Tasting. Careful not to cause her contused face further pain. When his tongue pressed against her teeth, she stiffened. He withdrew, sending kisses over her closed eyelids, along her bruised jaw line and then returning to her immobile lips. "Let me kiss you," he murmured against her mouth, but the sound of his voice snapped Christina from her daze.

She struggled free of his embrace and sat up, her face red with humiliation. "I can't do this."

"You are afraid?" He asked hoarsely.

"Yes. A little," she confessed breathlessly.

He raised his hand and ran his knuckles lightly down her arm. She shivered. His mouth twisted into an ironic smile. "You fear me, but your body desires me."

She placed a hand over his to prevent any further movement. Baying Wolf looked down and marveled at the difference in their skin. He brought his eyes back to hers, looking for affirmation of his statement, but saw only sadness, deep and painful. "I do not fear you, Baying Wolf, at least not nearly as much as I did. What I fear is...well, I do fear who you are, but what you are—not just an Indian, but also a man."

Baying Wolf's eyes narrowed in misunderstanding and Christina quickly explained. "My fiancé, now dead, tried to take by force that which you want now. One of your kind, raped and murdered my best friend right before my eyes. Indians savagely murdered everyone I hold dear. I don't blame you for what any of them did, and I know that you have some promise to protect me; however, I can't put the horror of what has happened behind me so soon. When you touched me, I forgot, but I'm not ready to forget."

Baying Wolf looked thoughtful for a moment, but when he spoke, she sensed a sadness in his tone behind the angry words he hurled. "You do not blame me, nor do you fear me. Your body desires me, but you will not have me because I am a man and Indian," he bluntly summarized for her. "In your eyes, I cannot win."

He waited for her to deny his words. Instead, he watched as a lone tear drifted from her eye, to follow the path that his lips had taken. When he looked into her eyes, he could see the battle rage within her, and knew she was trying to be strong, to fight against the desire she felt for him. But he did not want her to be strong. He wanted to make her weak, to beg him to take her, to make her cry out with pleasure in his arms. He wanted—what he could not have.

"Do not cry for me, white woman. I will not suffer your loss." Baying Wolf stood abruptly and stormed off into the woods.

"No, but I may suffer yours," she whispered to his retreating back, knowing that the chasm that they'd nearly mended this night had suddenly expanded to a width that might not be bridgeable again.

But could he really blame her reticence? Surely, he could see her point in the matter. What did he expect her to do? Throw away her virginity to a savage simply because he was aiding her? It was nearly sunrise before sleep claimed her disquieted mind.

CHAPTER 56

Baying Wolf knelt beside the white woman and watched the tears fall from her slumbering eyes. Obviously, something in her dreams was upsetting her a great deal. He felt a pull at his heart and wanted to wipe her sorrow away, but quickly hardened his heart before the action played itself out. She had rejected him for everything that he was without leaving a way for him to win her heart, so he most certainly would not give her his.

A part of him wanted to understand, knowing that she had suffered at the hands of men —both brown and white. It was that understanding that had caused him to reach out to her, to show her kindness even though her skin was that of his enemy. It was that understanding that pushed him to prove to her that not all men were heathens, but she continued to reject him. He'd thought, because of her intelligent words, that she was not one to hold ill will against the innocent, but perhaps her prejudice was too strong, and she'd allowed it to blind her to him. Well, he would no longer try to open her eyes. He would simply be what she expected to see and he would not feel sadness for her—or longing.

He shook her shoulder roughly, quickly removing his hand from the disquieting contact. Christina awoke with a start and cried out, but her heartbeat slowed at the sight of Baying Wolf kneeling beside her. The scowl on his face returned memories of the night before and she lowered her head in shame. What made the humiliation more unbearable was not that she'd acted like a brazen hussy, but that she *wanted* to act like a brazen hussy. When Baying Wolf kissed her—well, she had never experienced anything else like it before.

Other suitors had given her perfunctory pecks on the cheek or had stolen a kiss or two on the lips, but she'd felt nothing. Jeffrey had been the only man to kiss her like Baying Wolf, but his kisses made her angry and nauseous. Why then did this savage touch her and leave her skin hot where his hand had been? Why did a heathen kiss her and make her want to throw her arms around his neck and kiss him back? Her cheeks reddened when she noticed Baying Wolf kneeling beside her, studying her. *Well, he's obviously thinking just as intently about you,* she thought with a wry grin. His scowl deepened and he stood abruptly.

"We ride soon. Be ready," he commanded and then stormed off.

Christina arose shakily and moved dispiritedly toward the bushes to relieve herself. She knew without a doubt that she'd have to part company with Baying Wolf soon. No matter how kind he'd been to her, he had made his desire for her plain the evening before, and that was something she simply could never countenance. He was everything that she despised.

Then why is your heart hurting at the thought of the pending parting? Her mind asked. *And before you ask, I'm in your head which happens to be a part of your body. That means I'm not as detached as you sometimes wish I were. So why? Is it because his kindness has touched you more than you want to admit?*

"His kindness has touched me, yes," she responded readily, "but so has he and I cannot allow myself to bow to my body's desires when he isn't my husband. Since our cultures are so different, he's not likely to ever be my husband, and I don't even know why I'm dwelling on this." She continued talking to herself while she doused the fire and packed the meager supplies into the satchel hanging over the horse's haunches.

Baying Wolf had gone back into the woods shortly after waking her and she wasn't certain exactly how long he would be gone; however, he'd said they were leaving soon, so she planned on being ready when he did return.

Well, since you are dwelling on it, perhaps you could be feeling something more. Could that be another reason why you don't want to part company with our guide and protector? Her mind asked, refusing to let the subject alone.

"Why don't you stick to brain work, and I'll tend to matters of the heart, if you don't mind?"

Ah! The heart. Therefore, you admit that Baying Wolf has tangled the emotions in your heart into a huge mess. Why don't you just admit that you want him as much as he seems to want you, and that *is what's scaring you more than the color of his skin?* Her mind said bluntly.

"No."

"No, what?"

Christina jumped, dropping the plate and fork she'd been about to shove in the satchel. Baying Wolf looked at the utensils and raised an eyebrow in question. "Nothing. I was just talking to myself." His eyebrow shot up again, but he didn't question her further. He finished kicking dirt over the fire pit, and then turned to help her mount his horse.

"Baying Wolf," she began, placing her foot in the folds of his hands.

"I would prefer to talk very little today, white woman."

"I understand, but I'd like to know if you still intend to see me to my destination," Christina ventured in a near whisper.

Baying Wolf lifted her foot, releasing it when he settled her on the horse's back. "I am a man of honor. A man of his word."

"I know and I didn't mean to say you weren't. But you never got around to asking me where I want to go."

"I guess I got distracted," Baying Wolf said, his gaze lingering on her mouth.

Christina blushed, deciding it best to ignore his tone and obvious attempt at lasciviousness. "You wouldn't happen to know a rancher by the name of Peter Carthington, would you?"

"Carthington?" Baying Wolf questioned, his eyes narrowing slightly.

"Yes. He's my uncle, and if you know where his ranch is..."

"I know," he interrupted, his heart racing. He did indeed know Peter Carthington. Most of his people and those of the surrounding tribes also knew him well. Peter Carthington had come out west and driven many tribes off the land with guns and fire. He'd stolen what the Indians treasured and hired ruthless men to ensure that it remained in his possession. For the first few years, many tribes had risen against him, attempting to regain possession of the land, but his men outnumbered theirs and their brutality was unsurpassed.

Over time, the natives settled into an uneasy peace with Carthington, but some of the younger braves, still embittered over the loss of the land, made Carthington's life interesting by stealing stray cattle frequently.

"Baying Wolf?" Christina ventured, when his silence grew lengthy.

"I will take white woman to her uncle's house. It will take many days, but I will see you safely there. Now be silent."

"Aren't you going to ride too?" Christina asked when Baying Wolf moved to the front of the horse and picked up the lead rope.

"The one I'd like to mount is seated *on* my horse."

Christina's eyes widened and Baying Wolf smiled thinly. He shot her a look as if daring her to comment, but she merely looked away. Baying Wolf took the lead rope and tugged the horse, his heart beating loudly in his ears. It was going to be a long three days.

CHAPTER 57

They ate in silence, as they had for the last two days. Tomorrow they would be coming down from the mountains and heading into the plains that Baying Wolf called home. From there, he assured her, speaking only once earlier that morning, that they would be close to her uncle's spread. Tomorrow she would get her wish and separate from Baying Wolf, and he was doing everything he could to make that departure eagerly anticipated.

Their conversation had been limited on her end because the return conversation was nearly nonexistent. His entire manner was curt, bordering on downright rude. She took full responsibility for the shift in his behavior. She had unfairly cast him in the same light as those like Jeffrey Buchanan and the renegades that murdered her family. Rejecting his advances hadn't helped matters either, but surely he couldn't expect her to acquiesce after the trauma through which she'd suffered?

She'd tried repeatedly the last couple of days to set the record straight, but he'd walked away before she'd even finished uttering his name. Never had she met someone who harbored anger and resentment for as long as he did. She wondered whether he would still be cursing her name a year from now. He certainly didn't appear as if he'd be conversing with her anytime in the future. He'd even instructed her on the cooking of the pheasants he'd killed during his hunting trip, all without uttering a sound.

Although the pheasant looked juicy and delicious, she had very little appetite. She didn't doubt that desire for food would remain low until she sorted her emotions and a chance arose to clear the air with Baying Wolf.

With a determined resolution, she cleared her throat, "Baying..."

Baying Wolf shot to his feet and headed into the woods, returning long enough to snatch his dinner from the rock on which it had been sitting.

"That insufferable brute! Well, enough is enough. He can't keep pouting like a two-year-old." Christina tossed her nearly untouched pheasant aside and stalked into the woods after him. He wasn't likely to go far and she felt confident that she would have no difficulty finding him. How wrong she was. Natives must have built-in direction finders, she decided half hour later when she still hadn't found him and had no inclination about which direction he'd taken. Where could he have possibly gone in the time he left and she followed?

Now, with the sun lowering on the horizon and less light filtering through the trees, Christina decided that she'd been foolish in attempting to track an expert with nonexistent skills. She turned slowly in a circle trying to discern the direction of the camp, but everything seemed similar to her. Finally, she decided she had but one choice.

"Baying Wolf!" She yelled as loudly as she could, startling the fowl out of nearby trees. She waited for what she considered a reasonable length of time, and then shouted again. A twig broke behind her and she spun around expecting to see Baying Wolf maneuvering through the trees, gallantly coming to her aid.

"Hello, Wolf. Where's your owner?" The wolf stood watching her for a moment, and then turned and trotted off the way it came. "Hey, wait! I can't move as quickly as you can!" Less than two minutes later, she was free of the wooded area and back in camp. She hadn't been but a few hundred yards away—if that—so when she saw Baying Wolf sitting nonchalantly beside the dwindling campfire her temper flared.

"Didn't you hear me yell for you?" She stormed up beside him, stopping within a few inches of his side.

"I heard."

"Then why didn't you help me, you big buffoon?"

"I told you that if you left again that I would not come to your aid."

"You arrogant toad! I didn't leave. I was following you!"

"Why would you follow Baying Wolf?"

"You know what? Forget it. You can take my apology and shove it in your ear and if you never talk to me again it will be too soon!" Christina turned intent on returning to her side of the camp. Baying Wolf's hand snaked up and clamped on her arm, jerking her off her feet and straight onto his lap.

She opened her mouth to protest, but the only sound that emitted was a grunt, as his mouth descended on hers in a bruising kiss. Christina's heart pounded furiously in her ears. Instinctively, she lifted her hand and clutched his muscled arm. A desirous shockwave shot through her and she relaxed, sliding her hand up his arm and into his thick, coarse hair.

Baying Wolf felt her acquiesce, but wasn't pleased. He was trying to drive her away, not draw her closer. He lifted his head and shoved her from his lap. "Apology accepted." He turned and stormed toward the woods stopping only long enough to tell her not to follow him again.

CHAPTER 58

The flat grassy area stretched as far as the eye could see, but Christina still fumed over Baying Wolf's churlish behavior and found it difficult to enjoy the new vista. She tried to fathom what it was exactly that had happened between them, and when she thought she had it figured and would set to rectify it, Baying Wolf would not allow her the opportunity. It was if he had decided to be even more foul mannered, but why? What did he hope to gain by driving such a huge wedge between them? At least she was trying to amend their differences before they said their goodbyes, which could be any time today. His silent treatment had allowed her to think, if nothing else, and she felt horrible for the way she'd responded to him. It made her wonder if his churlish behavior was the direct result of her treatment of him. Of course, his not talking to her made it difficult to learn anything, but she was still determined to attempt reconciliation.

After a night of soul-searching, she realized that the color of a person's skin did not determine their character. Jeffrey and Chin Woo had been perfect examples of that. Jeffrey was from her world, but his soul was dark and evil. Chin Woo, on the other hand, had been from a strange culture on the other side of the ocean, yet his kindness and loyalty to their friendship touched her in a way that she would hold close to her heart forever.

She looked at Baying Wolf, still leading the horse after three days. He was from a world that the white people in the East called demonic heathens, yet he had come to her aid when she had needed him. He could have overpowered her anytime in the last week, as he'd proven he could do the few times he kissed her. Instead, he tried to teach her how to take care of herself, much as Chin Woo had with his weapons training.

The strange feelings she had when any part of her flesh met his, frightened her, but she had also come to terms with the fact that it wasn't him that frightened her, but the desire she felt for him. In fact, she had been wrong to treat Baying Wolf as she had and she only had hurt and anger over the loss of her family to blame.

She looked down at him again and was surprised to see him watching her. So intent was she on her thoughts, she had not even realized that he had stopped the horse. When he saw that he had her attention, he moved to the side of the horse and looked up at her.

"We will soon reach the land your uncle calls his," he said. "We should find a salve to put on your face. It will help the scratches heal faster." His eyes roamed over the scratches and the fading bruises that marred her face and marveled at how they failed to detract from her beauty. He should have offered to apply a salve sooner, but she was too great a distraction to him and his mind did not always think with sense. "Come and walk with me for a while?" He asked, and raised his hand to help her dismount.

They walked in silence for a short time, Baying Wolf chewing on a blade of grass. He was obviously deep in thought, so Christina remained silent.

"I would talk with you," he said after a while, and Christina merely nodded. "I have tried to push you out of my mind, white woman..." He began, and then stopped and turned abruptly to face Christina, surprise written all over her face. "What are you called?"

"I beg your pardon?"

"What are you called? What name do you use?"

"Oh!" Christina had become so used to being called 'white woman', she'd temporarily forgotten she even had a name. On the day she discovered his name, she should have thought to use the manners she'd accused him of lacking, indirectly, and introduced herself, but she was simply incapable of clear thought most times when in his presence. "My name is Christina."

"Chris...ti...na," Baying Wolf said slowly, savoring the sound as it rolled off his tongue. "I have been unkind to you, Christina, especially the last few days."

"No..."

"Please. Allow me to speak." Christina nodded and Baying Wolf continued. "The Great Spirit sent me to protect you. Why he sent me is a mystery. Fire Dreamer, the shaman of my people, said the answers would come to me in time; however, I have allowed anger and my lust for you to cloud any reason, so the answers have not come and we will part company soon." He stopped talking, as if trying to think of what to say next, and then continued slowly, "If the Great Spirit sent me to you, then I should have treated you better. I wish to say that I am sorry, Christina, before I leave you. Perhaps in time, I will grow to understand why our meeting was important to the Great Spirit. Perhaps in time, you will grow to forgive me for my mistreatment of you. Perhaps in time, you will not see me as your enemy, but your friend."

Christina placed a hand on Baying Wolf's arm and immediately removed it. The look he gave her made her blush.

"You feel what I feel, do you not, Christina?" He asked quietly, clasping her hand and returning it to his upper arm.

"Baying Wolf, I..." Christina stopped speaking when the smile vanished from Baying Wolf's dark face and his eyes clouded with anger. Had he not been gazing over her shoulder, she would have thought he was angry with her again.

"What is it?" She asked, turning. She placed a hand on her forehead, shielding the sun from her eyes, but could see only what looked like a cloud of dust far in the distance.

"Danger," Baying Wolf muttered.

"I don't understand." She spun around again to face Baying Wolf, but he had already turned away from her and was mounting his horse.

"Come. We must ride."

Christina did not hesitate to place her hand in his for he had proven himself repeatedly during her time with him and she knew that doubting him now would be foolish. He pulled her up behind him and clasped her arms firmly around his midriff. Baying Wolf spurred his horse to a gallop and Christina ducked her face between his shoulder blades, her arms tightening in fear, as the huge stallion bounded over the uneven ground.

When she finally heard the sound of horses' hooves in the

distance, she raised her eyes warily and looked back over her shoulder, afraid that the renegades had returned. She knew then why Baying Wolf had sensed trouble and felt the need to quit the area in all haste. The horses that were heading for them were quickly closing the distance. Baying Wolf's horse was fast, but her added weight was wearing on the mighty stallion, slowing his speed drastically.

The horse's nostrils flared and his haunches strained, but the riders soon overtook them. Baying Wolf reluctantly pulled back on his horse's mane when several riders skid to a halt in their path. Within moments, rough-looking men in cowboy hats surrounded them with rifles—raised threateningly.

Christina felt him tense in anticipation, certain that these white men would rather shoot him first without bothering to ask his business, but she was just as certain that her presence with him prevented it from happening immediately. A medium-built man on a chestnut sorrel moved forward, his hat pulled low over his head, the butt of his rifle resting relaxed on his knee. On closer inspection, Christina could see that his finger was on the trigger and that it would only take one movement to bring the barrel down to fire.

"This here is private property," the man said none too kindly, "and I don't take kindly to cow-thieving red skins riding through neither. Especially one with a white hostage."

Baying Wolf's back muscles tightened and Christina felt her own anger escalating. She may not be fond of Indians, but the man with her now was far from a heathen and to lump him in the same category as the savages that murdered her family didn't seem justified. She conveniently forgot that she'd once judged him nearly in the same way.

She was about to speak up for him when the leader of the group rode closer to her side and pushed his hat from his head. Red highlights shone through hair sprinkled with gray at the temples and the face was leathery and lined with wrinkles, but for some very slight differences the man before her was an older likeness of her father. She knew she'd found her uncle.

"Uncle Peter?"

The man's mouth drew into a tight line and his eyes narrowed, giving Christina pause. If this was her uncle, his reception was certainly unexpected, leading her to believe she'd made a mistake. This man couldn't possibly be related to her father. *Then again,* she thought after a moment, *perhaps he could.* If she reflected unbiased about her father's true character, he was not very different from what this man's face revealed. He had been narrow-minded, prejudiced, cold, and an insensitive cad. So far, the man before her held at least two of those traits—cold and prejudiced.

"Uncle, is it?" He looked her over slowly, disdain written all over his harsh features. "Do you know how many nieces and nephews have tried to lay claim as relation to me, since I became a successful rancher? Do you?"

"I must've been mistaken. It's just that for a moment you looked so much like my father," she whispered. Perhaps she'd best just forget trying to convince this man of her identity and go—but where? Her Uncle Peter had been her only alternative and without that, she had no one, anywhere.

"Who might your father be?" He asked. She could tell by his expression that he didn't really care and his disregard tempted her not to honor his question with a response, but the least she could do before leaving was to let him know that his brother was dead.

With that renewed memory, Christina's anger rose and she turned her torso as far as she could, raised her chin in defiance, and stared him straight in the eyes. "My father was Charles Henry Carthington, formerly of Savannah, Georgia, now lying dead beside the Red River somewhere east of here. Vultures, eating his carcass, were too numerous for me to count!" She said in a quaking voice, trying hard not to let him hear the pain behind her words.

"Well, there's no need to get your knickers in a knot, child," he said, his manner doing a complete about face. His hand reached over and took hold of her chin, and she had to force herself to endure his scrutiny. "You do have the look of your mother in your eyes. Can't see much else past the damage to your face. Is she gone too then?"

"Everyone is gone," she whispered and felt the tears begin to stream down her cheeks again as the memories flooded back. Peter Carthington slid from his horse and pulled her down into his embrace, stroking her hair affectionately as she cried into his shoulder. This was one trait her father never had—compassion.

When she'd calmed down enough to talk again, he put her away from him and grasped her shoulders firmly. "Mind telling me what you're doing in the company of this savage? If he's the one that marred your face..."

"He saved my life, and brought me here, and he's not a..."

"He saved your life, did he?" Carthington interrupted, which was a characteristic Christina was going to grow to dislike immensely in time.

"Yes, Uncle Peter."

Peter Carthington set his niece aside and moved to stand beside the man still seated stiffly on his mount. "It appears I owe you an unwilling debt of gratitude, Indian."

"You owe me nothing." His eyes, when he turned to look down at her uncle, bore a hatred that startled Christina, and she retreated from him a step. In all the time she'd spent with him, she'd never seen such hostility in his eyes. Anger, yes. Passion, definitely. Never pure unadulterated hatred and it unnerved her. Why would he despise her uncle so? *Or is it simply because he is white?* She wondered.

"So be it," Carthington agreed. "I owe you nothing; however, I'll give you your life if you ride away now."

So much for compassion, Christina thought, and then her uncle's words sunk in. Ride away! Christina felt close to panic. Her throat constricted and her heartbeat raced. He couldn't leave! He was the only person she knew in this place. Surely, he wouldn't leave her with a bunch of strangers. It didn't matter that one was her uncle. He was still a stranger.

Baying Wolf was her lifeline. The only stability, shaky as it was, that she'd had since the death of her loved ones. Now he was just going to up and leave! He couldn't do that to her.

Yet he did. With a swift glance in her direction, he spurred his horse toward the afternoon sun and soon vanished from sight.

"Why the long face, girlie? You're safe now," Peter Carthington said, staring at her grimly.

"Am I?" Christina whispered, her gaze still pinned on the horizon. Her dreams had played a hand in her destiny—partly; had brought Baying Wolf into her life –for a short time. Yet, it hadn't given her a map to follow from here.

Her dream was gone and so was Baying Wolf. Now she was depending on a man for whom contempt had already begun to sprout with their meeting just a few moments earlier. Was this the hand that destiny expected her to play? What had happened to that feeling, which she'd had on so many occasions, that her life was here in this place? That there was a purpose to her being here? Why wasn't that feeling still with her now that Baying Wolf was gone?

"Everyone, mount up!" Her uncle yelled, clasping her elbow and leading her to his sorrel. "You'll never see him again, child, so stop fretting," her uncle whispered before helping her mount.

"That's exactly why I *am* fretting," she whispered, keeping her gaze pinned to the horizon as her uncle spurred his horse toward her new life.

~ PART TWO ~
ARMS OF DESTINY

Love must have wings
to fly away from love,
and to fly back again.

Edwin Arlington Robinson
Tristram

CHAPTER 59

Early March 1861

"I have tried to push you out of my mind, white woman..." He began, then stopped and turned abruptly to face Christina, surprise written all over her face. "What are you called?"

"I beg your pardon?"

"What are you called? What name do you use?"

"Oh! My name is Christina."

"Is she going to be alright?"

"It's hard to say. I've done what I can, but..."

"But is not enough!"

"I'm sorry, Mr. Carthington, sir."

Christina heard the voices around her, but didn't have the willpower, or the interest, to acknowledge them. She turned her head into the pillow and allowed her mind to drift back to her dream.

"I have been unkind to you, Christina, especially the last few days."

"No..."

"Please. Allow me to speak. The Great Spirit sent me to protect you. Why he sent me is a mystery. Fire Dreamer, the shaman of my people, said the answers would come to me in time; however, I have allowed anger and my lust for you to cloud any reason, so the answers have not come and we will part company soon. If the Great Spirit sent me to you, then I should have treated you better. I wish to say that I'm sorry, Christina, before I leave you. Perhaps in time, I will grow to understand why our meeting was important to the Great Spirit. Perhaps in time, you will grow to forgive me for my mistreatment of you. Perhaps in time, you will not see me as your enemy, but your friend."

Christina placed a hand on Baying Wolf's arm and immediately removed it. The look he gave her made her blush.

"You feel what I feel, do you not, Christina?" He asked quietly, clasping her hand and returning it to his upper arm.

"I don't care what it takes! I lost my entire family to savages on their trip here, and I will not lose my only surviving relative! Do you hear me?"

Christina moaned. *I hear you!* She wanted to yell. She also wanted to place her hands over her ears to block out his voice, grating obnoxiously on her nerves. If she wasn't so tired, she would. If she could lift her arms to carry out that will, then she would. What was wrong with her?

The only thing she seemed able to do, was to listen as her Uncle yelled at someone in the room, and to curse at him in her mind for doing that yelling. *Drat him! Would someone please put a gag in that man's mouth?*

Thank you, she sighed inwardly, when the room fell silent. She welcomed the sudden peace, which allowed her to drift again into the welcoming arms of sleep.

"It appears I owe you an unwilling debt of gratitude, Indian."

"You owe me nothing."

"So be it, I owe you nothing; however, I'll give you your life if you ride away now."

"NO!" Christina sat up rapidly. The sudden movement was dizzying and stars dimmed her vision. A hand reached out and gently pressed down on her shoulder, urging her to return her head to her pillow.

"Don't fret, miss," a voice said softly near her ear. "Whatever it be that's troubling ye, will be well once ye're up and about. Now rest. I'll be here. Rest."

CHAPTER 60

Four days after turning Christina over to her uncle, Baying Wolf rode onto the land of his people—dirty and tired—his heart heavy and his spirits low. He'd only been able to spare her one final glance before riding away, but the pain he'd seen in her eyes, would hurt his heart forever.

If he'd been brave enough, he would have fought her uncle and stolen her away with him. Fought to keep her. Unfortunately, her uncle had not been riding alone, and his choices were limited to riding away, or taking a bullet to his skull.

He'd been lucky that the men hadn't shot him first and asked questions later. He expected it, so was relieved when they had allowed him to live long enough for Christina to explain whom she was and why she was with him.

It had spared his life...barely.

He had foolishly declared that her uncle owed nothing in exchange for saving his niece's life. Fortunately, for him, Carthington decided otherwise.

"So be it, I owe you nothing; however, I'll give you your life if you ride away now."

The memory of it still ate at him like diseased flesh. Leaving her was cowardly, knowing she didn't really want to stay. Yet spiriting her away would have been stupid, knowing he'd have died trying.

"It's best to just forget her," he told himself, as he turned over his equally tired mount to a young lad who'd run to greet him upon his return. With a distracted tousle of the boy's hair, he moved toward his tepee. Rest. That's all he needed—and time. Then she would be out of his mind and gone from his memory. Of course, time would help him forget faster if he didn't know where she was staying.

"Forget it!" Baying Wolf snapped, talking to himself. "That place is a fortress and you wouldn't get within a mile of the house before someone shot you. So, just forget it. Forget her." He needed nothing now but to fall onto his buffalo skins and sleep through to the next hunt. That's what he needed, but it isn't what he was afforded. Moments after entering his teepee, his uncle invaded his privacy and rest.

"Where is the white woman that the Great Spirit sent you to find?" Fire Dreamer asked sharply. "Why is she not with you?"

"She is with her uncle, where she belongs."

"You just left her there?"

"I did what the Great Spirit asked. I saw her to safety and allowed no harm to come to her. My task is done."

"Has hatred for the white man so blinded you, my nephew, that you cannot see?"

"Perhaps you should ask instead, Uncle, if hatred has blinded Christina. Not me. Do you know that Indians massacred her entire family? Did your visions tell you that? Did you know it took our entire journey together for her to come close to trusting me? Yet you expected that I would be able to ride with her into a village full of our people without her putting up a fight?"

Fire Dreamer shook his head sadly, as his nephew fled his teepee and stormed away. "Yes, I do think she would," Fire Dreamer whispered to the empty space in front of him, "and I think, maybe, so do you." He continued his one-sided conversation. "Perhaps you both need a clearer vision if neither of you can see your own destiny. Fear of each other is not going to help our people in the long run. That fear must be destroyed. The white woman cannot fear us for she is our hope for the future. Oh, foolish children! Now what am I to do? I must get her here."

CHAPTER 61

"Good morning, miss."

Christina awoke reluctantly to the sound of the voice and to the light streaming through the curtains, now drawn.

"I've done brought ye a wee bite to eat, I have," the voice continued cheerfully through the haze in her mind. "We were getting a might bit worried that ye weren't planning to wake up. After all, ye been nigh dead for the past three days, ye have. Oh, dear! I didn't mean 'dead', although ye were knocking on that particular door for a spell. Are ye feeling just so this morning, do ye think? Ye're still a might bit peeked, but at least your eyes be open now."

"Who are you?" Christina peered at the figure from beneath half-closed lids. Her head was throbbing, but she didn't know if the source was the sunlight or the woman's jabbering about her like a magpie.

"Oh, I be Katie, miss." The blur curtsied absurdly.

"Are you always this exuberant, Katie?" Christina rubbed at her temples as the throbbing intensified.

"Aye, that I am, miss." Katie bobbed again, and then set about tidying up, still chattering. "Me mum, God rest her soul, always said to start your day with cheer so that ye be better able to fight distress should it take a notion to come bothering ye."

And what does one do when the cheerfulness starts bothering someone else, Christina wanted to say, but refrained. After all, she couldn't fault someone else's cheery disposition simply because she felt far from sunny. Still, she would love it if the woman would slow her pace a bit.

"So, why are ye...I mean, *you*, why are *you* here, Katie?

"Your uncle hired me to look after ye. Only ye haven't exactly been awake for me to be doing that, now have ye?"

"My uncle?"

"Yes, miss." The woman continued moving swiftly about the

room, curiously and excessively tidying everything within sight, until Christina's head began to swim. "Would you *please* be still for a moment?"

"For certain, miss. Me apologies."

"Now that I'm awake," Christina said and pulled to a sitting position, "perhaps you'll explain to me once more who you are."

"Yes, miss." The woman curtsied again. "Me name's Katie, and your uncle, he hired me to look after ye."

"Uncle Peter?"

"Unless ye be having another uncle hereabouts, miss."

"How long did you say that I've been asleep?" Christina asked, rubbing her tired eyes.

"Nigh onto three days, miss, but I wouldn't be calling it sleeping. Do ye not recall what happened to ye then?"

"No, what happened?" Christina asked, her brain still trying to wake up enough to follow along with the conversation. It was definitely a trying task.

"Perhaps it best be your uncle that be discussing...no, it's no really something personal, so I suppose I could..."

"Katie, please! Just spit it out!" Christina continued to rub her temples, but the throbbing refused to ease.

"Oh, sorry, miss. Ye had a bit of a run-in with a rattler," Katie said with a wince.

"A what?"

"A rattler, miss, bit ye."

"A rattlesnake bit me?" Christina racked her brain, but it wasn't functioning well enough yet to remember where she was, much less what had happened prior to this morning.

"Well, it certainly didn't have the intentions of kissin' ye. Anyhow, ye were on your way here with your uncle, as I heard tell, when his horse shied and dumped ye. The rattler that scared the horse took a notion into its silly wee head to strike at ye. Unfortunately for ye, it didn't miss."

"And I lived."

"That much is apparent, miss. God was most definitely looking down on ye, he was. Your uncle is still out of his head with worry, seeing as how he blames his poor horsemanship for what happened to ye; and, of course, ye've been exceeding sick, but now ye're back, praise heaven. Ye already endured far more than one person ought to have."

"Endured?"

"This past month, aye. Do ye not be remembering that either, then?"

"Unfortunately, I do. Does everyone know about it?"

"Yes, miss," Katie bobbed her head rapidly, "and truth be told, we still don't know how ye managed to cross all that hostile country on your own."

"On my own?"

"Aye. It must have been awful for ye, what with your family murdered and ye having to make the crossing the rest of the way without a soul to comfort and guide ye."

"Alone," Christina muttered flatly.

"Yes, miss. Your Uncle, he done told us all about your harrowing experience."

"Harrowing."

"Are ye certain you be alright miss, or do ye always repeat that which someone else has already done said? I only ask because ye've been doing it since ye woke up."

"You've a sassy tongue on you, Katie," Christina observed sharply.

"Sorry, miss. That I do, and I'll be careful to curb me tongue in the future." Katie, subdued, turned, and started placing wood in the fireplace.

"I don't think I need a fire, Katie," Christina said, suddenly sorry for her boorish behavior. She knew that it had nothing to do with the woman now sullenly going about her chores, but with the fact that Baying Wolf had deserted her so easily, "and I certainly don't require a person to look after me. I've been doing that just fine my entire life. I *am* sorry however, that I snapped at you and am very grateful for your kind assistance. Let's just chalk it up to recovering poorly, shall we?"

"Very well, miss, and I be truly sorry if I said or did anything out of station. It was not me intention to be upsetting ye further."

"It's alright, truly. I do believe I simply woke up on the wrong side of the bed."

"Well then, now that we've said our apologies, why don't ye be trying to eat a wee bite. Oh, and I guess I should be letting you know that a package arrived for you some weeks back. I put it in your wardrobe..."

"I'll not be needing it anymore, Katie." Christina closed her eyes and felt tears slip from the corners. Her mother had ordered her that wedding dress before leaving Georgia, and it had arrived safe and sound—unlike her mother. She never wanted to see the dress, never wanted the box opened in her presence. What she wanted to do was burn it, burn the reminder of all that had gone wrong for her since leaving Georgia. "Take it with you when you leave, Katie. You can keep it."

"Um, might I be knowing what it is ye're giving me, Miss?"

"A wedding dress," Christina responded, her tone flat. She swiped at the tears in her eyes and sniffled indelicately. "I have no use for it now, nor will I ever."

"Aye, Miss." Katie wanted to refute her comment and leave the box where it lie, but the look in her mistress' eyes brooked no argument. She hefted the box and started for the door, "I'll go see about me other duties afore Mrs. Cavanaugh starts her fussing at me."

"Wait! What about my uncle?"

"Well, he did say as how he'll be wanting to speak with ye when ye be well enough, but I don't think he figured it would be so soon, so he be away in Austin at present. Besides, the doctor was saying that ye're not to be out of bed just yet. Not 'til he's had the chance to check ye." Before Christina could say anything further, a loud voice from below stairs shouted Katie's name and, after a quick curtsey, she bounded from the room. Christina looked at the food on the tray, but her stomach rebelled.

As she took in the room around her, with its pastel colors and lace trimmings, she felt her throat constrict and the tears threaten. She should be happy now. She had a roof over her head, was sleeping, apparently soundly, in a beautiful four-poster, feather bed. Katie was bringing her meals to her on a tray; and intended to wait upon her hand and foot. She also managed to survive a rattlesnake bite.

She should be ecstatic that she didn't have to endure Baying Wolf's company anymore, sleep on the hard ground, or take lessons on how to clean and cook her own food. Instead, she found herself remembering the day he rode away and left her, and anger replaced her sadness. *He didn't give a damn about me!* She thought—heart dejected. His Great Spirit had sent him to see to her safety, and the minute the deed was done, he'd gone away.

Did I really mean so little to him? She wondered. She'd thought that their relationship had somehow progressed into one of trust. A wary sort of trust, but at least she felt a basis of friendship had begun. Then, the moment the opportunity arose, he abandoned her to strangers. Rode away from her without even a backward glance; without so much as a by-your-leave. He was probably home already, enjoying his heathen life; not even giving her a second thought. Well, that suited her just fine.

"I mean, it's not as if I would have had anywhere else to go if I hadn't come here," she murmured to herself. "I certainly couldn't have gone home with him. Well, dwelling on it, certainly isn't productive." She would simply forget him—never think about him again from this moment on. "Just like he's doing, I'd wager," She sighed and dug halfheartedly into her rapidly cooling meal.

CHAPTER 62

Baying Wolf pulled the flap of his tepee closed and stopped short.

"I do not wish your company today, Prairie Heart." He moved to sit by the fire, ignoring the woman laying naked on his buffalo robes. He lifted the lid on the pot and sniffed deeply.

"The scouts said that you were on your way back, so I made you some buffalo stew. Perhaps after you eat, you would like to have me for dessert. Like the stew—I'm hot, delicious, and ready to be..."

"I said not tonight!" Baying Wolf cut her off sharply, not wanting his mind to envision the picture she was so boldly trying to paint.

"Why is Baying Wolf so angry with me?" Prairie Heart pouted. "I'm only trying to fill your appetites. All of them." Baying Wolf had no doubt to what she referred, but his mind was not on Prairie Heart. It angered him that all he could see was the red-haired, green-eyed she wolf in his mind now. In fact, she filled his mind with such totality that he could not even find a small nook with which to entertain thoughts of Prairie Heart and all that she offered him.

"What bothers Baying Wolf so much that he cannot spend time with his Prairie Heart? Do you not miss the companionship of your woman?"

"You are not *my* Prairie Heart. You are merely a woman that has shared my bed. Now I wish you to leave and never return."

Prairie Heart sat in stunned disbelief for the longest time, her mouth agape, her eyes wide and her heart thudding rapidly in her ears. Surely, she hadn't heard him right. She panicked, truly distressed. He couldn't possibly mean what he just said, she reasoned insanely. Something has just upset him, is all. "Baying Wolf..." Prairie Heart tried again softly, but was cut off once more by Baying Wolf's rage.

"I said out, woman!" Baying Wolf turned to face her, his fists clenched tightly by his sides. "Have your ears been stuffed so full of bear grease that you can only hear that which you choose? Leave me! Now!" Prairie Heart sprang to her feet, hugging the buffalo blanket to her breast like a shield. She grabbed her dress with her free hand and shimmied into it, lowering the blanket slowly, suddenly ashamed to have Baying Wolf stare upon her naked form. Not that he was looking at her at all. In fact, he kept his gaze pinned to the stew. Stew! Had he really been gone so long that stew held more appeal than she did? The tears she shed from having him snap at her turned to ones of anger. *He can't treat me like this! He just can't,* she thought angrily, yanking the dress down past her hips. She'd been there, as his woman, for months, but now when he leaves the village and returns...her gaze narrowed on him, "You have chosen another woman! Is that it? You unfaithful..."

"I made you no promises, Prairie Heart," Baying Wolf said without denying her claim. He turned to look at her now that she was clothed. "You came to me, remember?"

"But I thought that we would wed and..."

Baying Wolf snorted. "Do you think I do not know how you entertained yourself before entering my tepee, and you thought that I would marry you?" It didn't really bother him with whom she'd spent her time, but it was the only reason he could come up with on short notice. Unfortunately for him, it didn't work.

"You have been listening to rumors and lies. The other women are just jealous of my beauty. Surely you don't believe I have been unfaithful to you?"

"I do not think this, but I was speaking of your prior activities with Yellow Bear and Little Beaver, and...do I need to go on?"

"So, you listen to lies of men instead of women. What's the difference? They are only telling you that because they are jealous that I have chosen you and not them!"

"So everyone in our village is a selfish, jealous liar? Go away, Prairie Heart. I do not have time for your childish behavior." Baying Wolf closed his eyes and rubbed his neck. All he wanted was peace and privacy to eat and sleep. Instead, Prairie Heart wanted to debate honesty and integrity. When he opened his eyes, she was still standing there, her fists clenched at her sides. "Do you really want me to get angry?" He whispered between teeth clenched tight.

"I want to know who has taken you away from me, so I may fight for my honor."

"Either leave, or you won't have a life to fight for your honor."

"You're threatening me?"

Baying Wolf moved quickly, grabbed Prairie Heart by the waist, hoisted her over his shoulder, and tossed her onto her derriere...outside his teepee.

Activity stopped and faces gawked.

Prairie Heart squealed with humiliation, and then stood and ran from the village—tears pouring from her eyes.

Baying Wolf sank wearily to the buffalo blanket that Prairie Heart had used and lowered his tired head into his hands. He should feel sorry for the way he'd treated her, he knew, but for some reason couldn't summon the pity for her that she probably deserved. To have her out of his tepee actually brought a sense of relief that he had trouble comprehending. It wasn't as if he hadn't enjoyed her company, for he had—many, many times—so why not now? Why now did he not long to hold her and make love with her as he had so often in the past?

The answer was obvious and made his anger grow. He slammed his fist into the hard ground and winced.

"She is forgotten!" He yelled to the walls. "I will think of her no more!"

CHAPTER 63

One Year Later

The wind was gusting as fast and as furious as her heartbeat.

There's not enough shelter here! *Her mind yelled.*

"Now is not the time to panic!" *She whispered, rising panic evident in her voice. She was genuinely afraid, but she wasn't certain why; but whatever caused her fear was close. She sensed it. Sensed it was too close, but could not see who or what it was. Another gust caused her skirt to billow.*

"No! Stay put!" *She whispered harshly, tugging at the fabric, bunching it in her fists. The sound of footsteps drifted upon the wind and she stopped all movement; praying that her skirt would stop also—for if it did not, it would draw attention to her; attention she felt would be unwelcomed.*

It was difficult to determine through the howl of the wind, just how near or far the footfalls were, but she began a silent plea that whoever it was would pass her by or turn and head off in a different direction. She held her breath, and squeezed her eyelids tightly closed, her prayer intensifying as the sound drew nearer.

Then another sound reached her ears. Laughter.

She now knew that the threat was human, and they were nearby. Something was frightfully amusing to them. She felt anything but amused, for as long as they remained nearby, she remained trapped.

Then, as though the wind whisked the intruders away in a flash, there was silence.

She wanted to peer around the tree to see if they were still there, to determine why the sudden quiet on the heels of obvious gaiety. As if seeking to answer her question unasked, another sound began, as though a rumbling of thunder.

A hand was shaking her shoulder.

"What? What do you want?" Christina moaned, blocking the sun from her eyes.

"Good morning to ye miss. Time for ye to be rising and shining."

"Go away, Katie! I need..." Christina started and then paused.

She started to say that she needed to go back to sleep, that her visions had returned, but obviously couldn't without raising a whole lot of questions from the queen of inquiry. She stiffened, sitting up rapidly.

She was having another vision!

"Oh, dear!" She whispered softly. She knew that it was a vision because it was similar in realism as the one she'd endured last year; however, the content was very different.

"What did ye say, miss?" Katie asked, turning from drawing the second curtain.

"Nothing, Katie. Nothing at all," Christina murmured. *At least nothing that I can talk about,* she amended silently. With unconscious thought, she mentally braced herself, for though she knew not what was going to occur, she did not doubt that something would; that it was only a matter of time before her vision became reality.

This time she hoped it would be different; that she would be able to interpret its meaning early enough to take whatever action needed taking to stop whatever disaster she knew would occur. She had been ill prepared last year, unknowing that her dream was trying to tell her something. Had she been wiser, she may have recognized the danger the vision revealed and moved to save her family and friends from the massacre that took them all from her life.

You forget that the vision was confusing. You thought it was solely about danger to you. It was slow to reveal that the danger also was to those around you. Her mind offered in solace.

"I think, in reality, it was trying to warn me of the danger Jeffrey Buchanan presented to me and my family. After all, had he not convinced father to move, we would still be living safe and secure in Georgia; and yet, had he not convinced us to move, I would be his wife today and living in abject misery."

Perhaps it's time you realized that your vision last year was not meant as a measure of prevention, rather was meant as a revelation. Whoever sent that vision to you would have known you were unwise and ill prepared to interpret it, but wanted you to see what your future held in store, so that you could mature and strengthen your mind and body for what was, and is, to come.

"The sense that I had, many times, that my destiny somehow lay across the Mississippi, could have been a part of that which someone was trying to impart to me. Do you think?"

I more than think it. I am sure of it.

"Well, I wasn't able to glean much from this new vision before I was awakened, so don't know if it is revelational, and therefore unpreventable; or whether it is meant to be preventative, in which case I will need to interpret and heed its message far quicker."

"If you be asking me opinion, I'll need more information than that ye given thus far, miss," Katie said softly.

Christina lifted her head with a jerk. Katie was standing next to the bed with a tray in her hands, a confused curiosity on her face.

"So, you've taken to eavesdropping, is that it?" Christina snapped lightly.

"Well, truth be told, miss, I couldn't tell whether it was me ye were speaking to, so I moved a bit closer. Then I heard ye saying something about visions and such and...well, I take it ye were no talking to me then," Katie finished lamely, setting the tray on the nightstand, "but then as I couldn't tell if it were to me ye were talking, I thought it would be rude to ignore ye, so I waited for ye to take a breath, as it would've been just as rude of me to interrupt ye."

"Goodness, Katie. Well, it isn't exactly your fault that I was talking to myself out loud, I don't suppose," Christina said with a sigh.

"If you be wanting to, I'll be more than happen to lend you me ear," Katie offered. "I may be a talker, but I be an equally good listener."

"No, thank you, Katie. There's nothing to be done for it whether I discuss it or not, but thank you just the same. So, what's for breakfast this morning?"

"Oh, I've brought ye a bite of fresh fruit, toast, an over-easy egg, as well as some news."

"Ah, let the gossip begin," Christina settled the tray on her lap and took a bite out of her toast. Katie's bit of news, broadcasted every morning, had become a ritual during the past year, and it always began the same way: a listing of what she was having for breakfast followed by the 'as well as some news'. She had grown so used to the daily gossip that she wondered what would happen should all gossiping cease for a day. Would Katie find something to pass along were all sordid activities to cease? In that likely event, she'd probably turn the birthing of a foal into a melodrama.

"Well, ye heard talk of Marcie and Kevin, no?"

"How could I not? You've got the entire southern half of the state covered in your gossip chain, which trickles down to my ears every morning."

"Oh, aren't ye a smarty this morning?" Katie said, stabbing Christina in the leg with her elbow. "But never-thee-mind. As I was saying, Marcie finally consented to wedding Kevin, but I hear tell that she didn't have a choice in the matter, if ye know what I mean."

And so it went for the next quarter hour. Katie filling Christina in on the local gossip, and Christina sitting and filling her belly with food. It never stopped until Christina downed her juice and started on her coffee.

"Well, there were definitely some interesting tidbits this morning," Christina said, sipping on the hot brew. "I certainly won't be able to look at Charlene in the same light at the soiree this weekend."

"Speaking of which, we'd best get ye up and dressed," Katie said, bouncing off the bed. She removed the tray from Christina's lap and set it on the nightstand, and then moved over to the armoire. "Let's see! What's nice to be receiving callers' in, hmm?"

"What are you blabbering on about, Katie?" Christina asked, throwing her blankets aside and scooting off the bed.

"Oh, did I forget to tell ye that wee bit of news, then?" Christina sighed at the mischief in Katie's tone.

"Spit it out, Katie."

"Aye, well, it's only that there be a young man below stairs waiting to visit with ye," Katie said, and giggled at the incredulous look on Christina's face.

"Who?" Christina finally got around to asking.

"Well, it wouldn't be much of a surprise now, would it, if I was to be telling ye?" Katie said, throwing a simple, emerald green day dress over Christina's head. "Ah, green is definitely your color. Brings out the emerald in your eyes, it does."

"Forget my eyes, Katie," Christina snapped as Katie led her to the vanity and pushed her unresisting body onto the stool.

"Turn about now so that I can dress your hair for ye."

Christina snatched the brush from Katie's hand and waved it under the startled maid's nose, "If you don't stop playing and tell me who it is that's waiting for me, I'm going to whack you good on the nose with this brush!"

"Well, there's no reason to be getting your knickers in a knot. All ye need do was ask me," Katie laughed and Christina just shook her head in frustration.

"You're going to be the death of me, Katie."

"A little teasing is good for ye, miss. Keeps ye on your toes."

"So you say, now how about telling me..."

"Your caller be Barnabas Freely."

"Who?" Christina asked, the name not registering.

"What do ye mean 'who'? Why he's only the most eligible man in the county, and ye've caught his eye, ye have."

Not again, her mind sighed.

"Eligible or not. I haven't a clue who the man is and I'll not be the object of any man's eye that I don't know," she said sharply, and then added under her breath, "Not ever again!"

"Well, he's come calling to see if ye be free for the barbeque this Sunday, at the William's," Katie said with less enthusiasm, wondering if this man would go the way of the others that had dared attempt to court Carthington's niece since she arrived a year past. Either Christina chased them off or her uncle did with a declaration that they weren't good enough for his niece.

"And you know this because?"

"Because Susan overheard him talking to your uncle about ye when she took refreshments in, and she told Martha, and Martha told Betty, and...."

"Spare me, Katie," Christina sighed.

"Aye, well, it is a rather long list and ye need to be getting yerself below stairs now. All done!" She said, spinning Christina around to view herself in the mirror. "Absolutely beautiful, if I do say so meself."

Katie was right, Christina thought, she did look lovely. Green really was a good color on her, and Katie always managed to coif her hair in such a way that didn't portray her as supercilious.

"Thank you, Katie. A beautiful job, as always."

"Give him a chance, miss. He's only been in the area for a few months, but I've heard nothing but good about the man."

"I'll speak with him," Christina said, not promising a thing.

CHAPTER 64

Christina's heart was pounding when she stood before the solarium door and knocked, memories flitting across her mind of a similar moment in their home in Georgia. She'd been unpleasantly surprised that day—a day that had turned her world from a life of enjoyment to one of pandemonium.

"Enter." Christina jumped at the command. She drew in a shaky breath and ran her sweaty palms across the front of her skirt. She closed her eyes a moment, and forced her racing heart to calm. When she was certain she'd gotten her runaway emotions under control, she slid open the door and stepped inside. There was a man seated across from her uncle, who stood upon her entrance. Christina acknowledged him with a nod, and then turned to address her uncle.

"It was my understanding, uncle, that you wished me to see you, but as you have company at the moment…"

"No, no, come in, Christina," her uncle said, moving to take her hand, guiding her to their guest. "There's someone I'd like you to meet."

"Oh?" Christina said, attempting to sound surprised.

"Yes, indeed," her uncle said, stopping in front of the visitor. "This is Mr. Barnabas Freely. Barnabas, my niece, Christina."

"It's a pleasure to make your acquaintance, Miss Carthington."

"Likewise, I'm sure," Christina's remained unaffected as he lifted her hand and placed a light kiss on the back. His manner was social and gentle, and his voice soothing and pleasant, but Christina couldn't relax. He was too smooth, just as Jeffrey had been. Jeffrey had been the epitome of a gentleman, and had convinced her parents of his worth. Then, when her parents had fallen sufficiently beneath his spell, he changed, revealing his true nature in the span of one afternoon. So, while she felt a twinge of guilt at lumping all gentlemen into the same mold as Jeffrey, she could not prevent herself doing so. He simply couldn't measure up...

To Baying Wolf? Her mind concluded for her. *You do realize that 'gentleman' doesn't equate to evil? This man may very well be all that he appears, but because he isn't Baying Wolf, he isn't good enough. Did you ever stop to think why?*

At the reminder of the Indian that had been so prominent in her dreams last year, and had come to her aid after her family's slaughter, her heart started racing and the perspiration returned to her palms. She hadn't thought of him in a year, at least not with any consequence. She was thinking of him now, however. Remembering his kiss....

"Miss Carthington?"

"What? Oh, I'm sorry," A blush stained Christina's cheeks, "I drifted off in thought for a moment. What were you saying?"

"Actually, I was asking," Barnabas said, a grin on his face.

"Oh, well, then, asking...where's my uncle?" Christina asked suddenly, after a quick scan of the room.

"If I answer your question, will you endeavor to answer mine?" Barnabas asked, and laughed lightly at the embarrassment reflected on Christina's face.

"Oh, dear," Christina said, her blush increasing, "I'm not holding to my manners very well, am I?"

"Well, you did drift pretty far away for a bit, but now that you're back, maybe we can start again," Barnabas said amiably. "Your uncle thought we could spend some time alone to get acquainted. Now, it's your turn, but I'll need to repeat the question for you, won't I?"

"Unfortunately, yes." Her nervousness at being left alone with yet another potential suitor nearly proved her emotional undoing. It took a mental determination to stay focused to hear the question he posed, and an equal determination of will to answer civilly and not tear from the room in a panic.

"I was asking if you would like to accompany me to the barbeque at the William's on Sunday."

"I don't know. I hadn't really thought about attending."

Coward! Her mind snapped.

"I am not...certain," Christina hastened to amend, "that it would be fair to you to escort someone who is simply not ready..."

Admit it, he's not Baying Wolf!

"You know what," Christina said quickly, "I've changed my mind. I'd be delighted to have you accompany me."

Liar! Your mind didn't change anything. You are going to spite *your mind.*

Christina sighed and plastered a smile on her face. The look she was getting from her caller made her want to retract the acceptance. He eyed her as if she were twenty apples shy of a bushel. She blushed.

"I'd be delighted," she said to break the silence, "if you're still willing to escort me, that is. I assure you, I'm not nearly as imbalanced as I sound."

Barnabas' laugh was not genuine, rather an attempt at graciousness. Christina's blush deepened.

"Maybe I'd better let you go. I'm certain that there are plenty of young ladies who would be honored to have you escort them on Sunday." Christina curtsied lightly and then turned to leave.

"As confused as I am, I have to admit to also being a little curious," Barnabas said hastily, and Christina postponed her departure, "as to what it is that was going on in that head of yours. You seemed mightily preoccupied earlier, and just now it was if you were waging battle with yourself."

"You're very astute." Christina smiled without humor. The fact that he could read her so well was more than a little disconcerting.

"I'm not trying to pry," Barnabas smiled assuring. "My curiosity over why my presence bothers you so is just a part of who I am. In fact, my curiosity tends to get me in quite a bind now and again—as it would appear to have done now." Barnabas stopped speaking and bowed low at the waist, "I would ask that you please forgive my horrid manner, dear lady, and afford me one more opportunity to converse with you in the manner in which, I assure you, I am capable."

His exaggerated manner would normally bring a smile to her

face, as it so reminded her of her brother, Thomas. Moreover, Christina would normally be pleased at the thought that someone of her acquaintance held a similar annoying attribute as herself, someone who could possibly empathize with her about the many times her own curiosity had gotten her into trouble. The fact remained, however, that his manner—so similar to her brother— only served to sadden her heart; and though she didn't want to admit it, her mind was right about something. This man, though charming, was not Baying Wolf, and no matter how hard she attempted to focus on him, Baying Wolf's image continued to intrude.

I told you I was right.

"You've drifted away again," Barnabas whispered, watching the emotions, and indecision, flit across her face.

Still, this man seems a decent sort, and the fact that he reminds you of Thomas may prove him a man of good character. Why don't you at least entertain the notion of going with him?

"You're right," Christina conceded, "I did drift away again, and I have been waging a battle within my mind. If that trait disturbs you, I can assure you, your departure would not cause me grief. If you are still willing to converse with me a short spell, I'll try to remain here in this room and promise to conduct myself with the manners in which my mother raised me. Do we have an accord?"

Barnabas smiled and settled on the seat next to the window. "You are a curiosity, Miss Carthington."

Christina smiled and settled on the chair across from him. "It's just been a trying year for me, and thus I'm still attempting to regain my balance; trying to find my place in this world."

"You're uncle explained a bit about your upsetting journey," Barnabas said softly, "and you have my deepest respect for the courage you displayed in getting here safely."

Christina merely smiled again. She could say nothing about her journey without revealing details that would make mincemeat out of her uncle's version of events. Instead, she deftly changed the subject.

"So, what do you do, Mr. Freely?"

"I'm a captain in the army. My unit arrived last month. Some are only here for a short term, headed to Fort Bliss. Me? I hope to stay here for quite some time," he said. "Though far different from my home in Virginia, something about this region is fascinating to me.

It was another similarity to herself that Christina was hesitant to make much of.

"So why the increased presence in Texas? Is this anything to do with the rumors of war we heard prior to leaving Georgia?"

"A woman's company, Miss Carthington, is no place to discuss politics or war," Barnabas said.

And he just lost whatever spark of hope there was in getting better acquainted.

Christina nodded in agreement with her mind, but Barnabas took it as consent to change the subject, and thus the remainder of their conversation focused on how the weather differed between Texas and back east.

Despite her boredom, she did consent to accompany him to the barbeque that Sunday, wondering why she'd done so the moment he departed her company.

CHAPTER 65

"Marcie, Kevin, it's good to see you," Christina said, trying hard to keep her gaze from drifting to Marcie's belly. "I understand there are congratulations due."

"Oh, yes, well..." Marcie blushed. Kevin placed an arm around her shoulders and pulled her closer.

"We'd be honored if you were to attend, Miss Carthington," Kevin said graciously.

"I'm the one who's honored," Christina replied. "And I wouldn't miss it for the world."

Christina watched them leave and smiled. Then her gaze moved around the William's yard and came to rest on Charlene Thittlesmore, and her curiosity piqued. Was what Katie told her about Charlene true or merely idle gossip? If it was, then Charlene wasn't going to be able to stay in town for too much longer, or everyone would know her dirty little secret and her reputation would be in tatters.

Oh well, it wasn't her concern, for certain. It did make her wonder, however, just how many innocent-looking glances aimed her way were because of talk among the gossip queens. Did Katie talk to her friends about her? Was her arrival last year and her conversations about Baying Wolf, bandied about in the morning's daily gossip? She'd never thought that Katie would disclose that which they so freely discussed, but at the same time, Katie did freely discuss that information imparted to her about other people.

"Perhaps I need to censor my conversations with her, if I want to keep my own reputation intact," she murmured thoughtfully.

"Here's your punch," A voice startled her from behind and she jumped, knocking the punch away from the bearer.

"Oh, dear!" She said, eyeing the giant red stain that now covered Barnabas's white shirt.

Barnabas looked down and grimaced, "Well, at least we know the punch is *cold*."

"Oh, Mr. Freely, I'm terribly sorry," she said, pulling her handkerchief from her sleeve. "You startled me, is all."

"If I didn't know better, I'd say you had second thoughts about accompanying me today and thought of a creative way to send me home." When Christina didn't reply, Barnabas's eyebrows arched in question, "Humor me and tell me I'm wrong perhaps?"

"You're wrong," Christina said, her humiliation rising when she heard people nearby snicker and start whispering. "It was an accident, truly," she said, swiping ineffectually with her handkerchief at the stain on his shirt.

"I know, Miss Carthington," he said, placing a hand on hers to stop her efforts. "With your uncle's permission, would you like to accompany me back to the fort for a short while? It's a hot day to be sure, but if I'm going to cool off, it's not going to be with a dunk in the punch bowl. I'd really like to change."

"I didn't dunk you in the punch bowl," Christina grinned, "it's just a little stain."

"Little!" Barnabas said dramatically in mock horror. "That happened to be the largest cup available in the William's cupboard! *And* the entire contents are on my shirt. I may as well have taken a swim in the punch bowl."

"Oh, my, such dramatics from an officer," Christina said, genuinely amused by his antics. He truly reminded her of Thomas in many ways, yet in many ways was so different.

Barnabas laughed, flagging down her uncle. "Ride with me, Miss Carthington?"

"Very well, Mr. Freely," she said with a smile.

"Well, how're you two faring?" her uncle started and then stopped, eyeing the red stain questioningly. "Not too well, I take it?"

"Actually, it was an accident, Mr. Carthington," Barnabas said graciously, "but I am in need of a fresh change of clothing, and wondered if Christina could escort me back to the fort. I assure you that I am a man of honor."

"Well, I don't see why not?" Her uncle said, grinning. "Just make sure you bring her back before sunset, young man," he added in a stern voice that Christina knew was for show. She didn't have a doubt that Barnabas Freely could drag her off and force her to wed and her uncle would still welcome him with open arms.

Christina sighed. She wondered if all men had the innate ability to bamboozle the relatives of the woman in which they were interested.

Perhaps his interest in you is sincere.

Possibly, she replied, *but I'm not at all certain I appreciate the way he looks at me at times.*

Only you would be offended. Most women would be flattered.

Yeah, well, most women didn't go through what I did last year with a man that could out charm this fellow twice over, she continued her wordless debate, *so forgive me if I'm a little leery of men who turn on the charm too soon and too strong.*

At least try not to be cynical. Give him a chance, will you? Or you'll end up an old maid.

"Christina, are you ready?" Barnabas asked, placing a hand on her elbow. She felt a shiver of discomfort race down her spine, but didn't pull away.

"Ready as I'll ever be," she said with forced cheeriness. *Happy?* She snapped at her mind.

CHAPTER 66

Christina felt uncomfortable. She never visited the fort before, but now she was here pacing the boardwalk, waiting for Barnabas to change his clothes; sweat trickling between her breasts, beneath her arms, between her legs as the temperature intensified with each passing hour. To add to her discomfort, soldiers of every shape, size, and rank wandered by, their gazes ranging from curious to lustful, leaving her feeling miserable and exposed. However, neither of those were worse than the discomfort at having Indians swarming about the fort, chattering, laughing –staring.

She did her best to ignore it all, especially the Indians, but it was growing more difficult. She glanced at Barnabas' door ready to intrude upon his quarters, her reputation be damned, when his door opened and he sauntered out. Christina didn't hesitate. At seeing Barnabas exit his room, she immediately moved to mount her steed and headed for the entrance to the fort. She didn't doubt that Barnabas would catch up quickly, nor did she doubt he'd be looking for an explanation as to her abrupt departure.

The moment her horse exited the fort, she spurred her mare into a gallop, the need to flee overwhelming in its intensity. She heard horse hoofs bounding after her, but refused to slow, not until she outran the terror chasing after her.

"Miss Carthington!" Barnabas yelled, his stallion quickly catching up to Christina's mare. He pulled alongside, wanting to slow, but Christina's focus was so intent, the fear etched on her features so pronounced, that he merely met her pace and kept riding.

Within a few minutes, they crossed over onto the William's spread, and Christina slowed her horse to a trot and then to a walk. Barnabas shot by her and had to pull hard on the reins to slow his stallion's speed. He tugged on the reins and turned to move back alongside Christina's mount. Tears were streaming down her cheeks, her eyes glazed over, unseeing the scenery ahead, relying upon her mount to keep her safely headed toward the house.

"Did something happen at the fort, Christina?" He asked gently. She shook her head, and swiped the tears away. She shuddered and sniffled, raising her head in what appeared to Barnabas to be a defiant determination. "If nothing happened at the fort, why did you bolt like that?"

Christina let go a heavy sigh, "It's not anything I wish to discuss with you, Mr. Freely," she said softly, but her tone brooked no argument.

"Very well, Miss Carthington," he replied stiffly. "I think, perhaps, it's best if I return you to your home. I acted as escort to you today, and it's my duty to see you safely there."

"If it's all the same to you, I'd prefer to return alone. If you'll just let my uncle know of my whereabouts, your duty to me is done for the day."

Barnabas didn't argue. In his estimation, he'd tolerated her strange and impolite behavior more than many men would have. There had been signs of normalcy in her behavior that he'd hoped would become a regular occurrence, but she was simply too erratic in her emotional makeup to make a good wife for a military officer. With a brusque nod, he spurred his horse towards the house, leaving Christina alone with her thoughts.

She turned her horse towards her Uncle Peter's, but stopped when she reached the outskirts of the property. Just as she'd found a perfect spot to think near her home in Georgia, she'd located a spot here that she oftentimes visited to clear her mind. She wended through the trees until she entered a small clearing, and then slid from her saddle and sank onto the springy grass, her heart heavy, her body weary, and her mind in turmoil.

She had not encountered an Indian since the day she left Baying Wolf in the clearing; the day her uncle forcibly removed her from his company—or at least she'd felt as if she'd had no choice in what happened. Her uncle's assurance that day returned to haunt her, as it had done nearly every day for a year.

"You'll never see him again, child, so stop fretting."

For a while, she had put her past behind her; had only managed to think about Baying Wolf infrequently. For the past months, she had determined to move forward with her life, to put the past behind her and live for her future. Had she never visited the fort, seen the Indians milling about, she may have managed successfully never thinking about Indians again. May never recall the slaughter of her family. If she never saw another Indian again in her lifetime, it would be too soon by her estimation.

She lay back, plucked a piece of grass from beside her and wove a bracelet, while the movement of the clouds worked their magic and lulled her into a restless sleep.

CHAPTER 67

The sound she interpreted as thunder grew more distinct. It was growling, and it was just threatening enough to silence the amiable chatter of moments earlier. She continued to will her skirt to stay put, her hands pushing the material against her thighs; fighting a losing battle, as the winds continued to gust.

She remembered the last time she'd been in the middle of the woods, with no one nearby to assist, when people had come upon her. Had she not taken a chance and launched an attack against the lead trapper, she would have lost her virtue to three foul-smelling, hairy ogres. Her throwing star had hit its mark, giving her the chance to flee, and then she'd run headlong into Baying Wolf, and they'd dispatched the remaining two trappers with little difficulty. She reluctantly admitted to herself that they made a good team.

Another growl issued, and Christina shivered. She heard unintelligible whispers, as if the unseen people were trying to determine how to take care of the threat before them. Christina kept praying that they wanted to kill the threat, not because they knew she was there and wanted to get to her, but because the threat was blocking them from continuing along their journey. Were it not for the interference, the people would have trekked right past her hiding place, and have easily spotted her—or at least her billowing skirts. She needed to find a way to hide better, should they manage to outwit that animal. She silently cursed the pending storm, for it made hiding exceedingly difficult. If she made to move, they would spot her for certain, but to remain where she was, was foolish.

Perhaps if she was to ascertain the threat for herself, maybe then she could think more clearly upon a solution. She peered cautiously from behind the tree. Her heart skipped a beat, for standing amidst a circle of warriors—faces painted black as night—was Wolf; and from the way the spears were poised in deadly threat, Wolf was in mortal danger. Did Baying Wolf know...

Oh, my God! The wolf is Baying Wolf.

The realization struck her mind as a lightning bolt.

"She's over here!" The shout startled Christina awake, and she sat abruptly at the appearance of several horse and riders emerging into the clearing, surrounding her. Her heart palpitated, the fear from her dream still enshrouding her; a fear that refused to abate—until her uncle appeared through the trees. The anger emanating from his gaze spoke volumes—she'd not returned to the house as she'd told Barnabas she would do, and that had worried her uncle no end.

He did not dismount, merely sat glaring at her for a few moments before ordering her to mount up. She stood hastily and mounted her mare, following her taciturn uncle from the clearing, her own ire rising at his abrupt manner, and at the fact that he'd compromised her hiding place. She'd have to locate another.

When they exited the tree line, her anger departed quickly at seeing the sinking of the sun. She'd spent considerable time sleeping, so much time, in fact, that night was now falling. No wonder her uncle was so angry and had sent out a search party. She would have done no differently in his stead, for being outside at night was dangerous, even for a seasoned ranch hand. She suddenly felt like a silly child, and hoped he would not rebuke her too severely for her inconsiderate and imprudent actions.

She felt even sillier when they approached the house, and she spied nearly every staff member waiting on the porch. Katie's distress was most evident, as she paced, wringing her hands.

To Christina, their reaction seemed a bit extreme, but had she known the reasons behind their worry, her opinion would change as quickly as the weather on the plains. However, that reason was not to be imparted to her that day. The only thing imparted to her was a sharp-tongued lecture—from both her uncle and her maid. Neither of which she'd be forgetting any time soon.

CHAPTER 68

As the days turned into weeks, her uncle barely spoke two
words to her, and then, only when necessary, leaving Christina more
than a little confused. Her uncle, and Katie, had made her aware—
very loud and clear—that her actions on the day of the William's
barbeque had been beyond foolish, so then why couldn't he put the
incident behind him, as Christina was trying to do. Certainly, he had
forgiven her silliness. She said as much to Katie that morning.

"Oh, he no be worried over that no more, miss," she replied,
setting about in preparation of the morning gossip. As soon as
Christina took her first bite of toast, Katie launched into her news
bulletin.

"From what I've gleaned in the past couple weeks, ye're uncle
be a mite bit put out with ye for scaring off the only eligible
bachelor within nine counties."

Christina nodded in understanding. The last any of them had
heard from Barnabas Freely came in the form of a wire dispatched
to her a few days after the barbeque, which explained that he'd been
stationed elsewhere. Apparently—according to Katie's sources—her
uncle, displeased with this turn of events, had sought to have those
orders reversed, but was informed that Barnabas had made the
request, and that his commanding officer would not bring the man
back over affairs of the heart.

Christina blushed at that declaration, but Katie didn't appear to
notice. She continued with her delivery of the news, enjoying every
minute of her freedom of speech.

"But that not be his only concern, mind ye," Katie said.
"Apparently, word has arrived from back East that the war has
started, and ye're uncle be concerned over how it might affect things
here, which is why he's waiting to speak with ye in the parlor this
morning—after ye be finished eating, that is."

A short while later, Christina approached the parlor door and
braced herself—hoping that her uncle's disposition had improved

toward her. The last thing she wanted was another lecture—this one on how *not* to drive away a suitor. With a sigh, she lightly rapped on the door.

"Come in!" The voice shouted from the other side of the door. Christina pushed it open and stepped inside.

"You wished to speak with me, Uncle Peter?" She asked, moving forward into the room.

"Hello, Christina," a voice said from the shadows. Christina squinted and moved closer until the man came into focus.

"David Michaelson?" She asked in surprise. "Is that really you?"

"It's been a long time," David said, and placed a kiss on each of her cheeks. "I never fancied meeting you here, but when your uncle told me that you were living here now, I asked for an audience. I hope you don't mind."

"Of course not. You must tell me everything that you've been doing since we last saw each other. What's it been...over a year?"

"Shortly, Christina," Her uncle interrupted. "David brought a letter from his father. You remember Andrew Michaelson, don't you?"

"Of course. He opened a competing mercantile around the corner from Father's. David used to tease me mercilessly when we were younger, that his father would drive my father out of business one day. Of course, as it happens, he ended up buying us out instead."

"I'm truly sorry to hear about your family," David said quietly.

"Thank you, David. It was a trying time, for certain, but I'm faring better these days."

"Not to sound impertinent, but you look a might bit peaked. Are you sure you're well?"

"I'm faring much better, but sleeping not so soundly, I'm afraid."

"I'd have nightmares a good long while, if what happened to your family, ever happened to mine."

Christina didn't disabuse him of the notion that her tiredness had to do with the massacre a year's past. After all, she couldn't very well reveal the true cause of her tired state—her visions. She was about to agree with him when her uncle intervened with a none-too-subtle throat clearing. Apparently, socializing wasn't the reason for her summons.

Peter Carthington motioned for them both to take a seat in front of him, and then proceeded to fiddle distractedly with a missive for a few minutes before resuming. He looked up and surprised Christina when he addressed her directly.

"I've received a letter from Andrew Michaelson, as I said," Peter continued. "I want you to understand, Christina, that I would never engage you in matters of politics were it not relevant that I do so; were this not a matter that directly affects you—as it does us all."

"I understand, Uncle," Christina murmured respectfully.

"You've probably guessed by David's uniform that he's in the Army."

"Yes, I can see that." In fact, Christina hadn't noticed David's attire, so surprised she was to see him standing in her uncle's parlor. She took a moment to peruse the uniform, and decided it suited him; lent an air of confidence that had sadly been lacking much of his life. She turned her gaze back, when her uncle continued with his explanation.

"What you don't know is that a couple of weeks ago, a General by the name of Beauregard, fired on a place in Charleston Harbor, North Carolina called Fort Sumter and started a war between the Negro-loving abolitionists in the North and the slave owners in the South. Of course it doesn't help matters none that we elected an antislavery, Negro-loving president. What was his name again, David?"

"Abraham Lincoln, sir," David replied dutifully.

"Anyway, it's bad enough that they want to be telling the Southern states what they can and cannot do, but now they want to be telling us out here what our business should be. Not that I think they'll have much success. That's what David is doing here, isn't it boy?"

"I've been commissioned to Fort Bliss, hopefully to head off any problems that may head this way," David supplied. "I'm to meet up with my detachment in the morning. My commanding officer gave me leave to bring my father's letter to your uncle and then I'm to return posthaste. My father thought that maybe your uncle could use his influence to persuade the governor to stay out of the slavery issue."

"And I'll do my best to do just that. So, David, I hear tell that they'll be finishing them telegraph wires soon and people won't have to hand deliver messages anymore."

"I don't mean to appear rude, Uncle, but I'm not certain I see what this war has to do with me," Christina interrupted gently.

"Yes, well, it has a lot to do with you, my dear," her uncle cleared his throat and plunged ahead. "I have some cattle that I need to drive to the Abilene railroad terminal point, and I need to do it soon, before all hell breaks loose. This could very well be the last cattle we drive to market in some time. The men and I are going to be gone for a couple of weeks, maybe longer, and what with the war breaking out and them damned red-skinned Comanche and Apaches raiding across our borders on a regular basis, well things just aren't safe for you to stay here alone. You know, David, I do wish they'd get them red skins onto a reservation like they've promised, then that would be one less worry."

"Yes, sir," David replied. "I heard tell that they were thinking about sending out some Negro soldiers to help with the Indian problem but now with the war on, the Army is going to put those men to use elsewhere. In the meantime, the Texas Rangers are just going to have to handle things the best they can."

"Uh hmm." Christina cleared her throat gently, hoping to bring the conversation back on track.

"Oh, right! I was telling you about the cattle drive and got sidetracked."

"Yes, Uncle," Christina replied demurely.

"There's an old monastery of sorts just to the northeast of here that's been turned into a convent. It's not much to look at, but the accommodations should be suitable enough—especially since I'll be paying them a fortune to care for you. In all the time I've lived here, it seems to be the one place where respect is demanded and given. Never been an attack on the old place that I can recollect, so what better place to entrust the safety of my niece, eh?"

"Convent?" Christina nearly choked on the word.

"It's for your safety, my dear. Just until I return from the cattle drive. Then my men and I will be here to keep you safe from harm."

"But Uncle Peter! A convent? You said yourself that you aren't even certain that the war will come to Texas? Why can't we wait until we know for certain before shipping me off like this?"

"I know it doesn't sound very pleasant, but look at it from my point of view, will you? I've already lost my brother, sister-in-law, and nephew. I don't intend to lose you too, and if the war does head this a-ways, while I am off trying to get my cattle to market, there will be no one here to defend you. I won't leave my only surviving relative behind when I leave—war or no. Besides, I am certain as can be that there'll be trouble with warring Apache and Comanche raiders when I leave on the drive, and I'll not leave you at the hands of their mercy, that's for damn straight."

Christina shuddered at the thought of being taken captive by Indians, and nearly caved to her uncle's bidding; however, the thought of spending—what would undoubtedly be an interminable stay in an inhospitable environment—gave her courage to try one more tact with her uncle.

"Have you considered allowing me to accompany you on the cattle drive?" Peter was shaking his head before she'd concluded her sentence, and her hopes began to wither.

"It's completely out of the question! I will not have any niece of mine riding roughshod over a bunch of dirty, smelly cattle. Besides which, the men and I will be too busy seeing after the cattle to be watching after you."

"But what if I weren't actually riding with the men? I could ride on or alongside the chuck wagon; maybe help the cook prepare the meals. Besides, if we follow your logic about locking me away in an impenetrable convent, who would protect me if it were suddenly penetrable? The nuns? Katie? I'm assuming that you intended to send Katie with me as chaperone, right? Do you think any of us would be capable of defending our honor if the Indians or soldiers decided that a convent full of women would make a nice diversion?" Christina was pleased to see that her uncle's head had stopped shaking violently and he was gazing at her speculatively. She'd struck a nerve with that argument, and intended to create as much unease within her uncle as was needed to prevent his shutting her off for an indefinite period of time, inside a cold, dank, fortress.

"I know you and the men will be busy with the cattle," she pressed on, "but you won't have your hands full the entire time, and you or another of your men could easily check on my safety throughout the journey; and then there's the cook too. You may have hired him for the purposes of cooking meals, but he's also certainly adept with a rifle, right? He should be able to keep harm at bay." She didn't dare tell him that she had the skill at one time to shoot as accurately as any of his men; not that she was ashamed of that skill, but because she knew he would never approve. Not that it mattered anyway, as she hadn't practiced any of her skills since arriving in Texas. She only hoped that Chin Woo wasn't perched on a cloud somewhere, looking down on her and shaking his head in disappointment; especially since it would be highly unlikely she'd ever be afforded the opportunity to use her skill again.

"Wouldn't you agree, Uncle Peter, that it would be better for me to be near your side during this discouraging time? At least if I'm nearby, you would be in a better position to protect me, and you wouldn't have to spend so much money for Katie's and my long-term care."

When she finally stopped talking, Peter's brow cocked and he sighed. "I don't know, Christina. A cattle drive is hard on the body, and you weren't bred for that."

"Maybe I wasn't, Uncle, but have you forgotten last year already? I traversed some tough territory in a schooner, cooked over an open fire, bathed in creeks and rivers, and survived both an

Indian attack and a rattler bite. That should prove that I'm made of sturdy stock."

Peter sighed heavily. "We leave in two days. Be ready."

Christina sat there, slack-jawed, uncertain that she'd heard her uncle correctly. Did he actually just concede to her wishes? He'd certainly not done so to this day. She blinked rapidly, her mind unable to comprehend his concession.

Her uncle arched his brow and sighed, "If you don't get yourself out of here, young lady, I'm likely to change my mind about your going. I'm already beginning to question the sanity of my decision."

Christina bounded up from her chair and threw her arms around her uncle's neck.

"Thank you, Uncle Peter. Thank you." She skipped to the door, but turned when she heard her name. She'd forgotten all about David in her bid for the right to join the cattle drive. Apparently, time—nor a uniform—had changed his lack of appeal for Christina, for he was just as forgettable now as he'd always been.

"Christina, perhaps we'll have time to talk over old times after the evening meal?" David asked, turning in his chair.

"I'd like that," Christina replied, and then ran happily from the room.

"No disrespect intended, sir," David said, turning to address Carthington once Christina had left the room, "but do you really think it's a good idea taking her on a cattle drive?"

"She's right, you know. It's not that uncommon a thing...."

"Sir?"

"Okay, it's more uncommon than not, but she has some valid points, you know."

"Does she? And what points were those?"

"Well..." Carthington began, but couldn't quite put his finger on the answer. "Still and all," he hedged, "I'd rather have her close by my side where I can keep an eye on her."

"Although that's easy to understand, I think that taking her along is unwise."

Peter Carthington sighed heavily, hoping that he wasn't making the biggest mistake of his life, but worried that he was.

He looked toward the door that still stood open and watched his niece race happily up the staircase, wondering if was too late to retract his decision.

CHAPTER 69

Christina pushed open the door to her room a moment later and flopped onto her bed, startling Katie. Katie leapt up from beside the fireplace, nearly overturning the nearby bucket of ashes.

"It's a fright ye've given me, miss," she gasped, her coal-dust-covered hand flying to her bosom. "And what has ye tearing into this room in such a tizzy, if I may be so bold as to be asking?"

Christina giggled and rolled over on her back.

"Nothing much, but if you go wash up, I'll tell you."

"And why is it that I have to be washing for ye to be telling me what has ye so worked up?"

"Because you can't sit on my bed all dirty, that's why."

"So this isn't to be a quick telling then. I'll be back in just a moment."

Katie returned fifteen minutes later all scrubbed and clean, and plopped down on the bed beside Christina.

"If ye don't mind me saying so, ye look happier right now than ye have in the entire year ye've been here."

"I guess I am," Christina sighed. "I finally won a battle with Uncle Peter."

"And what battle might that be?"

"He's agreed to let me go with him on the cattle drive in two days, instead of shipping me off to some godforsaken convent for the next month or more."

"Whoa! Ye need to be backing up in ye're story just a wee bit, as I haven't a clue as to what ye're talking about. Does it have to do with the meeting he called ye down for earlier?"

"It does indeed. He's leaving on the cattle drive in two days and has agreed to let me come with him."

"And this is what's got ye all in a tizzy? What ye made me wash up to be hearing? A nonsensical story about a cattle drive and a convent? Ye've done little to explain just where your excitement stems from, if ye ask me. I can't make hide nor tails out of what ye done told me."

"I'm sorry, Katie. I guess I'm just excited that Uncle Peter finally allowed me to have my own way, instead of demanding that his way was the only alternative to be had."

Katie sighed loudly.

"Sorry again," Christina grinned. "Uncle Peter has to drive a herd to the railway station, and was concerned that—with the war breaking out, and the potential of raiding parties—I'd be none too safe remaining alone here, without his protection. So, he decided the best recourse was to ship me off to a convent until he was assured all was safe to return. I persuaded him otherwise."

"Why would ye be doing that?"

"Well, had he gotten his way about the convent, you'd have been none-too-happy either."

"He was going to send us *both* to the convent?"

"That's right, and then you would've had to spend a really long time away from that gorgeous Conan Connaughy.

"Ye're right. Still, I can't imagine why ye'd think that a cattle drive be the proper alternative. Ye're going to be miserable, to be certain."

"More miserable than being locked away in a convent?"

"I can't be saying, but after all that time ye spent last year trekking here from Georgia, and all the whining ye did in me ears about how hard that life was, I wouldn't think ye'd be eager to be repeating it."

"Two weeks will be a walk in the park, compared to God only knows how long being cooped up in a convent."

"I don't be arguing that point with ye, and I'm thankful I'll not be needing to go with ye, but as I am ye're personal maid, what will I be doing while ye're away? Egad! Mrs. Cavanaugh likely be taking advantage and putting me to work scrubbing the kitchen floors."

"Well, I'm certain that you'll not be coming with us on the cattle drive, since Uncle Peter will be acting as chaperone. Do you think that Mrs. Connaughy is need of a personal maid? Only for a short while, of course. That would put you in very close proximity to her son, Conan."

"Oh, would ye mind seeing to it, miss? That would make me even more happy than ye be right now, I'm a guessing."

"I'll certainly send out the requisite inquiry, but if she's not in need of a maid, do you want me to send inquiries to other households also? Might keep you out of the kitchens?"

"Any place where I can be a personal maid would be preferable to being in the kitchens beneath the constant scrutiny of Mrs. Cavanaugh. That would be sheer torture," Katie wailed dramatically, flopping back onto the bed.

"I'll draw up the missives to be sent out in the morning, and will ask Uncle Peter for his permission tonight at dinner."

"Thank ye, miss. Thank ye so very much. Still, I'll worry for ye out on that cattle drive. Won't it be dangerous for ye? Didn't ye get ye're fill of danger last year?"

"Better the possibility of danger mingled with a little bit of excitement and daily fresh air, than wilting away from boredom sequestered away in a musty old convent. Besides, this won't be anything like last year. We aren't moving our entire household across country. We're only driving a few hundred head of cattle to market."

"Point taken. Well," Katie slapped her thighs and jumped from the bed, "now that I'm clean, I best be helping you prepare for dinner and then get back to my chores before old prune-faced Cavanaugh comes storming up here and yells at me for shirking me duties. The last time she caught me lollygagging about with ye, she made me scrub the kitchen floor in the wee hours of the morning before tending to my regular daily chores."

"No!"

"For certain, miss." Katie pulled a lovely emerald-colored dinner gown from Christina's armoire and laid it across the bed. Christina shoved her arms into her corset, and then turned around so that Katie could tie up the strings.

"Well, maybe I should have a talk...."

"Don't ye dare be a doing that! I don't mind ye're friendship, but I be needing this job too much to be getting fired from it. Anyway, I'd prefer ye not say anything."

"Very well, Katie, it's your existence, and don't tie the strings so blasted tight, if you please. I can't stand it to begin with and I much prefer to breathe than present a fashion statement to the silverware."

"Isn't that handsome soldier going to be joining ye for dinner?"

"David?"

"Ah, already on a first-name basis, are ye?" Well, isn't that a fine how-do-you-do."

"We're on a first-name basis, Katie, because we've known each other since childhood. So as far as I'm concerned, he ranks right up there with the china when it comes to my concern over making an impression, so loosen up those strings a bit more, would you?"

"What if it were your Baying Wolf joining you?"

Christina looked at her reflection in the standing mirror and her cheeks colored prettily. "If it were Baying Wolf, I wouldn't need to dress so fancy, and mind your tongue. That's not a proper topic for you to be bringing up."

Katie chose to ignore the reprimand, "He'll find ye miss. I feel it in me bones."

"I'm all for feeling things in your bones—I think—but what makes you so sure that our paths will ever cross again if they haven't in over a year?"

"Well, like I said a minute ago, it be more like a feeling in me bones, and a good one if ye be asking me, and here's why I be thinking so. Before now, he couldn't have come and gotten ye, right? It's not safe for him to traipsing onto ye're uncle's property. Secondly, ye're dreaming of him again and ye haven't had a dream in a year. Lastly, ye're uncle is taking ye on a cattle drive...away from hearth and home...easily accessible to your warrior. So, something tells me the time be right for ye to meet your beau again. Think about it...what else but divine intervention could have gotten your uncle to agree to take ye where no woman should be—a cattle drive for heaven's sake!"

Christina sat staring at Katie for some time, an incredulous look on her face. "You drew that conclusion from the time I told you about the cattle drive until you started helping me prepare for dinner?

"Well, I be a wee bit wiser than most folks be giving me credit for, to be certain," Katie winked.

"Do you really think there's a chance he knows I'll be going with my uncle, away from the ranch?"

"Me bones haven't lied to me yet. Now, if ye'll be excusing me, I need to be getting onto me other chores."

"Very well. When you come back to help me undress this evening, I'll let you know what Uncle Peter says about lending you out to the Connaughy's."

"I be looking forward to that, miss. Ye have a pleasant dinner with ye're old friend."

"I will, Katie."

CHAPTER 70

"Dinner was delightful, Christina. Thank you for inviting me, Mr. Carthington." David wiped his mouth with the napkin and laid it on the table.

"We were delighted to have you with us, David. I'll be certain to let the staff know that dinner was to your liking," Christina said graciously.

"Join me in the study for a port, David?"

"If I could beg off, I'd really like to spend a little time with Christina before I have to leave in the morning."

"Very good. Then I'll leave you two to each other's company," Carthington said quietly, pushing back his chair. "It's probably for the best anyhow, since I have some important business to tend to."

"Oh, Uncle Peter, may I ask you a quick question before you retire to your study?"

"Do try to make it quick."

"Yes, Uncle. It's about Katie, sir."

"Katie who?"

"Katie McIntyre, Uncle. The young girl that you hired to help me."

"What about her? Is she ill or something?"

"No, sir. It's just...well, I was just wondering...."

"Spit it out, child. I can't stay here all evening."

"Yes, sir. I just wanted to know where she would be going once we leave day after tomorrow."

"She'll be staying right here to help Mrs. Cavanaugh with the house while we're gone. What else would she do?"

"But you said it wasn't safe for a young woman to stay here, what with the war and the renegades...."

"That was my niece, not my servant."

"I see. Well, would it be possible for her to stay to help another family with men folk around? Perhaps she could stay with the Connaughy's."

"And who will assist Mrs. Cavanaugh with the running of the house?"

"There are other servants, Uncle, and with us gone, there won't be overly much needing tended to. Katie's a bit nervous about staying here without any protection, and she'll come back just as soon as word reaches her of our return."

"I think this is utterly ridiculous. Fair or not, no one's going to bother my housekeeper."

"Do you think an Indian would know the difference? Would even care about the difference? To them, she's just another woman. Would you have her abduction or death on your conscious?"

"Servants are a dime a dozen. I may be displeased at having one removed from my service, but replacing her wouldn't be an issue. Now let the matter lie."

Christina decided to drop the issue, but she certainly would not let the matter lie. She would just have to see to Katie without her uncle's permission.

Without further comment, Peter stood and departed.

"It's hard to believe," David said in a whisper, pushing back his own chair, "that someone could hold someone else in such low regard. I hope my saying so doesn't offend you."

"Not at all, David. You're right. I find it hard to believe as well, but my Uncle does. He reminds me of my ex-fiancé. He too believed that a servant wasn't entitled to the same freedoms and regard as the upper classes."

"I didn't realize you were engaged at one time." David drew her chair back, and clasped her hand in the crook of his elbow. They walked slowly from the house and took a seat on the porch swing.

"You may not have realized it, but you probably won't be surprised as to who the man was. The man that made it abundantly clear that you weren't to call on me again, remember?"

"Jeffrey Buchanan," David hissed disdainfully.

"Precisely. We were to be married when we reached Texas, but his death on the way west prevented that."

"I would give you my condolences, but you don't sound as if

his death affected you poorly."

"It didn't. I do want to apologize to you though—albeit a little belated. It was uncouth of Jeffrey to intimidate you the way he did. You know, had the Indians not killed him, I would have been forced to do so myself. Fortunately, it's over now."

They sat in silence for a while. David wanted to talk to Christina about the cattle drive, but he wasn't quite certain how best to broach the subject. Still, the thought of her traipsing about this wild countryside had him worried and, as her friend, he felt that he had the right to voice his concern.

"It's getting a bit chilly. Why don't I step inside and request some hot tea? Would you care for some?"

"I'd like some, yes. Thank you."

"I'll be right back, then."

David watched her walk away and wiped the small amount of moisture that had broken out on his upper lip with the back of his sleeve. Sitting here on the swing with her, in the cool evening air was making him more than slightly nervous. He'd always been infatuated with her; and to find her here in Texas, so close to where the Army had him stationed was more than any dream could have conjured. Perhaps with Jeffrey out of the picture, he could seek to renew his courtship.

The moisture popped back out on his upper lip and he wiped it away again. Damn! He was nervous. He wanted to talk to her about the cattle drive, but more than anything, he'd love to take her in his arms and kiss her, and...the thought broke off as she came back out of the front door, holding two cups of steaming tea.

They sat in silence enjoying the tea, the cool evening breeze, and the myriad of stars that lit up the evening sky. David took a deep breath and reluctantly plunged forward.

"Are you certain you want to go on this cattle drive, Christina?"

Christina jumped at the sudden noise. The peace had been soothing. Although she was a bit surprised at David's tone and chosen topic, she decided not to take offense at her dear friend,

"More certain than I would be about a convent."

"But at least if you were to go to the convent, you'd have me and the whole of my regiment as escort there, and the chances of harm befalling you on the journey—or during your stay at the convent—would be lessened. On the cattle drive, you'd have only a few men with rifles to act as guardians. Do you really think that would be safer?"

"I appreciate your concern, David, truly I do, but I'd really feel safer staying with Uncle Peter. Besides, I can't help but seeing this as a grand adventure, and if I do well at it, then maybe Uncle Peter will stop looking at me as if I'll break apart in a strong wind."

David sighed. "Can't you see that there is bound to be a lot of risk involved, and I can't shake the feeling that something awful is going to happen? I mean, not only do you have to worry about the savage raids across the borders, but now there's a war going on. Don't you see how dangerous it's going to be?"

"Don't worry David; I know how to fend for myself."

"You're a woman, Christina." In that one statement, he made it clear that no woman could fend for herself; that all women required a man to tend to their needs and to protect them. Christina would have loved to disabuse him of that notion, but instead she shook her head and sighed.

"That I am, David, but I'm not ready to have anyone fending for me but me.

"Well, then." David rose from his chair and buttoned his jacket, his tea forgotten on the table beside the swing. "I guess the only thing left to do is to wish you Godspeed. I'll probably be gone by sunup and not likely to see you again for some time." Christina placed her half-empty cup on the table beside David's and stood.

"Must you go so soon? Couldn't we just sit and talk over old times some more?"

"I really wish I could, Christina, but I have an early wakeup call tomorrow morning, like I said, but it was a real pleasure sitting here and talking to you."

"Then may you have pleasant dreams this evening and a safe

and uneventful trip tomorrow." Christina placed a light kiss on his cheek. David blushed and moved around her.

"Christina...." David stopped and turned to face her once more. "Do you think that maybe I can come call on you again, should I be able to free myself from my duties at the fort occasionally?"

"That's a long way just to come to see a friend, isn't it David?"

"Of course. It's just that...well...I mean, that is...."

"I'd be delighted." Christina decided to help David get past his shyness. Here was the young man she'd known in Georgia who'd had a hard time communicating with her in anything but fragmented sentences. She'd seen the change that the uniform wrought, however. He carried himself with a pride she never saw before and with a confidence he lacked in his teenage years. Now, he was a soldier, but to Christina, he would always be shy, simple David. She wouldn't mind being his friend, but if he courted her and asked her hand, she'd have to turn him down. He simply did not turn her head in that regard. Only one man had caught and held her attention.

David smiled and with a final glance in her direction, opened the screen door and went inside. Christina stood on the steps of the porch long after everyone was abed. Her mind drifted to Baying Wolf and the dream she'd had this morning. The black faces of the Indians that had surrounded Wolf still terrified her, especially at the realization that Wolf and Indian were one, in her dream. She also noticed that the vision no longer presented as illusionary, rather each person was portrayed clearly.

She hadn't had a dream with Baying Wolf in it since last year. Did that mean that she would be seeing him again soon, or was it just trying to tell her that he or she or even both of them was in some sort of danger? If that were true, didn't she have some sort of obligation to contact him to let him know? But how? She wasn't exactly familiar with his people or the lay of this land. It would be suicide to set off on her own.

A shiver ran down her spine and she wrapped her arms around herself. *Why can't I just forget about him? I shouldn't give a fig about what happens to him.*

"But I do, blast his hide! He's the only Indian I can sincerely say that about," She whispered harshly into the night sky. "Besides, what if Katie is right. What if Uncle's sudden change from his characteristic stubbornness, in allowing me to do anything remotely difficult, signifies a possible change in my destiny? After all, Jeffrey's insertion into my family's life wrought a drastic change in my own, and that event was preceded by a dream."

Maybe whatever guardian angel was watching out for you has decided it's time for another change...one that involves Baying Wolf.

Christina sighed loudly, "It's all too confusing. Right now, all I know is that it would be best to warn Baying Wolf about my latest dream and there's only one way in which that is remotely possible." She bowed her head in prayer.

"Dear Lord above," she whispered, "I don't know how you look upon the warriors of this land, but I'm fairly certain that you consider them your children, too. So, if it wouldn't be any problem for you, Lord, would you mind warning one of those children...just in case. His name is Baying Wolf, and I don't really know where you can find him, but if you could try, would you please let him know that Christina thinks there is danger on the horizon? Thank you." Christina turned to walk into the house and then turned to look up at the stars once more. "Oh, and just one more thing, Lord. Could you please tell him...tell him that I love him."

CHAPTER 71

Christina's body ached clear down to the marrow in her bones. Every joint protested movement, and she was finding it extremely difficult to sleep. Each time she rolled onto her back, her tender posterior objected, but when she rolled onto her side, the hard, unyielding bed of the wagon sent shooting pains through her suffering limbs. Her adventure was turning out to be one of the few bad nightmares she'd had in her life, and she regretted her decision to join her Uncle, daily, though she uttered not one complaint; especially since she knew at the onset that this trip would be brutal on her body.

It wasn't as if she was unfamiliar with sleeping in uncomfortable quarters or riding seemingly endless days on horseback. She'd done all of that and more—first with the wagon train and then in the company of Baying Wolf.

Still, after a year of sleeping on a cozy feather mattress, her body had all but forgotten the hardship it once faced. It had become soft again, and being soft was making her life decidedly uncomfortable now. She truly preferred soft, over acquiring the traits of a man, as many of the neighboring women appeared to have done. To those women, this little outing would only serve to toughen their already toughened hides. And while Christina had learned to handle weapons, and was accompanying men on this cattle drive—she liked being a soft lady. Preferred it by far to attaining hands like a field worker or skin as tough as cowhide. What she didn't like was her uncle treating her like a simpleton, and so hoped her endurance on this drive would convince him to stop. She rolled over again and a splinter caught in her shoulder.

"Blast it all!" She muttered and reached over to pull it out. A hiss escaped her lips and she cursed again, complaining quietly in a seriously unladylike fashion. This was not going to be an easy next couple of weeks, but she couldn't let her uncle know how the trip was affecting her, since he'd only remind her that it was her idea to accompany him. She turned restlessly again, trying to find relief for her tired muscles. Sunrise was only a few hours away, and if she didn't find rest soon, she'd be falling asleep in her saddle come morning.

CHAPTER 72

Baying Wolf stormed from his tepee and collided with his Uncle.

"The sun will not rise for many hours, my nephew, yet you are awake. What troubles you?" Fire Dreamer asked, a knowing gleam in his eyes.

"You know what troubles me, Uncle, but know this! I will not go to her again! I will not help her again! Someone else can go in my stead."

"Then your dreams have returned?"

"Again you know this to be true, or you would not be out at this hour either, standing before my teepee with that all-seeing look in your eye!"

"I have seen trouble, but only you can see the woman clearly in your mind."

"But I thought that you could also see her." Baying was puzzled, "Did you not too see the trouble she is in?"

"I see *only* the trouble. I do not see the woman. Only you can see the woman in your dreams."

"But, why?"

"Do you not yet understand?"

"Will you never speak clearly?" Baying Wolf asked in return. "Will you always speak in riddles you think I can solve?"

"And must anger always cloud your mind?"

Baying Wolf opened his mouth to speak, but Fire Dreamer raised his hand for silence. "This talk is getting us nowhere. You will go to her again," Fire Dreamer said, and then raised a hand quickly at Baying Wolf's attempted protest. "You will go to her again," he repeated quietly. "This time you will fulfill the destiny that is meant to be fulfilled and bring her here like you should have done the last time the Great Spirit sent you to her."

"I did not know that I was to bring her here, Uncle. I only knew that I was to help her—and I did—but just how was I supposed to bring her here when men surrounded me, pointing rifles at me?"

"Perhaps you are right," Fire Dreamer acquiesced, "Perhaps the time was not right for her to come among us. There were too many obstacles in the way—your anger, her pain, and her uncle and his men; however, I feel that the time is right now, so you must clear your mind of your anger, and see what must been seen."

"And what am I to see, Uncle?" Baying Wolf asked in exasperation.

"Only you can clear your thoughts and see. I cannot do this for you."

"You think that because I see this woman in my dreams, and have gone to her in my dreams, and because the Great Spirit chooses me to help her, that she is my destiny, don't you?"

"Perhaps you are not as blind as I thought," Fire Dreamer grinned.

"How can my enemy be my woman? Her people have invaded our lands, killed our buffalo, stolen our women, massacred our warriors...she is one of them...she is my enemy!"

"You have seen her killing our buffalo," Fire Dreamer queried sarcastically, "and our warriors?"

"Do not play words with me, Uncle."

"No, no games. I am just trying to make you see that the wrongs of one—or even many—do not belong to all. She is not your enemy."

"How do you know this?"

"She can see you too," Fire Dreamer murmured, shocking Baying Wolf into silence. His face grew pale and his jaw slackened in astonishment.

"You know of that I speak." Baying Wolf nodded slowly, unable to find his voice. "It is her gift, as you feel it is your curse. She can see things in her dreams that go beyond what most can see. That go beyond what even you and I can see. For now, her gifts are but like children—still growing and developing. For now, she only has the sight to see her own destiny, and yours. She does not know that by allowing her gift to grow, instead of fighting against it, she will become a great seer. A great seer who is meant to help our people in the time of trouble that is to come. Right now, she is a lost child, wandering through her dreams in confusion; her only connection to our people is through your heart and mind. Can you not feel her there?" Fire Dreamer asked, pointing to Baying Wolf's heart and then to his head.

"Yes. Every minute of every day, she invades my thoughts."

"But not your heart?" When Baying Wolf didn't answer, Fire Dreamer sighed. "Soon you will clear your mind and see; but for now, she is the guide to our future and she will come to live among us, and you are the one that will bring her here."

"But what can a white woman bring to The People?"

"The color of her skin matters not. Why the Great Spirit chose her to guide us, I can only guess. Maybe he saw that she would lose her family and would need another, or perhaps he sent someone whose heart could not be blinded by anger and prejudice even though she has good reason to hate us all—only the Great Spirit knows. She is your destiny and the destiny of our people. You have fought against it so long, but now the clouds in your mind have cleared and you know I speak words that are true."

"You are right, Uncle," Baying Wolf sighed. "I have always known, but I felt that loving this woman would be a betrayal to my people. I did not know that she was meant to be *with* The People."

"Go get your horse, my nephew. You must leave immediately, for it seems as if danger follows your woman like night follows day." As if to confirm his uncle's words, a loud screeching sound rent the air and both men looked up to see Baying Wolf's eagle guide soaring high above.

CHAPTER 73

Christina watched bleary-eyed, as the men herded the cattle, their yips and cattle calls no more than a whisper across the vast distance. They had been on the move for six days, but to Christina's tired mind it seemed more like a year. She struggled to keep her eyes open and her derriere in the saddle, both of which became more of a struggle with each passing day.

"You can always jump up here with me," Cam called unenthusiastically from the front of the chuck wagon. He wasn't a man big on socializing and he didn't really care to have company on his wagon, but he knew that his head would roll if anything happened to the boss man's niece. That's why he went out of his way to accommodate her, even giving up his wagon bed to allow her a respectable, private, sleeping quarter. He shouldn't be held accountable if she fell off her horse and broke her neck because she refused to take advantage of the bed and actually get some sleep. He shouldn't be held accountable, but he damned well knew he would be. *Damnable woman!*

"Thanks, but I'll just ride," Christina called back, equally unenthusiastic. The thought of sitting next to his foul-smelling, unwashed hide made her stomach flip-flop. "Of course, it might help if you could simply talk to me. Keep my mind awake," Christina offered.

"I ain't never been much for talking," Cam said abruptly. The thought of willingly conversing with someone made his own stomach queasy. He had taken the job as cook for Peter Carthington because it afforded him the privacy he so craved. He despised humanity and did everything in his power to dissociate himself from their company. Even at mealtime, he ate apart from the rest of the cowhands, refusing to enter into even minimal conversation. Conversing with Christina these past six days were the most words he'd shared with any one person—at one time—in his whole life— and all fifty words—he'd counted—had been an effort to part with.

Those eight words spoken in invitation, startled his brain, and he had a difficult time figuring why he'd bothered to offer her a seat next to him in the first place. The only thing he could think of was that his fear of his boss outweighed his disgust for her company. His relief when she'd turned down his offer was as appreciated as a cold beer to a dying man.

Still he didn't want to risk her changing her mind, so he clucked his tongue and slapped the reins against his team's rump, sending them into a canter. She could follow along at her leisure. If he were lucky, he wouldn't have to look at her face, or hear her voice again, until the cattle drive was over, but even that would be too soon.

And so it was, that he didn't notice when Christina's horse stepped in a prairie dog hole and fell, trapping Christina's leg under its massive body. Christina yelled for Cam to stop to help her, but the wagon continued going, kicking up a cloud of dust in its wake. As she watched the wagon disappear over a rise, her anger turned to despair. Her Uncle's men had stopped for the noonday meal only an hour ago, which meant they wouldn't stop again until sundown; and since her uncle and his men always stayed a fair distance ahead of the chuck wagon, it was a good possibility that she wouldn't be missed for a long time. Unless, of course, that no-account cook decided to slow his team to look behind him, to check on her progress or her whereabouts; but that was about as likely to happen as a snowstorm in the middle of June. Christina fought back the tears that threatened to fall and struggled to free her leg from under the horse.

"Move, you big oaf!" She pushed against the horse with all of her might and was rewarded with a slight movement accompanied by a loud snort. "That's it, girl! You can do it!" Christina encouraged, pushing as hard as her arms allowed against the horse's side, ignoring the pain emanating from her calf down to her ankle. With a grunt of effort, the horse struggled to its feet and immediately fell back on top of her injured leg when its own injured leg gave way.

Christina screamed as the pain shot through her ankle, up her calf and straight into her thigh muscle. She pounded the dirt with her fist, angry with herself for not seeing the prairie dog hole and with Cam for riding off and leaving her alone, so she did what any other damsel in distress would do, she took it out on her horse.

"You've got to get off of me! Your weight is too much for my leg, especially against this uneven ground. If you don't move, my leg is going to snap like a twig!" Christina pushed again on the horse's haunches, deciding this time to roll away more quickly once the horse stood, regardless of the pain; for if the horse fell on her again, she knew her bones would surely break.

With another grunt of effort, the horse swayed upward temporarily, and Christina rolled her leg out from under its massive haunches. The horse snorted loudly and then returned to its position on its side, eyes glazed in pain. Christina scooted toward the horse, she herself unable to stand, and lay her head on the horses heaving flank.

"It's alright, girl. Everything will be all right. Someone is bound to notice us and return," she soothed, more for her own peace of mind than for the horse's comfort. "Don't worry. As soon as they come back, they'll fix us both up as good as new." She sat up, and tugged the boot from her rapidly swelling ankle and sighed heavily. "Of course," she murmured, remembering Cam's hasty departure, "I wouldn't hold my breath for a *speedy* return." She lay her head down against the horse again and stared at the sky, watching the sun move slowly across the horizon until her eyes closed and she was carried away from her pain into a world of dreams.

CHAPTER 74

"Where's my niece?" Carthington approached Cam angrily, his eyes darting from Cam to the horizon, where the sun was quickly setting.

"She'll be along shortly." Cam shrugged, unconcerned. "She said something about wanting to ride around a while and not to worry about her none. She knew how to find us." Cam was lying through the gap in his front teeth, and he knew that Carthington realized it as well. "Why not I get a meal going, and...."

"Mount up, men!" Carthington shouted, ignoring his cook. "We're heading back! Tom, Kendall, Joseph, you three stay here and mind the cattle. Matt, Jake and the rest of you be ready to ride out in less than five minutes!"

"We know how concerned you are, boss," Jake spoke up, "but it would be sheer foolishness to try to head back now, what with night falling already."

"I am not leaving her out there!"

"I have to agree with Jake," Harvey interjected. "It would be suicide for all of us to cross this country in the dark. We wouldn't be doing her a bit of good if any one of us gets injured, would we?"

"I am not leaving her out there!" Carthington yelled louder. "Do you realize what could happen to a female out in this country alone? If the animals don't get her, the Natives will! Now I said to mount up!"

"You're the boss man," Jake acquiesced reluctantly, "and we'll follow you out if that's what you really want, but Harvey's right. We won't be able to see squat out there once the sun sets in another hour, and then we'll be in as much trouble as your niece, sure enough. Then where would that leave her?"

"It's best if we wait until morning," Harvey offered with grunts of agreement coming from the men. "Besides, ain't we rushing things a bit? She may be okay and will show up any time now." Carthington stared at the men standing around him and waged a valiant war with reason. He knew the men were right. Christina could very well be riding around as Cam said—although he seriously doubted it. But if he waited until dark to find out...after dark, the land around them became a deadly rival. Scorpions, snakes—all manner of predators claimed the night as their hunting ground, and his niece was right in the middle of it, unprotected and for all he knew, injured. Damn! He had to think. If he rode out now, his men were right—they would do his niece no good. They would probably end up injured themselves, or worse, but the thought of his niece, alone, made his skin crawl. Shouldn't he risk his own neck to bring her to safety? *No*! His mind finally decided. If he injured himself going after her now, he would be no good to her when and if she really needed him. He would wait until dawn.

"Alright! We'll leave at first light." He informed his men and saw relief written on their faces. When Carthington turned to face his cook once more, there was fire in his gaze. "You better hope she rides in here in the next hour, Cam, because if anything happens to her tonight, your life won't amount to a hill of beans. Do I make myself clear?"

"Ain't nothing gonna happen, boss man. You'll see. She's gonna ride in here pretty as you please before dinner is done cooking," Cam assured him, but his assurances proved false, and by the time the men settled down for the night, Cam was mighty worried himself. Not for the boss man's niece, but for his own skin if they didn't find that no-account, trouble-causing female tomorrow.

CHAPTER 75

Why they stood just staring at Wolf created confusion in Christina's mind. They outnumbered the great beast, their spears at the ready, but they appeared undecided about how best to proceed. Did the snarling beast really incite a fear so great as to render them immobile? Were they simply uncertain it wise to kill a living thing simply for defending itself or its territory? She had heard that Indians held a high regard for nature and all its creatures, so perhaps they were just hoping to intimidate it into leaving; refused to attack it unless it launched itself at one of them. Whatever their reasons, Christina felt duty-bound to try to help.

She moved from her hiding place, approaching the group of Indians cautiously. She had to be out of her ever-loving mind to do this. The Wolf stopped snarling and shot her a look that agreed with her assessment, but she shot it one back that said she couldn't let it face danger alone. Not now that she realized that Wolf and Baying Wolf were one in the same; not after Wolf had saved her life. Exactly how she was going to handle this situation eluded her, but when she stepped on a twig, the matter was taken out of her hands.

She watched in horror as one of the Indians spun on his heels, raised his spear, and threw it at her. The impact knocked her backward against a tree, and she slid down its length, her eyes wide with disbelief—both at her injury, and how rapidly Wolf transformed from beast to man.

Her ears rang with the sound of Baying Wolf's cry as he attacked the man who'd harmed her; his own life no longer a concern. She heard herself scream as another Indian raised his spear and threw it at Baying Wolf, and then all went black.

Christina awoke with a startled cry. Sweat poured from her throbbing temples, as she slowly focused on the figures kneeling around, prodding her none-too-gently with the ends of their bows. With a cry of anguish, she pulled back against the horse, only to have one of the warriors drag her back, his opaque eyes laughing at her and his yellow-stained teeth leering at her through his black-painted face.

He twisted her leg around, looking at the ankle that had turned a dark purple during the nighttime hours. She grimaced and tried not to howl as searing pain shot up and down her leg. She gritted her teeth and felt tears prick the corners of her eyes, but she remained quiet.

The Native said something to the men surrounding him and then reached down and yanked her to a standing position. She squealed in pain when her foot impacted the ground, and would have fallen had the warrior not had such a tight grip on her arm. Instead, she pulled the leg up and stood unsteadily on one foot.

"You, inconsiderate barbarian!" She snapped and was rewarded with a sound slap across her face. She landed with a loud thump and tasted blood from her split lip. She glared up at the Indian standing over her, but wisely kept her mouth shut. He glared back at her, and then reached down and grabbed a fistful of her long auburn hair in one of his dark brown fists and pulled.

Christina squealed. She reached and grasped his hand, trying to loosen his hold, but it was no use. He tugged harder, until her body started sliding across the ground. The distance from her horse to his was short, but the journey took its toll on her body and her clothing—one battered and the other beginning to tatter.

She reigned in the urge to cry out with relief when he let loose her hair, but couldn't prevent the groan of pain when he hefted her from the ground and slung her across his horse's back, face down, and then quickly mounted himself.

Christina stared at the scrub grass only a foot or two below her face and cringed. She didn't relish the idea of riding in this position and hoped that the Indian that had mounted behind her would pull her to a sitting position before taking off. He didn't. Instead, he slammed his feet into his horse's haunches and they took off at a full gallop over uneven terrain.

She watched the ground rush by and barely had time to lift her head each time they rode past a small tree that could easily have sliced off her nose. The blood rushed to her face and her stomach hurt from being bounced about on the horse's back, but worse than that was the humiliation she felt at having her derriere stuck up in

the air for her captor to enjoy looking at, at his own leisure, were he
so inclined. She only hoped he paid more attention to where he was
going than to her body.

Now these are savages, she thought angrily. *They're nothing like
Baying Wolf.* That thought had fear racing throughout her body. The
fear mounted as that thought took root, and began to grow. These
men were definitely not like Baying Wolf, which left her mind
playing out all sorts of dishonorable intentions they could have in
store for her. *Oh, dear Lord! How am I supposed to get out of this one?*

*Maybe the somebody that sent Baying Wolf to you before will be nice
enough to send him again*, her mind offered, and she clung to that
thought, hoping it wasn't an insane hope.

She rode in her uncomfortable position for what seemed
eternally, but proved only to be a few hours before the warrior
stopped his mount and, unmindful of her numb body, took a
handful of her blouse and pulled her from his stallion. She landed
with a hard thud on the ground, but had no time to recover before
he grasped her hair again and drug her to a nearby tree. With
continued indifference to her comfort, he yanked her upright, pulled
her arms around the trunk, and bound her wrists tightly with a piece
of rawhide.

"I don't know which is worse," she mumbled as the warriors
took their bows and disappeared into the surrounding trees, "having
my abdomen jarred for hours on the horse, having my hair pulled
from its roots; being left tied awkwardly to a tree, or knowing that
my virtue is only a short time away from being stolen." To add
insult to injury, her bladder ached and she realized she hadn't
relieved herself since yesterday. She highly doubted they'd
understand her if she asked to take a visit into the trees—not that
she truly believed they'd allow her, even if they understood English.
"Blast their hides!"

She lowered her chin to her chest in exhaustion and then
snapped it up quickly as a thought struck her.

In honor of Chin Woo's efforts, she pocketed her last throwing
star and the knife he'd gifted her before leaving on the cattle drive—

just in case a situation such as this arose. She wriggled her wrists, uncaring that the tree scraped her delicate skin. She was determined to free her bonds and make these savages pay for adding more distress to her life, when she'd already had more than her fair share of grief.

CHAPTER 76

Baying Wolf knelt beside Christina's horse and let out a string of curses in his native tongue. *Too late again!* His mind shouted. Someone else had already been here and, if the signs surrounding him were any indication, had dragged her away. The only sign that she'd even been there was one boot near the horse's rear leg.

If the horse held any other marking but that of the Carthington ranch, he would not accept that his woman was missing and possibly in danger. A woman's boot nearby, in conjunction with the horse's brand, left him in no doubt that she'd been here and been taken, but where?

He examined the mare, petting its neck in sadness.

"I'm sorry you have suffered so, my friend." The horse neighed softly and tried to lift its head, but the pain and suffering were just too much and it lowered back down to the ground. "You were a good friend to my woman. Thank you."

The horse neighed again softly as if in understanding and then snorted loudly.

"You hear it too." Baying Wolf looked over his shoulder at the dust storm that signified many riders were coming. His instinct told him who it was. What he didn't understand was how Christina ended up on her own out in the middle of nowhere? Why hadn't her uncle been with her then? Why was he only now coming in search of her?

The one thing he could not do was stay to question him, for he didn't doubt that Christina's uncle would be none-too-pleased to see his face again. He stood and quickly scanned the area for any signs that would indicate where she'd gone. When he was certain that he'd ascertained the general direction, he mounted his horse and spurred it into a gallop, praying with each mile that he would not be too late to save her, as he'd been too late to save her family.

CHAPTER 77

The discharge of a rifle reverberated through the plains, startling fowl, and animals for at least a mile in all directions. Christina's mare was now out of its misery, but Carthington's misery was in full blossom.

"Where is she?" Peter Carthington's smoking Winchester hung limply in his hand, his fear mounting with each passing minute. His men withered beneath his glare and lowered their eyes to the ground, feet shuffling in the dirt as if they were somehow to blame for his niece's disappearance.

They grew more discomfited when the glare in the boss' eyes became one of distressed agony. Each embarrassed visage changed to incredulity when their boss—a man known for his hard and unfeeling character—fell to his knees, lifted his face heavenward, and released a tormented cry.

"Christiiiinnnnaaaa!" He yelled repeatedly, though his voice rapidly grew hoarse. Finally, having expended his efforts, he fell wearily against the horse, now dead from his single rifle shot, and bowed his head, feeling suddenly very old and weary. He clutched Christina's discarded boot in his arms as if it were a child.

"I should have come after her last night," he whispered in self-recrimination. "I shouldn't have left her to fend for herself. Lord help me, but I never should have brought her along. David was right—this is no place for a young lady to be. Too dangerous. Far too dangerous." He put his face in his hands and wept, his shoulders shaking with the intensity of his grief.

The men stared at each other, each shrugging in indecision. They had a difficult enough time dealing with a distraught female, so confronted with a distraught male was nearly too much for them to comprehend. None had suffered a loss as had Peter Carthington, so none were able to empathize with his current grief. To see this man, whose deportment was anything but genteel, forgiving, or soft was more than any of them could handle. When Carthington gave a strong sniff, straightened his shoulders, and swiped harshly at his eyes, each man let go an audible sigh of relief.

Carthington sniffed again, and pulled himself upright, breathing deeply to right his emotions. He straightened his back and glared at his men, "If any of you dare mention what took place today, I'll not just fire your asses, I'll burn 'em alive. Am I clear?" Each man nodded consent, uncertain anyone would believe them if they did happen to mention Carthington's temporary insanity.

"We got that you're grieving, boss, but we can't give up hope. For all we know, she may be on foot and most likely halfway home by now. Just because we came across her horse, lame, doesn't mean she was injured, right? The fact that she ain't here should be a good thing, yeah?"

Carthington nodded. "Matt, you head back to the men and tell them they're going to have to drive the cattle to the railroad terminal on their own. Take Jake with you and bring back as much food and ammo as you can carry. Enough for several days. Ride fast and hard. I want you back here before sundown."

"Yes sir, boss." Matt was glad to see his boss in control again.

"And Matt," Carthington called, stopping Matt in his tracks, "Bring Tecumseh with you."

"Will do, boss," Matt smiled, and shot Carthington a two-fingered salute, and then ran to his waiting horse. Jake was already mounted.

"What're you grinning at, Matt? I can't see that there's anything funny about any of this."

"I was just wondering," Matt grunted as he pulled himself into the saddle, "how much help Cole would be willing to give the boss if he knew how much the man despises him."

"The half-breed?"

"Yeah. Carthington calls him Tecumseh[1]. It's as plain as the

---

1 Tecumseh was leader of the Shawnee, whose members aided the British in the capture of Fort Detroit, during the war of 1812. He was killed by American forces during the Battle of the Thames in 1813, which ended his efforts to create an independent Indian nation. For more information, visit:

nose on your face that the boss man can't stand to be in the same vicinity as that half-breed."

"Why did he hire him on then?"

"Cause he's the best damned tracker in the territory, that's why? The boss may hate his Injun blood, but he shore ain't stupid. If anybody can find a trace of his niece, it'll be Cole." Matt tugged on his horse's reins, turning its head back the way they'd come.

"You don't really think we're going to find her alive, do you, Matt?" Jake asked, following Matt out of camp.

"Not really, and if you don't want to get on the boss man's bad side, I suggest you keep your thoughts to yourself. Man, I'd hate to be in Cam's shoes right now."

"As far as I can see, the son-of-a-bitch deserves whatever he gets." Jake leaned over and spit his wad of chew on the dirt.

"Yeah. Think we should warn him that we didn't find Carthington's niece?"

"Nah. We do that and he'll hightail it before Carthington can get his clutches into him."

Matt snorted and both men dug their heels into their horse's haunches, spurring them into a gallop.

"Alright men, listen up!" Carthington shouted. "We've already lost a day and we'll probably lose another one waiting for the men to return, but that doesn't mean we're going to sit here doing nothing. We're going to mount up, split up, and look for any signs indicating which direction they might have taken. Now get going." Each man nodded, knowing that failure to locate Carthington's niece was not an option.

Peter watched as the ten men surrounding him dispersed and ran to their horses. His mind drifted back, just seven short days ago, when he'd consented to letting his niece come along, and felt ill. He'd worried then that something might happen and now it had. His niece was gone. His whole family was gone. Lost to him forever.

He fought back the tears that threatened to fall anew and vowed that he would never give up the search for his niece until she was found—dead or alive—and if it did happen to be dead, then God help whoever took her, for when he found that person—and find him he would—he'd give him no quarter.

CHAPTER 78

"They rode that-a-way." Cole knelt beside a faint impression of a horse's hoof and pointed toward the direction of their target. "Five horses. One carrying two riders."

"How in hell do you know that?" Carthington looked at the markings in the dirt, but couldn't see anything that indicated that his niece had left on horseback. "And just how do you know you're looking at the right signs? Hundreds of horses ride this way every day. This could be my horse for all you know, or any of my men's. We've been riding around here the better part of a day now searching for signs and haven't seen anything definitive."

"You hired me, Mr. Carthington, for my skills as a tracker. To hunt for cattle thieves who have trespassed on your lands," Cole assured him unnecessarily. "I have never tracked them wrong, have I?"

"No, but...."

"There are many sets of prints. You and your men's are the freshest set I see. Besides your niece's horse, there are five horses coming in and six riders going out. They came in from the southeast and headed out going northwest. In addition, you and your men's tracks look sporadic, as if searching, while these next freshest tracks have a decisive heading away from the dead horse. The depth suggests a heavier weight on one of the horses than the single rider coming in. Five riders going that-a-way." Cole pointed again and waited for his boss to argue further. He didn't. "There is only one thing that doesn't make much sense, however."

"What's that?"

"One of the riders came later and left later. He is a single rider, and since he stopped here and then proceeded the way of the prior four riders, then the probability is high that he is also searching for your niece."

"There's no way in hell the signs could have told you that! I don't care *how* good a tracker you are."

"Not all of the signs told me," Cole grinned, "but look here. Four horses appeared to have stopped in a semicircle around your niece. There is a set of footprints that walk toward your niece," he lectured, pointing toward the ground, "and walk back to the horse, dragging your niece behind."

"He dragged Christina?"

"See these drag marks right here?" Cole pointed. "They indicate that your niece did not walk to her abductor's horse."

"Damn! I'm going to skin them alive when I get my hands on them. I'm going to attach every one of them to the back of my horse and drag them across the rugged terrain until they don't have any skin left on their savage bones."

"Now," Cole interrupted the tirade and walked over to where Baying Wolf had left his horse and continued to explain, "here is where our fifth horse stopped. The position of the hoof prints indicates he rode in from a different direction. He walked over and knelt by the horse, and then returned and rode in the same direction as your niece's abductors."

"How do you know he knelt by the horse, for heaven's sake?"

"There is only half an impression—the front of his moccasin."

"Moccasin!"

"They were all wearing moccasins. They were all Indians."

"Who do you think that person is, boss?" Jake asked.

"I can only think of one Injun who'd dare go after my niece, and he should have thought twice about trying to get his hands on her again."

"Again?" Cole's curiosity was aroused. He'd heard rumors that Carthington found his niece in the company of a warrior, but that Carthington crushed those rumors quickly and painfully— permanently dealing with any man who dared spread them further.

"Forget it! It doesn't matter. I guess I should just be thankful that she's alive right now."

"Do not ease your mind yet, Carthington," Cole continued, looking in the direction the riders traveled. "Just because she's alive doesn't mean she's safe. The direction they are headed lead straight through Apache and then Comanche territory. We did not find her body here, and that is a good thing—and it is not, for we may never find her body at all. Too many scavengers. And if she *is* alive," Cole continued, "she may wish she were dead."

Carthington looked into the black depths of his tracker's eyes and grimaced, his fears returning like a jab in the abdomen. He turned quickly and headed back to his waiting men.

"Mount up! Now!"

Cole followed behind, and grasped his boss' arm, "One more thing, Carthington."

"What's that Tecumseh?" Carthington barked. Cole's eyes darkened dangerously and he ground his teeth, but he had never let a white man, nor an Indian, provoke him with their whip-like tongues and he would not begin now. Ignoring the urge to punch his boss in the gut, Cole continued.

"Tracking your niece is not going to be an easy thing. It will be a slow effort through extremely hostile territory. Just thought you might want to give your men an out."

"My men are loyal to me. If I tell them to walk through Hell's fires, they will. Is that clear?"

"Just as long as you understand that I will not," Cole countered and turned away, mounting his own horse. His gaze locked combatively with Carthington's, and then Carthington looked away.

"Let's ride!" Carthington dug his heels into his sorrel's flank, praying with each passing inch of ground, that his niece would be safe and unharmed. He wasn't joking about the punishment he would mete out should they find her in any state other than breathing and intact.

CHAPTER 79

Baying Wolf spurred his stallion to greater speeds in a race against two clocks.

The first was Christina's abductors. If he didn't reach her in time, they could very well rape and dispose of her in a most inhumane fashion, especially if the Indians that took her happened to be Apache, as he suspected.

The second critical time element was Christina's uncle. He had no doubt that the riders he'd seen riding hell-bent toward him when he stopped beside Christina's horse, were Peter Carthington and his ranch hands. If Carthington caught up to him, Baying Wolf knew the man would stop at nothing to prevent his going after Christina—at rifle point, or by whatever means were at his disposal.

He had to find her, free her, and be in home territory before Carthington got close, or he could very well lose her again. That was something he could not allow to happen this time.

He realized now that Christina was meant to be with him and he would fight any man who tried to take her away from him. He just didn't want that man to be Peter Carthington. If he raised a hand in battle against her uncle, it may create a chasm between them, and if he killed her uncle in battle, the chasm could prove too great to close. She'd already lost too much, too many, at the hands of Indians, to lose one more could very well drive her over the edge and out of his life. Could she forgive him if it came to that?

Fire Dreamer suggested that she had a forgiving heart, which was why the Great Spirit had chosen her to guide their people, so perhaps she could forgive him if she understood his reasoning.

Right now, he just had to find her. He leaned far over his horse's neck, watching the terrain fly by, whispering encouragement to his quickly tiring mount.

A movement to the front and left of him caught his eye and he pulled back on his horse's mane, slowing him to a canter. The movement also stopped, and Baying Wolf grinned as his friend and spirit animal stepped from the tree line.

"I have not seen you in many weeks, my friend! Have you a woman somewhere that has kept you preoccupied?"

Wolf raised his head and howled, but not in response to the question posed. There was tension in the wolf that transmitted itself across the short distance to where Baying Wolf sat on his mount.

"What have you come to tell me, my friend?" His voice was a mere whisper, but he did not doubt that Wolf heard him, just the same. Just then another sound rent the air and Baying Wolf looked up as his eagle guide appeared, soaring in circles high above, a short distance into the trees from where Wolf stood. Wolf howled again and turned, disappearing into the trees and then reappearing, letting Baying Wolf know that he needed to follow.

CHAPTER 80

For several hours, the men followed Cole, who alternately rode his mount and walked beside it, looking for anything that would tell him where Christina's abductors had taken her. He hadn't lied about it being a slow process, and the agitation in the men's stances when Carthington called a halt for that night showed clearly their frustrations.

"No fires," Cole commanded, countermanding his boss's order to collect wood. "We cannot draw attention to ourselves. It is too dangerous."

Carthington wanted to slug the arrogance from the man's face, but he needed him too much to provoke him further than he already had, so he merely nodded in acquiescence and pulled some jerky from his satchel. He sank wearily onto a nearby log and munched quietly, looking from one fatigued, bearded face to another. He only hoped that his statement about their loyalty was accurate, for he doubted he could face what lay ahead without them to back him up.

"You realize that without a fire, we're opening ourselves up to the possibility of animal attacks," Carthington said quietly, when Cole settled nearby, chewing on his own bit of jerky.

"You realize that *with* a fire," Cole countered, "we're opening ourselves up to the possibility of attack by renegades."

"Not much comfort either way," Carthington laughed without humor.

"Can't say that there is."

"Where do you think they are taking her?" Carthington asked. "She *is* still alive, isn't she?"

"If the signs I am reading are right, your niece lives. As to where they are taking her? It is possible that they will return to their people, if they are not outcasts and have a people to return to. If they have no people, they may just be taking her back to their camp," Cole offered. "If they find her pleasing, they may keep her for their slave. Which may explain why we didn't find her body laying beside that of her horse?"

"You're just full of comforting thoughts, aren't you?"

"I only speak the truth. I have seen your niece, and if it had been me that found her, I would have taken her for my own as well."

"You son-of-a...."

"Maybe," Cole cut him off, "but at least I'm an honest son-of-a-...." Cole slid from the log and onto his bedroll. "I think I'll turn in." Cole rolled onto his side and placed his hands under his head to act as a pillow, his back to Carthington.

"We leave at sunup."

"I figured as much."

He lay for a while staring into the blackness of the nearby woods. He hadn't lied to Carthington about being an honest man, but that didn't mean he needed to reveal everything he knew. He was honest, not stupid. One of the things he knew that he refused to reveal was how difficult it would be to track one horse. Up to now, he had been tracking a group of riders, and felt fortunate that none worked to conceal their tracks. Should the lone rider catch up to the group first and take the woman with him on a lone horse, then the only sure way to track them with ease was if she left a trail; and the only reason she would do that was if she was with that lone Indian unwillingly. His senses told him that wouldn't be the case.

If he revealed any of that to Carthington, the man was just likely to kill the bearer of such news. Cole closed his eyes and willed sleep to find him. It did, and within minutes, his dreams were filled with visions of a red-haired, green-eyed lady and a dark-skinned native.

A booted foot woke him at sunrise, and he reluctantly pulled himself to a sitting position, wiping the sleep from his eyes.

"Time to ride," Carthington snapped, and then turned to mount his horse, the other men slowly moving to do the same. Cole stepped behind a nearby bush and relieved himself, and then took some water from his canteen and splashed it on his face. When he finally approached Carthington, all the riders were mounted and waiting.

Cole took hold of his own horse, "Let's go." He tugged on the reins, walking the horse beside him. His eyes trained on the terrain around him, Cole led the men through another exasperating and exhausting day. He knew that despite Carthington's obvious dislike for him, he depended on him to find his niece, and he would do his best. That's what Carthington paid him for—to track. He only hoped that when they found her, Carthington would be willing to let her go, for if she left with the warrior on her own, he had a very deep certainty that she wouldn't want to return.

CHAPTER 81

"Do you think the white woman will live?"

"She must."

"We must see to her wounds and return to our people quickly."

The discussion continued around her, but she could not respond. She felt her shirt and camisole taken from her body, and wanted to scream out in indignation, but her jaws wouldn't move. She tried to raise her eyelids again, but it seemed as if someone had taken adhesive and sealed them shut.

She felt a stabbing pain in her abdomen, and the prodding made it worse. She heard a moan in the distance and realized it had come from her, as large pair of hands scooped her off the ground.

"I will take her to the stream and wash the wound. Collect the plants that I will need and bring them to me," *A voice said near her ear.*

"What about him?"

"Leave him to the buzzards."

Christina's mind screamed and she tried desperately to cry out. Oh why couldn't she speak? Her mind fought against the pain, but then blessedly returned to oblivion.

Christina gasped as consciousness returned and the very real pain she'd felt in her dream gradually subsided. For a moment, disorientation consumed her mind and her sight. She rolled her head in circles, releasing the tension formed in her neck and slowly her vision and mind cleared. She licked at lips dried from heat and lack of fluids, and force-produced saliva to swallow to ease the dryness in her mouth. When a modicum of comfort returned, she took in her surroundings. As the memories flooded from the recesses of her brain, she looked around in search of the Indians who'd spirited her away.

"I must not have been asleep long," she murmured to herself and then set about working to free herself from her bonds again. Her arms and wrists hurt. The times spent pulling and tugging, in conjunction with the painful throbbing, left little doubt that she'd chafed her skin brutally, but her skin would survive the onslaught. She, on the other hand, was less likely to survive an assault and so overlooked the agony in hopes of attaining her freedom before her abductors returned.

A movement in her periphery startled her and she ceased all movement. Certain her time for breaking free had passed, she felt a shiver of dread race through her body and tears of anger well in her eyes. To her amazement and relief, the Indians didn't emerge from the trees, Wolf did.

"Where did you come from, boy?"

"He's with me," A voice said from behind her. She felt tugging and pulling on the ropes that bound her wrists, and her joy mounted.

"Baying Wolf? Is it really you?"

"Hush, my woman. We must be quiet, for the warriors who took you could return at any moment."

"We're in a lot of danger, Baying Wolf. Please hurry."

"You will be free in a moment."

"I would ask how you found me," Christina laughed quietly, "but I'm sure I already know the answer. The Great Spirit sent you, right? That's how you found me so easily, and why you're not surprised to find me tied to this tree."

Baying Wolf freed the bonds, and then moved to stand before her, a playful scowl on his face, "You think you know me so well, you, green-eyed she wolf?" Christina merely nodded and then threw her arms around him, hugging him tightly. Baying Wolf lost his balance and nearly toppled. He braced himself, laughed softly, and embraced her tightly in return. "Why is white woman so happy to see me? The last time we parted, we were not even friends."

"I think it may have to do with the fact that you've probably saved me from a fate worse than death, and we are friends, aren't we, Baying Wolf?" Christina looked intently into his opaque eyes, searching them for the assurance that she needed.

"More than that, Christina," Baying Wolf murmured, his palm caressing her dirt-streaked cheek, "but that is a discussion for another time. Now we must leave here quickly. Can you walk?"

"If you want honesty, then the answer is no."

Without hesitation, he scooped her into his arms, and then quickly made his way toward the tree line, but their departure was interrupted when the four Apache warriors returned, carrying their kill. Without hesitation, the warriors dropped the venison and pulled their spears from across the sheaths on their backs. Christina cried out as her vision came to the forefront of her mind.

"We mustn't attempt to fight them, Baying Wolf. If we do, you will die and I will again be a captive—an even more injured captive."

"Your vision has told you this?"

Christina nodded, tears blurring her eyes.

"I cannot see how we will leave here without a fight, my woman."

"Please, we have to find a way. I can't bear the thought of losing you again."

The four warriors appeared in no hurry to attack, but their stances remained threatening. Christina could only surmise that they wished her alive and preferred that Baying Wolf deposit her on the ground so to make it easier to kill him and keep her.

That's exactly right, her mind concurred.

"Whatever you do, Baying Wolf, do not put me down."

Baying Wolf let out a sigh of frustration, "You are making it difficult to defend you."

"You are defending me by keeping me in your arms."

Baying Wolf's brow knitted quizzically, "I hope your interpretation is correct."

"Me too."

"If I attempt to leave..."

"They will spear you in the back. I can feel them in my mind. The leader is trying to devise a plan to maim you into dropping me. Why they want me, I cannot guess."

"They must know you are a special woman. Perhaps their medicine man knows of you and wishes you among their people, as our shaman wishes also."

It was Christina's turn to don a quizzical expression, but knew this was not the time to seek answers to the questions whirling about in her head. Instead, she focused on an idea forming in her mind.

"Can you summon Wolf without raising too much suspicion; somehow communicate that we need a distraction? Can it provide one without getting injured? I don't want one tiny gray fur on that wonderful creature harmed." Christina didn't bother to whisper any longer, as the four natives were also busily conferring on the current state of affairs. They seemed perplexed at Baying Wolf's lack of action, at his apparent nonchalance when confronted by men with spears —by the entire situation. As with her and Baying Wolf, it seemed as if they'd decided a conference was in order to determine the next course of action. Christina felt relief sweep through her at knowing that they were hesitant to kill her; that they apparently preferred her alive.

"Wolf and I are one. I must only call for my spirit animal in my mind for it to appear, and since Wolf is already nearby, we will not have to wait long." Baying Wolf's confidence brought Christina a much-needed reassurance. She felt the tension leave her as Wolf slowly and cautiously appeared at the edge of the trees behind the Apaches. It broadened its stance, lowered its head, bared its teeth, and emitted a threatening growl. The sound had the desired effect, and all four Indians turned to look.

It was the distraction needed, and Baying Wolf did not hesitate for even a second. He turned and fled through the stand of trees, stopping only when he reached his mount. He flung himself onto the horses back, and then reached down to pull Christina up behind him. He muttered a quick apology when he slung Christina onto the horse's back, jarring her damaged leg.

"Hold to me tight. It will be a long, hard ride," He said and then dug his heels into his stallion's haunches.

CHAPTER 82

Baying Wolf kept at a steady gallop until he was certain they were out of range of danger. He knew that it was still possible that the four Apache would come for Christina; that the distraction Wolf provided may have been very temporary. He also knew that Christina's uncle would not give up searching either; that the man's obsessive, possessive nature would keep him on the trail until world's end. That filled Baying Wolf with a profound sense of insecurity, and he would not feel safe again until they reached the People and had the whole of its might as protection for his woman. He finally reigned in his stallion just before nightfall; in a clearing, several hours ride from their origination. It wasn't the idyllic secure location, but it was near water and the wooded areas always provided better opportunity for hunting food.

He also worried over Christina, who fell limp against his back shortly before stopping. She had suffered much in the past twenty-four hours, but he felt pride in how strong she'd been despite all she'd been through. He turned to catch her against his side before carefully sliding from his mount and pulling her down into the cradle of his arms. It worried him that she remained unconscious.

He gently deposited her in the clearing and quickly set about collecting wood. He hesitated to light a fire, but he had nothing for which to provide his woman warmth. Even more than warmth was the need to prepare food. He knew that she was unused to feasting on meat, freshly slaughtered and uncooked, yet wondered if she would object if he asked her to do so. He doubted she would question him in matters related to their safety, but decided not to put that assumption to the test. She'd suffered too many indignities to endure more at his hand. Right now, she needed all of the physical and mental comfort he could provide.

When the fire was sufficient to provide warmth, he gently lifted Christina and deposited her closer, laying her head upon his lap. He stroked her hair and face gently, willingly her to waken. When she remained still, he lay his head back on his shoulders and looked up at the stars above.

"You brought her this far with me; do not take her from me now." The words drifted away, no more than a whispered plea. Baying Wolf closed his eyes, weariness overtaking him. Only his mind remained alert, thoughts jumbling about in confusing succession: He needed to remain by her side; he needed to hunt for food. He needed to linger and let her rest; he needed to get her to the safety of his people. He needed to move slowly so she could heal; he needed to gallop non-stop until they reached the haven of home.

A moan caused him to jerk. His eyes opened and he apprehensively scanned Christina's features. Never had he felt such relief as he did at that moment when she opened her eyes and their gazes met.

"I thought you would sleep until morning," He said softly. A warrior did not cry, but he felt close to tears when she smiled up at him. "Do you hurt bad?"

Christina's nod was barely perceptible.

"Will you be okay while I go in search of food and the plants I need to help you feel better?"

Christina smiled, but it vanished quickly, replaced by a wince, when Baying Wolf shifted and lowered her head to the ground.

"I know you are in pain, Christina, but you must remain strong. We cannot stay here long, for there are too many who search for you. I will do what I can to ease your pain, but we must leave soon. When we reach my people, my uncle will see to you; he will make you better."

"I understand," Christina whispered.

"And do you understand that I will never let you go again?"

Christina smiled softly. She knew he sought confirmation that she belonged to him—not a possession, but as his woman. She knew he sought confirmation of the understanding that he would kill any man who tried to take her from him—including her uncle.

Baying Wolf smiled back and stood, vanishing into the woods

beyond the fire. Christina closed her eyes, but did not sleep. Her body ached too much for sleep, but more than that, she needed to listen for any signs that her uncle or the Apaches had caught up to them.

CHAPTER 83

"Baying Wolf?" Christina spoke his name, her face pressed against the rippling muscles of his back, as they bounded across the uneven terrain. She needed a break from the ride and only hoped that this second stop would not make her appear weak in his eyes.

"Let us reach that stand of trees," Baying Wolf said simply. He did not need to ask what she wanted, for her tight grip around his waist spoke of the mounting pain in her body.

He slowed his horse to a walk, guiding the animal through the trees until he located a sufficient clearing for which to rest. As he'd done prior, he shifted on his mount's back so he could provide a measure of support before sliding off and pulling Christina into his arms.

"I will search for the plant which will provide you relief," he said, lowering her carefully to the ground. "You will be well again soon."

"I know. Thank you for caring for me."

Baying Wolf nodded and went in search for medicine and food, leaving Christina alone again with her thoughts. They drifted back to when they'd first encountered her uncle, which reminded her of the hatred she'd seen flash in Baying Wolf's gaze when he'd discovered who'd barred their flight. Initially she'd thought the color of the skin of the men surrounding them brought the look of hatred to his eyes; but quickly realized it was a look reserved for her uncle. Baying Wolf abhorred Peter Carthington. That she knew. What she didn't know was what her uncle had done to him to create such enmity. It hadn't been because of her. That look told of a long-standing hatred, simmering just beneath the surface waiting to explode. She'd wanted to ask him then about the reasons.

Perhaps you can ask him now, her mind supplied when Baying Wolf returned—sooner than she'd anticipated. She felt her spirits lift at the sight of him.

"I have found what we need," Baying Wolf said, depositing a

skin full of berries and leaves near her head.

"Which are to eat and which are to take this pain away?" Christina asked, but not truly caring; for what she wanted to do was shove the entire contents into her mouth to ease the grumbling in her stomach and the aching in her leg and arms. She just didn't know if all were meant to be ingested, or she'd do just that.

Baying Wolf laughed softly, kneeling to sort through their meager supplies. Once again, Christina looked at his face in awe. When he smiled or laughed, his face went through an amazing transformation. Gone was the austere, replaced by little laugh lines around the eyes. She hesitated to bring up the subject of her uncle now because she knew it would erase the beautiful smile and hatred would once again cloud his vision. Still, she wanted to know what had created the hostility, in the event her uncle caught up with them. Despite her lack of affection for him, he was still her uncle and the only family she had left in the world.

"Baying Wolf, can I ask you a question?"

"Ask what you need and I will always answer, but do so while you eat, for we must be on our way." He slid a portion of the leaves and berries beside her and then settled down to eat his own.

"I understand," Christina said softly, then reached down to pop a few berries into her mouth. "I guess I am just curious as to why you despise my uncle so much."

"I do not hate the man so much as I hate what he has done," Baying Wolf admitted freely, and Christina was pleased that his tone remained amiable. "He came here many years ago, when I was but a young man. He used guns to take our lands and violence against our people to hold onto that land. He, and other's like him, make it harder every year for my People to hunt for food because they fence in the land and shoot anyone who crosses over those fences."

"So, it's not just because he's white?"

"If it was because he had white skin, I would also hate you, would I not?" Baying Wolf smiled and stood, then bent and lifted Christina into his arms. Her heart flipped over. "You are the woman of my heart; the woman of my dreams. You did not come here to destroy, but to mend and to heal. To help our people. I was angry at one time that the Great Spirit sent me to help a woman with skin the color of those who would seek to destroy my People, but I was wrong to be angry." He bent his head and placed a soft kiss on her lips, and then set about kicking at the dirt to extinguish the flames. "We must go. Are you ready?"

"I am."

He lowered her next to his stallion and leapt up, then lowered a hand to pull her up behind him. Baying Wolf spurred his horse into a canter and she grabbed hold of his thighs in an effort to stay upright.

"Do you know why we are going to my People, Christina?" Baying Wolf asked after a while.

"Because I dream," She replied simply.

Baying Wolf nodded. "The council wishes to speak with you about your gift."

"I haven't seen it as a gift. I knew it told me things, but until today, I was never able to interpret them properly to prepare myself, or to prevent something from happening, or use them to alter what would happen."

"My Uncle says that your gift is young and will grow and mature in time, but that it is very important to The People."

"I wish it had grown fast enough to prevent the massacre of my family."

"And I am sorry that I was not able to help you on that day, but we must try to put what has happened behind us or we will not be able to move toward our future."

"How long before we get to your village?"

"We should be there before the sun sets tomorrow."

Christina grimaced as her swollen foot banged into the horses haunches, but did not complain. She could manage the pain for one more day.

CHAPTER 84

"How do we know that this is where they stopped? There is no sign anywhere that she was even here."

"You talk too much, Carthington. I cannot concentrate with your mouth running." Cole attempted to focus on the signs around him, but with Carthington standing over his shoulder—nagging him like a female—it was extremely difficult. "Go stand somewhere quietly and I will let you know what I find—when I find it."

"I want answers!"

"And I want silence, or I will not be able to give you any answers! Now be quiet!"

Carthington stalked over to where his men sat in agitated silence. They were tired and hungry and wanted to give up the chase, and it was written all over their faces.

"Cole is certain that we're getting closer," he said as he approached. "It won't be too much longer before we find her and can head home again."

"The men have barely slept in two days boss," Matt piped up, "We're going to have to rest ourselves and our horses for longer than it takes to pick up the trail again or we're all going to collapse."

"Every second we waste, is one second less that my niece has to live. Do you understand that?"

"Yes, boss," the men answered in weary unison.

Cole walked over and gestured for the men to follow. "Over here." He led them to the tree to which the Apaches tied Christina. "Looks like someone was tied to this tree and did a lot of damage to their skin trying to break the bonds, and over here," Cole continued, walking to where the ground was spattered with blood, "it looks as if someone was seriously injured, and over there too."

"Who?"

"I cannot say who was injured, only that the blood shows injury. A fresh injury."

"Is the single injun still chasing after them? Which way did they all go so we can mount up and continue our pursuit?"

"Things have changed," Cole explained, "and before you ask how I know that, come and look at the signs for yourself." Cole stopped beside a set of prints in the dirt, "Here," he said simply and then moved to a spot across the clearing, "and here. The four warriors stood in a semi-circle facing the lone warrior. By the smeared impression, something startled them and they turned suddenly." Cole moved back to the first set, "That distraction gave the lone warrior time to flee." Cole walked through the trees, stopping to examine broken branches before exiting on the other side into another clearing. "Here is where they mounted. See here? The single imprint means that your niece stands on one foot, her other most likely injured, which may explain the blood. They are now headed in a more northerly direction, and the multiple horse prints following tell me that the Apaches want your niece back. What is it about your niece that makes everyone desperate to possess her, I wonder?"

Carthington shook his head, "That's a good question. I have had enough run-ins with the natives to know that if they lose their prey, they aren't likely to put themselves at risk retrieving it, unless it belonged to them in the first place."

"Yeah, you're an expert alright," Cole said sardonically.

Carthington glared at him, but held his peace, "How far ahead of us do you think they are?"

"They still have a day on us, but it should be easier if your niece is injured," he continued, "since the man who took her from here may move slowly to protect her from further injury—unless you think he doesn't care what happens to her."

"He cares. Too damn much."

Cole's brow lifted, but he didn't comment, "Or, he may sense that the Apaches are still after them and ride harder and faster, despite her injury. If the former, we should be able to catch them easily enough."

"Then let's ride." Carthington mounted his horse and headed out behind Cole. His gaze darkened as he remembered his niece riding behind Baying Wolf, a year earlier. The look of possessiveness in that warrior's eyes told more than any words could have. Baying Wolf wanted his niece and now he had her. Well, he wouldn't keep her for long—not as long as he drew breath.

CHAPTER 85

"They camped here recently," Cole stated confidently, kneeling beside the cold embers of recently burned wood, "and they ate berries and leaves for their meal."

"Good God, how could you possibly know *that*?" Carthington had never actually seen his best tracker in action and was unnerved by Cole's ability to accurately read signs around him, when all he could see was a cold fire pit. It made him feel inadequate in a hostile world in which inadequate could get you killed.

Cole sighed; tired of answering the same question over again each day, but Carthington would not be satisfied in just knowing that he was right. He had to know every little detail as if hoping to catch a mistake or a flaw in Cole's estimations. After all, for a mix-breed to be more capable than a white man was inconceivable to him.

Cole picked up some of the berries in the soot near the fire pit and gave them to Carthington. "It is not hard to see when one knows where to look."

"Right." Carthington looked at the dirty berries lying in the palm of his hand. He dropped them on the ground, smashing them with the heel of his boot.

"They have also changed direction slightly," Cole continued, ignoring his boss's tantrum. "Headed straight into Comanche territory."

"Damn!"

"That's a good way to put it."

"If they make it to Comanche territory, we're going to need reinforcements. Matt! Grayson! Get over here!" Matt and Grayson rode over, their weariness evident in the way they sat in the saddle.

"Yes, boss," Matt grumbled, unenthusiastic about following his boss man's next dictate and with good reason when he heard the orders issued. He'd already been sent to get reinforcements once, he thought petulantly, and wasn't eager for another hard ride.

"I'm sending you east to Fort Bliss. When you get there, seek out a Lieutenant David Michaelson. I'll have a missive for you to give him and his commanding officer in about five minutes. Until then, pack up what you'll need in the way of food and supplies. It's a long haul, so ride hard. You should be able to meet up with us day after tomorrow. We'll hold up for you at old man Warner's cabin about a day's ride north of here. Any questions?" Both men shook their heads wearily. "Good, then get ready to leave."

When both men had mounted up and ridden away, Carthington turned back to face Cole. "If we hole up and wait for reinforcements, will you have any problem picking up their trail again?"

"Not unless we get a solid rain that washes it away."

"You do realize that I've put my niece's life in your hands."

"I wouldn't do that, if I were you, Carthington. I'm just a tracker, not a god. I can neither predict nor prevent what will happen to your niece in the hands of the warrior she's with, so don't look to me for any miracles."

"I have nowhere else to look," Carthington admitted in quiet weariness. His boss looked so defeated at that moment, Cole almost felt sorry for the old man, but then he remembered how this man treated others with the same blood as himself, and the feeling vanished.

"Then I pity you." That comment snapped Carthington out of his doldrums quickly and he glared at Cole.

"Save your pity for someone who really needs it!"

"I usually do," Cole retorted.

"You have a smart mouth on you, breed."

"That's better than the chip that you carry on your shoulder."

"Listen, Cole," Carthington started and then stopped suddenly, a heavy sigh escaping from deep inside. He ran weary hands through his unwashed graying hair, "it's no secret that I don't like you none, but you're the best tracker I've got, and like it or not I've got to depend on you to find her. So what's say we try to put our differences behind us long enough to do that." Cole could see that it took a huge effort on Carthington's part to try to find a middle ground for them to stand on, but Cole didn't feel like being amiable. Carthington treated him like dirt, unless he had a need for him—like now. Then he actually elevated Cole to a higher position—breed in need. They would never be equal and Cole wasn't about to pretend otherwise.

"Our differences will never disappear, Carthington, but I would never allow an innocent woman to suffer because of them. I will track your niece, and I *will* find her. I only hope you'll be able to face some hard truths when I do."

"What truths?"

"The truth according to someone else besides Peter Carthington. Now let's go. We have to reach that cabin you were talking about before nightfall tomorrow." Cole turned and walked toward his horse, leaving a perplexed Carthington glaring after him.

CHAPTER 86

"What in blue blazes is taking them so long? They should have made it back before now." Carthington paced the small cabin, his anxiety mounting as the hours slowly ticked by. They had stayed holed up at old man Warner's cabin for two-and-a-half days, plenty of time for Matt and Grayson to arrive with reinforcements.

"Try not to worry so much, boss," Jake said. "Cole is out right now, checking out the trail to make certain he doesn't lose them. He's even offered to bring us back some fresh meat for dinner tonight."

Carthington shot his employee an angry glance. "I'm sure that Cole is a mighty special man, but all his abilities will mean nothing if we get slaughtered by savages. We need those reinforcements!"

"Yes, sir." Jake lowered himself into a nearby chair making a mental reminder to keep his mouth shut. His boss was in too foul of a mood to help and he didn't want to get his head bit off over every little statement.

"When I get my hands on Cam," Carthington continued to rant, "his hide is toast."

"Uh, boss man?" Jake stammered cautiously, forgetting his mental reminder to remain quiet. He knew this next bit of information was more likely to get him shot than his head chewed off, but despite the warning bells going off, he felt he owed his boss the information.

"Damnation! What is it now, Jake?"

"Well, it's about Cam, sir." Jake's whisper was barely audible. He'd avoided the subject of Cameron Hawthorne since he and Matt had gotten back that very first day. Now there was no more stalling to be had. He had to let his boss know.

"Jake! If you have something to say, then stop hemming and hawing like a woman and spit it out!"

Jake turned red at the insult, but he wisely kept his mouth shut at that jab. "Cam's gone. He was gone by the time Matt and I got back for supplies. The others say he hightailed it the minute we left camp in search of your niece. Guess he didn't want to deal with you."

"Well he's going to have to deal with me. All he's done by running is buy himself a short reprieve. As soon as I find my niece, I'm going after him, and I'm going to make him pay for putting her life in danger." The door banged open against its hinges; bringing Carthington's pacing and raving to an abrupt halt. "Damn!" He turned away when Cole stepped through the door, hauling the skinned flank of a buck behind him.

"Yeah, well, I ain't none too happy about seeing you again either." Cole had been gone most of the day, tracking and hunting, and wasn't in any mood to put up with his boss's bad-tempered behavior. "Somebody get a fire going and get this meat cooking," Cole ordered, dropping the meat on the table, and then turned and left the cabin again in search of a bath. He could care less that there wasn't a man in that cabin who knew how to cook. He'd had his meal on the trail. Carthington and his men could starve for all he cared.

The men in the cabin looked at the bloody carcass with disgust and wondered how the hell they were supposed to eat the dead thing lying sprawled on the dining table.

"What are we supposed to do with that thing?" Matt looked at the deer and felt his stomach roil.

"Oh for heaven's sake! Take your knives, cut off a chunk, and hang it over the fire to cook!" Carthington stomped toward the carcass with his knife drawn and sliced a large section from the leg quarter. He placed his meat on a poker sitting near the fireplace and propped it up to where the meat hung a few inches above the flame. The men looked at the blood droplets trailing across the floor and their eyes widened. "What a bunch of females! You can take a man's life and watch him bleed to death, but you can't handle the sight of a dead animal?" The men turned from Carthington accusations.

"We ain't never had to eat the men we killed," Jake answered boldly. "And we've never had to kill a deer for our food. Cam's always done the cooking."

"Well Cam ain't here, so you can either cut your own meat and cook it, or toss the carcass out the door and starve. I don't particularly give a damn. At least I'll eat tonight."

"Yeah, thanks to Cole," Matt murmured under his breath.

"What did you say?"

"Not a thing, boss man." The derision in Matt's voice was clear, but he kept his tongue in check. The smell of roasting deer caused his stomach to rumble and he drew his knife. "Better than starving to death," he said to no one in particular. He stuck the point of his knife into the side of the deer and almost gagged. Blood spurted with each slice and it took a Herculean effort for him to cut a piece large enough to fill the hole in his belly. He squatted in front of the fire and stretched his meat out over the flame, beside Carthington's. Before long, the other men overcame their disgust in favor of eating and were soon crammed around the fireplace.

When they'd had their fill, Carthington ordered the remaining pieces of the carcass be dragged a good distance from the cabin and the blood cleaned out. Without running water, the men had to make several trips to the nearby river and haul buckets back to rinse the table and floor. By the time they were finished, they were too exhausted to complain anymore, but at least their bellies were full.

Cole watched the men hauling buckets of water from the river from his vantage point in the middle of the still water. He could see the frustration in their every move and wondered just how much longer Carthington would be able to drag them around by their noses before one of them bit him. Grumbles of discontent were already being voiced when their boss man went to sleep, but all Cole could do was reassure them that he'd find Carthington's niece as soon as possible. He didn't really care about Carthington or his niece, but if the men deserted them, he didn't fancy facing Comanche warriors alone.

The rumble of hoof beats drew his attention. He climbed from the river and shook out his long black hair, and then dressed quickly and made his way back toward the cabin. When the cabin was in sight, he dropped to a crouch, the hairs on the back of his neck standing erect. He counted fifteen strange horses tied to nearby trees and could hear Carthington's loud voice booming from inside.

He approached one of the horses carefully and examined its flank, confirming by the army insignia branding the horse's rump that the men Carthington had been waiting for had finally arrived.

Cole took a deep, cleansing breath and stepped reluctantly inside.

"Are you telling me, Michaelson, that these men are all your commanding officer could spare me?" Carthington was standing on the far side of the room, his face as red as his hair and his mustache twitching in irritation, his hand waving toward the pitiful number of men filling the room.

"Mr. Carthington, sir," David said with a quiet authority that Cole appreciated immediately, "no disrespect intended, but there is a war going on. Not only with the Indians, but also between the states. That's a lot for the good soldiers of this nation to handle. Running after missing women isn't high on my commander's list of priorities at the moment, and if it wasn't for the fact that I know your niece personally, he probably wouldn't have sent anyone at all, sir."

Carthington's face turned even redder and the veins in his neck bulged in displeasure at the apparent dressing down, but he wisely held his tongue.

"I asked—no, I fairly begged him to send me and a small detachment," David continued, placing a hand on Carthington's shoulder. "I know it's not much, but it's the best I could do, and it's better than nothing. These men are some of the best that the army has to offer. You couldn't ask for better men to help search for Christina."

"How long do we have before you have to return to your post?" Carthington asked, enervated.

David looked down, his shoulders sagging as if a sudden burden had been placed upon his medium frame. "One week's time," he said quietly, as if afraid by speaking the words, the time would suddenly be gone. He glanced up, saw the incredulous look on Carthington's face, and empathized. One week was no better than a day when tracking someone, and if hostiles were encountered along the way then they would lose precious, valuable time. He couldn't think about that right now. Right now, all he could do was offer encouragement, and pray that God guide and protect them.

"If that's all we have, then that's all we have," Carthington said, his tone resigned. "Where's Cole?" He turned and began searching above the heads crowding the room and found Cole leaning against the door jam. "What say you?"

"About what?" Cole asked, knowing full well what Carthington was asking.

"Can you find her before weeks end?"

Cole looked at the anticipation lining the men's faces and didn't like having so much dependent upon his skills. Not that he doubted his skills. He was, in his humble opinion, damn good, but any number of things could happen to delay finding Carthington's niece, not the least of which was attack by renegades. Still he had to try, and it helped that he had an ace up his sleeve. His tracking over the last couple of days had developed an interesting, if not completely reliable, lead. He hadn't wanted to raise false hopes with the information, but looking at the faces around him now, he knew what he had to do or these men would likely desert Carthington and go home. The time constraints were just too great for any man.

"I can find your niece within the week," he began, a small smile forming on his usually tight lips. "In fact, I can tell you with a great deal of certainty, that you'll find her in one of three Comanche villages located about one day's ride northwest of here."

CHAPTER 87

"I'm not sure I can do this." Christina looked at the activity of the village a short distance away. "What if they don't accept me?" She drew nervously closer to Baying Wolf's chest.

"They will accept you," Baying Wolf grinned and wrapped his arms tightly around her. He placed a light kiss on the back of her neck and felt a tremor go through her in response. "My uncle has already prepared them for your arrival. They know that you are special and will be very important to The People. Besides, you are my woman."

Christina shook her head at that last statement, as if that was the greatest reason why his people wouldn't kill her the minute they rode into camp. Still, if his uncle had spoken to them, perhaps they wouldn't view her as an enemy, but as an ally. One look at her though would easily frighten the small children and the animals. She looked a fright, and said as much.

"My clothes are ripped and filthy, my hair is matted and tangled, my ankle is swollen and purple; my wrists have been rubbed raw and are bandaged—thank you for the salve you put on it, by the way, it helped a lot—and I look as if I've done battle with every element and creature Mother Nature could hurl at me."

"Is my woman done talking now?"

"I don't know, am I?" Christina replied sheepishly.

"I think so."

"It would help a great deal if you could just ease my mind a little and tell me that I'm not going to lose my scalp."

Baying Wolf threw back his head and laughed. "You may lose your scalp to me, woman, if you aren't silent real soon." Christina turned and slapped his arm, but did as he bade and quieted. "Now hear me well, Christina," Baying Wolf ordered gently, "I was sent to you by the Great Spirit and with the blessing of the shaman of our people. I'm the son of the chief and no one would dare to show their displeasure over my actions whether I brought you here by your own will to be my wife or against your will to be my slave. Anyone who dare speak out against me, risks the wrath of my father and banishment from our people. Do you understand?"

"Yes."

"Good. Besides, I already told you that everyone is expecting you—with welcome in their hearts, so, shall we continue on toward our home?"

"Yes."

"Still scared?" Baying Wolf asked as he nudged his horse forward.

"I'd be lying if I said I wasn't, but knowing you're beside me helps a great deal."

Christina's confidence fled as they approached and found a woman angrily blocking their path. She was older than herself, Christina observed, but very beautiful. Her long black hair fluttered in the light breeze along with the fringes that lined her brown buckskin dress. At first Christina thought she'd come to greet the returning warrior, but the fists pressed firmly against her hips, her wide stance, and her lips pressed into a thin line told Christina that she was extremely irate.

So much for welcoming you with a happy heart, her mind said, and for once Christina did not argue with herself. This woman was definitely opposed to her being there.

"Step aside, Prairie Heart." Christina heard the anger in Baying Wolf's tone, even though she couldn't understand the words he spoke, for he was speaking to the woman in that strange language she'd heard him use before when speaking to Wolf. She wondered if she were going to have to learn this strange language as well or if he would continue speaking to her in English.

"I will not!" Prairie Heart stomped her foot defiantly. "You cannot think to bring that woman here, Baying Wolf. She is our enemy!" Christina blushed furiously as the woman's contemptuous gaze raked over her disheveled appearance. Although she could not understand this woman any more than she could Baying Wolf, it was obvious that she had no desire to let them pass. Christina wondered whether she was someone of importance in the tribe that she would dare stand against Baying Wolf. For hadn't he just told her that no one would dare take a stand against the son of their chief? Didn't he just moments ago reassure her that he had the blessing of his shaman in bringing her here? So then, who was this that defied the very words that Baying Wolf had spoken to her?

Christina glanced about nervously as other members of the tribe stopped their work and moved to stand nearby, listening with growing interest to the argument going on between warrior and maiden.

Some of them watched the spectacle with amusement, some with growing alarm. Those watching the encounter nervously shot incredulous glances at Prairie Heart. It appeared to Christina that they were shocked by the woman's daring.

Baying Wolf also became aware of the growing numbers surrounding them and had enough. He dismounted and stormed up to where Prairie Heart stood. The crowd backed up a step and Christina stiffened. She couldn't understand why the woman standing there didn't turn and run, for if Baying Wolf approached her in that manner, obviously angry, she would have turned into a coward very quickly. Or would she? Her memory returned to her first meeting with Baying Wolf and her own daring at standing up against him when her mind argued the intelligence behind the action. She looked with renewed interest at the woman standing in heated debate with her man and wondered if her anger prevented wisdom as it had once done with her.

"Your behavior is unbecoming, Prairie Heart," Baying Wolf said loudly, hoping to embarrass her into moving, but it didn't work. Instead, she seemed to grow angrier.

"How could you bring this white eyes into our midst?"

"She is not our enemy. She is here to help our people," he explained unwillingly. Christina was not Prairie Heart's concern, but if he allowed her to taint Christina's presence with her wayward tongue then others may begin to question his decision in bringing her here as well, a decision sanctioned by the council. Sanctioned or not, his actions should never be questioned. He was the son of their chief, and this woman's impertinence was beyond forgivable. She'd entertained him in his teepee, but had no rights as a wife. He understood that his rejection is where her anger stemmed, and so tried to treat her with calm and logic, but she was having none of it. Her anger clouded her mind and made her actions foolish—another thing with which he could empathize. Still, if she did not calm soon and move, he would have to physically move her, for he could not allow her words to cast skepticism upon him, his actions, or Christina.

Fortunately, all decisions or actions were removed with Fire Dreamer's intervention. He insinuated himself between Baying Wolf and Prairie Heart and though his tone brooked no argument, Prairie Heart's mind seemed incapable of good judgment.

"Prairie Heart," Fire Dreamer said acrimoniously, "your actions today bring shame to your people. Silence your tongue now and leave our presence or you will suffer severe consequences." *Two against one*, Christina thought, *and yet the woman continues running off at the mouth*. Whereas she'd been angry earlier, it was evident in her stance and her eyes that she now resorted to pleading. Still, if she didn't shut up soon, she worried that Baying Wolf may do something foolish.

"But how can you allow Baying Wolf to bring the enemy here among us?" Prairie Heart's eyes darted around for anyone who would stand with her, but those whose gaze met hers quickly lowered them, showing their lack of support. Tears filled Prairie Heart's eyes, but still she didn't move.

She's either very brave, Christina thought, *or very stupid*. She cringed visibly when the elderly man standing beside Baying Wolf spoke again, for it was evident that he was ready to commit bodily harm upon the woman.

"You dare question me and the council who have brought this woman here?" Fire Dreamer raised his hand as if to strike Prairie Heart. Prairie Heart's face paled and she fell to her knees. "Your jealousy has clouded your heart and mind. If you do not trust the elders of this village, then leave and never return."

Prairie Heart gasped. Her gaze widened in disbelief and she looked at Baying Wolf, pleading silently with him to intervene on her behalf. When he remained silent, she stood quickly and fled to her tepee, crying loudly in her distress.

Slowly, the villagers also departed and returned to their tasks, eyeing Christina curiously, but without the hostility that Prairie Heart hoped to incite. When all was calm, a man stepped forward to embrace Baying Wolf.

"Welcome home." Chief Running Elk stepped forward as soon as the crowd had dispersed and stood proudly before his son. "Introduce me to this woman of dreams." His kind, gentle glance sought Christina's worried one and he smiled. The resemblance between father and son was striking and Christina liked this man immediately.

Baying Wolf turned and helped her dismount, carrying her toward the two men waiting to meet her. He lowered her gently to the ground and allowed her to lean against him as the introductions were made.

"Christina, I would like you to meet my father, Chief Running Elk, and my uncle, Fire Dreamer, the shaman of my people. He is the one who ordered me to go to you last year," Baying Wolf added, a twinkle in his eye.

"Ordered?" Christina placed her available hand on one hip in mock annoyance. "You had to be ordered to come to help me? What happened to dreaming about me and the Great Spirit sending you a guide to help find me?"

"Well, that was true," Baying Wolf squirmed playfully. "But I never said I wanted to listen. Even the son of a chief can be very stubborn."

"A truer statement was never spoken," Running Elk laughed, "It is good to have you here, my daughter. I look forward to speaking more with you tomorrow at the council of elders. I have heard great things about you and am honored you have come to live among us. Let Fire Dreamer take a look at your foot and hands.

Perhaps there is something he can do to help speed the healing."

"Thank you," Christina smiled.

"Does the pain hurt you much, child?" Fire Dreamer asked.

"Not overly much," Christina lied gracefully, for indeed the ride here had caused her foot to swell more than before and the constant pounding created a pounding in her head that had yet to cease. "I'm doing what I can to keep the pressure off my ankle and Baying Wolf put a salve on my wrists."

"She is already depending on me too much to help her get around. If she is not careful," Baying Wolf teased, "she will turn into a lazy white eyes."

Christina reacted to his sarcasm with a solid blow to his belly and was rewarded by his swift intake of breath.

"She will make you a good wife, my son," Running Elk laughed, and a blush crept into Christina's cheeks. Running Elk turned and strode to meet a beautiful woman standing some distance away, watching their every move intently.

"That is my mother," Baying Wolf whispered in her ear, following her gaze. "You will never be permitted to speak directly to her."

"Why ever not?"

"It would be a sign of disrespect. You must never forget."

"Your way of life is so confusing, Baying Wolf. I'm not certain I'll ever adjust."

Fire Dreamer stood listening, and laid a hand gently on Christina's shoulder. "When the moon first took its place beside the sun, it was disheartened because the sun's light shone more brightly than its own. Its value seemed as dim as its light, and it felt it would never be of any use. Because of that distress, it decided to extinguish itself, so that it would not have to face its growing feelings of inadequacy. Until one day, the sun explained to the moon why its light was important. The sun said that after a time of lighting the earth, it grew tired and needed rest, and thus relied upon the moon to provide light the rest of the time. The sun and moon split the time evenly and thus the moon felt its importance regained and it performs its duties with great honor and pride to this day.”

“I’m not sure I understand completely, although it was a very sweet story,” Christina said politely.

“You are like the moon, and although you cannot see your importance to our people at this time, you are significant. You will adapt, because you have to, and because we need you. In time, your gift will grow and you will find your place. Bring her to me, Nephew, as soon as you are settled, and I will see to her wounds. I am not certain that I can do anything for her foot, but I will make an herbal tonic for her to drink that may take the swelling away.” Fire Dreamer removed his hand from her shoulder and smiled at them both, and then turned and walked away, leaving them standing on the outskirts of the village, alone.

Baying Wolf lifted Christina into his arms again and gave her a fierce hug.

“My uncle is right. You do not yet see the importance you hold in my people’s eyes, but you will in time,” he kissed her gently. “Are you still afraid?”

“I was truly afraid,” Christina replied softly, wrapping her arms around his neck, “when that woman started carrying on so. Who was she, Baying Wolf? Why does she despise me so? Is it simply because I’m white?”

“It is partly because of the color of your skin, but I think more than anything she is jealous of you.”

“Of me? Why? I’m hardly anything to look at, at the moment, and hardly worth getting jealous over.”

“Her name is Prairie Heart, and she was my lover before you came.”

“I’m sorry I asked.” Christina blushed and tried to squirm from his arms.

“Before you came, my woman,” Baying Wolf repeated against her ear. “That is why she is so distraught.” He tugged at her earlobe with his mouth. “Because she will never visit my tepee again.”

“She’d better not.” Christina punched Baying Wolf playfully in the shoulder, “or else I’ll be the one getting jealous.”

Baying Wolf lowered Christina carefully to the ground and then pulled her hips firmly into contact with his arousal. "Jealousy is not a pretty trait in most people, but it makes your eyes sparkle like the stars and your cheeks flush like a rose."

"Does that mean you intend to be a good boy?" Christina asked coyly.

"Only outside our teepee, my woman. Now no more talk, so I can get you comfortable. My uncle needs to tend to you."

As he carried her through the village to his tepee, her embarrassment increased and her blush deepened as the young women and children of the village giggled at their passing. She buried her face in his shoulder and felt his chest rise and fall in silent laughter at her discomfort.

Baying Wolf ducked into his tepee and carefully lowered Christina to the ground.

"This will be *our* home now," he whispered against her hair, wrapping his arms around her waist from behind, "does it please you?" He placed a light kiss on her shoulder.

"It does." It was not her feather mattress back at the ranch, but it had its own comfort and charm. "Did you draw all of these pictures?" Christina gaze took in all of the depictions lining the walls of the teepee. "Are you an artist among your people?"

"What is an artist?"

"Someone that draws pictures that other people look at and admire, to decorate their home with."

"Ah, no. These pictures represent my life. See there?" Baying Wolf pointed to a stick figure kneeling beside a rock in a meadow. What appeared to be a wolf was standing opposite him, howling at a drawing of the moon, "that is where I became a man; and over here, I will draw a picture of a green-eyed she wolf pointing a revolver at my chest..." Baying Wolf started laughing when Christina pushed back hard against him, flattening him against the skins.

"I had every right to be afraid of you," she replied.

Baying Wolf carefully rolled her off of him, and moved to lean over her, "Do you fear me now?"

Christina shook her head, a blush staining her cheeks pink at the look in his eyes. He leaned down and kissed her gently, and then rolled away from her and sat up. He smiled gently, and held out a hand to assist her in returning to a sitting position. "I want to take you but do not wish to begin something that I will have to stop." At her quizzical expression, he laughed, "My uncle will arrive soon with medicines. I do not want him to walk in when I am making love to my woman."

Christina blushed again and Baying Wolf laughed. Once more, Christina was in awe at how much joy transformed his features.

"I don't know if I ever told you how much I love your smile. It makes you seem less fierce," Christina said.

"Am I really so fierce?" Baying Wolf inquired.

"When I first met you, your countenance was so daunting that my knees refused to stop knocking and I was certain that I would die just from the intensity of your gaze."

"Yet you bravely stood against me and brandished a revolver in my face, threatening to shoot me. Why didn't you?"

"Shoot you?"

"Yes, you green-eyed she wolf."

"I probably would have if you had attacked me or if I had felt threatened by you. I can't really say what it was, but as scared as I was of you and as scary as you looked, I didn't see you as a threat, just an angry man who didn't want to be where he was anymore than I wanted to be where I was."

"That is good, but I hope my enemies always see me as fierce as you did, or they may build enough confidence to attack my people."

"It's your reputation that keeps them away?"

"Mine and that of all the warriors."

"Well, I'm glad you're all on my side," Christina said sincerely, and then looked up into her warriors beautiful opaque eyes. "And to answer your question, no, you no longer frighten me. Can I ask you a question?"

"Anything."

"Why do you call me a green-eyed she wolf?"

"Because you are," Baying Wolf laughed. "If you ever see a female dog defending its cubs, you will know why I call you that. There is fierceness in its stance and a daring in its gaze that defies logic at times, since one arrow can kill it with little effort. You are the same. You stand bravely against unreasonable odds in opposition to those that could easily overtake and harm you. It is truly remarkable." Baying Wolf planted another kiss on her lips and then stood.

"Where are you going?" Christina asked, when Baying Wolf moved to rise.

"Did you not hear the knock on the teepee?"

Christina shook her head, astounded that someone would knock on a skin and expect to it to be heard, and that Baying Wolf heard that knock.

"It is my uncle here to tend to you. He must help your body heal so that you can sit with the council tomorrow—and also to become my wife."

"I like that."

Baying Wolf opened the flap to the teepee and Fire Dreamer bent to enter. For the next hour, he tended to Christina and instructed her on all that would take place tomorrow. The expectations were great, and her mind would have been in turmoil at everything he said had he not given her a tonic that had her drifting off into a dreamless sleep.

CHAPTER 88

"Well, we know the first two villages weren't the right ones." Carthington paced back and forth in front of Cole. "Your promised one day came and went yesterday and we don't seem to be any closer to finding her. And now you sit and tell me that you've lost their trail!"

Cole watched as he paced back and forth as a caged animal. He had been ranting and pacing for the better part of fifteen minutes while Cole sat and watched, sharpening his knife blade.

He wondered if Carthington would treat any tracker in this manner, or if was because of his mixed blood that he continued to lambaste him so. He wasn't certain of the answer to that one, but he did know one thing—he could hand Carthington his niece on a silver platter and still he would despise him. It was times like these, that Cole wondered why he even bothered working for the man.

Money, he thought grimly. Carthington paid the best wages in all of Texas. He needed the money and Carthington needed a tracker; and so they tolerated each other, circling warily around one another like two coyotes after the same carcass. After they found his niece, however, Cole determined that enough was enough. He'd saved sufficient wages to start a place of his own, far away from the likes of Peter Carthington.

"Well, what have you to say for yourself, breed?"

"I never promised you a damn thing, Carthington. I only said that I was reasonably certain we'd find your niece yesterday. However, we still have one more village to search, and I am almost as sure as I can be that we will find her there."

"How can you be so blasted positive?"

Taking a deep, calming breath, trying to remember from where Carthington's impatience stemmed, Cole explained again. "The trail led me in this direction. There are a limited number of tribes in the region because of the rocky terrain. We've already encountered two of them. The third lies a little further north in a slightly higher elevation. I've lost their trail because of the terrain, which only confirms the fact that they were heading this way. If they'd headed away from here, I'd have spotted the trail easily enough."

"Tarnation, Cole! What if they headed further north to another village? What if she's not at the village we'll be paying a visit to tomorrow?"

"She will be."

"How...?"

Cole raised a hand to stop the repetitive question. "I just know. You know, if this warrior had not already known your niece, he would not have ridden such a great distance to retrieve her. I cannot say how he knew where she would be, but he did, and made certain to be there. You taking her on the cattle drive gave him a chance to abduct her away from the safety of your ranch. Your decision to allow her to ride along with you afforded the Apaches that same chance. We are fortunate that the Apaches decided it was too far from home territory to continue their own pursuit. It was as if fate determined her destiny and used you as the tool to see it come true."

To hear the words spoken that Christina's abduction was his doing, angered Peter. He knew his decision had been a poor one and had kicked himself daily as to why he'd allowed it. Cole called it fate; he called it plain stupidity. No matter the reasons for her abduction, he was determined to turn his stupidity into his victory. He'd get her back.

"She'd better be at the last village."

"Or, what, Carthington?" Cole's eyebrow arched at the implied threat, but instead of answering the challenge, the fire in Carthington's eyes diminished and his shoulders slumped.

"I don't know, but I'll think of something."

"My assurances stand, Carthington. Unless the tribe has moved locations, we'll be at the village in another day. You can also be certain that if the tribe has moved, I'll find them."

"I know. I wish all red skins were as venerable as you."

"Maybe it's the white blood in me that makes me so honorable." The sarcasm was not lost on Carthington. He opened his mouth to reply, but no words came out. His eyes bulged and his jaw went slack as he stared over Cole's shoulder.

"What in blue blazes is wrong with you?" Cole stared at his boss's countenance for a short moment, and then turned slowly to follow Carthington's obviously distressed gaze. His own jaw slackened momentarily as he stared into two opaque eyes watching them intensely from a nearby shrub. "It's obvious that you've been discovered," Cole shouted to the crouching form, "so why not come out slowly before my boss forgets himself and yells for reinforcements." Both men's faces registered shocked amazement as the figure slowly and warily emerged, a fine bone-handled knife clutched tightly in a brown fist.

"What the...?" Cole raised a hand to silence Carthington before he said something to frighten their visitor away.

"What's your name and why are you spying on our encampment?" Cole's eyes scanned the horizon for any further surprises.

"She looks like him. The one you seek," the intruder said shortly, nodding in Carthington's direction.

Cole's eyes narrowed slightly, and his glance went to Carthington who was trying hard to maintain his own calm. If Cole was any judge of character, Carthington was aching to get his hands on the Indian standing before them and extract answers to questions that hadn't even been asked yet. He shot him a warning glance, and then turned his attention back to the interloper.

"How do you know we are searching for someone?" Cole asked, trying to keep his stance and his voice casual. He, too, wanted answers quickly. The intruder laughed shortly and harshly, as if the question was lacking intelligence.

"I overheard you talking, and since that man looks a lot like the woman that was recently brought to my village, I made the connection easily enough. She has his hair, his eyes."

"They sent a woman to ensure that we did not reach her?" Cole laughed sardonically.

"My people did not send me," Prairie Heart snapped irately. "They banished me for speaking out against the white eyes. I was on my way to join my uncle's people when I stumbled upon your camp and overheard you talking."

That confession brought both men up short. Each looked from Prairie Heart to each other trying to weigh the honesty of the woman's words.

"Then you're telling me that my niece is being held in your village?" Carthington found his voice and forced the same calm tone that he'd heard Cole use. "And does your village lie just north of here?"

"Held?" Prairie Heart queried perplexed.

"Prisoner," Carthington clarified.

"My village is a day's ride to the north of here," Prairie Heart was suddenly pleased to have stumbled on these two men and to answer their questions, "but the woman you call 'niece' is not being held there."

"But you just said that a woman, who looked like him," Cole said, pointing toward Carthington, "was at your village?"

"I did," Prairie Heart grinned wickedly, "but she is not a prisoner there as you wish to think." She watched as her next words affected the man in front of her and her heart soared. She may not be able to hurt the white woman that took Baying Wolf away from her, but she could strike at the man that calls her niece. "Why do all white eyes think that their women leave them against their will? Even as we speak, the woman you call 'niece' is laying with the son of our chief, Baying Wolf, accepting his seed—seed that will be as mixed as yours," She concluded, sending a scorching glance at Cole.

"You lie!" Carthington forgot his attempt at restraint and struggled to push past Cole, whose strong grasp prevented him from attacking the startled maiden. "You lie!" He repeated, his struggle intensifying.

"Only white eyes have lying tongues." Prairie Heart turned to leave, suddenly wishing to quit their presence in all haste. She'd had her fun, and her revenge, but it was time to go before the white man decided to take his displeasure out on her. She couldn't resist one last parting remark and turned to face the man whose face was now a mottled red, his anger so intense she could almost feel the heat slamming into her body. "You will see tomorrow, white man, when you ride into the village that I used to call home. You will see the white woman clinging to the man that I used to call mine. She will not be happy to see you." She turned quickly and hurried back the way she'd come, not slowing her pace until she'd traveled several hours. As she lay beside a small stream, watching the moon slowly rise in the sky, her laughter turned bitterly hysterical and it was sometime before sanity returned. "I wish I could be there to see Baying Wolf's face when the white eye's storm the village and takes his precious woman away. At least now I can live with my uncle in peace knowing that his happiness will be destroyed."

CHAPTER 89

"Your dreams are gifts, that not even you were aware of, my child," Fire Dreamer spoke, addressing Christina before turning to speak to the village elders. Baying Wolf had carried Christina into the meeting hall earlier. She sat and watched as the elderly men of the village entered one after the other, eyeing her with a mixture of interest and suspicion. Now she listened with them as Fire Dreamer spoke. "The Great Spirit guided my nephew to the white woman seated next to him, and commanded that he keep her from the many dangers that surrounded her life," Fire Dreamer spoke in his native tongue.

"And what is to keep that danger from following her here and bringing it among us?" An elder countered.

"It is my belief that my nephew was sent to guard her because the evil one wanted her destroyed before she reached us," Fire Dreamer countered. There was a collective 'Ahhh', and all eyes turned toward the woman who sat near Baying Wolf, her eyes wide with nervous tension. "She has faced many horrors on her way to us," he continued to a now captive audience, "all to test her strength, her gift, her resilience, and her heart. Renegades attacked her family—an attack revealed to her in a vision; and while they butchered everyone around her, she lived. She could have let her anger against our kind grow and kill her young gift, but she overcame that anger and thus was able to see yet again through a vision, her abduction by Apache warriors. Because of her gift, she was prepared when the Apaches captured her, spiriting her away from her uncle. Again, as with the first time, the Great Spirit sent Baying Wolf to her aid and after a year of turmoil and struggle, he brought her here to live among us, so that her gift can help us see what our future holds." Fire Dreamer stopped speaking for a moment and allowed his gaze to rest on each member of the council.

"You say that she can see her own danger, but what makes you think her gift will be of use to The People?" Fire Dreamer turned and was surprised to see Chief Running Elk had asked the question. A gleam in his eye reassured Fire Dreamer and he relaxed. Fire Dreamer realized that, although Running Elk stood with him, he must also voice those concerns brought to him by his people.

"Her gift is young. It is growing daily. An ability must begin somewhere. Hers began with warnings and guidance about her own fate. Because her life is intertwined with that of Baying Wolf, I believe that her gift will soon encompass dreams of his fate. When she has developed her gift and when The People accept her as family, she will dream of the destiny of us all. We all know that change is coming because of the white man, which we all know will affect our lives. It is my belief that this white woman, who will soon become a member of our tribe by marrying the son of our chief, will be able to see what will be; and that will help us in making the proper preparations instead of fumbling around in the darkness."

"Can you not see what the future holds in store for our people any longer, Fire Dreamer?" Another council member asked. "Why must we rely on a woman of our enemy to guide our people? Is she so special that she has been given the sight to lead us? How do we know this gift is for the good of The People and will not be used against The People?"

"This is a good question. She is young, and her heart and mind are pure. She is connected to our people through Baying Wolf and her love for him. It is that pure love, I believe, that will lead her never to harm that which she cherishes. More importantly, I have become aged and my sight is growing dim," Fire Dreamer admitted reluctantly, embarrassed to admit his own shortcomings. Still he held his head high, as he continued to address the council. "I believe this is the final reason that the Great Spirit brought this woman among us. She has been given my gift of sight, and she will take my place as shaman of our people. She cannot use the gift against us, as she will soon become one of us."

The strange language began flying around the council chamber, deafening in its intensity and strength of conviction. No one had expected this turn of events and they were all eyeing Christina with a strange light in their eyes. When Fire Dreamer was speaking to them, they expected she would hold a place on the council not take a senior place of authority.

"What is it?" Christina leaned close to Baying Wolf, shouting to be heard above the din. "What has happened?"

"It's Fire Dreamer," Baying Wolf paused, staring at Christina as if seeing her for the first time, and then his gaze shifted and locked with his uncle's. *You knew all the time why I had to go to her,* he thought in awe. *Didn't you, old man?* The challenge was issued without words, across the great expanse of the chamber, above the roar of the elders, but Baying Wolf could tell by the expression on his uncle's face that he knew what Baying Wolf had said, what he'd asked, and a sly grin crossed his narrow lips.

"Baying Wolf. Please, tell me what's wrong. Why is everyone suddenly so agitated?" Christina tugged on his arm frantically until he looked at her again.

"Fire Dreamer is no longer the shaman of our people. He is giving the honor to someone else to take his place."

"I don't understand. Who? Why? What?" Baying Wolf placed a gentle finger over her lips, silencing the questions that poured out.

"It is the first time that an outsider has held such a position of honor and authority among our people. It is even rarer that it will be held by a woman." He watched as Christina's eyes widened. Her lips moved to form words, but no sound came out.

She jerked her head around and scanned the faces until her gaze came to rest on Fire Dreamer. He nodded slightly and smiled gently as if he had been expecting her to seek him out, and then turned to speak with the person standing next to him.

A thundering command rent the air and the talking ceased abruptly. Running Elk moved to the center of the room, and stood beside Fire Dreamer.

"What will be has been spoken," he said loudly, "and there will be no more discussion in our chambers about it." Running Elk pointed at Christina and held out his hand for her to join him.

Baying Wolf stood proudly by her side and led her carefully toward
where his father waited. Christina moved gingerly, leaning heavily
against Baying Wolf. Her heart was pounding in her ears and her
knees were knocking nervously. As she walked toward her future
father-in-law, he continued speaking. "This woman will become our
new shaman. Her words will be held in high esteem and honored in
the chamber of elders. Because she is a woman and forbidden in
council beyond today, my son will hear her words and carry them to
our ears." He looked at Baying Wolf to confirm his new position
within the council. Baying Wolf bowed slightly, accepting the honor
with a pride that reflected in his stance. "From this day forth,
Christina will be known as Dreamer of Destiny."

Everyone sat in stunned silence as Running Elk faced Christina
and removed his amulet from around his neck. With great
ceremony, he raised the amulet high in the air and said a prayer that
the Great Spirit would guide Christina's heart and mind for the good
of The People. He lowered the amulet over her head and placed a
kiss on her cheek.

"She will learn the ways of our people and the language of our
ancestors. She will follow in Fire Dreamer's steps and learn to use
her gift to aid our people as Fire Dreamer has done faithfully for so
many years. You will look past the color of her skin and past the
fact that she is a woman. This is a command that all will obey for as
long as they remain a member of our tribe. Now, we will leave here
and return to our village, for there is much to plan before my son
and our new shaman say vows that will join them together forever
in this life as husband and wife."

Christina watched as the elders filed by slowly, her mind still
too numb to do more than nod at the ones who passed with
greetings and well wishes. Some continued on their way, refusing to
look at her at all. Their chief had spoken and they would not argue
with his decision, but it was obvious by their demeanor that they did
not readily accept her and would be watching for her to make a
mistake.

When everyone had left the building, Baying Wolf came up and placed a reassuring hand on her shoulder.

"I'm honored that the Great Spirit has chosen me to be your husband, and I am pleased to have you as my wife. I will be a good provider for you and will make you happy always. This is my vow."

"Oh, Baying Wolf!" Christina placed her palm against his bronzed face and smiled, her love for him growing stronger every day. "I never had a doubt that you'd care for me. My doubt, right now, is how I can ever expect to be a shaman to your people when I don't even know what a shaman is."

"A shaman," Fire Dreamer answered, moving closer to where the couple stood, "is a healer. The people come to me when their bodies have been hurt."

"Like a doctor?" Christina asked.

"Yes. Similar to your white man's doctor."

"But I don't have any medical training!" Christina was alarmed, and her voice began to rise in pitch as she spoke. "I wouldn't even begin to know how to care for sick people. Besides, you said that the reason I was taking over as shaman of your people was because I could sometimes see things through my dreams, not because I was capable of curing sickness."

"Relax, my child and I will try to explain to you." Christina took a deep breath and let it out in a rush. "Come, we will sit." Fire Dreamer took her arm and guided her to the stone bench that he'd occupied during the meeting.

Baying Wolf took a seat nearby, but not close enough to interfere with their conversation.

"I'm not only a healer," Fire Dreamer continued. "I'm also a seer."

"I don't understand."

"As you can see into the future through your dreams, so can I. It is a rare and special gift."

"I see," Christina nodded in understanding.

"Yes, you do," Fire Dreamer quipped and Christina smiled. "The gift of healing is a simple one to learn, and you will go with me every day to learn which plants to use for curing the sick, and which to use on the enemies of The People. The gift of sight is much harder to understand because sometimes the dreams that come to us are not clear. Sometimes we do not know if it is simply a dream or something of importance that we must act upon. This gift I cannot teach you or train you in its use. You will simply learn to read your dreams as time goes on. Do you understand all that I have said?" Christina nodded.

"Good, then come." Fire Dreamer stood and held out his hand. "We must prepare for your marriage. The women of our village have worked hard to prepare a wonderful feast for you both."

"I will take her to my sister. They will be waiting to prepare her for the ceremony." Baying Wolf appeared by her side and took her elbow, guiding Christina from the council chamber.

CHAPTER 90

"My brother did not want to come to you last year," Little Bird confided. "He was very angry when the Great Spirit told him that there was a white woman that needed his help," she giggled as she washed Christina's hair for the second time. Little Bird had been chosen to be Christina's helper because she spoke English, as did Baying Wolf. She had also been given the task of instructing Christina in the language of her people. Today, however, she concentrated not on lessons, but in preparing her shaman for marriage to her brother. Little Bird had taken a liking to Christina immediately and was pleased to have been given the job of serving her. "He stomped around the tepee like a little child who did not get his way," she confided, and then lifted the skin of water, pouring its contents over Christina's head.

"He must have hated me a great deal,"

"No, my sister," Little Bird corrected hastily, "he did not hate you. He just did not wish to be told what to do. Especially when what he had to do concerned leaving his home and helping a white eyes—even if that white eyes is a beautiful woman."

Christina blushed. The blush deepened when Little Bird reached for her shirt and began tugging the buttons loose. Her pale hand instinctively reached up and brushed the bronzed one away.

"I'm sorry," Little Bird apologized, noticing her discomfort. "I only need for you to remove your clothes so that you may bathe."

"But we're out in the open with no shelter!"

"Do not worry, my sister," Little Bird reassured her, "the men of my village know not to watch when we bathe, but if it will make you feel more comfortable, the women will provide a shield for you." Little Bird snapped her fingers and instructed the other women standing nearby to fan out. When Christina felt that no prying eyes would be able to see her, she relaxed her guard and shed her clothes. "Wash quickly, my sister," Little Bird called from the bank when she heard a splash from the water. "The time for you to be wed is getting closer and we still must get you dressed."

Christina returned to the bank after a quick scrub, and searched frantically for her clothing.

"Where are my skirt and blouse?" She asked Little Bird.

"It has been taken to the community fire, where it will be burned."

"What? But those are the only clothes that I own?"

"No part of your white world will remain after today. You are one of The People now."

"Well, what exactly am I supposed to wear to the wedding—nothing?"

Little Bird shrugged off Christina's concerns and wrapped a buffalo skin around her nude form. "Come. The women have prepared something special for you."

Christina entered the tepee a short time later and was quickly ushered over to the small fire that burned low in the center. Several women were waiting there with an assortment of things with which to fix Christina's hair. Christina knelt by the fire, wrapping her blanket protectively around her as the women moved in closer. It took a while for them to work all the tangles free from her hair, but when they were done, it shone with a radiance that it hadn't had since leaving her uncle's ranch.

The women paused their work when the flap raised and Little Bird ducked in carrying a buckskin dress over her arm. It was a pale cream, accentuated sparsely on the shoulders and front with brightly colored, turquoise beadwork, unlike anything Christina had ever seen before.

The moccasins, that she carried in her other hand, were slightly darker in color, but the beadwork was no less elegant. It was the most beautiful raiment that Christina had ever seen, but she had her doubts.

"How do you know that the dress will fit me?" Christina asked in awe.

"Baying Wolf let us know when you arrived yesterday how big to make the dress," Little Bird explained with obvious pride. "The women have been working most of the night to make sure this dress would be ready for your marriage today." Christina wanted to stand to try on the gown, but the women behind her pushed down on her shoulders, returning to their work. "They have also made you several other items to wear for a while until more clothes can be made for you."

"It looks so soft. Can't I try it on now?"

"The women need to finish your hair, and then you will dress."

"I see." Christina was disappointed, but did not argue further. "What did you mean, until more clothes can be made for me? Aren't I going to learn to make clothes for myself?"

Little Bird quickly relayed this question to the women surrounding her. Christina blushed as the women giggled behind their hands.

"You are to be Baying Wolf's wife and the shaman of our people. You will not work. You will have women work for you," Little Bird explained. "It would be an insult for you to labor, when you will have many other things that will keep your days busy."

"I see."

"Good, now you may come to try on your dress. The women have completed your hair. It is time to see if the dress we made for you will fit. If it does not, then Baying Wolf is not as good at sizing a woman's body as he thinks he is." She held up the dress and Christina rubbed her hand over it, marveling at the softness of the material. When Little Bird moved to place it over her head, Christina stepped away.

"But what about underclothing?"

"What are underclothing?"

"I don't have a corset, for one."

"I do not know what this thing is, but the dress is all you have need for." As it turned out, the dress fit like a glove, which made the women giggle more and Christina blush. "Obviously," Little Bird commented, "Baying Wolf knows your body well. Come. Let us go meet him now."

Christina was led from the tepee behind a procession of

tittering females. The men lined the path, smiling broadly at Christina, and then closed in behind the females as they passed.

She caught sight of Baying Wolf standing proudly beside his father at the head of the crowd and Christina blushed at his heated perusal. His passionate gaze held hers as she limped toward him, her heart swelling with love for the man that would soon be her husband.

She blushed pleasurably at the thought, and her heart smiled as she remembered this time last year when she'd have preferred his death to his company. She tried hard to suppress a giggle as memories of their conflicts played through her mind and she wondered how so much could have changed in so short a time to bring about this glorious day.

"You look very desirable, my woman," Baying Wolf murmured against her ear as he took her hand and turned her toward Fire Dreamer, who would be performing the ceremony.

"So do you, my darling," Christina whispered back, a blush creeping into her cheeks at her own audacity.

"The blush that tints your cheeks is beautiful, but after today you will learn much in our tepee that you will have no need to blush. That, I promise."

Christina's blush deepened and she heard Baying Wolf laugh softly over Fire Dreamers words as the ceremony began.

Christina heard the words that Baying Wolf's uncle spoke, but they did not register in her mind. All that she could think about was Baying Wolf's promise of their wedding night and the things she would learn. When the ceremony ended, loud shrills accompanied them as Baying Wolf carried her to his tent—her new home and her new life.

He lowered her carefully, and then knelt to stoke the fire in the pit. "How is your foot feeling?" He asked, adding more wood as he spoke.

"Much better." Christina watched him work with the fire and felt a shiver of anticipation crawl down her spine. "At least now I can put a small amount of pressure on it," she lowered herself onto their bed of buffalo skin, "but it's not good for me to stand on it for too long."

Baying Wolf moved over to where she sat and lifted her leg. He gently removed her moccasins and examined her still swollen ankle. "It is not as bad as it was, but will still take many days to heal." He bent and kissed the appendage in question.

Another shiver worked its way over her body as his hand stroked her ankle, then made its way up to her calf, and on up to the back her knees, followed by his warm lips.

"Does this ease the pain?"

"Yes," Christina breathed. It did more than ease her pain; it lit a fire deep inside her. If the look in Baying Wolf's eyes were any indication, that fire was burning inside him also.

He lowered her leg and moved to kneel behind her head, "Sit up. I wish to tend to you."

Christina didn't know what kind of tending needed to be done while sitting up, but she was too aroused to ask, so she timidly did as he bade. Baying Wolf stood and removed his clothing, and then knelt again behind her. He slid his hands beneath her buttocks and grasped her clothing, lifting her and sliding the material up and over her head in one fluid motion. An action that left Christina even more breathless.

His hands expertly moved through the braids, removing the flowers and beads, laying them at the head of their bed. Then he gently tugged the braid loose and ran his fingers through her long satiny tresses. His fingers ran in and out of the auburn curls, alternately rubbing her scalp and neck. When he finished admiring her hair, his hands moved over her shoulders, beneath her arms and cupped her full breasts in his hands.

He leaned over and gently nipped at her neck, his hands moving lower to caress her quivering abdomen. She moaned and Baying Wolf moved from behind her. She lie back and he stretched out beside her, lowering to claim her mouth in a kiss that bespoke of the desire placed on hold for too long.

When he joined with her, it was as if they'd known each other forever; and even in her innocence, her body moved in unison with his. She now recognized that this was but one way in which a couple expressed love for one another; for the joining of a man and a woman ripped away all pretenses, exposing all weaknesses. Without love, it became an act in which neither would risk revealing too much of themselves; for any revelation, any sign of weakness, could never be welcomed or accepted by the other.

Baying Wolf's body arched with the release of his seed. He tensed and then fell limp atop his wife, energy depleted. He wanted to stay; resting on the comfort of her breasts, but knew she would not welcome his weight for too long. He rolled to her side, slid his arm beneath her neck, and pulled her into his embrace. It was sometime before either of their heartbeats slowed and they were able to speak.

"I did not hurt you?" He asked quietly, placing a kiss on her head.

"Only for a short moment, after that it felt as if I were shooting through the clouds on a giant eagle—a breathless and tingling feeling enveloped my entire body."

"Hmmm. I take it that you are pleased with your husband."

"You would be right about that." Christina traced a finger over his hairless chest.

"When we begin to know each others' bodies, there is much to discover that can bring pleasure. We did not even come close to learning each other tonight."

"When do we begin that?" Christina asked and blushed at the eagerness in her question.

Baying Wolf laughed. "You are greedy. Allow an old man to rest, and then I will be happy to accommodate you again, wife."

"I like that. Wife."

"Hmm."

Christina lifted her head and grinned. Baying Wolf had fallen asleep. She returned her head to his shoulder and willed her own tired body to rest, but what she'd experienced over the last few days had her too restless. With as quiet a movement as she could, she slipped from beneath his arm and stole to the river to wash. She sat on the bank for a long while, staring at the rippling reflection of the moon upon the surface of the water. Fire Dreamer had said that she was like the moon, and that she would soon find her place among the stars. She hoped so, for never had she had so many conflicting feelings bounding about her body as she'd had since this new adventure began.

She knew that her destiny had brought her among these people, strangers to her; and hoped that they would learn to accept her and that she would learn to accept her own fate.

A nose nuzzled her arm, startling her. She laughed when Wolf moved around her and laid its massive head atop her lap.

"If you think I am going to stay here and provide you a bed to sleep upon, you're sadly mistaken." The animal gazed up at her, gave a giant yawn, and then stretched out beside her on the bank. "Keep us safe while I sleep?" Christina asked, rubbing the gray fur affectionately. The wolf looked at her again, and Christina had a sense that the big brute understood her perfectly. "Thank you, my friend," she whispered, then stood and made her back to Baying Wolf's embrace.

CHAPTER 91

Cole held tightly to his boss long after the Indian woman vanished, afraid that he'd follow her and beat her to within an inch of her life, just for being Indian.

"Let me go, you misbegotten son of a savage!"

Cole chose to ignore his boss's comment, realizing that he was trying to provoke him. Carthington needed an outlet and Cole refused to acquiesce. He would just have to duke it out with a tree trunk.

"If I release my hold, will you at least attempt to calm yourself?"

"I said let me go!"

"And I said I won't unless you calm down." Cole's grip tightened stubbornly.

"Alright, you mixed-breed miscreant. I'm calm!"

"That's doubtful, but I have no choice but to let you go since I can't very well detain you indefinitely." Cole took a couple of steps back as soon as he released his hold, his stance prepared for the punch that was certain to follow. When Carthington merely stomped away toward camp, Cole breathed a sigh of relief and followed at a distance.

"Carthington. Hold up a minute!" Cole called, falling into step beside Carthington's fast-moving form. "I think we might better discuss what's happened before you go storming into camp and then running off half-cocked."

"What in hell are you talking about?" Carthington asked, not slowing his pace.

"Options. Now that we know your niece isn't being held against her will...." The fist that connected with his jaw sent Cole sprawling in the dirt. He lay there a minute, shaking his head and rubbing his chin. Finally, he looked up into the furious countenance of the man standing above him, hands raised, ready to punch him again.

"I didn't think you had it in you, old man," Cole laughed harshly, "but if you think I'm going to let you take your frustrations out on me, think again."

Carthington lowered his fist and stretched out a hand to help Cole from the ground.

"I'd apologize yet again, if punching your lights out hadn't felt so damned good."

"I'm sure." Cole rubbed his sore jaw and watched Carthington with a wary glance.

"You don't think that Indian squaw was lying, do you?"

"You have to ask yourself what her motivation for lying would be, Carthington, and as far as I can see, she doesn't have one." Cole waited and watched as a dozen emotions played across Carthington's face. When he finally stopped pacing and looked at Cole once again, Cole stepped back in astonishment. Standing before him was no longer a man full of strength and determination, but an old man that looked as if he'd been beaten down.

"I have to find out for myself, Cole. I can't just leave her there without knowing. I can't believe she'd accept life with a heathen, especially after what they did to her family."

"I doubt it would make any difference what I say, Carthington, but not all Indians are evil, blood-lusting, women-snatching, devils."

"You're right. It doesn't make a difference." Carthington turned on his heel and walked into camp, leaving a bewildered Cole staring after him.

CHAPTER 92

"Good morning, wife." Baying Wolf stared down at the woman outstretched beside him and smiled. "How are you feeling this morning?"

"Like the cat that ate the canary," Christina murmured sleepily. She lifted her arms and drew her husband down next to her. "Like the cat that is hungry for more canary," she whispered seductively, planting a soft kiss on his lips. Baying Wolf moaned and deepened the kiss, rolling over until Christina lay prone on his body.

A knock on the tent flap distracted them. Baying Wolf pulled Christina off of him and covered her with the buffalo hide. He stood quickly and donned his skins, and then bade the visitor to enter.

"I would not intrude on your privacy if it were not important, Baying Wolf," Gray Fox said quickly, his eyes averted from the bed.

"It is okay, my friend. Speak what must be spoken, so I can go back and attend my wife." Christina blushed and squirmed deeper under the skins.

"That will not be possible, my friend," Gray Fox said, casting a quick glance in Christina's direction. "There are men approaching the village."

"My uncle!" Christina gasped, sitting up quickly, the buffalo hide clasped to her breast like a shield. "Oh, Baying Wolf, I knew he would find me!"

"How far out?"

"The scouts spotted them less than an hour's ride from here."

"Thank you, Gray Fox. Go and await their arrival. Have the men in the village prepare in the event we need to defend ourselves and our families." Gray Fox nodded and ducked back out of the teepee.

Baying Wolf removed his skins and returned to the bed, pulling a still shaking Christina into his strong arms.

"They may have found you, but they cannot have you. I told

you once, Christina, that I would never let you go, so calm yourself. I still have a canary to feed you, my green-eyed she wolf."

Baying Wolf claimed Christina's mouth in a desperate kiss that belied his calm words.

They lay in each other's arms, a short while later, their limbs weakened and their desire spent.

"Are you ready to meet those who are coming?"

"You mean you're not going to order me to stay hidden in my teepee?" Christina's finger drew a lazy circle over Baying Wolf's bare chest. He grabbed her hand in his and brought it to his mouth, kissing each fingertip slowly.

"I would do so if I thought it would keep you from harm, but it will not. It is best that your uncle sees that you are happy and then maybe he will turn away in peace."

Christina sighed. "This is one time that I wish you would boss me around. I might actually listen." Christina burst into fits of uncontrollable laughter when Baying Wolf flipped her over and threatened to whack her bottom end.

"Are you telling me," he growled playfully, "that you will only obey me when you choose to do so?" Christina giggled, until she glanced behind her and saw that Baying Wolf had grown serious. He turned her back over into his embrace. "I know that you joke, but understand, my woman, that if I ever order you to do something, you must obey. Your life could very well depend on it."

"I understand."

Christina lifted up and placed a light kiss on her husband's lips. His response was immediate, but a knock on the flap drew them apart.

"Come."

Gray Fox stuck his head through the door flap. "They are waiting for you at the edge of the village. There was anger in their leader so your father would not permit them to enter, not that the white man *wanted* to come any closer," Gray Fox said with a sneer. "He has brought many men with him. Some of them are soldiers."

"Thank you, Gray Fox. It would seem," Baying Wolf turned to

face a nervous Christina as soon as Gray Fox left, "that there is more hatred in your uncle toward my people than we hold even for him."

"I wonder why?"

"Perhaps we will know when we go to meet him, but remember one thing, my woman," Baying Wolf stared intently into Christina's eyes, "I will not hesitate to kill him should he try to take you from me. Do you understand this? I do not want you to hate me for killing your uncle, but I will if I must."

Christina wrapped her arms around her husband's neck and squeezed tight. "I do not want you to kill my uncle, Baying Wolf, but I'm your wife now and I will not leave with anyone freely. If my uncle tries to take me from you, I may very well kill him myself."

A short time later, a nervous Christina sat atop her mount, beside her husband. She watched as her uncle and a detachment of soldiers slowly approached.

"It would appear that they were even further away than Gray Fox mentioned. Perhaps they fear that we may kill them with our eyes." Baying Wolf's angry sarcasm was not lost on Christina and her nervousness mounted. Here she sat, smack dab in the middle of a hatred war and she was the prize to be given the victor. She could feel the tenseness in the atmosphere grow as her uncle neared.

When the riders were only a short distance away, they stopped, and after a short conference, only three of the riders continued forward. Her uncle, a soldier, an Indian brave. They brought their mounts to a stop a few feet from where Baying Wolf and Christina sat mounted on their horses.

They all sat there for a minute or two watching each other warily. Christina recognized the soldier as David and smiled weakly. She should have known when Gray Fox mentioned soldiers that her uncle would have enlisted David's help. She only hoped and prayed he would stay out of the final conflict, or he could very well end up a casualty of this bitter encounter.

It was Baying Wolf that finally broke the uneasy silence that hung over them like a storm cloud, speaking not to her uncle, as she would have thought, but to the Indian brave that sat mounted to the left and slightly to the rear of her uncle. She looked at the brave and couldn't help noticing the differences between him and Baying Wolf. His features were less sharp and his hair less course. Although his skin had the same hue, the most striking difference was in his eyes—they were a blue as bright and clear as a summer sky. Christina knew at once that this was what she'd heard referred to as a half-breed.

"You have brought them here?" Baying Wolf asked Cole condemningly.

Cole chose to overlook his accusatory tone. Baying Wolf was an Indian; he was part Indian. To Baying Wolf, Cole had betrayed that Indian blood by bringing the white men to his village.

"I did. I felt that her uncle had a right to see her once more, so he could assure himself of her safety. She is here of her own free will, is she not?"

"She is," Baying Wolf stated simply, turning his opaque gaze toward Peter Carthington's acrimonious one.

"I should have shot you in that prairie a year ago, and would have if I'd known you were going to abduct my niece."

"Uncle Peter!" Christina gasped. Carthington turned his grim visage toward his niece.

"Don't worry about collecting your things, we're leaving here and going home. We'll keep this little incident a secret...."

"Like you did the 'little incident' last year, when you told everyone that I'd trekked across hostile country all on my own."

"If no one knows about this, then I won't have any trouble finding you a good husband."

"A good *white* husband, you mean? Well, no thanks. I've found me a good husband and he's sitting right here next to me."

"Are you telling me you prefer this savage to a decent, God-fearing...?"

"Wife-beating, drunken-minded, deceiving, lying...."

"Stop it! Your mind has been drugged somehow, otherwise you would never speak in this manner."

"Let me tell you something, Uncle Peter. The last man I was engaged to...."

"You were engaged?"

"...forced me into it by means of deceit and brutality," Christina continued, ignoring her uncle's interruption. "He used my brother's weakness for gambling to blackmail me into the engagement and used threats of violence against me and my family to keep me from breaking it off. He was, by far, more of a heathen than any of the Indians I've ever encountered while I've been here."

"What about what they did to your family? What they took away from us both?"

"In a way that was Jeffrey's fault too," Christina said in quiet sadness, "since it was him who persuaded daddy to make this journey, and if daddy had stood his ground and refused, my whole family would still be alive, but he also did me a favor, Uncle Peter. He brought me to the place I belong. He brought me to my destiny."

"You belong with us, child. Among civilized people."

"Look around you, Uncle, and tell me what is so uncivilized about what you see? What is it about these people that offend you so much? Why do you hate them?"

"I'll tell you why! Because they killed my wife! They killed my darling Annabelle!" The bitterness in his voice was a testament to the fact that he may have buried his wife, but he had never buried the past.

"I'm truly sorry, Uncle Peter." Christina was sorry, but she had learned that you could not blame a whole race for the villainous actions of a few. She too had lost loved ones to the renegades that raided across the Texas border, but unlike her uncle, she'd learned to forgive and move forward.

"I came home to our little cabin," her uncle continued talking as if seeing into the past. "The one we had before the big house was built. It had been a long week on the cattle drive. I was tired and dirty, and all I wanted was to come home to a nice fire in the hearth, a warm bath, and my wife's arms. Instead, I come home to find my house burnt to the ground and my Annabelle lying dead with an arrow through her back."

"It must have been awful for you, and I can empathize, truly I can, but..."

"Then leave with me. Knowing how I feel about these people, knowing what their kind did to our family. Shouldn't that be enough to persuade you that they aren't like us?"

"I don't love Baying Wolf and his people because they are like us. I love the man because of who he is, and he's not a savage."

"Christina," David broached carefully when Carthington clammed up and refused to speak, "do you really think you'll be happy living this kind of life? Living without the luxuries you've grown accustomed to?"

"I'm happy, David. Happier than I ever was being treated like a fragile simpleton. Here, my life has purpose and meaning. I know it's not the life I was raised to, but I'm not helpless, you know. I survived more in the last two years than most women endure in a lifetime, and it made me a stronger person."

"You really mean that, don't you?"

"With all of my heart, David, which now belongs to Baying Wolf and his people. God sent me here for a definite purpose and I intend to stay and see that purpose fulfilled, no matter what it is."

"You realize that in a few years, all these people are going to be forced from their homes and onto reservations? There's already talk in Washington of doing just that, once this war is over. What will you do then? The army will never let you stay with Baying Wolf on a reservation. They are already removing white captives from the tribes."

Christina gasped and stole a quick glance at her husband, who had been sitting quietly until this time.

"My people," Baying Wolf spoke softly, "will never accept life on a reservation..."

"Baying Wolf." Christina placed a gently restraining hand on her husband's arm. The last thing she needed was for him to make threats that would send the entire army after them. She also knew that what David spoke was true. She wasn't sure how she knew, for she'd never seen anything in her dreams, but a feeling crept into her heart and confirmed his words as surely as if they'd been written in stone and delivered straight into her hands. "I will never leave my husband, David," she stated resolutely, "and they will never be forced to live anywhere that they are not free. If the army comes for us, we will leave and find a place where war and government cannot influence or interfere with the life that we were meant to live."

David spurred his horse closer to Christina's horse and placed an encouraging hand on hers. "I only want what's best for you, Christina, just as your uncle does, and we just can't see how this is it?"

Christina stole a glance at her uncle's grim visage. He had clammed up tight, refusing to even look her way.

"I'm sure you both do, but I'm also certain that once Uncle Peter and you, David, realizes that this is what's best for me, you'll be happy for me, and allow me to live the life I was meant to live—and do so in peace."

David smiled grimly, "I can see that there is no changing your mind, so I will take my leave of you. May God be with you, and you too, Baying Wolf," David said, smiling shortly at the man who sat tensely beside his wife.

"I am glad that you see what must be seen, and will not try to take my wife from me."

"I cannot take what is not mine to take." Turning his horse, David stopped momentarily beside Christina's uncle and whispered something she could not hear, and then spurred his horse into a gallop. He signaled his men as he approached them and they turned to follow, disappearing a few minutes later over a small ridge.

Carthington's men looked around them nervously, suddenly insecure in their small numbers. As if it would make a difference, they closed ranks and moved their horses closer to where Carthington sat, forming a semicircle behind him.

"It's a long way home, Uncle. Would you like to stay, eat, and rest your horses?" Christina offered graciously. She wanted them to comprehend that she was truly safe and trusted those with whom she now resided.

The men got the message and glanced uneasily from her to their boss, waiting to see what his reaction and his orders would be, but by the look on their faces, not a one of them fancied the idea of going head-to-head with any of the warriors in camp. Not that they'd seen any since approaching, which made them all the more nervous.

"What I would like is for you to ride away from here with me."

"We've already been over this, Uncle Peter," Christina sighed in frustration. "I'm not leaving my husband. Don't you understand that we're married now?"

"Not in the eyes of God, you're not. You don't actually think He'd bless your marriage to a heathen, do you?"

"And do you really think that our God is so narrow-minded that He doesn't consider these His children also?"

"I didn't come here to get into a religious debate with you, Christina. I came to take you home."

"I am home, Uncle Peter."

"If you ride out with me now, then everything I own will be yours when I die. We'll find a good man that will run the ranch and you'll be rich beyond your wildest dreams."

"Everything that I've ever wanted is right here. All my hopes. All my dreams. Oh, why, can't you see that I'm where I want to be?"

It was evident in his scathing perusal of her husband and the few people scattered about the village watching the dispute with interest that he didn't. His hatred for these people was blind and ignorant, and nothing she could ever say would change that. She was suddenly grateful that the massacre of her family had not rendered her heart useless, and that she'd been able to heal and learn to love again.

"The invitation to dine still stands. Maybe if you spend some time..."

"I will never sit and eat with a bunch of dirty barbarians, and I'll be damned if I'll watch my niece do the same! You are coming home with me!" Carthington made a grab for Christina's reins, startling both horses. Christina's mare reared and she slid from the rump, landing hard on her derriere, her ankle throbbing as it landed with a thud.

Baying Wolf jumped from his own horse and knelt beside his wife. "You are okay?"

"I'm getting used to being banged up, I think. Don't do anything foolish, husband. I'm fine," Christina begged, noticing the anger mounting in her husband's dark eyes.

"You may be fine, but your 'husband' is going to be dead if you don't mount up and move out right now." Christina heard the soft click of the rifle before she laid eyes on it, and paled when she saw it pointed right at Baying Wolf's head. "Thing is, if I leave you alive," Carthington said to Baying Wolf, obviously glad to have resumed the upper hand in this little conflict, "then you'll just come after her again, won't you?"

"Whether I live or die is not important." The soft, threatening tone in Baying Wolf's voice sent a shiver down Christina's spine. "If you take Christina from here, my people will hunt you down and feed you to the wolves, piece by piece."

"Mount your horse now, Christina, if you don't want me to fill him full of lead."

"No, Uncle Peter. I can't do that." Christina crawled on her knees and moved slowly to kneel in front of Baying Wolf. "I can't let you hurt him, and I won't leave him."

"Christina, don't be an idiot. Stand up and let's ride. Days a wasting, child."

"Why are you being so stubborn?"

"*I'm* being stubborn! You're the one who's insistent upon living with savages! You're the one who thinks being a squaw is appropriate for a girl of your upbringing and social standing! You're the one who's trying to throw her entire life away on someone who will never be worth anything more than cow fodder! And you say I'm being stubborn!"

"I am where I want to be! Why can't you just accept that and leave me in peace?"

"That's just it, Christina. I can't fathom you truly wanting to be here. There's got to be something wrong with your brain, child. Maybe he put something in your food, I don't know, but there is no way in hell I can believe that any niece of mine would willingly choose this kind of life over the life I can provide. It's just not sane."

"Then call me insane. Call me anything you please, but I'm not leaving my husband!"

"And I can't leave you here," Carthington rejoined harshly, "I can't live with the knowledge that I let my only surviving relative remain among savages. If you won't mount up willingly, then I'll just kill you both and remove your dead body from this godforsaken place. At least you'll be *buried* among civilized people."

Christina froze at her uncle's words. Surely he wasn't irrational enough to carry out his threat. Perhaps he was just bluffing, using the threat to get her to acquiesce, but what if she called him on that bluff and he shot them both. Then she would never feel Baying Wolf's arms around her again; never know the joy of bearing his children.

Her decision made, she stood slowly, careful to keep her weight off her ankle, which was swelling once again. She could not take a chance on hers or Baying Wolf's life. She would return peaceably with her Uncle.

She took an unstable step toward her horse and froze in astonishment. She shot a quick glance at her uncle's face and was relieved to see that he was unaware of the activity going on behind him. She lowered her eyes to the ground so she wouldn't accidentally give anything away and had to work hard to suppress a smile.

The Indian cavalry had arrived. How the braves had managed to leave camp and sneak around to the rear of her uncle and his men without being noticed, she didn't know, but never had she been happier to see a bunch of half-dressed, bow-and-arrow-wielding natives in her entire life.

Baying Wolf also stood slowly. He'd watched the exchange between Christina and her uncle with growing trepidation. The man was imbalanced, and he worried that Christina's efforts at persuasion would not work. He'd wisely held his tongue, knowing that Cole had slipped away sometime during the exchange and had gone to warn his warriors that their help was going to be needed after all. Now that help had arrived.

"Look behind you, Carthington."

"Why, so you can jump me? Well, let me just warn you, Injun, you'll be dead before you step one foot in my direction."

"Uh, boss man?" Matt said nervously, swallowing deeply. "You might ought to put that rifle down."

"Shut up, Matt. I ain't putting nothing away, and I ain't leaving here without my niece."

"There's just one problem with that plan, boss," Jake spoke up next.

"And what might that be?"

"Them," Matt and Jake said in unison, both pointing at the warriors standing guard to their rear, their bow and arrows drawn, ready to shoot.

When Carthington shot a quick glance over his shoulder, Baying Wolf lifted Christina by the waist and pulled her quickly behind a nearby tree, using his body as a shield should Carthington get off a round before he was brought down by his men, but the shot never happened.

Carthington may be unbalanced, but he was not a witless man. He liked his life way too much to give it up now. He slowly lowered his rifle and placed it back in the holster attached to his saddle.

"Do I ride out of here with my life?" He asked, when Baying Wolf and Christina cautiously moved from behind the tree.

"If you do so now with the promise that you'll never set foot near our people again."

"You have my word," Carthington said with quiet resignation. He pulled the reins on his horse and turned to leave. "Let's ride," he said quietly to his stunned cowhands.

"Uncle Peter?" Christina pushed past Baying Wolf and limped to her uncle's horse. "Would you deliver a message to Katie for me? We became very close in the short time I was with you and I don't want her worrying about me."

"Why should I deliver a message for you? I don't even know who you are." Carthington clicked his tongue, dug his spurs into his horse, and galloped away.

Christina stood in stunned immobility for several seconds and then turned into the waiting arms of her husband, but even though her uncle's words had stung, she found herself unable to cry. She knew that he could be a cold man and now his frigid heart had turned on her. To him, she deserved no more consideration that any of his servants. She also realized that, before many years had passed, not even a trace would remain in her memories of the man she'd once called Uncle.

As she watched him ride away, realization struck. She had finished the last page of the first part of her life. In her mind, she closed its worn cover and shelved it as she would a beloved novel. As she remounted her mare and followed her husband's stallion back toward her new home, she mentally pulled another book from her life's bookshelf, opened its pristine cover, and knew before she even began the prologue, that it would be a story full of adventure, love, and happiness. A story she hoped never to finish.

"Will you be okay?"

"I never really knew him that well," Christina sighed, "but the man that I came to know over the past year, is not a man I'd suffer the loss of too greatly. He was nothing like my father after all."

"Then you do not hate me for sending him away and ordering him never to return?"

Christina stopped her horse next to her husband's and turned to face the man who'd risked his life for her on more than one occasion and whose love for her was as deep as any ocean.

"Would it matter if I did?" Christina teased.

Baying Wolf looked intently into her eyes and then his mouth split into a wide grin. "You are joking with me."

"There's hope for you yet, my husband."

EPILOGUE

January 1868

"Little Bear! Little Wolf! Come here this instant!" The two four-year-old twin brothers came running from the trees covered from head-to-toe in mud. Christina fought to keep the smile off her face as they bounded across the grass and came to a screeching halt in front of her, mud slinging from their bodies onto her bare legs. "I thought I told you to keep an eye on your little sister, and instead I find you've run off to play."

"We're warriors, not girl watchers. We were going to go on a vision quest like White Elk."

"White Elk has gone with Fire Dreamer to learn the ways of the shaman. Your brother has a special gift that needs to be developed. He hasn't left here on his own or against his parent's wishes. And, seven years old or not, he would not have left at all if he hadn't learned to obey his parents first."

She could see that her precious baby boys were thinking hard about what she had said, and that pleased her. They were strong-willed and stubborn like their father and older brother, and she wanted to make certain they grew up with an understanding of obedience and respect before they got too unruly and out-of-hand. As with White Elk, however, she knew she had to tread softly. She had learned in the last seven years that Indian braves, no matter their age, took their manhood and manly duties very seriously.

That's why she had given Fire Dreamer the task of training her eldest son, even though he was old and infirmed and she was the shaman of The People now. She still felt he needed the guiding hand from another man.

"You have to understand that we have a lot of things to do over the next couple of days if we are going to be prepared to leave. Your father left strict instructions that we're to be ready before he returns, and I can't do it all by myself, not and watch your sister too." She turned and looked at where her two-year-old daughter,

Dancing Deer, sat playing with her doll beside the teepee and smiled warmly. "You know, it takes a lot of courage to obey your parents and watch over your little sister."

"It does!" Both little boys gawked at their mother through widened eyes.

"Of course! Only a coward runs out on his duties."

"We will watch Dancing Deer, mother! We're not cowards!"

"I know you're not, my brave young men, but you need to go and wash off first." She laughed as they bounded back into the trees, headed for the stream. "Come, Dancing Deer. Let's get you some lunch before those two whirlwinds return."

"Lunch," Dancing Deer repeated happily, clapping her hands.

Christina bent and hefted her daughter in her arms, but stopped short of going inside the teepee when she noticed riders approaching. "It looks as if lunch is going to have to wait for a few minutes, darling. I think I see your daddy coming."

Christina lowered her daughter gently back down to the ground and straightened her buck-skinned dress and then patted her long red tresses. Assured that her hair had not escaped her braid, and she was dressed reasonably well to meet her husband's return, she bounded across the grass.

She smiled widely as her husband rode closer, but the smile faded at the sight of his grim visage. All it took was one look at his demeanor and she knew that the dream she'd had night before last had been confirmed. The buffalo soldiers had finally arrived.

It had been seven years since she'd joined the tribe, and during that time, her dreams had prevented many disasters from taking a grip on The People she had come to claim as her own. But the dream she'd had a few nights ago scared her more than anything she'd dreamt of in years. Not since the first dream she'd had of Jeffrey under the guise of a white beast.

She had been sleeping fitfully beside her husband after a wonderful night of lovemaking when the dream came, stealing into her heart and mind, driving all sense of security from her. She had awakened with a scream and cried on Baying Wolf's shoulder for a long time thereafter.

"What has happened, my wife?" He asked in hushed tones, afraid to wake the children.

"I had a dream again. It was horrible to me."

"Tell me."

"There were soldiers with black skin. They had The People of this village surrounded and were forcing them into the back of wagons that looked like prisons. The time has come to leave this place, Baying Wolf. Danger is coming. I know it is." The tears started up again as she spoke of the dream. "What David said about the Indians being forced onto the reservations is true. I felt it long ago when he spoke of it, and now I see that it will come about—and soon."

"I will call a meeting of the elders tomorrow and we will discuss what is to happen now. Try to sleep until then." And she had tried, but sleep eluded her.

The meeting of the council had been the reason behind Baying Wolf and several other braves departure. Christina had asked Baying Wolf to convince the elders for proof. They were to go in search of the buffalo soldiers, hopefully to bring back evidence that her dream was prophetic and not just a dream.

Now they had returned, and the expressions they wore could not mean good news.

"My wife." He lifted Christina into his arms and kissed her long and hard. "I have missed your company at night."

"And I yours." She kissed him back for a long moment, and then stepped away. "What have you discovered, Baying Wolf?" She was almost afraid to ask, for if she didn't ask then he wouldn't find the need to answer, and she could hold off the inevitable for just a little longer.

"They are coming. We saw many of The People we called friends and they were riding in caged wagons, just as your dream said. A detachment of soldiers, with skin the color of night and hair as course, black, and curly as that of the buffalo was guiding them, and guarding them. Our people looked—defeated," Baying Wolf finished, nearly choking on the final word. "It is true, then, what you said. Our life here is over. The life that the brave men of my village know will never be passed down to our sons. The art and beauty of our women will die before reaching our daughters."

"Only if we remain here, Baying Wolf, and allow them to take us away. Only if we remain here," Christina reiterated, her heart aching for her husband and her people.

"Perhaps we could take a stand. Fight for the right to remain free on the land of our ancestors."

"No, Baying Wolf." Christina placed her palm against his cheek. She couldn't stop the tears streaming down her face. "Believe me when I say that fighting would prove fatal."

"Perhaps we would rather die than..."

"Don't even say that! You have to think about the children, Baying Wolf. Not only ours, but all of the children. What kind of future will they have if their fathers are killed in a battle that cannot be won?"

"You are right, my wife. Sometimes I allow my anger to cloud my thinking."

"Like it did when you were forced to come after me?"

Baying Wolf laughed and pulled his wife close, "At least I am easily persuaded, or I may never have cleared the anger from my heart and mind and seen clearly our destiny."

"I love you."

"I love you, too. Now come. I will call a meeting of the council and advise that we leave, as you have suggested."

"I was so hoping that this time it was just a dream. Not a vision."

"Do not be sorry for your dreams, my wife. If not for them, we would lose everything we love. Because of you, we have a chance to go to a new place and continue to live together in peace."

"But where will we go?"

"North. To Canada."

Two days later, Baying Wolf and Christina, their four children—White Elk, Little Bear, Little Wolf, and Dancing Deer—

began their long trek across North America to their new home, with the tribe following unfailingly. Not one member had stood against Christina's vision and denounced her. They knew, as did she, that leaving their home was the only solution.

It was a long journey fraught with many dangers, and they lost many of the elderly along the way—including Baying Wolf's father, Chief Running Elk and his uncle, Fire Dreamer.

Christina shed a lot of tears for the loss of Fire Dreamer, for if it hadn't been for him, Baying Wolf never would have become a part of her life and she would never have known the happiness she had now.

She pulled her daughter closer, seated before her on her mare, and then looked down from her perch at her sons, walking beside her, and thanked God that this chapter in the book of her life was not the final page. This was a story that she never wanted to return to the bookshelf in her mind. She preferred to continue writing new pages until her life's end, and thanks to her visions, she knew that her life would go on for many years to come.